D0089186

VICKY PETERWALD

REBEL

MIKE SHEPHERD

ACE BOOKS, NEW YORK

ACE

An imprint of Penguin Random House LLC
375 Hudson Street, New York, New York 10014

VICKY PETERWALD: REBEL

An Ace Book / published by arrangement with the author

ISBN: 978-0-425-26659-5

PUBLISHING HISTORY
Ace mass-market edition / June 2016

PRINTED IN THE UNITED STATES OF AMERICA

10 9 8 7 6 5 4 3 2 1

Cover illustration by Scott Grimando.
Cover design by Diana Kolsky.
Interior text design by Kristin del Rosario.

Penguin
Random
House

ACKNOWLEDGMENTS

As we complete the third book of the Vicky Peterwald trilogy (exactly three books, count them), I'm also coming up on twenty-five years since my first short story was published. It's been a great ride, and now seems like a good time to thank all the people who helped me along the way.

I will always be thankful to Sheila Simonson and the group at the Novel Writing class at Clark College, Washington. They helped me through those first stumbling efforts, taught me how to do dialogue (you know, Mike, that stuff in quotes), and gave me the discipline to write ten whole pages a week. Mary Rosenblum and her writers group helped polish me. Mary also gave me the benefit of her Clarion experience.

Thank you, Stan Schmidt of *Analog*. You were the first to see the writing potential in me and give me the approval I desperately needed. Like with all writers, that approval came in the form of a check.

Jenn Jackson has been the best agent that I could hope for. She's given me all I needed and kept out of my way when I needed that. My longtime editor at Ace, Ginjer Buchanan, picked me up and gave me a second chance when others might not have. She was a perfect match for twenty years. I hope she enjoys a long and fun retirement; she surely deserves it. I appreciate Diana Gill's contributions to *Rebel* and my other latest books. I'm grateful to the whole gang at Ace for the work they've put into the production that turns my manuscript into the finished product you readers enjoy. Oh, and I do love Scott's cover art.

The folks at Lincoln City, both at the Historic Anchor Inn and the Sunday brunch bunch, have supported me through a lot and helped me keep going. I'm sure you will keep me going for a long time to come.

I really want to thank my first readers, Lisa Muller and Edee Lemonier. They do a great job of cleaning up my typos and nits. Oh, and occasionally backing up my wife that "I really need to change that section."

At home, Nikki and Danny are not only interesting sources for inspiration, but they've also come to understand what it's like to have a writer for a grandpa. They've learned to enjoy the ups and put up with the downs with accepting smiles.

And then there's Ellen. She's devoted years to learning how to be the best first reader that a writing husband could hope for. Thank you, honey, for everything.

CHAPTER 1

═══

H ER Imperial Grace, the Grand Duchess, Lieutenant Commander Victoria of Greenfeld felt the pressure in her ears change ever so slightly. The battleship *Retribution* had sealed locks with High St. Petersburg Station. She should be getting herself off to pay her respects to Admiral von Mittleburg.

She stood and faced the door.

Commander Franz Boch, the latest officer to swear that assassins got to Vicky over his dead body, and the one to survive the longest, cleared his throat.

"No need to go anywhere, Your Grace," he said.

Vicky raised an inquisitive eyebrow.

"The admiral is on his way to pay his respects to you."

Vicky paused to examine what the commander had just told her.

It was loaded with meaning.

Admirals sent their compliments to junior officers such as lieutenant commanders. Junior officers sent their respects to their seniors. Was Admiral von Mittleburg really on his way to pay his respects to Vicky?

If that was true, Vicky had succeeded in making a Grand Duchess worth a great deal in this dance with life and death.

Princess Kris Longknife had once told Vicky that modern society had little experience in valuing creations such as her, a jumped-up Rim princess, so she was making the best of it. Vicky had been doing much the same of late, trying to determine the value of one Grand Duchess.

Apparently, some people had come to consider her worthwhile. Certainly, Admiral von Mittleburg was treating her as if she had taken on greater value in this slow minuet toward rebellion that they were dancing.

Dancing for their lives and those of so many other desperate people.

Vicky settled into a comfortable chair in her quarters on the Imperial Greenfeld Battleship *Retribution*. During more normal times, they were the in-port cabin of any admiral who might find himself aboard one of the most fearsome battleships of the Imperium.

No admiral being aboard, Vicky had taken them over for herself and her staff.

Captain Etterlin had not objected. Vicky had counted that for a success.

Vicky took a moment to examine what she had to offer Admiral von Mittleburg in the way of hospitality. Against the far bulkhead was a metal desk, rarely used, but painted to make it appear like wood. In front of it was a conference table, also metal, also painted to mimic wood. Vicky, her two miniature assassins, and the commander often sat around it, examining how Vicky might next stick her neck out and maybe get it chopped off.

Vicky chose to settle into the more comfortable overstuffed chair of the conversation group. Across a coffee table that doubled as a computer display was a second armchair for the admiral. Anyone else would have to settle for the two sofas around the table or one of the straight-backed chairs arrayed against the closest bulkhead.

The not-airtight door opened. Everyone jumped to their feet and snapped to attention. The commander opened his mouth to call all present to attention, a superfluous announcement if ever there was one.

"As you were," Admiral von Mittleburg said to those standing already. "I understand congratulations are in order," he continued as he marched for the empty seat reserved for him.

"Metzburg has signed a trade agreement with St. Petersburg, Admiral, if that's what you mean," Vicky said.

"Signed, sealed, and delivered," the admiral said, beaming happily, a rare event for a Navy officer of his lofty rank. "They took all the crystal and electronic products you brought, and I've already gotten a request to loan out the landing craft tanks from both the *Crocodile* and the *Anaconda* to drop the newly arrived heavy fabs down to St. Petersburg."

"The mayors of St. Petersburg aren't going to argue over who gets which of the heavy fabricators?" Vicky asked, surprised that that group of politicians could agree on anything.

"No, it seems you have brought enough back to leave their industrialists sated, for the moment."

"No doubt that will be temporary," Vicky said. She'd rarely found either businesspeople or politicians satisfied for very long.

"The battlecruiser *Smiter* just came in from Brunswick with a long wish list and an equally long list of nice things they can offer. Prepare to be waltzed through the streets of St. Petersburg the next time you drop down to the surface."

Vicky could not restrain a chuckle. "Whereas, a few months ago, they were threatening to shoot me out of the sky if I darkened their doorstep."

"How times change."

"I'm glad it's for the better," Vicky said.

"At least on St. Petersburg," the admiral added dryly. The admiral turned to a civilian who had followed him into Vicky's quarters and taken a chair against the wall with Vicky's two diminutive assassins. "Mr. Smith, if you will join us, please?"

Mr. Smith, whose actual name was likely something quite different, rose and joined the commander on the sofa, giving Kit and Kat the honor and trust of turning his back on them. Mr. Smith had started out in the service of Kris Longknife, keeping her alive against the law of averages.

In that endeavor, he had managed to save Vicky's life at least once. When Kris had been hustled off to points unknown, Mr. Smith had offered his services to Vicky to be billed at his usual outrageous hourly rate. He had saved her life enough times to make his pay a bargain.

And to earn himself a shopping spree to Longknife territory.

"Did you manage to buy some of those spidersilk-armored body stockings for me?" Vicky asked.

"Kris Longknife's Grandmother Trouble was very helpful in that. I got several for you as well as Kit and Kat," Mr. Smith said, nodding over his shoulder. "I also got a couple of them in my size and two for you, Commander," he added, now smiling at Commander Boch.

"Thank you," Vicky said.

The commander seemed rather relieved to have been included, even as an afterthought.

The admiral cleared his throat. "That, however, is not the reason I brought Mr. Smith with me. He has some messages for you."

"Messages?" Vicky echoed.

"While at Bayern, arranging for your, um, message, to be delivered to your loving stepmother, two messages arrived for you from the palace."

"Hmm," Vicky said. "And who were they from?"

"The first was from your father, the Emperor."

Vicky eyed the admiral. "Have you seen it?"

"Yes," was voiced in the most neutral manner Vicky had ever heard.

Vicky glanced around her quarters. Only her most loyal assassins were present. "Will you play it for me now?"

The admiral nodded to Mr. Smith and the bulkhead screen in front of Vicky came to life with the Imperial seal. Kit, Kat, and the commander turned with Vicky to watch it. Vicky noted that neither the admiral nor Mr. Smith bothered to turn toward it.

They were watching her watch it.

Her father the Emperor appeared. He was in his courtly dress though at least he was not seated on his gilded throne.

"Daughter," he began. "We are hearing strange reports about you here at the palace. Very troubling stories. We know they can't be true. You will always be Daddy's little girl. Still, what *we* are hearing *is* troubling. We request and require that you immediately convey yourself to our court, here, to answer allegations of a most deplorable nature. You will do this immediately, without delay. Do you hear me, dear?"

The screen held the visage of a most troubled man, whether that of an Emperor or father it was difficult to tell.

"Interesting," Vicky said. "He makes no mention of my leaving because I was kidnapped and threatened with death."

"That does appear to have been overlooked," Mr. Smith said dryly.

Vicky allowed her father's words to percolate for a few moments, then said, "You mentioned another message?"

The admiral nodded.

The screen again showed the Imperial seal. This time, it was replaced by a very pregnant woman in full rage.

"You little bitch," the loving stepmom nearly screamed. "So you think you can play in my game? You think you can stop me from taking what is mine?"

She paused, face red, to scowl out of the screen. "Your tits are in a real wringer now, you little bint. I'll have your guts strung out on the palace lawn and pound your boobs flat with a croquet mallet. You get your stupid ass in here immediately, and I may just let that doting fool of a father let you live. Stay out there one minute longer than it takes to run home, and you'll not just be dead. You'll be begging my people to let you die."

The screen went blank on a truly horrible glare.

"You know," Vicky said, "if she's not careful, she's not going to pop like most pregger women. She'll just explode."

"All over the place," Mr. Smith added. "By the way, the word is that she has delivered the promised baby boy."

Vicky puzzled over what she'd just watched. "Did that message come in the mail like the other one?" she finally said, eyeing her spy.

Mr. Smith shook his head. "That message was embedded in your father's message. When the one file was turned over to me, I noticed it seemed too large and had my newly upgraded computer examine it. It stripped out the one from the other."

"While you were on Bayern?"

"Yes, Your Grace," he answered.

"Did you view it then?"

"Yes, Your Grace. I viewed both messages and shared them with certain former Navy officers that had met with you on a previous occasion. They have a third message for you."

"Have you seen it, Admiral?"

Admiral von Mittleburg nodded.

"Should I clear the room?" Vicky asked.

"I believe the commander should see it," the admiral said. "He is *trying* to keep you alive."

"Then Kit and Kat will stay as well. Mr. Smith, if you will?"

The screen came alive. In place of a seal, it showed the rolling green hills of Bayern with some very lovely horses grazing peacefully. Then the view panned to a retired admiral.

"I understand that a well done is in order, Your Grace. A very well done, if I may say so myself. None of us here expected anything of the high order that you have achieved. It almost makes me believe that you Peterwalds do have some stern stuff in your bones. At least one of you. Please continue to surprise us, and we will do our best to keep up with you and give you what support we can."

Here he paused, took a deep breath and let it out slowly. When he began again, his face was stern but loaded with commitment. "When you were last here, we spoke of a certain rag. Matters have gone downhill faster than even our worse fears allowed for. That rag is yours. Feel free to do with it what you may."

And on that note, the screen went blank.

Vicky leaned back in her chair. She had met the man in the last message only once, during a quick stop at Bayern. They had returned the body of the first officer who died for his error of getting too close to her. She had met with a good score of retired officers and wives. They had debated among themselves whether to kill Vicky, as her stepmother wanted, or return her safe to the palace. It had been a close run thing, but they had agreed to let Vicky live.

All the while, in the background of their discussions had been a rag. Actually a flag. The flag of rebellion. Should it be raised? Should Vicky be used to wave it, and should the Navy back her in that rebellion?

Then, Vicky had been adamant that she was no rebel. Then, the Navy had been sure that, while matters were bad, they weren't *that* bad. People were not ready to rebel against the Emperor.

A lot had changed since then.

Vicky had returned to the palace and seen for herself why a shadow Navy staff on Bayern made policy for a Navy staff on Greenfeld that was just too close to the palace to keep any secrets. She had barely made it off Greenfeld with her life.

Even distant St. Petersburg hadn't been far enough away that her stepmother couldn't hire assassins to do their best to rid the Empress of one troublesome Grand Duchess who stood between her now-born son and the throne.

Vicky let the content of all three messages roll around in her head. She had permission from the Navy to rebel. With her father's summons so clear, failure to attend to court immediately would be rebellion, plain and simple. Equally, to attend to court was to put herself in her stepmother's murderous embrace.

"I *must* go to court," Vicky said softly, and to the consternation of all listening, even Kit and Kat.

"However, I can *not* go to court. That would be my death."

Those around her settled back into their seats.

"So," Vicky said, smiling at those around her, "how do I spin out my journey to court for as long as possible? The more time we have to prepare our rebellion, the more likely it is to succeed."

CHAPTER 2

POLICY established, the Grand Duchess turned to evaluating her options.

"I guess my little message really got to my stepmama."

"I told you, mademoiselle, zat ze second nipple slip was just too too," Kat offered slyly.

"You might be right," Vicky agreed, absently.

"Ah," Mr. Smith said, delicately clearing his throat, "I didn't deliver your message."

Vicky raised her eyebrows in surprise. "My dearest darling stepmom was that far around the bend without a word from me?"

"It may be that your actions spoke louder than words," the admiral put in.

"Do you think she had time to get the word about us turning around her little invasion fleet at Presov?"

The admiral shrugged. "It is hard to say how fast news travels in these times, but I would strongly suspect that bad news flies to her without delay."

"Your father was hearing stories about you," the commander put in. "I doubt if he was reacting to word that you'd been kidnapped and staked out to die of thirst."

Vicky nodded slowly. "Knowing him as I do, I suspect that

you are too right. Me nearly killed. 'Oh dear.' Me with just the hint of rebellion. 'Damn it, you will answer me immediately.' Or so it went when I was getting into this cookie jar or that boy's pants. Now, I suspect it will be worse."

"No doubt," the spy agreed.

"So, what are your plans?" the admiral asked.

"We will have to somehow buy me time to stay out of the palace's loving clutches."

"But how?" the commander asked.

"Maybe ze mademoiselle was more hurt in ze latest mad escapade?" Kat put in.

"Not a bad idea," the admiral said. "Not a bad idea at all."

"Considering how bad my feet hurt, I could easily have stepped on something that gave me the roaring heebie-jeebies," Vicky agreed.

"I suggest you answer the Emperor's demand from sick bay, after some serious bandaging and, ah . . ."

"I believe I can apply the makeup," the spy offered.

"We have pictures of all her lovely scratches and bug bites," Kit offered.

"Maybe the answer should best be taken from a planetside hospital," Vicky said. "It would be easier for me to claim I can't take a shuttle ride up here than that I can't take a starship ride home."

"Good point," the spy said. "I will make an operative out of you yet."

"Thank you, but I think Grand Duchess is dangerous enough for my tastes. So, how are we set for ships?"

The admiral's shrug was burdened with fatalism. "The *Attacker*'s damage report grows by the day. It is not that the pirate ship did more damage than we thought but that the ship was in much worse underlying shape than we were led to expect. I find myself wondering what we would turn up if we put any of our ships in the docks here on High St. Petersburg."

"Is nothing what it seems in the Greenfeld Empire?" Vicky asked, not expecting a reply. She did not get one.

"The *Kamchatka* is now in our second newly equipped refit dock," the admiral went on. "We have replaced it with the *Azov* and *Orsk* on patrol above Presov. They are old but serviceable. It appears that we got the old *Kami* into dock just in time. Her reactors are being torn down and totally rebuilt as we speak."

"Are the *Retribution* and the *Rostock* all we have in port that could respond to anything?" Vicky asked, trying but failing to keep the incredulity from her voice.

"It would seem so. Two laid-up liners are just about through being converted to armed merchant cruisers, but until you got back, we were kind of thin here," the admiral admitted.

"We will not leave St. Petersburg that unprotected again," Vicky snapped.

"Yes, Your Grace," the admiral answered.

Vicky realized what she'd done only after she had done it. It seemed that the admiral also was only now tasting how he'd responded to her coming the Grand Duchess with full intent.

She chose not to apologize, and he chose to move on.

"Will you be dropping down to Sevastopol to meet with the local power brokers?" the admiral asked. "It would seem that they may feel a need for a say if you are intent on using their planet as your base for a slow boil to revolution."

Vicky sighed. "No doubt I have more politicking to do. Oh, for the days when my father or grandfather could snap his fingers and people would jump."

"Or appear to jump," the spy pointed out.

"Ah yes, we do seem to be deep in discovery of how things really went, don't we?" Vicky agreed.

She left others to do what they did and headed out to do what she did best: listen to people talk and talk and talk until they agreed with her. However, before she headed down, she called a time-out so everyone on her team could take advantage of the new spidersilk armor.

Which turned out to be a lot tougher to get into than Kris Longknife ever mentioned. After much pulling and yanking, use of talc, and not a few nasty words as hair was pulled out of delicate places, Vicky, Kit, and Kat were ready to dress again.

"I wonder how the men are making out," Kit said, through a giggle.

"We should have offered to help them," Kat giggled back.

"But then we'd never have made it down to Sevastopol. At least not today," Kit insisted.

"We would so jump them," Kat agreed.

Vicky was only too aware that she had not jumped or been jumped by anyone in far too long. She was trying to persuade herself that a real Grand Duchess didn't jump men or women at every convenient moment of the day or night.

At least Mannie didn't seem to behave that way and, so far, Mannie was her best example of how someone with power used it, and used it in ways that got people behind him.

Vicky took a deep breath, suppressed the image of Mannie sandwiched between, among, and within Vicky and her impulsive assassins, and donned her undress whites. She had a lot of work ahead of her.

Mannie was waiting at the spaceport with a limo for her and her team.

"I was expecting you as soon as I got word that fabricators from Metzburg were raining from the sky as fast as those marvelous heavy-lift LCTs could drop. Things must have gone quickly."

"Your advance men did a lot of prework. My stepmom made her usual threats to do horrible things to people if they talked with me. That didn't stop them; though it did make them a bit reluctant to shake hands on any deals. Then stepmommy dearest had the usual attack made on my life, and folks on Metzburg got angry. Things moved faster after that."

Mannie shook his head. "I don't know what to react to: her trying to throttle anything we do for our own good or her trying to kill you."

"Thanks for thinking of me a close second," Vicky said, and pulled what bit of spidersilk armor she could from her throat. "I now have some of Kris Longknife's miraculous body armor. Nothing's getting at me now."

Mannie seemed delighted at that. Vicky searched his smile for any hint that he might have wanted to get at her, even a little bit. If it was there, he hid it well. With them sharing the back of the limo with the commander, the spy, and two tiny assassins, he didn't so much as rest his hand on hers.

"I have a meeting scheduled in an hour. We need to talk about how things are developing and head off any problems before they get too bad," the mayor of Sevastopol said. "I'd heard that the *Retribution* was in system and that you might be available, but I didn't want to bother you with just our local problems."

Vicky couldn't think of anything Mannie might do that would be a bother, but she ignored that for the moment. "It appears that I do have some problems to lay before your committee."

"Problems?"

"Mr. Smith, run the Emperor's message to me."

"Immediately, Your Grace," and his computer began to project a small hologram of the Emperor in front of Vicky and Mannie. He went through his fatherly concerns again.

"Nice computer you have there," Mannie said.

"I just had it upgraded in Longknife space," the spy answered.

"So," Mannie said, turning to Vicky.

"There's more."

Now the spy projected the Empress in all her pregnant roundness and red-faced rage.

"Oh," Mannie said, when the Empress's threats vanished back into thin air. "She is not a nice woman. And your father wants you back there with her, huh?"

"So it would seem. There is one more message you should see."

"I don't think so, Your Grace," the commander put in.

"I don't intend for this message to be shown at the coming meeting," Vicky answered back, "but Mannie needs to know all the cards that are in our deck."

"You are risking a lot," the Navy officer said.

"I have a lot at risk," Vicky countered.

The commander sat back in his seat, and the spy played the third message.

"I don't recognize the man," Mannie said when it was finished.

"I prefer that you don't remember his face."

"He seems to speak for the Navy."

"In a manner of speaking, he may," Vicky agreed.

"What is this 'rag' he spoke of?"

"Substitute flag of rebellion and how does the message go down with you?"

Now it was Mannie's turn to sink back into the thick leather seat.

"So, when you dropped down here the first time, you *were* planning rebellion?"

"No," Vicky said, as forcefully as she could. "I could not be planning rebellion because I had nothing to rebel with, and I was not willing to even consider rebellion. What I told you that day was true."

"For that day," Mannie pointed out.

"For that day, yes. And forever more if I could have managed it. I love my father for all his faults and for all that his middle-aged folly is causing a disaster. I still don't want to rebel."

"But you kind of like living, don't you?"

"Very much. It offers all kinds of opportunities for tomorrows," Vicky agreed.

"Yes. There is that. And those first two messages, they don't seem to promise you many tomorrows if you do as you are told," the mayor said slowly.

Vicky nodded.

"And I don't see us getting a whole lot of good done for ourselves if you stick your head into that noose."

"I can't agree with you more."

"So, if you go there, you die. If you stay safe out here, you are in rebellion. Did I miss any other option?"

Vicky shook her head.

"Then I think we will have to persuade my associates that we would lose too much if we send you back home as requested and required. We will gain far more by keeping you out here than the Empress can take out of our hide."

Vicky had never felt so much support and acceptance in her life. She wanted to throw herself into his arms and kiss him. She wanted to, but he had turned away to watch the city flowing by his window, seemingly lost in thought.

Gnawing her own lower lip, Vicky did her own turn away. Civil war was not something covered much in her education. It had also not had a section in the ship's library on the *Fury* or any other Imperial ships she'd been on. Civil war was not even a whisper in Greenfeld territory. Now she was left to wonder what a civil war might do to the lovely city of Sevastopol.

"I had planned a quick lunch," Mannie finally said. "Have you eaten?"

"Not since breakfast," Vicky admitted. "I'm not really hungry."

"Love letters like those would kill any appetite. Still, our meeting may go long now that I'll be adding this to the agenda. There's a deli I ordered sandwiches from. I've reserved a room for us to eat under the watchful eyes of my security team."

They were taken up the tall glass tower that Vicky had been in before. This time, they stopped a floor below the conference room; she was escorted to a suite of rooms under heavy guard.

The ham and cheese sandwiches waiting for them were quite delicious. The pasta salad that came with it reminded Vicky of something she'd tasted as a kid when Maggie would take her for a picnic on the palace grounds, and the cooks would outdo themselves.

The guards took turns wolfing down sandwiches while staying on high alert. She and Mannie talked about her most recent voyage. He enjoyed the part where the Golden Empress ships turned and ran from Presov.

"I don't think their 4-inch popguns and 18-inch pulse lasers were ready to take on a battleship," Vicky said with a laugh.

Several of the local guards shared in Mannie's enjoyment of that picture. Vicky was prepared to let this go on as long as Mannie was willing, but one of his aides came to whisper in his ear.

The mayor stood. "The meeting is ready to begin," he said, and offered Vicky a hand to help her to her feet and an arm for the short walk to the elevator. Again, the view from the conference room was beyond impressive.

This time, some forty men and women sat around the table; the seat at the head was left empty for Vicky. Sadly, that gave her the worst view in the house, looking back at the one wall with only the elevator and a pair of large landscape paintings beside it.

Mannie opened the meeting. "All of you have had a chance to review the agenda. Shall we get started?" he began without mentioning that Vicky needed to add another item.

An agenda appeared on a screen inlaid into the table before Vicky. Most of it was too cryptic for her to make sense of though it helped her follow the conversation.

The industrialists were quite happy with what Vicky had brought back from her "smuggling run," as they called it. They seemed especially delighted that a Peterwald was doing their smuggling. There was one problem; Kiev would be slow to install and staff several of the fabs they had ordered.

St. Petersburg was only too willing to take the delivery and promised to have them up and running within the week. They were updated versions of fabricators that they had traded for food from Sevastopol during the worst of the troubles. The industrialists from St. Pete promised to let Kiev have their delivery when it came in from Brunswick in a month, two at the most.

Kiev, however, was very unwilling to let go of the machinery. The distrust was palpable from the previously agricultural hinterland for the industrial powerhouse that had kept them as a cheap resource for food and fiber while charging them an arm and a leg for finished goods.

Mannie raised an eyebrow to Vicky.

"I think I can speak for the Navy in this," Vicky said. "Since it is our heavy landing craft that are delivering the oversized loads for the fabs, I can assure you that the next delivery will go as we now agree to. If we agree today that Kiev gets more of the Brunswick cargo, I can give you my word that that is exactly the way it will be distributed."

"Is the word of a Peterwald any good?" someone Vicky didn't recognize opined.

"The word of this one is," Vicky said flatly.

"That settles that," said the mayor of Kiev, whom Vicky recognized from his profuse apology for her being kidnapped while visiting his city. He glanced at the industrialists and bankers around him. They nodded agreement.

"We accept your word, Your Grace, and we *will* be ready for the *next* delivery, won't we?" he said, eyeing his own.

The men of business did not argue with the elected representative of their workers.

The rest of the agenda was handled without Vicky saying a word.

The room was taking on the air of finishing up early and on a happy note, when Mannie leaned forward. "There is an extra item I have to add to our agenda. I only found out about it an hour before we were scheduled to start."

"Can't it wait for next time?" the mayor of St. Pete asked.

"I'm afraid not. I beg your indulgence. Your Grace, will you share the two messages you received? I'm sorry, when did you say you got them?"

"This morning, about four hours ago," she told the gathering.

"You see, this really is something we couldn't plan for," Mannie said.

"And won't delay?" came again.

"I think you'll understand once you see it. Your Grace."

"Computer, please play the first message for these people."

The computer synced with the table's computer and both of the landscapes in the wall murals suddenly changed into screens, showing the Emperor as he ordered Vicky home.

A puzzled "Oh," seemed to be the general reply.

"You will, of course, go," the mayor of Moskva said.

"One moment before we get to that," Mannie said. "The second message, Your Grace."

Vicky played the Empress's message into a deadly silent room.

"Oh," said the Kiev mayor when that tirade was done. "I guess she is not happy that her last bunch of assassins failed to kill you."

"Or that I stopped two shiploads of security types from landing on Presov and taking over the crystal-mining operations. Or should I say, taking them back over."

Vicky watched as the men and women, elected officials, bankers, and industrialists eyed each other in silence.

She cast Mannie a quick glance, but he was busy studying the others in the room. *Are you going to leave me hanging out here to dry? Why haven't you jumped to my defense?*

If this is democracy, then Kris Longknife can have it.

Still, Vicky kept her mouth shut.

These people didn't need to be reminded of what she'd done for them. They didn't need to be told what would likely lie ahead for her if she went back to Greenfeld. Stepmommy dearest had done a very good job of laying that on the line.

What is going through your minds?

Vicky had a pretty good idea of the answer to that question.

Just what good is this Grand Duchess to me? Can I take care of me and mine without her? What will it cost to save her life? Can I afford it?

What will the price of a civil war be? What will the price of just laying down and taking it be?

Mannie let those in the room do their own thinking. He made no effort to rush them. Neither did he step away from his place at her right hand.

"Well, that's not going to happen," the mayor of St. Pete finally said.

"No way," said the mayor of Moskva, after taking the census of those closest to him.

"She tried it before, and we damn well stopped that crazy bitch from killing our Grand Duchess," said Kiev's mayor.

"Then we stand united on this," Mannie said.

"Yeah," a manager drawled. "I guess we do. Assuming you can come up with a plan that isn't suicide."

On that note, the room turned to attacking this entirely new problem.

CHAPTER 3

"**Y**OUR Grace," Mannie said, turning to Vicky. "You've known about this for a bit more than the rest of us. What are your thoughts about a draft action plan?"

Vicky noted how Mannie deftly handled the turnover to her. He was asking her for a "draft" action plan. She would propose. They would dispose. She'd heard that was how it was done in a democracy. At least for the moment, she would go along with it.

"Thank you, Mr. Mayor," Vicky said. "I would like to thank all of you for considering my problem. No doubt, it will prove to be a most interesting challenge," she added dryly.

That got a chuckle from most in the room. Not all. Several intense men were leaning forward, serious to the point of deadly.

"His Imperial Majesty has requested and required me to return to the palace. Not to do so would be stupid, suicide, and treason. Therefore, my next message to him must be one of compliance. Or at least expressing the greatest desire to comply."

"Expressing it," one of the deadly serious men echoed. "Expressing one thing but doing another. How will you manage that?"

Vicky smiled slyly. "As you may have heard, there was an attack on my person. I managed to rescue myself, with a lot of help from all of you, but I did wander, shall we say, in the wilderness, for a day or so. My tender feet, as befit a Grand Duchess, were subject to rough treatment by rocks and thorns. My delicate skin was assaulted by bugs and all sorts of sharp denizens of nature. I might even have taken an infection or contracted something worse out in the wild."

"I take it that you propose to answer your father, our Emperor," Mannic said, "from a hospital bed? In intensive care, no doubt."

"No doubt," Vicky readily agreed.

"A good opening gambit," the deadly serious man agreed. "Some might point out that our peripatetic Grand Duchess has been seen at Presov and Metzburg since the attack."

"Someone might," Vicky said, "but one of the pains of travel among the stars is that dates can get so very confusing for people who live on one planet and never set foot off it. If I say I am sick from this dastardly attack by men only just arrived from Greenfeld, then it will be easy for others to assume some date has slipped. At least my father, Your Emperor, can easily persuade himself. No doubt my blackhearted stepmum, Your Empress, will do her best to correct him.

"With any luck, that will only add to the confusion," Vicky added.

"That may buy us time," another serious type said. "What will we use that time for?"

"During my recent visit to Metzburg, whenever it was, I suggested to them that they arm any available merchant hull with 6-inch lasers and good fire control systems. I also suggested they might put many of their unemployed to use in forestry work, under the guidance of retired military men who might also teach them, while working in the great outdoors, the more basic points of light infantry tactics. Such skills in the proper use of firearms might come in very handy if you suddenly found yourself in need of repelling lightly armed security personnel who were interested in anything but securing the peace."

"So you've got Metzburg doing pretty much what we're doing," the first serious type observed. "Where will Metzburg get these retired military types to help them train their, ah, irregular guardsmen?"

"The same place you are getting your training officers and NCOs," Vicky said.

"But our training cadre are taken from active duty Marines."

"Active duty, retired," Vicky said, diffidently, "no need to put too fine a point on it."

"Oh," one serious type said.

"Oooh," said the other. "Just how much is the Navy in on this?"

Vicky let that trial balloon float around the room for a long moment before she shot it down. Sort of. "I would not know," she said, as innocently as she had managed when she was five and caught with her hand in the cookie jar. "I do not speak for the Navy. As a Grand Duchess, I do what I am able. As a lieutenant commander, I do what I am told. I do my best to keep my different roles straight and not confuse them."

"I imagine that you do," said the first serious man.

"I think I get your meaning. For the moment," the second one added.

The two serious types glanced around the room, polling others of their mind-set, then the first turned back to Vicky.

"When I first heard that you had landed here, I strongly suspected you had come to start some sort of rebellion. I considered Mannie a fool, maybe a lovestruck fool, for letting you survive the drop. However, over time, you convinced me that you really were intent on doing good deeds. Was I as foolish as Mannie here?"

Vicky eyed Mannie. Lovestruck fool? He was managing not to meet her gaze. Vicky turned back to her inquisitor. She was getting rather good at answering inquisitors.

"I had no thought of rebellion when I landed on that day, not so long ago. You may find it hard to believe, but I love my father. My first choice was, and will always be, to remain loyal to him. You, the people of St. Petersburg, allowed me to do what I wanted to do. Save two planets. Save their people. You have seen my stepmother's answer to those deeds. She tried to kill me and now threatens to kill me if I don't docilely place my head under her axe.

"What I intended to do that day is one thing. What I find myself having to do today is another."

"And what you will do tomorrow may well be another," one of the intent men said. "Tell me, young woman, if it will save your neck, will you sacrifice the lives of all those in this room?"

Vicky gnawed her lower lip. That had to be the question

foremost in every mind around the table. She chose her words carefully.

"Today, I plan to respond to my father's summons with a message asking for delay. Soon, I intend to lead a trade convoy to Brunswick to open trade between them and you. When I return, I will examine all my options to see what I do next. What I will not do, not then, not ever, is to break faith with those who today swear on their honor to stand with me against the evil that the Empress and her family have brought to this, our beloved Greenfeld. I will fight them until their evil is banished from our lands or until I am dead. This I swear. This faith I will not break."

"Will we swear this with her?" Mannie asked.

"I will swear it," Kiev's mayor said, shooting to his feet.

"I will swear it," said the Kiev delegation as they followed him to his feet.

Even as they pushed their chairs back, others from other city delegations were shouting, "I swear it," and standing with them.

Around the room, the collection of serious men were eyeing their enthusiastic brothers and sisters towering above them, and polling themselves. Then, the two who had questioned Vicky got slowly to their feet. The others followed their lead.

"This we swear," they said, and someone began a cheer, and soon the entire room was cheering.

Vicky slowly came to her feet as the room quieted.

She let her eyes rove the room, blinking back moisture that threatened to fog her vision. "You have sworn with me, and now I swear with you. I will see a new dawn for Greenfeld, or I will die in its attempt."

CHAPTER 4

"**D**ADDY, I just got your message. I can't believe anyone would tell you I am not your most loyal subject," were the first words Vicky spoke to the message recorder.

It had taken three hours to get her ready for the camera.

The hospital where Doc Maggie had worked was only a short drive from the conference room. The rest of the time had been spent getting her camera-ready.

Her left leg, the one closest to the camera, was in an open sling. The foot dangling from the sling was about twice as big as normal and purple, with yellow pus draining down. That had been thanks to a makeup artist that Mannie just happened to know.

This rather lovely makeup artist reminded Mannie that it had been a while since he dropped by the studio, and the other girls missed him.

Maybe Mannie's not the monk I took him for.

After spraying on an underlayer of sunburn, the artist helped Kit and Kat get the scratches and bug bites back onto every inch of her exposed skin . . . quite a bit of exposed skin that Daddy would, no doubt, enjoy looking at once more.

Two young doctors, obviously attracted by all the lovely

women, turned up and added medical advice on just how bad infected bites and other insect activity could get.

They produced horrible pictures in vivid color.

Vicky ended up looking horrid.

The girls loved it.

Mannie looked on, grinning. "I have never seen a woman quite as ugly as you."

"Is that an offer to take me to dinner?" Vicky cooed.

"After you wash all that off, maybe," he answered.

"Oh, but shouldn't I be seen in public to strengthen my story?"

"We need to do something about her vocal cords," the makeup artist observed professionally. "If she's supposed to be dehydrated and sick, we can't have her sounding like she's ready to seduce the mayor, now can we?"

"Definitely not," Mr. Smith agreed, though Kit and Kat were clearly undecided.

As the scribe arrived with the camera, the movie magician had Vicky breathe in something from a can.

"That tastes horrible," Vicky growled, but her voice came out cracking and just as horrible to hear as she was to look at.

"Now it's showtime," the makeup artist said, and stepped back, out of sight.

Vicky adjusted her body in bed and her mind to corkscrew. "Daddy, I just got your message. I can't believe anyone would tell you I am not your most loyal subject,"

She paused to fall back in her bed, gasping for breath. The scribe took the time to play the camera over her body, moving slowly over every ugly cut, bruise, and bite before ending at her pus-oozing toes.

"I will come as soon as I can," Vicky got out as she struggled up a bit on one elbow. "I will answer every slander."

Again, she collapsed back onto her pillow. The scribe brought the recorder in close to her bare chest, her breasts now covered with light patches of bandages with truly ugly green and yellow ichor leaking through.

No nipple slip today, girl.

"I would come immediately, but I was kidnapped last week. They stripped me naked and left me chained to a bed in a hut back in the woods to die of thirst."

The camera swung to cover her hands and the truly appalling gashes on her wrists.

"Daddy, I'm a Peterwald. I escaped and trekked through the woods until they found me, but it was horrible. The rocks cut my feet, and they got infected. There were bugs and brambles and all sorts of things that got at me."

Vicky collapsed again into her bed, gasping for breath.

"I don't understand. The men who did this. They had just arrived from Greenfeld. Why would someone come out from Greenfeld to try to kill me?

"I am getting better, but they tell me that I can't fly in a shuttle yet. Here, let my doctor explain."

A mature doctor, not one of the kids that had helped get Vicky ready for the camera, now came to stand in front of Vicky and deliver a report. They'd made him go through his spiel four different times before he got it right.

"My father does not understand technical," Vicky had warned him after his first two tries. "You can include a full medical write-up for any doctor he brings in to check on this, but your report to him has to be aimed at a fourth-grade science level."

His next two tries were better. This, his fifth, was great.

"Your Imperial Majesty, the Grand Duchess has suffered major contusions and cuts, both to her wrists and ankles in her escape from her restraints and to her feet during her walk out. Most of them have become infected. I do not think the restraints were very clean.

"Here on St. Petersburg, we have several insects that bury their eggs inside other animals for them to incubate. When hatched, the larvae eat their way out of their victim. In the event of a high-gee shuttle launch, there is the chance of these eggs being sucked into the bloodstream and carried deep into the body. Larvae eating at heart or lung tissue would be fatal.

"Besides that, we need to care for the blood infection from her foot injuries. I'm afraid I cannot certify the Grand Duchess for flight. I do not know when I will be able to. We are still searching her body for bug bites and larvae infestations. She is a fighter, but all of this is taking a toll on her.

"I will attach my complete report for your own doctors to examine."

The scribe cut the recording.

"You will give me that report?" he asked the doctor.

"I should have it ready for you in an hour. We're pulling the photos and tests from other patients' files and making sure they all fit smoothly into the Grand Duchess's medical report."

The scribe grinned. He would be affixing his seal attesting to the truth of everything within. This one was young, and quite excited to be involved in pulling the wool over the reviled Peterwald's eyes.

And doing it for a Peterwald at that.

"If we're done here, can you clean me up?" Vicky said, getting her foot down out of the sling, before pulling herself up.

"Oh, please," Mannie said, covering his eyes from a view that might have been vile except she was now flashing him quite a bit of her lady parts.

"Excuse me," the commander said, in a voice that froze Vicky's blood. "I think we have a problem."

"What kind of problem, and can someone give me something to make my voice sound right."

"It will wear off in an hour," the makeup artist said, helpfully.

Vicky scowled, but turned her full attention to the commander.

"Three cruisers and three large attack transports just jumped into the system. They are setting a point seven five gee course for St. Petersburg and refusing to answer our hails."

"I think we have a problem," Vicky agreed. "I need this room," was pure Grand Duchess. "Kit, Kat, let's clean me up and get me back in uniform. Commander, have a shuttle waiting for me as soon as I am ready."

"I'm going with you," Mannie said. "You may need some local political cover for what comes next."

"Thank you, Mayor," Vicky said. "Now, folks, clear out. I need to clean up."

CHAPTER 5

V ICKY had her shuttle dock directly on the *Retribution*. She apparently was expected. Admiral von Mittleburg met her at the door of her quarters with Captain Etterlin of the battleship in tow.

"What have you got so far?" Vicky asked as she led them and her entourage into her day quarters.

"Not a lot," the admiral growled. "What looks to be three heavy cruisers are leading in three ships that have declared themselves the *Golden Empress 1, 2,* and *3.* The cruisers have throttled their squawkers so we can't identify them, but the *Golden Empress*es are being quite bold, even if they aren't talking to us."

"You can't tell me anything about the ships but that?" Vicky asked.

"What more could we tell you?" Captain Etterlin countered.

Vicky rolled her eyes. "Computer, get me Lieutenant Blue."

"Yes, Your Grace," came immediately in the voice of the enthusiastic young officer.

"What can you tell me about the six ships that just entered the system?"

"The three heavy cruisers are not telling us anything, but we have identified them as *Wittenberg, Augsburg,* and *Ulm.*

According to our data files, they carry twelve 9.2-inch lasers. Interesting enough, none of their capacitors are charged."

"And the three other ships?" Vicky prodded.

"They identify themselves as the *Golden Empress 1, 2*, and *3*, but they were, until lately, the *Germanica*, the *Europa*, and the *Constantinia*, all eighty-thousand-tonners of the Greenfeld-Earth lines. Our sensors show them armed with six 18-inch pulse lasers and three 5-inch long guns. Their capacitors are charged; however, their fire control systems, assuming they have any, are inactive."

"Thank you, Lieutenant Blue. Will you please report to me in my cabin."

"On my way, Your Grace."

Vicky rang off and faced her two superior officers. Admiral von Mittleburg had a quizzical look on his face. Captain Etterlin looked in danger of a heart attack.

"And who is this Lieutenant Blue?" the captain demanded.

"I believe he and his staff and equipment came aboard at Bayern, a gift to me from some retired admirals."

"Why wasn't I informed?"

"No doubt you were," Vicky answered the steaming officer. "No doubt you didn't know what you had been given," she added.

"Captain," the admiral said, stepping between the Grand Duchess and the skipper of her putative yacht. "Why don't you get the *Retribution* ready to sail. No doubt, there is a good chance we will be in a fight soon."

The man saluted, happy to have something he understood handed to him, and left.

"He is a good ship handler," the admiral noted.

"But I need a man of imagination, not a plodding cow."

"Yes. Now, if you will, just who is this Lieutenant Blue?"

"He heads a sensor team with capabilities that go far beyond what our usual sensor suites can produce. I noticed that Kris Longknife had a major sensor suite on her ship. Her corvette was much better outfitted than one of our battleships. I put that down to the nosy Longknifes wanting to know everything. Then I watched her in action. Information is power, and she had more information at her fingertips than I have ever seen.

"I might have mentioned that to our friendly neighborhood spy. Possible he passed it along to someone in the Navy. Or maybe I dropped a hint to Admiral Waller. I don't know how it happened, but I was delighted to be invited into Lieutenant Blue's inner sanctum and shown what his toys could do. My own computer had told me more about the two *Golden Empress*es we ran into that were intent on recapturing Presov than the ship's systems. Mr. Blue's, however, actually stripped data off their computers, which gave me an update on what was happening in the Empire while I was out here."

Vicky finished with a simple, "It was most informative."

Tired of standing, she offered the admiral his chair and took hers across from him. Mr. Smith and the commander settled into one couch between them. Mannie took the other. Kit and Kat found chairs against the wall and took up alert stations.

"I want Lieutenant Blue to have a station on the bridge where he can keep me informed of what is happening as it develops. I suggested he do that, but, last I was on the bridge, nothing had been done."

"No doubt he would be quite useful. Assuming the captain does not keelhaul him," the admiral said dryly.

"Is there any chance I could have Captain Bolesław of the *Attacker* as my captain, Admiral?"

"My immediate answer to that is no, but I doubt that was what you wanted to hear."

"In that, you are correct."

"Let me consider this. If we can lay our hands on enough ships, I might actually get a chance to take a squadron to space and command it from this ship. That might open a lot of opportunities to you and put a cushion between you and Captain Etterlin."

"It would be appreciated. You understand the value of a Grand Duchess. I fear that Captain Etterlin can only see a lieutenant commander."

"That will, no doubt, be his mistake," the admiral said.

At that moment, Lieutenant Blue presented himself. He was delighted to have a chance to explain to an admiral how he had managed to strip the IDs off three cruisers that were not squawking and how he knew what was and was not charged in the weapons they might be facing. When he'd finished, the admiral eyed Vicky with raised eyebrows.

"If the Wardhaven princess has this kind of information at her fingertips, no wonder she is such a pain in our behinds."

"Yes." Vicky agreed. "That is just the pain I wish to be if it comes to a fight."

"I believe the *Retribution* has a flag bridge," the admiral said.

"It does, sir," the lieutenant reported.

"Please arrange to have a sensor station with feeds from your instruments located on that bridge. If you need any paperwork signed, contact my chief of staff."

"I will contact him immediately, sir."

"By the way, Lieutenant," Vicky said. "What is your name? Blue is a nice code word, but if we are going to work together, I would like to know whom I am addressing."

"Blue *is* my name, Your Grace. Lieutenant Odo Blue, at your service," came with a bow from the waist and a full click of his heels.

"I am glad to have you in my service," Vicky answered, and the lieutenant went on his way.

Vicky turned back to her admiral. "It seems we must find you a fleet to command so I can stand at your elbow and not someone less impressionable."

"We have the *Rostock*," the admiral provided.

"What kind of a battle can one battleship and one light cruiser put up against three heavies and a trio of armed liners?"

The admiral stared at the overhead. "It all depends. If the battleship can open fire at its maximum range, it could do a lot of damage before the others got close enough to lay a finger on it. If, however, politics or something else allowed the cruisers and jumped-up merchant ships to close to within their range before a shot is fired, it would be a bloody brawl. No matter who was left standing at the end, they'd be in a lot of hurt."

"I kind of figured you'd say that," Vicky said. "So, we either fire first and start this war without any defiances given, or we let them get in close and start the war, and maybe make it a very short one, at that."

"None of that sounds good to me," the admiral admitted.

"I remember you telling me you had two armed merchant ships of your own fitting out."

"Yes, the *Sovereign of the Stars* and the *Sovereign of the Sky* are both about ready to sail. They are now armed with six 21-inch pulse lasers and six 6-inch long guns."

"Better than the blackhearted Empress's ships, but we only have two to her three."

"Yes," the admiral agreed. "It might be better for us, but it would still be a bloody mess."

"It seems to me that we need to figure out some way not to fight this battle."

"That would be my first choice," the admiral agreed, "but how?"

"What if the two *Sovereign*s pass themselves off as *Attacker* and *Kamchatka*?"

The admiral frowned at Vicky. "*Attacker* has twelve 8-inch lasers. The *Kamchatka* is older, but she has twelve 9.2-inch lasers in her main battery. Older. Slower to recharge. Still, with the *Retribution* backing them up, I'd be reluctant to get in a fight if I only had the three *Wittenberg*s. But how would anyone mistake the *Sovereign*s for heavy cruisers?"

"Computer, get me Lieutenant Blue."

"Yes, Your Grace."

"I need to pass off two armed merchant cruisers as the heavy cruisers *Attacker* and *Kamchatka*. Any suggestions how I do it?"

"Well, Your Grace, it's against the law for a ship to squawk as another ship."

"What if I didn't care about that law?"

"Assuming the sensors aboard the cruisers coming in aren't any better than the sensors on most Greenfeld ships, it should be pretty easy to mess with them. I've always wanted to try it, but, you know, ma'am, it being illegal and all that, I'd never think of actually doing it."

"Which is to say that you've never done it for very long and gotten caught," Vicky said dryly.

"Not more than a few seconds, ma'am."

"Can you do it for several long hours?"

"Most certainly," sounded boyishly eager.

"Admiral, could you advise the skippers of the necessary ships that we will be making some unusual modifications to them in the next hour."

"Unusual or illegal?"

"No need to put too fine a point on it, is there?"

"Of course not, Your Grace." With a grin, he tapped his

commlink. "Bruno, have I got some work for you, and it's not even all that illegal."

Vicky went over to the bulkhead that separated her day cabin from her night cabin. "Computer, show me the system with all the ships under way in it."

The bulkhead screen came to life. There was only the one dot representing the incoming six ships from her stepmother.

Mannie now came to stand at her elbow. "What are you thinking of?" he asked.

"How to not fight a battle but win one anyway," Vicky said vaguely.

"To use cunning rather than brute force; huh."

"Something like that," Vicky admitted. "Kris Longknife does this all the time. This is the first time I'm trying my hand at it."

"You going to go charging out at them?" Mannie asked.

"If I did, the admiral here would tan my bottom, right?"

"I don't know about your bottom," the admiral said, carefully, "but I would strongly recommend against you charging at the incoming ships. Once you shot past them, you'd have a hell of a time turning around, and they'd be closing on St. Petersburg and this station with a free hand."

"I did learn something following Admiral Krätz and Kris Longknife around," Vicky said. "Never let the enemy get between you and the base you have to defend. No. We stay here for as long as I dare. I just wish something would force them to tip their hand . . . give away their intentions."

The admiral's shrug was full stoic.

Then the jump coughed out a new set of dots.

"The heavy cruiser *Biter* has just entered the system," Vicky's computer announced.

"I think I hear a hand tipping," Vicky whispered.

CHAPTER 6

"THE *Biter* was escorting a trade convoy on a swing through Good Luck, Finster, Ormuzd, Kazan, and Presov," the admiral said, as freighters followed the cruiser through the jump.

"So those cargo ships are loaded with crystal and rare earths," Vicky said.

"Among other resources," the admiral agreed.

"Which we need."

"Definitely," Mannie said.

"Your Grace," came from Lieutenant Blue, "the *Golden Empress 1* has just ordered the *Biter* and the arriving convoy to match course and acceleration with them."

"Thank you, Lieutenant."

"I wondered why those ships were only accelerating at point seven five gees," the admiral said. "They were waiting for the convoy to come through so they could shanghai it."

"Apparently. How bad are the odds against the *Biter*?"

"She has twelve 8-inch lasers. She faces thirty-six 9.2-inch ones. Not good."

"Admiral, if you will, please advise the convoy and its escort to comply with the threats being leveled at them."

The admiral raised a quizzical eyebrow.

"One could say that they are being attacked by pirates, could one not?" Vicky said, oh so delicately.

"Assuming the color of the demands is piratical and not official," the admiral agreed.

"Only time will tell, but we don't want to fire the first shot, do we?"

"No," and the admiral tapped his commlink and sent the suggested order to *Biter*.

It took a while for all the messages to pass through space this way and that. While Vicky went about her own work, messages came in from the *Biter* demanding to know who was ordering her and her convoy to deviate from their course. The three Navy cruisers stayed quiet through the exchange. A Lord High Commissioner for the Safety of St. Petersburg aboard the *Golden Empress 1* informed them he held a warrant direct from the Empress's hand and that all must comply with his commands. The skipper of the *Biter* delayed answering that one, but he did accelerate away from the jump at one gee and slowly overtook the early arrivals.

Once they got close enough, the Lord High Commissioner for Safety announced that they should prepare to be boarded. The *Biter*'s initial answer to that was a strong negative. Luckily, the admiral's instructions arrived about that time, and *Biter* then matched its course and acceleration smoothly with the other convoy. Longboats quickly covered the distance between the freighters and cruiser from the armed merchant ships or maybe pirates.

"I would call that an attack, wouldn't you?" Vicky said.

"I doubt if the Empress would," the admiral pointed out.

"Mannie, what do you call it?"

"Interference with the free trade of ships registered to my planet," the mayor snapped.

"I think we might give his opinion on this matter some weight," Vicky said.

"Maybe we can," the admiral agreed, rubbing his chin. "Maybe we can. Now what?"

"We wait until they are close enough," Vicky said slowly, "then we loop out to do our own matching of orbits with them. You and your task force of three cruisers and a battleship."

"Since all we can do is wait, I'm hungry," Mannie said. "Don't you sailormen eat?"

"I'll have the galley send a meal to my wardroom, or the admiral's wardroom," Vicky said. "If he's coming aboard, I imagine I'll have to find someplace else to hang my dainties out to dry."

"I suspect it will be a quick in and out, all in one day," the admiral said. "No doubt you can leave your dainties drying where they are."

"You are most gracious," Vicky allowed.

"Is she always this nice?" Mannie asked the admiral.

"I think she's trying to pull the wool over someone's eyes. It's certainly not working on me," the admiral answered.

"Hmm," was all the mayor said.

The commander announced that supper was served in the admiral's wardroom, and the seven of them adjourned next door to taste a decent goulash the cook was rumored to be famous for. If you didn't believe it, you only had to ask the chief petty officer yourself.

Kit hunted up a screen they could glance at during supper. It continued to show the progression of the ships closing in on High St. Petersburg.

After his second spoonful of goulash, the admiral put down his spoon and turned to Vicky. "How would you fight this coming battle?"

Vicky had a spoon of the quite tasty stew halfway to her mouth. She put it down, patted her lips with the linen napkin, and thought for a moment more. "First, the objective is to overawe the other side into not fighting. Somehow, I would want to put them in a position where they knew they were in trouble and would be badly bloodied if it came to a fight, and thus, would call it quits before it came to one."

"A commendable objective," the admiral said, "considering that some of my friends are on those ships. So, how would you do that?"

Vicky leaned back in her chair and stared at the overhead for a long moment. She found herself worrying her lips as she thought. Clearly, the admiral was not about to turn his fleet over to a green lieutenant commander. This was an exercise to see if a Grand Duchess could be trusted on his bridge as he figured this one out for himself.

Still, this was a test she very much wanted to pass.

"Kris Longknife had a battle very much like this one,"

Vicky finally said, remembering a very long analysis that someone had added to Kris's file.

Vicky wondered how many friends the man writing that analysis had lost when Kris Longknife won that battle.

"Which one was that?" Mannie asked. "She seems to have fought a lot of battles if the stories are to be believed."

"It was in defense of her home planet," Vicky said, "when pirate battleships suddenly appeared and demanded its surrender."

"Oh, that one," Mannie said.

Vicky had noted the slight wince from the admiral when she said "pirate battleships." No doubt he knew the real reason for the empty seats at Greenfeld Navy Academy reunions of late. In present company, he kept his silence.

"Yes," Vicky said, "that one. Six battleships headed for her planet. Only twelve mosquito boats to defend it because of an unbelievable blunder by some politicians."

Again, Vicky had a pretty good idea who had encouraged those Wardhaven politicians to make such a botch of matters, but it was not something to talk about here and now. The look the admiral gave Vicky told her he wanted that talk, and soon.

"So, Kris Longknife had this same problem," Mannie said, playing the straight man to Vicky. "What did she do?"

"She put her fast attack boats, along with anything else she could scrape together, kind of like us and our armed merchant cruisers, in a high orbit that reached out to meet the incoming battleships without charging right past them. That put her in a position to fight them all the way in. Is that what you intend to do, Admiral von Mittleburg?"

"Gravity tends to limit our options in situations like these," the admiral said, "but yes, that would be my choice. The incoming ships will be braking toward an orbit. We will meet them at a point that allows us to bring them under fire at the extreme effective range of our lasers, where their guns are barely able to heat water. That will give us time to talk. Hopefully, to talk them down."

"You might be able to talk the Navy down, but I'm not so sure about that Lord High Commissioner for Safety on St. Petersburg," Vicky said.

Mannie scowled. "We can take care of our own safety, thank you very much."

"Yes, but can you keep yourself safe from a Lord High Commissioner for *your* Safety?" Admiral von Mittleburg asked.

"I'm hoping you will save me from that problem," Mannie said. "We've smuggled some books on irregular warfare in from Longknife territory. It makes interesting reading. The Lord High Commissioner may have no idea what he's in for, but then, suppression of guerrilla wars can be very bloody to all concerned."

"We will try to save you from that," Vicky said.

"If your Lieutenant Blue is correct, and *Wittenberg* is leading the cruisers in, its skipper, Staale Sandback, will not be enthusiastic about firing the first shot, not on his own Navy, but he is an honorable man. Speaking of your Mr. Blue, it is one thing to switch squawkers from one ship to the next. It is another thing to have sensors report that the reactors match those the database has for those ships. How will he manage that?"

Vicky shrugged. "I have no idea. I certainly have no idea how to do it myself. Do you know anyone on board more likely to come up with such an idea?"

The admiral chuckled. "Not on my life."

"So, sir, shall we enjoy this delicious goulash before it gets too much colder and trust more twisted brains than ours to come up with what we need?"

"I doubt," Mannie said, "that there are more twisted brains in the worlds than those seated around this table."

That got a general laugh, and they returned to their dinner with a hearty appetite.

CHAPTER 7

E ARLY the next morning, the *Retribution* led a small task
force away from High St. Petersburg Station. The *Rostock*
quickly slipped into the lead while the putative *Attacker* and
Kamchatka pulled up the rear.

Vicky and Mannie stood beside Admiral von Mittleburg
on the flag bridge of the *Retribution*. Lieutenant Blue had a
station just off to their right. Mr. Smith had pulled up a seat at
the lieutenant's elbow and was dividing his attention between
the sensor station and his own computer.

The admiral eyed the spy but kept his opinions to himself.

"Tell me, Lieutenant Blue," Vicky said when the young officer
paused from what he had been so intently doing. "The reactors on
the *Sovereign*s are not the same as the heavy cruisers they are
trying to pass for. How do you propose we pull that off?"

"We can't, Your Grace. Reactors can't be faked."

"So, as soon as their sensor team gets a good look at the reactors on those ships," the admiral snapped, "they will know we are
faking it."

"Yes and no, sir."

"That is not an answer, Lieutenant," the admiral growled,
his poor humor getting worse.

"It's the only answer I can give you, sir. What the other ships' sensors will actually get off all our ships, including the *Rostock* and the *Retribution* will be hash, sir. One of my petty officers came up with this noisemaker idea that we've installed in all four of our ships. They will generate all sorts of static where a sensor usually finds data on reactors. When the captain of the oncoming cruisers asks his sensor officer to identify the ships coming at him, he will have to painfully answer that there is something wrong with his instruments. He has some data, but it might be right. It might be wrong. He just isn't sure."

Mannie barked a laugh. "I've never met a Navy officer who didn't like to be sure of himself. That is going to be one painful report to make and receive."

"No doubt," the admiral admitted dryly.

The short line of ships decelerated to pass close aboard St. Petersburg, then accelerated into a much higher orbit. At apogee, it would bring them close to the incoming ships, putting the decelerating convoy's vulnerable rears in the *Retribution*'s crosshairs while the cruiser's guns were far out of range.

That would be the critical time for this battle. If it was to become a battle.

The *Wittenberg*, *Augsburg*, and *Ulm* continued to lead the transports, each ship keeping a comfortable five-hundred-kilometer interval. The trade convoy from Presov now docilely trailed the first group, a thousand kilometers from *Golden Empress 3* to the *Biter*, then five hundred klicks between each freighter.

The clock ticked off the seconds as the ships closed.

"*Retribution* will be in extreme range of *Wittenberg* in one minute," Lieutenant Blue reported.

"Very well," Admiral von Mittlburg said. "Open a communications channel between me and *Wittenberg*. Wide beam and in the clear for anyone who wishes to listen in."

"Done," a chief communications tech answered, and a small window opened on the main screen.

"Hello, Staale. I hoped to meet you in better times."

"Hello, Admiral von Mittleburg. Are these not the best of times?"

"My lasers are charged and yours are not."

"As I have told those with me, I see no reason to charge my lasers. Should I?"

"Time will tell."

A new window opened on the forward screen to show a red-faced balding man with three chins. "Charge your guns, Captain. Charge them, damn you! I have ordered you to power up, and you keep refusing."

"And I have told you time and time again, Lord High Commissioner for Safety," Captain Sandback said, as if to a tiresome child, "that it would be suicide for us to come in here threatening to fire on the *Retribution*. This must be worked out. To use force is only to commit suicide for all of us."

"We have the right," the red-faced man shouted.

"You are interfering with the free trade guaranteed by the Empire between planets of the Imperium," Mannie said, tossing his oar into the troubled waters. "Boarding free-trading freighters of St. Petersburg is tantamount to piracy."

"We did it to protect them," was smooth as oil on silk . . . and just about as worthless.

"A Navy cruiser was escorting them. I saw no threat to them," Mannie spat back. "Unless, of course, the threat was you."

"I am the Lord High Commissioner for Safety on St. Petersburg. I have a warrant signed from the hand of the Empress."

"But not the Emperor," Mannie pointed out.

"They are one and the same," had a lot of bluster behind it.

"We have received no such Imperial Proclamation to that effect," Mannie pointed out.

"Maybe I'm carrying it." The Lord High Commissioner seemed suddenly less sure. "What I do know is that I am backed up by three regiments of security specialists, and I will assure that St. Petersburg remains safe and law-abiding."

The commissioner's eyes seemed to narrow. "Oh, I see that you have the Grand Duchess Victoria aboard. Good. We understood that her safety was in some question. You will immediately transfer her to my ship for her own safety."

"Strange," Vicky said, "it was the people of St. Petersburg who secured the safety of my person. It was recent arrivals from Greenfeld who did me harm."

"Canards, no doubt. Lies and damn lies to cover up the danger you are truly in."

"Little man, I am on a battleship of the Imperial Navy. I doubt I could be more safe."

"Nevertheless, you will obey my order and report immediately to the *Golden Empress 1* for safekeeping."

"Or tight imprisonment?"

"Do not risk the ire of the Empress."

Vicky half laughed. "Sorry, little man. I have risked her ire and dodged her assassins ever since she became pregnant, and I became one too many people between her child and the throne."

"Is that the way the wind blows?" Captain Sandback said.

"I'm afraid it is, Staale," Admiral von Mittleburg answered. "The Navy has protected Her Grace through over a dozen assassination attempts, most of which could be traced back to the palace. There is no chance that I would turn her over to someone holding a warrant from the Empress's own hand."

"I believe I begin to understand better many of the things I have been told or overheard. Admiral, my squadron will stand down. Mr. Lord High Commissioner, this is between you and the, ah, people you say you have come to protect."

"I'll have your head for this. I have three regiments, over ten thousand men at my beck and call." The red in his face was reaching new heights. In any cartoon character, this would have anticipated a truly glorious explosion. All Vicky could hope for was a heart attack.

"Yes, good High Commissioner," Captain Sandback said, so very evenly, "but you are there, and I am several thousand kilometers of vacuum removed from your guns. If I was not worried about sending the wrong message to my old friend, Admiral von Mittleburg, I would charge up my lasers. Then you would see how your ten thousand machine pistols stood up to a mere dozen 9.2-inch Navy lasers."

A new window opened. "Captain Hans Wirtz of the *Biter*, Admiral. We have, ah, recovered our freedom of movement, sir. I am advised that the guard detail that St. Petersburg has attached to each of its freighters has also regained full control of their ships."

"Mannie?" Vicky said, nudging the mayor of Sevastopol.

"So we put a squad of Rangers on each ship. It seemed like a good idea."

"And your Rangers," Captain Wirtz added, "have full

battle armor, something the security detachment that boarded our ship did not. Confronted by the prospects that they would bleed, and those with guns facing them likely would not, the security people surrendered to the obvious."

"Well, I will not surrender," the Lord High Commissioner spat. "Captain, your course is for the space station."

"I beg to differ," Admiral von Mittleburg said. "You will not come alongside my station with your lightly armed men. I like the air in my station, and it is hard to maintain it when there are bullet holes all over the place."

"Captain, increase your speed," the commissioner demanded.

"Your Lordship, I can't increase my speed," came from off his screen. "We are decelerating toward the station. If we go any faster, it won't be there when we get there."

"You know what I mean. Get us there and shoot anything that gets in my way. You have lasers. Use them."

"You use them," Admiral von Mittleburg growled, "and we will blow you out of space."

"Admiral, Captain Wirtz again. I'm the closest to those transports. While the *Biter* doesn't have the greatest of shots at his engines, I do have a decent one. More likely I'll put them off-line than blow them all to hell. Of course, with his rocket motors perforated, he's likely to miss the station and head off to freeze in space. After their air goes bad, of course."

"Captain! Fire on that man," the Lord High Commissioner screamed.

"Fire," the captain ordered.

All three of the *Golden Empress*es fired all of their pulse lasers and long guns immediately.

Of course, no one took any time to aim them, so they dissipated their lasers into empty space although one shot from the *Golden Empress 2* did come close to the engines of the *Golden Empress 1*.

"Blow Reactor 2 to space," came over the net in what Vicky took to be the voice of the skipper of the *Golden Empress 1*. Immediately, all three transports dumped one of their two reactors.

"Now, my Lord High Commissioner of blowhards," that voice continued, "we have one reactor. We can use it to slow this tub full of your asses so that it ends up close to the station and we all get out of here alive, or we can use it to reload our lasers. No doubt we will be blown out of space before we finish the reload, but the call is yours. What will it be?"

The red face tried to say something, but suddenly, he was speechless as he clasped his chest. A moment later, he collapsed and disappeared from the screen.

"My God, I think he's having a heart attack," came from a man in a merchant captain's uniform now visible on screen. "Medic! Do you goddamn security guards have any decent medics with you? Damn it! Somebody help him!"

"We will send our ship's surgeon," Captain Wirtz of the *Biter* announced. "Hold your deceleration and course steady so we can make the transfer."

"You better make it quick. I don't see this guy lasting too long."

"The longboat is away with a medical team," Captain Wirtz announced.

Vicky turned away from the screen. "Well, I didn't see that coming," she admitted.

"We created the situation," Admiral von Mittleburg said softly, "and a lot of good men, and at least one bad one, provided the miracles. Interesting, is it not?"

"Are all days in the Navy like this?" Mannie asked.

"Some are more exciting than others," Vicky allowed.

"Now, about those ten thousand lightly armed thugs wanting to dock at my space station?" the admiral asked.

"Ah, yes," Mannie said. "If you will allow me to borrow one of your communication circuits, I will see what I can do about having a lot of off-duty cops and not a few Rangers in full armor brought up on the next shuttles. There are plenty coming up with cargo for Brunswick, and there's still stuff coming down from Metzburg. There should be plenty of room for troops."

"Good. I've got Marines, but not nearly enough to keep that number of people of unknown moral standards under control. Oh, Mayor, do you have jobs for them?"

"Given a choice between letting them wander around idle," Mannie said, "and us getting them to work, we'll find something, though it may be farmwork in the outback and by."

"Just so long as they're out of my hair."

"Well, Vicky this has been a most interesting day," Mannie allowed after he'd finished his calls.

"We must do this more often."

"We'll be putting the finishing touches on the first shipment to Brunswick. It means meetings. Likely not as exciting as this one, and it may all go so smoothly that they just might bore you. Still, you and I might arrange for a quiet, candlelit dinner."

A shiver went up Vicky.

Is this really me?

"I doubt the admiral will miss me," Vicky said, sounding almost coy.

"Oh, no. I won't miss you at all," Admiral von Mittleburg put in, enthusiastically.

"Then I guess I'll go dirtside with you."

"Good," Mannie said. His smile seemed more than pleased. Vicky found herself wondering just what thoughts might be behind that smile and found she liked the mystery.

CHAPTER 8

THE trip back to High St. Petersburg got more than a little
exciting as the jump point spit up a powerful task force.

Lieutenant Blue did the honors of calling them back to the
flag bridge. "Admiral, Your Grace, we have company."

"What kind of company," the admiral demanded.

"Big company. It's squawking as the battleship *Scourge*."
Mannie shot Vicky a worried glance.

"It's almost as big as the *Retribution*," Vicky said.

"Twelve 18-inch lasers for a main battery to our sixteen,"
the admiral filled in.

"Whose side is it on?" Mannie asked.

"It was here a month ago, but they pulled it back for some
odd reason," Admiral von Mittleburg answered. "Who has it
now is anyone's guess."

"The battlecruiser *Stalker* followed it through," the lieutenant added. "And now we have the *Slinger*."

"Those were Admiral Gort's ships when he picked me up
on High Chance," Vicky said.

"Gort was a good man," the admiral said.

"A good man who took a bullet intended for me," Vicky
added.

"One of those twelve assassination attempts the Navy has messed up for the Empress?" Mannie asked.

"It was just luck. My good luck. His bad luck," Vicky said mournfully, feeling the desolation of it again.

"The old heavy cruiser *Kasimov* just jumped in, trailed by its sister the *Yamal*."

"They're as ancient as the *Kamchatka*," the admiral said. "The *Scourge* is nearly new. The *Kasimov* is over twenty years old. What have they got in common?"

"Admiral, commlink opening to the *Scourge*," announced the chief petty officer.

"On main screen."

"Hello, Admiral von Mittleburg. I was hoping to see you again," came from a sandy-haired captain of middle years.

"Willy Brandl, I'm glad to see you again," the admiral said, "although I admit to being a bit surprised. I'm not sure I'm prepared for such an influx of ships."

The time delay made for a slow conversation, but it did not stop it. "Sorry to pop in on you so unexpectedly, but it was either come here or report to High Homburg to be decommissioned and scrapped. Assuming the ships were actually scrapped and not put to another use."

"They are scrapping battleships and battlecruisers in midlife!" Vicky exclaimed in shock.

"Some of us suspect they need bigger pirate ships. The Navy's light cruisers have been shooting up heavy cruisers that seem to have transitioned from scrap to pirates in an amazing sleight of hands," the newly arrived captain said dryly.

"May I ask who sent you?" Vicky asked.

"Not on an open channel," he said. "But Admiral von Mittleburg, we are just the first of several. It's preferred that we come out here. Putting us in orbit around Bayern would be a clear signal to some that the Navy is not doing as ordered. Really, I must ask, can you put us up?"

The admiral looked at Mannie and Vicky. It was Vicky who stepped forward.

"We will support you. We need you. Certain decisions have been made recently. They also can't be talked about over an open comm line. However, we need you as much as you need us." She glanced at Mannie.

"Arrangements will be made," he said. "I am the mayor of one of St. Petersburg's largest cities. I don't know *how* we will do it, but we *do* need you, and we *will* support you."

"Thank you," the redheaded skipper said, and cut the circuit.

"It seems that we really must get below," Mannie said, "as quickly as possible."

"Yes, I think we must," Vicky said.

CHAPTER 9

I T is a law of physics that what goes up must come down. In space, a similar law insists that what goes out comes back no faster than it went there. Or at least not all that much faster.

The *Retribution* fell back toward High St. Petersburg Station with a slowness that almost drove Vicky to chew her well-manicured nails.

Mannie called ahead to set up meetings that people were already clamoring for. They knew about the new ships in the system and wanted to know what they were doing there and what would be done about them.

The mayor admitted that some of the ships were an invasion fleet that had been dissuaded. Others were a trade convoy coming back, and the rest were Navy ships seeking refuge.

Yep, the leaders of St. Petersburg definitely wanted to talk. Mannie explained why he couldn't call a meeting right that moment. After a long talk, Mannie broke the commlink.

"That could have gone a lot better."

"How could it have gone worse?" Vicky snapped.

"They're worried. They need to talk."

"And they are going to talk behind our backs."

"You want to hold a meeting on a commlink and have it recorded and shot off to your stepmother?"

"Not really," Vicky had to admit. "Then again, will we have any better luck keeping the contents of a meeting out of her hands?"

"What we say among ourselves risks all of our necks. What some hacker picks up and sends off for payment is another thing. They want to talk, but they aren't going to talk on net. Your father's late-lamented State Security Police taught us our lessons about that."

"So, what happens now?"

"They are all heading to St. Pete for a meeting of all interested parties, and then some. We will get there as soon as we can. No doubt, we will be behind the curve when we do."

"Will you have a representative there when they start?"

"I'm no neophyte. My lieutenant mayor, a very competent young man, will cover for me and take copious notes. However, he is not me. The businessmen and bankers will walk all over him, and the other cities will ignore Sevastopol. Here I thought sticking my neck out to stop an invasion would make me a hero. Now I'm out in left field playing catch-up."

Vicky could only sigh. "Strange how the world works. Commander, please check on how soon we can cut loose from the *Retribution*. Don't worry about using the captain's gig or the admiral's barge. Any longboat that gives us a larger window for landing at St. Pete is just fine with me."

"Yes, Your Grace," the commander said, and left them.

Mannie and Vicky spent the next few hours sweating over every number they could find. Food would not be a problem. Finding tritium to fuel the extra ships' reactors might be. "Finding docks for them may also be difficult," Mannie said. "We were getting more freighters moving. If the warships are parked permanently, that could affect trade."

"Then we'll just have to keep the ships doing something," Vicky said. "I'm headed for Brunswick with a trade delegation and half a dozen freighters."

"A dozen," Mannie corrected.

"A dozen!"

"Yep. Brunswick had a longer wish list, and what with all the shipments of crystal and rare earths, we can meet their needs. Oh, and we need to look at a second convoy to Metzburg."

"Half dozen or a dozen?"

"A full dozen this time. It may not sail in the next few days. That load of rare earths we just got in will need to be processed into product before we send that convoy out."

"I'm starting to think that keeping enough ships at High St. Petersburg to protect it may be more of a problem than you're thinking."

Mannie shrugged. "You could have a point. By the way, are we just protecting convoys and St. Petersburg from pirates, or is it something bigger?"

"That depends on how many skippers turned their ships over to be junked, doesn't it?"

"How good will the skippers be that the Empress hires for her new battleships?"

Vicky sighed. "Your guess is as good as mine. How much of the flexibility that we saw in the crew of the *Golden Empress 1* was because they were so outgunned and how much was because they thought they were on the wrong side?"

"As you said, your guess is as good as mine," Mannie agreed.

They went over more numbers and found more options and more challenges. It became clear that they were guessing at their problems and guessing even more wildly at their solutions.

Mannie leaned back on his couch, spread his arms wide, and put his feet up on the coffee table that doubled as a computer screen. He let out a huge sigh. "Don't things around you ever slow down?"

Vicky gave the question all the time it deserved—about two seconds, then shrugged. "They don't seem to although I will point out in my defense that I don't have a lot of control over them. As a case in point, I give you that invasion fleet or the refugees."

"Yes, yes, yes," Mannie agreed. "But don't you ever want to lean back on a sofa, kick your shoes off, and curl up in front of a nice fire?"

She wanted very much to curl her legs around him, fireplace or not. With regret, she deflected that thought.

"There aren't that many fireplaces on battleships. I don't think they're allowed."

Mannie scowled at her. "Not even for Grand Duchesses?"

"Especially not for Grand Duchesses. Oh, I don't know. Maybe for a Grand Duchess who doesn't spend all her time running for her life. I don't know about those kind, never having met one."

"You have a point. Not a good one, I allow you, but a point. When we get you back to Sevastopol, you are going to have to let me take you up to a place I know in the mountains. It's great when it snows. There's skiing and maybe even a snowball fight or two if you're really daring. It has the most wonderful fireplace. Gray fieldstones all the way up to the ceiling. Beautiful high wooden ceiling. Or would you call it an overhead?"

"Houses have ceilings," Vicky allowed. "Warships have overheads. It's the same with walls and bulkheads."

"You sure? Would a real Navy officer give me a different answer?"

"I don't know. If my commander/lifeguard ever comes back, you can ask him. Maybe if you're third-generation Navy, even walls are bulkheads, but I've only been at this Navy thing for a few years."

"And someday you'll be a full-time Grand Duchess and not part-time Navy and part-time Grand Duchess."

"Oh." Vicky sighed. "It would be so wonderful not to have to check each footstep, each word. Am I Navy right now, or am I whatever a Grand Duchess is?"

"You don't know what you are by now?"

"My dad seems to know what Emperor means. He can do whatever he damn well wants to. The Empress seems to think she can kill whomever she damn well chooses. Me, I can't tell the difference between Grand Duchess and Grand Target."

"Probably because they appear to be one and the same at the moment."

"Apparently."

"You want to sit over here, or is there something in the Grand Duchess Handbook that says you may never share a sofa with a subject?"

"Is there such a handbook?" Vicky said, letting her eyes go wide. "Have you got a copy I can borrow?"

"So, you just like to keep your own chair."

"I didn't say that," Vicky said, and stood to walk toward the offered place beside Mannie.

There was a knock at the door, and the commander entered, a chief boson's mate right behind him.

Vicky turned her slink to the couch into standing tall like a good Navy officer.

"Yes, Commander?"

"The chief is the most experienced man aboard at handling longboats. Chief?"

"Your Grace, we got a picket boat aboard that we usually just use as a liberty launch. However, it does have more powerful engines if we want to use them and can carry extra reaction mass if we don't need to carry a lot of junk, if you take my meaning, Your Grace."

"I've got five people plus me I need to get to St. Pete as soon as possible." When the commander started to object, Vicky cut him off. "The admiral can send as many Marines down when he gets in range. For now, Mannie and I need to be there, and I think you, Mr. Smith, Kit, and Kat can take care of matters well enough."

"I have already called ahead and have an extralarge security detail going along with my lieutenant mayor," Mannie put in.

"If you insist," the commander said.

"I do. Chief, how soon can we detach from this battlewagon?"

"I've double-checked my orbital calculations with the ship's navigator as well as the captain and admiral. If I may say so, they agree the earliest time to depart is in"—he glanced at his wrist—"thirty-three minutes."

"Then I think we need to toss a few things in a bag, don't we?" Vicky said.

Mannie left to get the tiny overnight bag he'd brought up with him. The commander allowed that his baggage was already aboard the picket boat. Mr. Smith was back in five minutes, a bit before Kit and Kat managed to pack Vicky a couple of uniforms, a little red dress, and her toothbrush.

They were aboard the picket boat well before it dropped away.

CHAPTER 10

VICKY could not recall a wilder shuttle ride in her life. Nor had she ever put on such heavy gees.

Kit wryly suggested they all needed to lose weight.

Vicky was haunted by the doctor's words about bugs in the wild outback of St. Petersburg that laid eggs under your skin. He thought a high-gee shuttle ride just might knock those eggs loose into her bloodstream so the larvae could dine on her heart. She dearly hoped she hadn't actually run into any of those little buggers during her naked wandering through St. Petersburg's wilderness.

Assuming us Peterwalds have hearts.

The picket boat groaned and moaned as the chief put it through some sharp S turns during reentry. Vicky found herself praying to any god willing to listen to her blackened soul that the wings would stay on. Beside her, Mannie was fingering a rosary.

Despite all the bumps and thumps, the wings stayed on, and the flight ended with the shuttle's coming in for a smooth landing at the St. Pete spaceport.

A limo awaited them with a large police escort.

"I told you I phoned ahead for security," Mannie said.

"Let us hope no one in the Empress's pay was listening," Mr. Smith said with no softening smile.

Kit and Kat kept their heads on a swivel. Vicky was glad she had on her spidersilk under armor.

The drive through St. Pete showed a city recovered from its economic death spiral. Everywhere Vicky looked, traffic was thick on the streets, and people were walking with purpose. Several new buildings were going up.

Their ride ended at an older building, built of marble in the classic style. They drove past the columned entrance and disappeared into underground parking. From there, it was a short elevator ride to the fourth floor. They walked down a thickly carpeted, marble hallway to a pair of tall wooden doors that guards swung wide for them.

Inside, a huge room had walls covered in tall windows or equally tall mirrors veined in gold. The sun through the windows was reflected back, leaving the many crystal chandeliers with little need to shed their light. In the middle of the room was one long, thick, wooden table with several dozen people gathered around it. Many looked all too familiar to Vicky. They stared at her and Mannie in heavy silence.

Again, chairs at the head . . . or maybe foot . . . had been left for her and Mannie. She didn't need any suggestion but made for the empty seats.

The meeting started before she was halfway there.

"You told us nothing would happen, that this would be a secret rebellion to start with," came from somewhere in the middle of the table. It was supported by "Yeah," "Yes," "I told you we couldn't trust a Peterwald," and worse.

Vicky schooled her face to neutral and continued her walk. When she got to the chair at the end of the table, head or bottom, she sat down and surveyed the people around the table.

Some had fallen silent, but others kept on with their own comments on recent events. She did not interrupt them.

She sat there, stiff and attentive, keeping her silence until a question rose above the babble. "Aren't you going to answer us? Or are you going to pull that Peterwald thing? You know, 'You peasants, me Emperor, so shut up and do what I want.'"

Vicky stood up on that note, and the room slowly bubbled down to silence. Then she sat down again.

She took a deep breath of the silence, and said, "I told you when we last met that I wanted to take it slow. I wanted to feel my way into whatever it was that we were doing. I also made it clear that my stepmom had *her* own agenda, and it would unfold on *her* timetable."

Vicky let that circulate around the room. She was still facing some very hard looks, but other heads began to nod. "She did tell us that," was whispered by several people. Vicky found it interesting that all three of the women at the table were in that group.

"I don't know if you realize it, but St. Petersburg was invaded a few days ago. Did you notice three regiments of the Empress's best, or should I say worst, security specialists strutting around your streets?"

Several heads shook slowly. Someone finally said, "That was an invasion?"

"Yep," Vicky said. "Three heavy cruisers and three regiments of security thugs. If the negotiations on Metzburg had dragged out, and my battleship had been in orbit there rather than here, there would have been nothing between you and them."

The room was deadly silent as the obvious became blatantly clear to even the densest heads.

"As it is, Mannie here drove M'Lord, the Lord High Commissioner for Safety on St. Petersburg into a heart attack rather than a planetary attack."

"I knew Mannie was good for something," came from the mayor of Kiev.

"I had a little help from our Grand Duchess," Mannie said, wryly.

"But I'm gracious," Vicky said, innocently batting her eyes.

"In a pig's eye," Mannie said, under his breath for all to hear.

The tension in the room broke up in a good laugh.

Vicky let them enjoy their release for a long moment, then leaned forward as the silence returned.

"The blackhearted Empress tried to take your planet. As luck, and only luck would have it, I and my battleship were between trade missions, and we put a stop to that. It could have ended very differently."

Vicky saw her words hit home, and continued, "Instead, we have acquired the invasion fleet. Some ten thousand thugs will need employment that doesn't involve swaggering around with guns. However, we have a problem.

"The Empress is thinking about St. Petersburg. You may be far from Greenfeld, but you are, no doubt, in every waking thought of the blackhearted Empress. That could be a problem. However, what might otherwise have been a problem now appears to be a gift."

Several heads snapped around to give her some really strange looks.

"The Imperium, be it my father or my stepmother, has been ordering battleships and battlecruisers to be scrapped in midlife. Strange how they are soon showing up in different hands doing their best to pirate merchant ships going about their proper business of carrying trade between planets. The Navy has fought and captured those ships. Now, captains with orders to sail their ships to the scrap heap have strong suspicions that what is left of the Navy will all too soon be facing those guns crewed by pirates."

Vicky relaxed back in her seat, but she chipped her next words from hard flint. "Several of those captains have chosen to sail here and place themselves at our disposal. I now lay before you a proposal that you accept their service in our mutual defense and do what we can to feed their crews and maintain their ships."

Vicky paused to see how that idea went over. It hung there in the air, neither accepted nor rejected. "Not too long ago, there would have been no way for St. Petersburg to maintain a fleet of battleships. You, however, have recently upgraded the docks on your station. Now you have the choice of maintaining them or not. A few weeks ago, you did not have the heavy industry to repair such ships. Now, with newly arrived fabricators from Metzburg, you do."

Vicky let her eyes rove those seated around the table. "You have made the decisions that have led you to this moment. Will you now make the decision that you can, not just for yourselves, but for your children?"

It was Mannie who broke the silence she left her listeners frozen in.

"We have a proposal before us to accept the services of the offered ships. Need I say, some were actually captured. It is proposed that we create the St. Petersburg Division of the Greenfeld Imperial Navy Reserve Fleet. I motion that we open the floor for discussion."

"St. Petersburg Division of the Greenfeld Imperial Navy Reserve Fleet, you say, Mannie?" the mayor of Kiev said. "That's quite a mouthful. Did you just come up with it, or did Her Grace, here, help you?"

Mannie grinned. "That name is my very own creation. Me being a loyal subject of the Emperor, I don't want anyone to get the idea that we aren't just as loyal."

"Whatever you call it," a banker midway down the table put in, "it's going to cost. And it's going to take scarce resources I'm not so sure we have. Food, for one thing."

"I'm looking for a great crop this year," a rancher put in. "I was expecting to use it to trade with some of the mining planets out there. Am I going to have it taxed away so someone can feed Navy mouths that don't contribute nothing?"

"May I point out," a woman in a bright red business suit interjected, "that the security thugs the Navy just intercepted would have confiscated most of your crop, and you wouldn't have seen a pfennig for it."

"Being robbed for my own good is just as much robbery as when the Empress does it," the rancher shot back.

"About those security thugs we seem to have acquired. Are any of them good for a day's work?" another rancher drawled.

Vicky took that question. "The Navy will do a security check and interview each, ah, detainee. They'll cull out the worst cases, but I suspect a lot of them were just looking for a job when they found that one. We haven't had any trouble with them so far."

"Kind of docile little doggies, huh?" the optimistic rancher said.

"A greenhorn ain't no good on a working ranch," the other spat. "They're more trouble than they're worth."

"Well, Slim, I got land I could open up if I had some cowpunchers and plowboys. If you don't want any of them, I'll take your share."

"Who said I didn't want 'em? I got land to open up, too."

"Gentlemen," Mannie said, "the Empress's foul deeds can

open up many opportunities for us. I think we're up to them. Still, the only thing that she seems willing to drop in our lap is a bunch of thugs to take us down. If we're to have something to face her next move, we need our own reserve fleet."

"Okay, tell me this," came from the banker. "How come we need all these extra ships? That nasty battleship the Grand Duchess has was good enough to handle things. Why can't it stay parked in orbit while we lay up these other ships? Yes, I see that we don't want them laid off where they can be turned against us, but why do we need them all crewed and fixed up?"

Mannie glanced at Vicky.

"As I mentioned," Vicky said, "I'm headed for Brunswick with a convoy of freighters to open trade with them. The last time I rode a cruiser, it got shot up bad. My Navy superiors want me in something a bit more powerful. They still haven't fixed the last ship that I got busted up."

Vicky's offhanded delivery of that line drew a chuckle from many.

"Anyway, when I leave for Brunswick, the *Retribution* goes with me. Possibly, I'll also take one of the battlecruisers as well as a couple of cruisers. There's also a convoy leaving for Metzburg. It will need an escort, too."

"Can't any of those other planets pay for some ships?" came from the banker.

"No doubt, I will broach that topic with Brunswick. It is quite possible that they will want to keep a couple of ships in their system for their own protection." Vicky grinned at Mannie. "I see no reason why St. Petersburg should be the only planet with its very own division in the reserve fleet."

Now the debate began in earnest, with a lot of people talking and few listening. At first, this experience in participatory decision making was a bit frightening to Vicky. Mannie kept a restraining hand on her arm. Anytime she started to open her mouth, the pressure would grow.

For a reason she was never quite sure of, she let him keep her quiet.

No, he kept her listening. Slowly, through the din of so much talk, she began to make out the thread of where the talk was leading. There were a few wanting to debate whether or not to accept the ships. However, most of the talk now was how to manage a fleet, to feed it, pay for its upkeep, and spread its costs to other planets.

Since this was what Vicky really wanted to hear, she found it easier to listen. After a while, Mannie took his hand off her arm and gave her a smile.

It was a nice smile. She'd have to see about getting more smiles like that from him.

CHAPTER II

T HE meeting broke for lunch when stomachs began to rumble louder than the babble. Everyone adjourned to a restaurant across the street that had a back room reserved for them. It was simple fare of various sausages served with a variety of potato salads and sauerkraut. The beer was excellent, but Vicky hardly touched it.

Or her food.

Her table had six chairs. One each for her and Mannie, the commander and Mr. Smith. A succession of people dropped into the two empty chairs and asked Vicky a lot of questions, starting with how the invasion had been stopped. She and Mannie told it as humorously as possible without making too light of how badly it could have gone.

The next-most-frequent question was when she'd be leaving for Brunswick and what she'd be taking. Vicky was not about to give away operational details but left it at the *Retribution* and maybe a few cruisers.

"Any chance Brunswick will chip in for operations and maintenance of those ships?" came on the heels of that answer.

"We're swapping their goods for our goods," Mannie

pointed out. "It's kind of hard to put an excise tax on barter goods that will support the ships convoying the stuff."

"I never realized how much easier things were with real money," was the usual answer to that, even from bankers.

The lunch hour was almost over when the mayors for the three other major cities on St. Petersburg took over the two chairs and pulled up a third.

"We really need to know what this St. Petersburg Reserve Fleet is going to look like and what it's going to be up to."

"Can I ask why?" Vicky said.

"We need to figure out how to pay for it. To do that, we have to know what part of it to charge off to the trade side and what will be devoted to keeping the Empress out of our hair. We're getting gripes from those who don't see themselves getting all that much from the trading business. 'Why should I pay for convoys?' So, what's the story?"

"You know, of course, that any answer I give you today may change tomorrow if more refugee ships show up. It could get a whole lot worse if we have a shoot-out. You know how the *Kamchatka*'s repairs have gone."

That got winces from the three. Make that four. Mannie didn't look any too happy to be footing the bill for another major ship repair job.

"She warned us that we were dealing with a moving target," Kiev's mayor pointed out.

"Have you ever tried to get a project through the finance committee with a price tag marked 'to be determined later'?" the mayor of St. Pete grumbled.

"I don't think a revolution is something you do to a plan or a budget," Mannie pointed out.

"That might explain why so few of them succeed," the mayor of Moskva grouched.

"No doubt we must try to win all our victories with a few words that induce heart attacks in our attackers," Mannie muttered softly, so everyone could hear.

That drew a few dry chuckles.

"If we could only be so lucky," Vicky admitted.

"So how many ships do we have, Your Grace? How many of them will be in trade and how many standing guard in our sky?" the mayor of St. Pete demanded. "And yes, I know that there is such a thing as security, but I also know that I cannot ask people to write checks without telling them something. This is not the palace where Harry demands and everyone says, 'But of course, Your Imperial Ass.'"

"No offense intended, Your Grace," Kiev's mayor put in.

"None taken," Vicky allowed. "Maybe I should have asked Kris Longknife how this democracy thing worked. It seems that I am going to experience it or something like it, no?"

"Or something like it," Mannie allowed.

Vicky tapped her commlink. "Admiral, I am talking to several mayors who are trying to draw up a budget for the St. Petersburg Division of the Greenfeld Imperial Navy Reserve Fleet."

"The what?"

"Please don't ask me to repeat it," Vicky said. "That is what we're calling the refugees presently under your command. The people down here need to have something with their name on it if they are to foot the bill for it."

"Oh. I guess that sounds logical," the admiral admitted.

"To work up their tax accounts, they need to have a rough guestimate of which ships will be escorting trade convoys and which will be allocated to the direct defense of their system against things like the Empress just sent our way."

"Your Grace, I'm not even sure what ships I have now. Do you know what shape the old *Kasimov* and *Yamal* are in? When will I get the *Attacker* and *Kamchatka* back available to answer bells? You might as well ask me how many angels can dance on the head of a pin."

"If you can't tell us something," Mannie said, "your budget may very well be the number of angels that can dance on that pinhead."

"Your Grace, this is starting to feel dangerously like Longknife democracy."

"Admiral, I could not agree with you more. Shall we just call off whatever it is that we are doing and present ourselves to the Empress for whatever she might wish to do with us?"

There was a long pause.

"Some bean counter in the Navy who never held a command once told me that the true power in the Navy lay in the hands of the man who held the purse strings. I am beginning to see his point."

"Admiral, I, like you and these sincere men of government, are taking this journey one step at a time. I have no idea where we will end up. I do know where the Empress wants us. I do not want to go there. Shall we do what we can today and worry about tomorrow when it comes? Who knows, we might not live long enough to worry about it."

"Well, the Lord High Commissioner could have taken your advice. I was just informed that he succumbed to his blackened heart. I am told that several of his subordinates were amazed to find that he indeed had one. I have been talking to them, He appears to have had few friends."

"It's amazing how few friends losers have," Vicky said.

"Something I must remember," the admiral admitted. "Now, about your ships. I propose to keep the *Scourge* pierside here while the *Retribution* is on convoy duty with you, Your Grace. Count one battleship for trade and one for defense. I propose to send the *Stalker* with you and the *Slinger* with the next convoy to Metzburg. It is possible that she might stay there. It is possible that you may find Brunswick interested in keeping the *Stalker*. Only time will tell."

The admiral paused for a moment. "We have ten heavy cruisers: one damaged and in the yard. Five are old, one of which is already in dockyard hands, and the others may follow. Of the four new cruisers, I propose to send two with you and two to Metzburg. The one light cruiser, *Rostock*, will likely go with you to test the jumps, so I imagine that puts her on trade.

"Now, about those merchant cruisers. We have five. The two we recently converted and are now squawking like heavies. I propose to use them for local trade, escorting freighters out to our nearby planets. May I point out that the Navy colony on Port Royal has not seen a freighter or any supplies in three months. I have quite a long list of goods they want. I hope we can get a shipment out to them before too much longer.

"The three ships, the *Germanica*, *Europa*, and *Constantinia*, if I may return them to their proud old names, are way underarmed. There are some 6-inch lasers due up here soon from the shop in Sevastopol that we think should be added to them. It will be a small matter to upgun them. They could use an extra reactor, but we can put that off until we have more time. I'd keep them in system although if more trade blossoms, we might see them escorting convoys.

"Does that answer your questions?"

"Ah, how much will it cost to keep those ships in service?" the mayor of St. Pete asked.

"Oh, for crying out loud," the admiral exploded. "Why didn't you start with that?"

"We didn't know we should have," Mannie said. "Remember, this is new to all of us."

"Can you tell us what it takes to feed your crews?" Vicky said. "Then you might give us an idea of what spare parts a ship runs through in a month. I think most taxes will be paid in kind."

"Let me have my bean counter get back to your bean counter," the admiral said. From their end, it sounded like his commlink got thrown against a bulkhead.

"We really have no idea what we're doing, moment to moment?" the mayor of Kiev asked.

"I seem to have missed the course in rebellion when I was at college," Mannie said.

"I suspect we all did," Vicky admitted.

"We want to know the things that are important," Mannie went on, "but just what is important to us is hard to figure out. What an admiral needs to know and what a mayor or banker or industrialist needs are different, aren't they?"

"And don't forget the rancher or farmer," Vicky put in. "If the Navy doesn't eat, you won't have many Sailors for your ships. Of course, if you don't have lightbulbs or spare parts for lasers or reactors, you won't have a warship for very long either."

"And we have to do it without any real tax system in place," Mannie said. "We can't just tell those people to give us this part of their paycheck, then tell these others to give us a widget or a steak for this much tax money. I knew I should have been a house painter. I was a very good house painter working my way through college. Maybe I could get my old job back."

"Sorry, Mannie," the mayor of Moskva said, "I think we're all locked into our jobs until we either win or they hang us."

Mannie looked sad.

Vicky tried on her most vacant grin. "Look on the bright side, guys. If we all hang together, it will be one hell of a date."

"Only if you go up the scaffold stairs first. And in a short dress," Mannie suggested.

"No doubt, my stepmother would be only too happy to oblige you," Vicky said, then put her most impish look on her face. "But I live by the old saying, no noose is good noose."

That got a groan from the mayors, who went back to their own groups. With hardly a silent moment, the group reconvened in the conference hall. Gradually, as the afternoon shadows grew longer, the venting became less and the practical suggestions bubbled their way to the surface.

"Yes, we need a committee to see that the fleet gets fed."

"And one to see they get spare parts."

"Do we lump spare parts in with the major overhauling of the older cruisers and arming of the merchant ships? Shouldn't that be a separate account?"

"Do we really need to put a lot of money into those old ships? Who decides if a wreck of a ship gets rebuilt or just junked for parts?"

A lot of people ended up looking blankly at each other.

Mannie stood up. "Ladies and gentlemen, I think we're asking the wrong questions. Rather than asking what gets done, we need to be talking about how it gets done and who does it. As I see it, we need a Navy Committee to see that all of these questions get answered. Within that committee, I see a couple of subcommittees to tackle most of those questions specifically. Do you see where I'm going?"

"Kind of," the mayor of St. Pete said.

"But we need a Finance Committee," a banker said, "unless you're going to let the Navy Committee raise taxes, and let's make no mistake about it, we are talking taxes here."

"Svin, we've been paying taxes all our lives," a farm representative said. "Now at least I can see where my taxes are going and decide for myself if it's worth it, and from what I just saw up there in space, Navy ships parked on our space station are worth a whole lot more than some extra marble on a palace on Greenfeld."

Vicky could see the shape of how these matters would end, but she had to sit through another two hours as the haggling turned to this specific or that general question, which committee or subcommittee could decide what and what would be referred to this, the committee of the whole.

Her bottom could not take much more. When someone moved to adjourn and meet again in a week, Vicky could only hope that she'd be in some faraway place even if she was outnumbered and fighting for her life.

"I have reserved a suite for you at the Imperial Hotel across the street," Mannie whispered. "What do you say we adjourn to there and order room service?"

"I hope it has a hot tub because my tushy needs a nice soak," Vicky said, and gave Mannie a smile that she hoped promised more.

CHAPTER 12

B Y the time Vicky left the conference that evening, there was a Marine security detachment waiting for her. The captain in charge listened to Mannie's security detail's advice, formed an outer perimeter, and shared the inner circle with the local detail.

They stopped traffic but no bullets on their way to the Imperial. Vicky discovered that Mannie had not only reserved the Imperial Suite, but he'd also ordered ahead for a light dinner. Room service was waiting for them.

Vicky, Mannie, the commander, and the spy settled down to dinner around an elegant table that could have easily served double their number.

"I hope I never have to go through a day like this one again," the commander grumbled as he served himself an Oriental salad.

"Democracy is certainly messy," Mr. Smith said as he buttered a roll. "However, it is surprisingly strong and resilient at times."

"You like the way they do things in Longknife space," the commander spat.

"I like the way people tend to their own knitting," he said, taking a nibble. "For example, the Army looks to its duty. Navy officers fight their ships. Farmers raise the food to feed them. Ranchers raise their beef. And conducting them all in their own expertise are elected officials who can do nothing that they do," he said, bowing sardonically at Mannie, "but, if they do their jobs well, they all can do their jobs smoothly."

The commander "harrumphed" at that.

"You doubt me. Consider, for a moment that Admiral von Mittleburg found himself with all those extra mouths to feed and a few dented ships to repair. How successful do you think he'd be if he dispatched a battalion of Marines to Sevastopol with orders to collect enough food to feed his hungry crews for a month? How would it work if he sent down a Navy detachment to rummage through the shops of St. Pete and find the odd part the fleet required?"

"Not successful at all," Mannie muttered to his own shrimp-bespeckled salad.

"What did you say, Mr. Mayor?" the spy said.

Mannie looked up. "The Marines might succeed in stripping our supply chain of a few days' worth of food, but they'd never do that again," he said in a voice firm with resolution. "We aren't dumb. We've been getting around State Security since before most of your Marines were born. We will get around whomever we have to."

"I rest my case," Mr. Smith said, putting down his roll. "The mayors here will orchestrate a system that allows the Navy to be Navy, the industrialists to make things, and the farmers and ranchers to do what they do best. Who knows, they might even get the bankers to do what they're supposed to do, manage the planet's financial system for the betterment of all. Such miracles have been known to happen."

That drew a chuckle from everyone around the table.

The commander put down his fork. "I need to make a report to Admiral von Mittleburg."

"I hope you will tell him about the more productive parts of our day," Mannie said.

"What do you think I should tell him?" the commander asked, with amazing gentleness, Vicky thought, for a fighting man who'd lost a day of his life to interminable meetings.

"I would suggest that he arrange to have some officers

assigned to our committees to coordinate the Navy's needs with our resources. We may have gotten off on the wrong foot, butting into his area of expertise, but I think we ended on a good note. You give us people who can tell us your needs, and we'll do what we can to meet them."

"That may work or be the best way we can work this mess out." The commander stood. "Your Grace."

"Go with my blessing and good luck."

The commander left. The spy seemed to be taking his own measurements of the situation. "I think I will call it a night. Not that I suspect I will get a lot of sleep. I will be checking in with your security detail," he said, nodding toward Mannie, "and your Marines regularly through the evening."

"Thank you, Mr. Smith. I always feel safer when you are somewhere in the shadows."

"Thank you, Your Grace," the spy said, and likewise withdrew.

Vicky found herself alone in a room with just Mannie, and, of course, Kit and Kat. It seemed the night held all sorts of possibilities. She played with her salad for a few moments while watching through veiled eyelashes as Mannie attacked his.

"So, what do you do for excitement around here?" she finally said.

"I'm hardly the one to ask. My ex-wife said I was about the most unexciting man on the planet."

"Ex?" Vicky said.

"High-school sweetheart. I guess she didn't know me as well as she thought. Anyway, enough about me. What does the Navy do for excitement?"

"Oh, blow up this or shoot up that," Vicky said, moving her salad from one side of the plate to the other. "After I got caught in the paint locker with a junior officer, excitement has been limited to official excitement the Navy approves of."

"And the paint locker is not approved of?"

"Oh, very much not approved of," Vicky said with an arched eyebrow.

Mannie sniffed. "This room certainly does not smell of paint."

"I have noticed that. I think the hot tub could be most exciting."

"Those two young women look only too eager to be lifeguards," Mannie said, half laughing as he nodded at Kit and Kat.

They grinned back most willingly.

"I haven't seen them as enthusiastic for a job since the last time they almost got to kill someone," Vicky said.

"Are you offering me what I think you are?" Mannie said with a significant gulp.

"A dip in the hot tub with three lovely young women and not a swimsuit in sight," Vicky said, casually. "I do think so."

Kit and Kat nodded, obviously well into the thought.

"An adolescent boy's dream of heaven," Mannie said.

"And only seconds away for you," Vicky said.

Kit and Kat kicked off their shoes and began removing their pants.

Mannie watched them with a happy smile, then sadly shook his head.

"I don't think so."

"Why not?" Vicky said, startled at the very first no she'd encountered since puberty hit her like a ton of feathers.

"Correct me if I'm wrong, but can't most of the trouble we are in be traced to a certain Peterwald falling into bed?"

"I'm not my stepmother," Vicky said with edge.

"I don't see you that way, but I need to make a lot of things happen here on St. Petersburg. To do that, I need the goodwill of a lot of people who aren't sure they can trust anyone outside their own small circle of friends. How will they look at me when they see me in bed with a Peterwald?"

Mannie put down his fork and stood up. "As much as I would love to stay, ladies, I fear that I must trudge my way to the door. I assure you, I will have fond dreams of all of you tonight."

Kit and Kat had finished stripping. They stood, hands on hips, giving Mannie a spectacular view of what he would be only dreaming about.

Vicky said nothing as Mannie made his way to the door, not looking back. He said he had to go, and she would let him.

"Well, that was not what I expected," Kit said. "But the tub, it is so nice and warm."

"It would be a shame to waste it," Kat pointed out.

Vicky gave the firmly closed door one last look. Should she have done more to undermine Mannie's self-control? Did she respect his judgment of their situation enough to let him decide for the both of them that they had to be off-limits to each other?

She sighed. Mannie was off-limits. The commander was off-limits. That did leave the two delightful assassins.

"Last one in has to massage the rest," Vicky said with an eager grin full of evil intent.

"But we are ready now," Kit said, backing toward the balcony, where the pool bubbled.

"Then I'll get my hands all over you two," Vicky said, reaching with clawing hands for the two of them.

They charged her, bowling her over, and began stripping her right there on the carpet. There were a lot of fingers going here and there as well. Just who splashed into the hot tub last was never determined.

CHAPTER 13

VICKY spent the next couple of days touring the major cities on St. Petersburg, smiling for the camera while it replayed the Battle of the Heart Attack. She quickly developed a standard speech that highlighted the danger their homes and planet had been in, the Navy's rapid movement to their defense, and their sudden acquisition of a fleet of ships with hungry Sailors and many other needs.

Mayors thanked her, a gratitude Vicky accepted in the name of the Navy. Little girls gave her flowers and jars full of copper pfennigs toward the maintenance of the fleet. Vicky smiled and said nothing about her hope that their parents might be willing to give a lot more.

Vicky slowly came to the understanding of the true value of a Grand Duchess. She didn't so much do as allow others to do things in her name. She was the physical embodiment of other people, both those giving and those receiving. She imagined that a flag might have worked better, but her smiling face and hands to give and take seemed to work quite well.

It kept her busy, almost enough not to notice that Mannie was nowhere in sight.

When she thought about it, she realized that his disappearance was inevitable. He had a job to do, and she had what she was doing. Their duties took them in different directions.

If they had become entangled in a scandal, neither one of them would be as good at their jobs as they were right now.

Mannie knew his people. While Vicky might consider it just fun to fool around in the hot tub, he made a call, and she had to respect him for it.

The Navy had taught her the Navy Way. Now Mannie was introducing her to the political way.

The fact she didn't much like either way had nothing to do with anything that mattered.

Four days of smiling and saying just the right thing had her about ready to sign on again as a boot ensign under Admiral Krätz's heavy and demanding hand. She was not at all disappointed when Admiral von Mittleburg called to say the convoy to Brunswick was fully loaded.

"Oh, and I have created a new job to coordinate dealings with St. Petersburg or other planets for the logistic needs of the reserve fleet."

"You have. Did you pick anyone I might wish horrible things upon?" Vicky said.

"Captain Etterlin, formerly of the *Retribution*."

"I can't think of a man more deserving of the promotion," Vicky said, fighting a laugh but not very successfully. "Will he be sitting in on meetings and saving my tush from long hours in hard chairs?"

"No doubt. The *Attacker* is not yet out of the yard. I've offered the *Retribution* to Captain Bolesław."

"He did a good job of bringing in the *Attacker* when it could have easily been lost with all hands, and my head as well."

"Yes, I thought you might say something like that. Anyway, all joking aside, Your Grace, you need to be under way and quickly. As I might have mentioned, I'm sending the battlecruiser *Slinger* and the newly acquired large heavy cruisers *Wittenberg* and *Augsburg* along with you. I'm holding back *Rostock* for here, so you'll be using *Sovereign of the Stars* for your jump-point scout."

"How soon can you send a shuttle for me?"

"I have my own barge on final approach to the Kiev spaceport."

Vicky looked around the limo she was presently in. The commander and Mr. Smith, Kit and Kat were there. "Did we leave anything in the room this morning?"

"Everything you own dirtside is in the boot," Kit said.

"Commander, tell the driver our destination has changed. It is now the shuttleport."

Four hours later, they were on their way, leading a convoy of fifteen freighters to Brunswick. The voyage was quick. Their arrival was the shock this time.

———

CHAPTER 14

A week later, *Retribution* followed *Sovereign of the Stars* through the jump point to the Brunswick system. In only a moment, Lieutenant Blue was reporting on what was in orbit around Brunswick.

"It seems we are not the only fleet in this system," Captain Bolesław said after Lieutenant Blue finished his more in-depth analysis of what was ahead of them.

"How bad is it?" Vicky asked. She had a pretty good idea it was bad, but it was the captain's prerogative to say the worst, and she needed to know just how bad he saw it.

"Two battleships are tied up to High Brunswick Station," her captain said. "The *Savage* and the *Ferocity* according to your Mr. Blue although they are squawking as the *Reprisal* and *Revenge*."

"Do we have any battleships of that name?" Vicky asked.

"Not since they were scrapped ten years back."

"What about the *Savage* and the *Ferocity*? Were they scheduled for scrapping?"

"Not that I know of, but we aren't getting the most up-to-date news out here."

Vicky couldn't argue with that. "So do you know anything about the skippers of those two battleships?"

Captain Bolesław eyed his own commlink. "Yes. I know them."

"We'll just have to wait until we get in closer to see if you can do anything with them. About the cruisers?"

"The *Koln* and *Emden* are heavy cruisers, though not as strong as ours. Their main battery is twelve 8-inchers. We have twelve 9.2-inchers on the *Wittenberg* and *Augsburg*. In a fight, though, the quality of the crew might be more telling than the extra power of the lasers."

The commlink came alive. "Put it on screen," Captain Bolesław said.

"Ships entering Brunswick space from outside the Imperial Security Zone, you are forbidden any contact with those protected by Imperial Security. You will attempt no contact and return immediately from whence you came."

Captain Bolesław eyed Vicky.

She nodded. "So that's the way it is. I guess my stepmama got here ahead of us. Lieutenant Blue, how strong is the Empress's grip?"

"I can't honestly say at the moment, Your Grace. I'll need more time to analyze the communications I can hack off the station and planet."

"While he's doing that, Captain, why don't we close on the Imperial Security bubble?"

"Dare we risk popping it?" the captain asked, an eager grin playing at the edge of his lips.

"God forbid I should do such a thing."

"Yeah, right," the captain muttered, but he turned to his navigator and had him set a course for High Brunswick Station. "One gee if you will."

"One gee it is," the helmsman answered, and Vicky's tiny fleet headed in to stick their heads in the Empress's maw.

CHAPTER 15

FOR four hours, they accelerated toward Brunswick, and nothing happened.

The *Sovereign of the Stars* maneuvered over to lead the column of fifteen freighters; now the *Retribution* led the *Slinger*, *Wittenberg*, and *Augsburg* in a second column fifteen thousand klicks to port. Vicky organized her small fleet, but from the ships docked on High Brunswick, there was not a sound.

"No communications at all between them?" Vicky asked.

"Not so much as a time check on their net," Lieutenant Blue replied. "I've never seen a net so silent."

"Could they have done something to jack up their net security?"

The lieutenant shrugged. "With them, it's always possible, Your Grace, but I really can't believe that our best has been left totally facedown in the mud."

Vicky hoped he was right.

"There is a second possibility," Captain Bolesław said softly, his hand over his mouth.

"I'm all ears," Vicky said, and even Lieutenant Blue leaned close.

"There is old-fashioned shoe leather. If you send a runner

to call a meeting, there is no net traffic. You get all your interested parties in one room, and there is nothing for the good lieutenant to eavesdrop on."

"How tacky," Vicky said. "You'd think they don't trust us."

"As hard as that might seem," the captain said.

They continued to wait for several more hours. On the one hand, Vicky didn't mind the delay. Conversations in space with speed-of-light delays were so ineffective. How could she talk someone into a decent heart attack if it took an hour or more for each verbal jab to cross space?

The longer it took them to start talking, the shorter the delays between verbal sallies.

Still, it was nerve-racking to wait, wondering what they were up against.

"You know the skippers of the ships tied up at High Brunswick," Vicky finally said to Captain Bolesław.

"Yes. The skipper of the *Savage*, now *Reprisal*, spent four years just down the hall from me during my Academy years. He was a bit of a rounder. If there was a prank going on, he was likely at the bottom of it. He finished below the middle of the class. I never would have expected him to get a battleship in my Navy. But then, maybe the *Reprisal* isn't in my Navy now. Time will tell."

Yes, time will tell.

Vicky decided she might as well spend some of the time getting a good nap. She was asleep when they reached midpoint in their approach, and the convoy flipped over and began to decelerate toward Brunswick.

The nap had turned into a good night's sleep and she felt well rested and refreshed by a fast shower and a new set of whites when she returned to the bridge.

"Anything happen?" she asked the officer of the deck.

"Not a thing, Your Grace. The captain is in his in-space cabin, and I have orders to wake him if anything new develops, but it's been a very quiet watch."

Vicky turned toward the sensor station. A chief had the watch there.

"Anything to report?"

"The ships at the station are still observing strict emissions control, Your Grace. We have made a thorough analysis of the planet's public network. It appears normal. The media is reporting the usual stuff. Cat up a tree. Dog bites dog. We have successfully hacked the police net. There's nothing like a security presence. The lieutenant told me to tell you that he doesn't think the Security Consultants have actually landed on Brunswick."

"Is he absolutely sure of that, Chief?"

The senior countermeasures tech looked pained. "Beg your pardon, ma'am, but there are no absolutes in this game."

"Pardon me for showing my ignorance. Thank you, Chief."

"You're welcome, Your Grace."

"Would Your Grace care for a cup of tea?" the OOD asked.

"Please."

Vicky noted that sometime during her nap, a command chair had been added next to the captain's. On its back was stenciled: GRAND DUCHESS.

Vicky settled in and soon found a steaming mug of tea at her elbow.

She sipped it while staring at the main screen; it showed the planet ahead of them getting larger. Still, it stayed a mystery.

Then the screen lit up. "Stand by for a formal declaration by Count Korbinian, Lord of Karenhall."

"Runner, wake the skipper," the OOD ordered, and a seaman striker dashed off.

Captain Bolesław was back on the bridge in a moment, still buttoning up the shirt of his fresh undress whites.

"Has the message come in?" he asked.

"Only the alert," the OOD said. "Nothing of substance."

The captain settled into his chair. A chief steward's mate had a steaming mug of tea waiting for him when he absentmindedly put his hand out while staring at the main screen as if to will it to give up the next message.

So, of course, the screen obeyed the will of the skipper and did.

A man appeared. He looked thirtysomething; his face was yet unlined by age and experience. The red uniform he sported would have been comical for all the gold and silver dripping from it . . . except for the large silver death's head on each lapel.

As he spoke, Vicky's eyes were drawn back repeatedly to those two grinning skulls.

"I am Count Korbinian, Governor General of Brunswick, and the Lord Protector of the Imperial Security Zone in which all good subjects of Brunswick reside. Unknown ships approaching Brunswick, know that we hold your silence to be clear evidence of hostile intent and we will use deadly force on you if you approach this station. Return from whence you come, or face the most serious consequences. This message will not be repeated."

And the screen went back to its view of still-distant Brunswick.

"It took him *that* long to come up with *that* little," Vicky said, scowling at the screen.

"OOD, am I mistaken, or hasn't the *Retribution* been squawking that it is a ship of the Imperial Navy every moment since we entered this system?" the captain demanded softly but firmly.

The commander standing the watch took time to verify his answer before he replied. "Yes, sir. Both the *Retribution* and the other warships have been identifying ourselves properly. No squawker has broken down. One of the freighter's IFF went on the blink for an hour, but they got it back up, and we're all right and tight, sir."

"Silence, my eye," the captain spat, but softly and for Vicky's hearing only.

"So, they've had their heads together ever since we entered this system," Vicky said softly, "and a claim that we are silent is all they can come up with."

The captain nodded agreement.

"Captain," came from Lieutenant Blue who had joined the chief at sensors. "The warships tied up to High Brunswick have begun to charge their capacitors and power up their lasers."

The captain's head snapped around to take in sensors. Lieutenant Blue didn't so much as blink at the glare the skipper threw his way.

The captain opened his mouth but snapped it closed just as quickly. Again, he leaned close to Vicky. "No one powers up their lasers while in port. God, think of the mess one slight twitch of the wrong finger could do. This is asinine, even for Engel, if he hasn't taken total leave of his senses."

"So let's go to the root," Vicky said. "Captain, could you have Communications replay the message. Lieutenant Blue, I don't recognize this Count Korbinian. Run a facial recognition program and see if you can get a match."

"Yes, ma'am," and "Yes, Your Grace," greeted Vicky's

request, and with a somewhat delayed nod from the skipper, the recent transmission reappeared on screen.

"Sorry, Skipper," Vicky whispered.

"It's my own fault for having a Grand Duchess on board," he shot back, but his eyes were on the screen, and his lips had an upward curl at the edges.

The facial recognition program operated as the putative "Count" spoke his terror in a monotone voice. He had hardly finished his threat again before Lieutenant Blue announced, "I have a match."

"Put what you got on screen," the captain ordered.

Vicky was careful to keep her mouth shut. She'd gotten her one free order in for the day. She hadn't asked for it, but no doubt about it, the crew had given it to her, and the skipper was counting it. She'd have to be more careful in the future.

"We've got a ninety-six percent match on Kurt Corbin. He married one of the Empress's cousins and rose without distinction to be a minor vice president in one of the family banks. He rather enthusiastically volunteered to oversee a composite commando of Navy and Security Consultants that gunned down a lot of State Security. We've got a match with him and Karenhall. It was a hunting lodge owned by the major general commanding State Security's Internal Operations Bureau. Kurt seems to own it now. He was created a baron for his efforts against State Security and was raised to Count a year ago for his pacification of several planets while commanding one, then two brigades of Security Consultants." Lieutenant Blue paused as if not knowing whether or not to go on.

"Is there more?" Captain Bolesław growled.

"One of the private computers we hacked off the *Golden Empress No. 34* had correspondence in it, one friend to another. It said that Kurt was up for a dukedom if he did well on his next job. The reply said that Kurt would never get a duke's ring, not after some drunken mouthing off he did at a cocktail party about the Empress's dad sleeping with all his daughters."

"Oh, ho!" muttered the captain through an evil grin. Then again, Vicky's face was far from angelic at the moment.

"So the hell the palace has become begins to eat its own," Vicky muttered, doing her best to suppress thoughts about just how hellish it had always been.

"But how can we put all of this to our own ends?" the captain said, rubbing his chin.

"The good Count Korbinian has got himself far out on a limb and sawn it at least halfway through," Vicky said. "He can't afford to fail this assignment, or they will hand him his head."

"Apparently literally."

"No doubt, in that court," Vicky agreed.

"He's under pressure."

Vicky grinned. "Let's raise that pressure. Lieutenant Blue, can you tell us more about this fellow?"

"He's pretty bland. He seems to have enjoyed killing State Security commanders rather gruesomely and sending video back to the palace."

"Sadistic twit," the captain muttered.

"Oh, when he acquired Karenhall, he seems to have also gotten a string of polo ponies. He likes to win. He actually shot a pony that failed him once."

"Quite a temper," the captain observed.

"We will have to make him lose it," Vicky said.

CHAPTER 16

VICKY didn't get a chance to try her hand with Count Korbinian until they were almost to the orbits of Brunswick's two small moons. Her computer had taken a quiet moment to bring Vicky up to date on the fellow. His last name, Corbin, meant little crow or raven. He'd chosen the old Frankish German form of that name for his noble name.

Either way, he was a carrion eater, surviving off the rotten meat of those he'd killed.

What say we leave you rotting by the road this time?

Vicky was coming back from a light supper. She dropped by her stateroom and collected her high-gee station. If things got exciting—and she expected they would—she wanted to be prepared.

Kit and Kat had it tuned up, recharged, and waiting.

"Thanks, girls," Vicky said, giving them a kiss.

"Have no fear, Your Grace. We will be here when you come back, and you can give us more than a peck on the cheek."

With that, they sent their warrior on her way.

No surprise; as Vicky motored onto the bridge, much of the watch was either in a high-gee station or had one parked close by. Even the skipper.

"My, Your Grace, you are getting quite adept at this Navy Way."

"I'm getting quite adept at staying alive," she growled.

"Either one works for me."

Their comradely chatter was interrupted as the main screen came alive.

There stood Count Korbinian, in all his red, gold, and silver glory, on the bridge of a warship. Captain Bolesław's softly whispered "Oh, Engle, my lad, what have you gotten yourself into this time?" suggested that it was his friend standing a bit back from Korbinian and the ship must be the *Reprisal* nee *Savage*.

"You should have taken my warning. Now I will slaughter you. *I* take no prisoners."

Captain Bolesław raised an eyebrow. Vicky sighed and moved to take center stage before the main screen. "Put me on screen," she said.

"We are no threat to Brunswick," Vicky said, evenly. "We come bearing trading goods, escorting a convoy of merchant ships through the snares of pirates."

"We have no trade with outies," the Count spat, then seemed to blink twice and look hard at Vicky.

"You're the outlaw who sometimes styles herself the Grand Duchess Victoria."

"I *am* the Grand Duchess Victoria. And I am *no* outlaw."

"Yes, you are. You've been proclaimed outlaw by the Empress's edict."

"But not by the Emperor's decree. I am called to court, and I come."

"Like hell you do. Not on a battleship." Then Kurt seemed to see his salvation handed to him on a platter. "Or maybe you'd send those battleships away and come alongside the station in a shuttle."

"Not even a captain's gig?" Vicky said.

"Gig, barge, boat," Count Korbinian spat. "What do I care so long as you come here unarmed?"

Behind him, several Navy types failed to keep scowls from flitting across their Navy-bland faces as the little Lord of Karenhall demonstrated his total disdain for the Navy.

Vicky noted that. *I can use that against you, you carrion-eating crow.*

"I will return to court at a time and place of my own

choosing," Vicky said, cutting Kurt off. He let his disappointment show on his face. "For the moment, I am doing what I can to improve the free flow of trade within the Empire."

"There is no trade between the Imperial Security Zone and those who have refused to submit," Kurt snapped.

"We are all loyal subjects of Emperor Henry I," Vicky shot back, "with a right to his protection and to prosper in free and open trade that is ours by right of the Imperial Charter."

Vicky had heard her father laugh derisively at all the platitude that got dumped into the charter by the "fools and do-gooders." Still, he'd allowed it to be written and signed it with a flourish. If that was the cost of his being declared Emperor, that was cheap. Vicky's surprise wasn't that these vultures were stripping the flesh off the charter, but that her father hadn't declared it null and void before this.

"To hell with a scrap of paper," the Count snapped.

"So," Vicky said, "you are restricting trade between planets of the Empire."

"You ain't nearly as stupid as they told me you were, little girl. You finally got it. Now turn those ships around and head back to where you came from."

That was the second time he'd said that. Turn the ships around and go back. Didn't he know that ships couldn't just turn on a dime like polo ponies?

Maybe you don't, bullyboy.

"Or, I could take up a trailing station, say a third of an orbit behind the station," Vicky said, lightly. "There I could pick off any ships coming in or going out. If you won't let me trade with the planet, I can always close down your trade."

"And you call yourself a loyal subject of the Emperor."

"Yes, I do."

"Well, we decide who is loyal to the Empire," Kurt growled. "You've gotten in the way of the Empress's Security Forces one too many times, little girl. Now you're in my way. People either get out of my way quick, or they die. You've been warned twice. Now you die. Captain, the fleet will mount up on my command and ride out to trample the enemies of the Empire."

Had a Navy squadron ever been ordered to space on orders so far from the Navy Way?

"But," the skipper of the *Reprisal* tried to get a word in.

"Don't you 'but' me, Captain. You have your orders. Get these ships out there. You have a battle to fight. Or don't you have the stomach for one? Shall I have you shot and get someone with more guts to put spurs to this bunch of cowards?"

From the rear of the bridge, several men in red coats and white trousers with machine pistols slung over their shoulders stepped forward, menace in their eyes.

"Poor Engle," Captain Bolesław was heard to murmur softly from his command chair.

"No," was not quite spat by the Count's captain. "I will take the squadron to space. Communications, pass the word to the ships of the Brunswick Security Squadron. We sortie in fifteen minutes. I will issue more precise orders when we are no longer talking to them," he said, raising a shoulder to the camera.

"Yes, yes," Kurt said, eyes locked on Vicky. "Pretender, prepare to be blown to hell." And the screen went blank.

CHAPTER 17

LIEUTENANT Commander Vicky Peterwald turned to the skipper of the battleship *Retribution* with a huge grin on her face. "Did I just do what I think I just did?"

"We will have to wait to be sure," Captain Bolesław said, "but I think you just got one stupid landsman to take a squadron to space in the worst way."

"When we had to stop the last attack on St. Petersburg, we used a partial orbit, the same that Kris Longknife used to defend Wardhaven against those pirate battleships we won't talk about," Vicky said. "That was the way for them to defend Brunswick. Instead, I think our no-account Count is going to do a cavalry charge right down our throats."

"Oh, I'd love to be a fly on the bridge when Engle has to explain to that idiot that you can't wheel an accelerating fleet about the way he turns his polo pony on a dime. I just hope the damn fool doesn't shoot poor Engle just because he can."

"Your friend Engle should have taken retirement when he had the chance."

"I'm not sure he was given any choice, Your Grace. He's on an Imperial ship, no doubt under some sort of confused chain of command, but the renamed *Reprisal* is squawking as Navy, not pirate."

"God help us when we can't tell the difference between the two."

"That, Your Grace, is one reason why they say a civil war is the worst war possible."

As the conversation with the Count came over the net, several members of the bridge crew had been seen to share furtive glances among themselves. That was nothing like the dismay that ran around the bridge when the skipper spoke the words "civil war."

The captain tapped his commlink. "All hands. A squadron of battleships and cruisers is about to head our way. The security honcho giving the orders to them says the blackhearted Empress doesn't want us trading with Brunswick. Our Grand Duchess has pointed out that the Imperial Charter the Emperor has granted says we can."

Captain Bolesław paused for a breath. "Division heads and leading chiefs, please take a few minutes to discuss this matter with the crew. If anyone has a problem with returning fire when fired upon, you may dismiss them to their bunks. Now, I am not asking for a Longknife vote on this. I stand with our Grand Duchess. I've fought with her and brought one shot-up ship home with her standing right there at my elbow, not running for the first lifeboat. If I have to fight the *Retribution* with my own two hands and hers, I will, but let's clear the air if we can."

Captain Bolesław paused. "Now, as soon as you can get a work team together, I hear that turret Dora is flat on her ass. I'd like to see her ready to shoot back at anyone taking a shot at me. Chiefs, are you going to tell me we can't fix the *Retro* as good as any yard clowns?"

A cheer went up as soon as the captain clicked off. Whether it was for his willingness to fight the ship all by his lonesome, with maybe a bit of help from Vicky, or his challenge to the chiefs of the ship to patch the turret with no help from a yard, it was hard to say. Then again, it might have been his use of the crew's pet name for the *Retribution*. Vicky didn't even know that the new skipper knew that belowdecks his ship was proudly called the *Retro*.

Whatever it was, the cheer started fast and lasted long.

When it calmed a bit, the skipper turned to Communications. "Send my last All Hands message to the rest of the fleet. Were they tracking the message traffic between High Brunswick and the flag?"

"Sir, all comm watches have been guarding the main comm-link and following everything we've received and all that the Grand Duchess sent back, sir. I think you may have had your finger on the All Squadron button as well as All Hands. I have logged acknowledgments from all of the warships and half the freighters. They range from simple 'acknowledge,' to 'yes,' to 'hell, yes.'"

The comm chief paused for a moment, realizing he'd broken communication protocols. "*Slinger*, *Wittenberg*, and *Augsburg* are in the 'hell, yes' category."

Captain Bolesław looked a bit abashed by the reception his words had gotten around the fleet. "Well, let's take some time to see that anyone who wants to stand down is given that chance," he said.

On the bridge, the chief boson's mate went from station to station, muttering softly to each rating. The XO did the same with the watch officers. Done, the XO left to do his polling of the division heads. He was back with the command master chief in less than ten minutes.

The command chief spoke for both of them. "Other than two layabouts who are taking the chance to malinger in their bunks, all hands are with you, Skipper. And I got a good dozen chiefs that say they can have *Dora* on her feet and dancing a jig before those flat-ass dandies from the Greenfeld Squadron can get on their feet. If it pleases you, sir."

"It pleases me very much, Chief. Carry on."

CHAPTER 18

F OR the next several hours, the battle developed. Vicky's ships continued to decelerate toward Brunswick . . . they could hardly do otherwise. The freighters bore away to starboard, opening the distance between them and the battle line to a good thirty thousand klicks. Captain Bolesław brought the *Wittenberg* forward to the head of the line but kept the *Slinger* and *Augsburg* trailing the huge battleship.

"If I'm reading the Count dude, he'll order everyone to concentrate on the *Retribution*. Engle might even suggest it though I doubt that stupid crow would listen to anyone."

"Why?" Vicky asked. "Won't that give our other ships free shots at theirs?"

"Yes. Admiral Krätz taught you well. Still, we are the biggest target. Take us out, and the rest are easy pickings. Then, there is you. Kill you, and they win all the chips."

Vicky swallowed hard. Assassination attempts were quick and over before you knew it. Most of them. It looked like she'd spend the next few hours waiting to die.

She glanced around the bridge. A lot of good people would be waiting with her.

Captain Bolesław went on. "Of course, the *Retribution* will be a tough nut to crack. The *Reprisal* and *Revenge* have ice armor three meters thick. Ours is six meters where it counts. Their 15-inch lasers will spend a lot of time nibbling at us. If, however, we concentrate our 18-inch salvos down tight, we might get burnthrough after a broadside or two."

"You going to try to blow one of them out of space?" Vicky asked.

"I'd rather not. I've got friends on those ships. The *Wittenberg* and *Augsburg* were against us last trip, and now they're with us. I'd rather persuade Engle to come over to our side, or at least to leave here with fond memories."

Vicky listened to the skipper of her flagship. No doubt her father would have his head for being so soft. Vicky wondered if now was a time for such softness. Part of her was only too glad to leave the decision to the experienced Navy officer. He knew the men who'd be on the receiving end of his guns. A civil war was a war of brothers against brothers. She should trust his instincts.

On the other hand, someone was about to start a shooting war. Wasn't now the time to pack away all milk of human kindness? No question, her loving stepmom was rubber-stamping death sentences by the hundreds. Count what's-his-name was only too quick to crow he'd take no prisoners.

Should I let the other side have a monopoly on slaughter? Is it better to offer everyone two solid choices? Should I stand for something different from the evil Empress?

Her father's choices had led the entire Empire to this. Where would her choices lead?

"Captain Bolesław, make this Engle's lucky day."

"As you would have it, Your Grace," came with a new edge to the skipper's voice.

I just hope this works. Vicky sighed.

The opposing squadron got away from High Brunswick Station in reasonable order, did a deorbital burn, and ducked down toward the planet. When they came back around, they headed straight for Vicky's squadron, accelerating at one gee.

"It seems that our idiot of a Count is indeed conducting a cavalry charge," Captain Bolesław observed dryly.

"Isn't that the way it's done in all the videos?" Vicky pointed out through a grin.

"And, as Admiral Krätz no doubt told you, in the videos, the other side is kind enough to be blown to bits. In real operations, the two passing sides are only in range of each other long enough for a few salvos, then the defender is headed off into the void and the attacker is closing rapidly on what the defender was supposed to defend."

"I do recall Admiral Krätz hammering that into my thick skull a dozen times or ninety," Vicky said.

"Defense, warn the crew we are about to put five revolutions on the ship."

"Aye, aye, sir."

Warships had ice armor. The more the better. It absorbed laser hits and ablated away the heat. Occasionally, it mucked up space between the battle lines so that lasers bloomed and did less damage. However, even the six-meter-thick armor of a super battleship like the *Retribution* couldn't stand solid hits.

So all warships rotated along their long axes, spinning their iced hide away from a laser hit. Instead of burnthrough, the laser had to burn up a lot more ice.

It frequently worked. Not all the time, but often enough that warships lugged around a lot of extra weight, coating their skins with frozen water.

There were, however, problems with all that heavy ice. The ship had to be perfectly balanced. You put a spin on a hundred-thousand-ton warship that was out of balance, it could tear itself apart.

Captain Bolesław was following the advice Admiral Krätz had hammered into Vicky. "Test the ice. Test the ship. Put your spin on slowly."

The *Retribution* slowly spun up to five RPMs. Vicky listened as pumps worked to move reaction mass around the ship, balancing it out.

"The ship is solid at five revolutions per minute, sir," Defense reported.

"All hands, this is the captain speaking. We are about to go to battle stations. We'll likely stay at battle stations for the next couple of hours. If you have to hit the head, now would be a good time."

Suddenly, Vicky felt a strong need to void her bladder. "If I may be excused, Captain."

"By all means, Your Grace."

Vicky motored down to her quarters. It was that or the nurses' quarters. Kit and Kat were in their high-gee stations but were out in a flash to help Vicky get out of hers and make her way to the head. With the ship spinning at five RPMs, it was no easy operation.

Done, they helped Vicky back into her cart, this time attaching the necessary fixtures to her plumbing. The high-gee station was designed with a man in mind. No doubt, the adjustments to accommodate Vicky would leak under high gees and rotations. Still, it was all she'd have until the battle was decided.

Kit and Kat provided quick pecks on her cheeks, and Vicky rolled out to see what the day would bring.

CHAPTER 19

O N the trip back to the bridge, Vicky reflected on the battles she'd been in with Kris Longknife. Vicky had always been the cute little girl in the new dress. As she maneuvered her cart through traffic, it dawned on her she was likely one of the few battle veterans aboard.

Now that's a frightening thought.

She reviewed what Kris Longknife would be doing to get ready for battle and found that Captain Bolesław might be missing something.

On the bridge, Vicky motored over to the skipper and leaned her head close to his. "Sir, have you got any evasion plans in your computers?"

"Evasion plans?" had the question mark Vicky had feared.

"Kris Longknife in her battles has her ships follow a pattern of zigs and zags, ducking up and down, juggling the throttle back and forth. Jinking to confuse the enemy's firing solution."

"It would mess up our own firing solutions," Captain Bolesław muttered.

"Not if your fire control computer knows where the pattern will take you and adjusts your fire accordingly."

Now the captain seemed intrigued.

"Computer," Vicky said to her own personal computer, made of the same self-organizing matrix as Kris Longknife's Nelly, but without the attitude, "show the captain some of the moves you captured when you were with Kris Longknife's ships."

The image of a small corvette appeared. It did a wild jig in space for a half minute.

"Kris says the idea is to never go the same direction for more than two seconds, three at most."

"And she gave you this evasion scheme?"

"Not exactly," Vicky admitted. "Kris was very much into not sharing too much with anyone she thought might become the enemy. No, my computer captured this during one situation when we were on distant approach. I've tamed it down a bit. Some of the more energetic ones were downright frantic."

"I imagine they were," the captain said, rubbing his chin. "I remember reading histories of the Iteeche War that mentioned evasive actions, but none of the historians seemed to know what they were talking about. Now I'm beginning to understand. No wonder this got lost in the long peace. I bet this is hell on bad backs."

"I believe our files on Kris Longknife mentioned that she retired almost an entire Navy back in the days when she was with Training Command introducing Navies to the fast attack boats and her tactics for them."

"We may have to adjust this a bit, hold course for at least three seconds, maybe four. Our maneuvering jets restrict just how hard we can zig and zag. Still, this beats doing nothing," he said. "Let's see if your computer can come up with a program for three minutes of jinking that the squadron can do together when Count Crow is at his closest."

For the next five minutes, Vicky and Captain Bolesław jiggered Kris Longknife's stolen evasion plan. When the skipper was satisfied, he sent it to the squadron with a request for comments from the other captains.

The general response seemed to center on, "So that was what those old after action reports were getting at," followed by, "We can do that."

"Now, let's get back to our RPM drill," Captain Bolesław said, and jacked up the RPMs to ten, then fifteen, and finally twenty. The *Retro* bumped and groaned a bit, but they moved reaction mass around to calm her down. The real test would come when hostile lasers were slicing gashes in her hide, and the pumps had to make adjustments in fractions of a second.

Satisfied, the skipper took the rotations off the ship. "No need to stress the *Retro* or give anyone coming at us any ideas."

Vicky raised a questioning eyebrow.

"Sensors, have you seen the Brunswick squadron doing any RPMs?"

"No, sir. They are steady at one gee and no battle tests," Lieutenant Blue reported.

"Idiot landsman," Captain Bolesław growled.

The four onrushing ships, the battleships *Reprisal* and *Revenge* trailed by *Emden* and *Koln*, bore down on them on a course that would sweep them past at a closest range of seventy-five thousand klicks.

"That should be just inside the 8-inch range of their cruisers. Maybe time for two broadsides unless they hold their fire for closest approach. I wonder who makes that call."

"Count Crow said 'charge,'" Vicky said. "He didn't say anything about how they do it."

"At least not while we were listening," Captain Bolesław pointed out.

Vicky shrugged.

"Comm, send to *Sovereign of the Stars*, 'Reorganize the freighters into two columns, twenty-five and thirty thousand klicks off our starboard side.' That should keep them far enough away to avoid becoming targets yet close enough to not become targets of opportunity once that carrion eater's battle line is out of range."

Together, Vicky and Captain Bolesław watched as the two forces closed rapidly. The Brunswick fleet was accelerating, which allowed them to bring their forward battery to bear. Vicky's fleet was decelerating to make orbit around Brunswick. Unfortunately, that left their vulnerable sterns with unarmored rocket engines hanging out there for the Count's ships to shoot.

Vicky was pretty sure what Captain Bolesław would do then, but it was kind of him to explain it to her beforehand. "Just before we come in range, I'll flip ship and present them with our bow armor to shoot at. Bow on also makes us a harder target to hit. Usually, for a school problem, I'd cut my engines to idle. With your evasion scheme, I must keep some way on the ship, say a quarter gee to start with, then juggle it to make hash of their firing solution. Likely, my aft batteries will be brought to bear if I need them."

"Or you could do what Kris Longknife does," Vicky said.

"And what would the inimitable Wardhaven princess do?" the captain said, evenly.

"Wait until the forward batteries fire themselves dry, then flip ship and give them the aft battery."

"Hmm," the captain said, rubbing his scalp. "That might work if they keep their full broadside to us, but if I know Engle at all, he'll be as edge-on to us as I'm trying to get to him. If I flip ship, he's likely to learn from me. Do you really want to teach your opposition so many new tricks the first time we go at them? This could be a long war."

And Engle is your friend. If you can hit his ship as light a blow as possible . . . Vicky did not finish the thought.

"Just a thought you might use," Vicky said.

"I might. We'll see what we shall see." Captain Bolesław glanced at the screen. "When do we get in extreme range?"

"For us, sir, fifteen minutes," Nav said. "For him, sixteen at the most."

"Guns, do you recognize my voice?"

"Your voice is recognized and logged."

"You will not open fire until I give you an express order. No one else may give you that order."

"Understood, sir. We are not weapons free until you say we are weapons free. Sir, may I ask a question?"

"Ask."

"If we are fired upon and the bridge is hit, what are your orders?"

The captain glanced at Vicky. "Guns, if you aren't hearing anything from this bridge, you can assume that it has been a very short war."

"Understood, sir, and thanks for taking us off the hook."

"Guns, starting a war is way above your pay grade."

"And it's not above yours, sir?"

Bolesław almost snorted but answered with a curt, "Captain off."

Now Vicky eyed Captain Bolesław. "I thought starting a war was reserved for my pay grade."

"I considered that, and letting you give the order, but this is a Navy thing. I'm the captain, Lieutenant Commander, and you're just a passenger aboard my ship. One overweight political elephant, but still just a passenger. I will decide when and where my ship fires."

Vicky glanced down demurely. "I try to watch my cellulite, but it so does stick to my hips."

"If it makes you feel better, you as the Grand Duchess may order me to return fire. I assume you're only talking about returning fire after they started this shindig."

"Most definitely."

"Then you say your piece and I'll give my order and we'll get to Scotland together."

"We have *got* to get better jokes," Vicky said.

"After we win this war, we can hire a writer. Until then, we'll just have to make do with what we can come up with in our stressed-out situation."

Together, they stared at the screen.

"Ten minutes until we are in extreme range," Nav reported.

The ship got very quiet.

"Five minutes until we are in extreme range." Guns had taken over the litany on net from his station in fire control. At four, three, and two minutes, he updated the report.

"Guns, cancel all reference to our time to firing range," Captain Bolesław said. "Report me the range to the approaching battleships with reference to the maximum range of a 15-inch gun."

"Aye, aye, Captain. One hundred thousand klicks to maximum 15-inch range."

"Guns, I want you to concentrate the two lasers in each turret at a single spot on the *Reprisal*. For the four forward turrets, pick four targets well apart."

"Aye, aye, sir. Seventy-five thousand klicks."

"Fifty thousand klicks. We have dialed in the *Reprisal*, sir."

"Very good, Guns."

"Twenty-five thousand klicks."

"Defense, put a full battle spin on the ship," Captain Bolesław ordered.

"Spin is five . . . ten . . . fifteen . . . a full twenty RPMs. Ship is stable."

"All squadron ships report battle RPMs and stable," Comm announced.

"Five thousand klicks," said Guns.

"Helm, one-quarter gee, put us bow on to the approaching ships. Begin Evasion Plan Addled."

"One-quarter gee. Helm over. Commencing Evasion Plan Addled, sir."

In her high-gee station, Vicky felt the ship slow hard, then swerve.

"We are taking laser fire, forward," Defense reported. "One hit. No burnthrough. I am moving reaction mass to balance."

Captain Bolesław turned to face Vicky.

"Captain, you may fire when ready," she said without even taking a breath.

"Guns. Fire. You have weapons release," the captain said with utmost calm.

"Fire," Guns replied over the rest of the captain's words. "We have weapons release," was an afterthought. Admittedly, an important one, but firing circuits were closed on the order, well before weapons release was echoed.

"Comm. Order the fleet to open fire. Concentrate on the *Revenge*."

"Squadron replies they are firing. *Revenge* is the target."

The war Vicky so wanted to avoid had started.

CHAPTER 20

"P ER your orders, sir, we are concentrating all four turrets forward in tight, two-shot spreads," Guns reported.

"Very good."

On screen, the *Reprisal* had turned bow on to the *Retribution*. It glowed as lasers boiled ice to steam and sent waves rolling off it into the space around the battleship. Now it was easy to see the invisible lasers as they showed bright red in the roiling gases. The *Reprisal* was taking one concentration of hits to the right of center and two others widely scattered to left and right of the bow.

There was no evidence of burnthrough.

The lasers fell silent as capacitors ran down and began to recharge.

The *Reprisal* finally began to spin. Even Vicky could see the deep hole in the ice on its bow as it began to revolve around the battleship's bow. *Reprisal* did a drunken jig; it was way out of balance and struggling. Still, it rotated.

"Good, Engle, you're learning," the skipper whispered.

"Damage Control here. We took only one glancing hit. Our spin reduced its impact, and we jinked out of it before it took off more than a few centimeters."

"Lucky us," the captain observed dryly. "Have they hit any of the other ships?"

"No, sir. It appears the *Revenge* missed entirely."

"Give me a rundown until they finish reloading, Defense."

"Seven . . . six . . . five . . . four . . . three . . ."

"Helm, jink down, now."

"Helm down now."

"One," Defense finished. There was a pause. "We are not taking hits at this time."

"Guns, concentrate our fire on four points. Two guns for each one."

"I was going to aim for the hole we made."

"Aim for a new place. Peel him, don't gut him."

"Aye, aye, sir. Retarget. Fire."

"Peel him, don't gut him?" Vicky asked.

"He saw what I did to him last time. He'll know what I'm doing to him this time. I've only got three, maybe four shots at him. He will understand what I am telling him."

I hope I understand what you're telling him. But Vicky said nothing.

A lot of steam came off the *Reprisal* this shoot. Sensors got a good view of the lasers aiming for the *Retribution*. Both hostile battleships fired their forward battery. None hit.

"The cruisers are coming in range of us," Defense reported.

The captain ordered a jink up, but the cruisers didn't fire. A second jink down didn't draw fire from them either.

"The battleships are coming up on reload time," Defense reported, "in five . . . four . . . three . . . two."

"Helm, go left with all you got," the skipper ordered.

"Going left hard," the helmsman answered.

"One," Defense said.

"Both battleships and both cruisers fired. All missed to the right."

"Yes," Captain Bolesław said excitedly, but softly. "Guns, concentrate everything you got on the *Revenge*."

"*Revenge*, aye, sir. Retarget. *Revenge*. Four tight salvos."

The second battleship in line began to light up. The *Slinger* had been trading blows with it for the last half minute, but its four forward 15-inchers had only scarred the surface. Now a big gouge opened up at the lower center of the ship's bow.

Steam shot off in geysers. It was hurt, but there didn't appear to be any burnthrough.

The battle paused while both sides reloaded.

"You got any preference for the next salvo, sir?" Guns asked. "I figure they get one good shoot before we get out of their range. We get maybe two more while they run from us."

"Give the *Revenge* four tight hits, Guns. I'll tell you what I want to do next after this salvo."

"Aye, aye, sir."

Captain Bolesław leaned close to Vicky. "Do you have a preference, Your Grace?"

"You clearly don't want to blow either of those battleships out of space."

"Not really. Today's enemy may be tomorrow's friend."

"I've heard that can happen. Okay. I'd kind of like to give Count Crow a good-bye kiss."

"I'm inclined to do the same. Some concentrated hit where we haven't hit before."

"Can you do that?"

"Only fools think they can control a battle, but it would be fun to put the fear of the Lord in that yahoo."

"Anything that scares him, that leaves him worried that someone else might not take prisoners, is fine by me."

"Then let us see what we can do."

Captain Bolesław once again did his dance with the other ships, dodging down. One cruiser seemed to have guessed down, but its 8-inch guns were barely in range, and they did little more than warm the ice.

The battleships got off one weak broadside expending what they had managed to get into their capacitors as they slipped toward the limit of their range. They caught the *Retribution* between jinks, slashing maybe three meters of ice that would have burned through another ship's armor but only made the *Retro* do an urgent jig.

Captain Bolesław had Guns finish reloading before ordering him to aim for the *Reprisal*. "Aim four concentrations for somewhere you haven't pounded them before if you will."

"The range is long, but I think we're good enough to do that."

The distant battleship began to burn in the lower left corner of its bow. It hadn't taken a hit there though it might be close to one of the smaller punches. Steam exploded. Huge chunks of ice flew off. The *Reprisal* was in trouble but lucked out as the lasers expended their stored charge.

"Well done, all hands," the captain said on net. "Defense, secure from rotations. Helm, secure evasion actions. All hands, secure from general quarters. Damage Control, let me know what we need to do to assure the ship's safety."

A series of rapid-fire "aye, ayes" greeted his words.

For the ship's crew, it had been the peak of a career. A live fire exercise that they came through with flying colors. They'd tell their grandkids about this day.

For Vicky, it was a kick in the gut.

I am a rebel against my father. I didn't fire the first shot, but I fired nevertheless. I didn't want war. Dear God, if you are above, I never wanted war.

But I've got one now.

CHAPTER 21

VICKY sat in her high-gee station, her gut too roiled, her knees too weak, to get up.

Around her, the ship's crew went about their business. Defense coordinated with Damage Control to get robots out to hose water into the gashes in the armor. They were few and shallow, but they were there, and no good skipper allowed armor to go unpatched.

First reports showed no casualties other than a few people who fell out of their high-gee stations when the ship zigged, and the Sailor zagged. There was a lot of laughter at their expense.

The captain was concentrating on making orbit, and Vicky was thinking about what she'd tell the station crew if they were under the thumb of some stay-behind security guards, when Lieutenant Blue cleared his throat.

"Pardon me for interrupting, but the Brunswick squadron is reversing course."

"Nobody does that," the navigator snapped.

"I don't think anyone told the Count," Blue answered, "because I'm looking at four ships that just flipped ship and are doing their wild-ass best to decelerate."

"Poor Engle," Captain Bolesław muttered. "Now he has to attack us."

"They are indeed trying to return to the station," Nav reported. "Give me a few minutes, and I'll get you an estimate of how long it will take."

"Please do so, Nav."

"Can we catch the station?" Vicky asked the skipper.

"Yes. We may need to go to 1.25 gees to do it. I believe the freighters were specifically chosen because they had the legs for some hard tacking."

For the next hour, they tacked hard. They were on final approach when the screen came alive. They found themselves looking at a middle-aged man with a large paunch in Security Consultant reds with a bit less gold and silver but large death's heads on his lapels. Behind him stood a ramrod-straight major in undress Marine greens and a station boss in civilian clothes.

It was the Security Consultant who spoke for them all.

"You will not approach this station. It is under the Empress's protection."

With a nod from Captain Bolesław, Vicky stood to give the reply for their side.

"You may have noticed that the squadron providing you protection is all to hell and gone."

"I hold this station with a brigade of Security Associates," came back fast.

"We intend to dock," Vicky said calmly.

"You can't."

"Ah, excuse me," the station boss said, clearing his throat, "but dock tie-downs are automatic. Any ship that comes alongside can dock."

COMPUTER, IS THAT TRUE?

NO, YOUR GRACE. PIER TIE-DOWNS ARE CONTROLLED FROM THE PORT CAPTAIN'S OPERATIONS STATION. THERE ARE NO REPORTS IN MY DATABASE OF THIS STATION BEING ANY DIFFERENT.

So, maybe the Empress's security goon doesn't control this station as much as he thinks.

"Then I will have my security technicians, and, oh yes, Marines, shoot down anyone who tries to leave your boats."

Vicky gave the head honcho a fatalistic shrug. "Then I'll

just have my flagship perforate the station with a few well-placed shots. Unfortunately, this will empty the station of air, but we can have our Marines in battle armor go aboard, block the holes, and refill the station with air. It will be one messy station, though. I understand dying in vacuum is a horrible death. All that blood and shit and eyes popping out of their sockets. It's a bitch to clean up."

The security goon's eyes had gone huge, his face matched his white trousers, and his Adam's apple was bobbing alarmingly.

"You wouldn't do that?"

"Your Count fired on us. No matter what you may have been told, his ships are a whole lot worse for the wear. Six meters of ice armor does a lot better job of stopping 15-inch lasers than three meters does against 18-inch lasers."

The security honcho gave a panicked glance at the men behind him. The Marine replied with a curt nod. The station boss's head was bobbing up and down.

"I surrender the station. Major Burke, handle the surrender details." And the man in the bloodred uniform bolted from the screen, no doubt for the head.

Vicky waited while the two on the station watched their lord and master depart, and only when they turned back to her did she say, "Your surrender is accepted."

Captain Bolesław joined Vicky on screen. "How bad is it, Wenzel?"

The major gave one more glance off screen at the departed redcoat. "It hasn't been good, Ališ. My wife and kids are still on Garnet, and my former boss regularly made the point that if I don't follow his orders to the T, my family would pay the price."

"Then we'll have to do this by the numbers and get your family out."

"Mine, and all my officers' and NCOs'."

"I will personally see to it immediately," Vicky said.

Now the major eyed Vicky. "So, you are in rebellion against the Emperor."

"Say rather, that I am loyal to the Emperor, my father, and in rebellion against the Empress and her grasping family."

"Said that way, I'd give a hearty amen if my family weren't held hostage to my following the Empress's orders."

"That's the way we're saying it, Wenzel," Captain Bolesław

said. "Now, about that brigade of redcoats. Any chance your troops can corral them?"

"I sent the order when Jo-Jo the Baboon bolted out of here. A few of his officers had a hard time agreeing to surrender, but several of my officers have resolved their doubts with a few well-placed shots." The major glanced off screen. "As I suspected, the rest are following the instructions my Marines are giving and will be locked down in the next quarter hour. Once that's done, I'll have all my troops stack arms on the station's A Deck and the Gunnys will march my men to quarters except those keeping an eye on the redcoats. My officers and I will await you on A Deck."

"We will land our ship's Marines to take your surrender. That means docking my ships. I'd planned just to dock the freighters, but I doubt you want to surrender to St. Petersburg Rangers."

"What are they, some sort of half-ass security types?" the major asked.

"The 1st Rangers fought side by side with the 34th Armored Marines and 54th light battalion on Posnan and Presov," Vicky put in. "You may ask the Marines from the 54th what they think of them."

"Dear God, it really has started if planets are raising militia that can stand in the line with Marines."

"Yes, Wenzel, it really has started. That Count joker may have fired the first shot, but we've been getting ready for a while now."

"Just get our families out, and you'll have another battalion of Marines, Ališ. So help me God, if they harm our kids, you will have a battalion that will storm hell to gut the Empress and take no prisoners on the way."

Vicky and Ališ nodded with the Marine. Inside, Vicky was fighting horror.

Was this what makes civil war so bad? Does this game of hostage taking spawn hearts so burned-out that body has to be piled on top of body? I didn't want this war. Now I've got it. How do I keep it from running away with me?

The look Ališ gave her told her she wasn't the only one gnawing on that thought. Only when the commlink was closed down did he say, "I hope the evil Empress is not giving you any ideas about joining in the hostage game."

Vicky shook her head. "I do not want to go there, and I hope the Navy won't touch it, either. Still"—she paused—"if your friend's family is harmed, I don't know what others will do."

"If Major Burke's family is harmed, I will do my level best to see him assigned to staff work where he can't get his hands on a weapon."

The two exchanged nods.

We can hope, was Vicky's final thought on the matter before the captain got busy elsewhere.

Several hours later, the *Retribution* docked on High Brunswick, followed quickly by the rest of the squadron and the convoy. No sooner were docks locked down than the freighters were disgorging their cargos. No surprise, there was no cargo waiting for them.

A few quick calls, even as the first of St. Petersburg's cornucopia of trade goods flowed down the space elevator, and there were return loads headed up. The Empress might have controlled the station, but her sway had not spread beyond its air locks.

Vicky caught a glimpse of the beginning of trade when she went ashore to take the formal surrender of Major Burke and his officers. Captain Bolesław left that to her.

"Now I begin to understand Admiral von Mittleburg's comments about some rag that some girl might wave," he said. "Am I correct to decode it as the flag of rebellion that the Grand Duchess might wave?"

Vicky nodded. "It had been long under discussion as to whether or not the flag existed and whether this Grand Duchess could or would wave it. It seems that the debate is over and if I can't carry the flag, my stepmom will use it for my shroud."

"She'll use it for a lot of us," the captain muttered.

"Then we must win this. I assume you have plans for when the Count of Crows makes his way back."

"I'm working on them. Why don't you take Wenzel's surrender?"

So it was that Vicky found herself in the dress whites of a lieutenant commander taking the surrender of a Marine major.

"I thought battalions rated a lieutenant colonel in command," Vicky said after the initial formalities were done.

"The 16th Marines *had* a lieutenant colonel, but he refused the job offer when we were mustered out. He died in a car crash on the drive home that evening. I was told I'd suffer a similar fate if I didn't take the job." The major glanced away. "I figured the men deserved someone decent between them and the shitheads I've been dealing with."

"Well, then, stand down with your men. I will do my best to see that your POW status is respected and goes easy on you. I have already gotten a message off to see that your families are freed from their captivity."

Actually, Mr. Smith was the one that got a coded message off to Bayern to alert the Navy high command that the 16th Marines were no longer obeying the Empress and their families were in harm's way. Hopefully, the Navy would succeed in moving heaven and earth to free them.

"Thank you, Your Grace. I won't ask to whom or where your message was directed." Then the major saluted and led his officers off to their quarters. They were trailed by one sergeant from the 54th Marines. The officers and men of the 16th were now under their protection.

Whether the 54th could control them if matters got out of hand was another matter entirely.

Vicky returned to the *Retribution* just in time to hear the air locks close down behind her. Her tiny battle fleet was getting under way for yet another fight.

CHAPTER 22

As Vicky joined Captain Bolesław on the bridge, he muttered, "Now we show the Clown of Crows how you properly defend a planet."

"Are we going to follow a long elliptical orbit like Kris Longknife did at Wardhaven?"

"Precisely. I've timed our departure to intercept him right where I want him."

The St. Petersburg squadron detached smartly from the space station, formed up, and did a deceleration burn that dropped them down, swung them close to the planet, then hurled them out into the long reach of an elliptical orbit. Even as they reached far toward the stars, Brunswick kept them in its gravity well . . . but not by much.

At the most distant reach of their orbit, they began to fall back toward Brunswick just as the squadron ordered about by the Count decelerated toward the station. This time, there would be no short shooting pass that left only time for a few salvos from the bow guns. The ships now would slam each other with full broadsides as they plunged toward the planet and its station.

Just who would be left alive when they got there was anybody's guess.

Vicky's recent studies, induced by Admiral Krätz's taking away her other nighttime activities, had included a lot on the history of warfare. She'd been startled to discover that there had been entire centuries with only a few major battles in Europe. She'd shared her dismay with the admiral.

"No one wanted to fight a battle. They'd raid each other's territory and lay siege to this or that town or castle, but even those trying to relieve a siege would usually just ravage the besiegers' lands, and they'd break the siege to defend their own."

"That sounds crazy."

"Is it, Ensign?" Admiral Krätz said, his eyes gleaming.

"It seems so," Vicky had answered, suddenly less sure.

"Who wins a battle?"

"The winner?" Vicky answered, her puzzlement growing.

"And did they know it the day before?"

"Of course. Who'd go into battle unless they expected to win?" That seemed obvious to Vicky.

"And do you suspect that maybe the other side, the one that lost, expected to win when they marched into it?"

"Oh," said Vicky, something dawning, even if it wasn't all that clear yet.

"If there is a battle, it happens because both sides see that they must fight, and both sides think they will win it. Now, what happens if one or both sides don't see that they need to fight here and now, or one or both sides don't think they can win the fight, or afford the casualties that even a win might cause them?"

"I see," said Vicky, establishing a grid in her mind and seeing how two commanders might answer its questions. "So, for a couple of centuries, at least one commander, or both, felt that victory was elusive or the cost of a victory might be more than the benefits."

"You begin to think like a great commander," Admiral Krätz said, and shot two more books to Vicky's reader and assigned her reports on both of them before the week was out.

Under Admiral Krätz, it was easy for Vicky to stay out of the paint locker. She was too busy to hunt down a fellow ensign and jump his bones.

She was learning again, and there seemed to be just as much celibacy involved.

Life's a bitch, but it's better to stay alive than not.

They were closing rapidly into extreme range for the 18-inch guns of the *Retribution*. "Do we open fire this time?" Vicky asked.

"That remains to be seen," Captain Bolesław said, eyes firmly on the screen as if it might show him not the ships they were closing on but what was happening on their bridges. "Come on, Engle, don't make me have to kill you," was a softly whispered prayer.

"Defense, prepare to initiate defensive spin. Take us up smartly over the next two minutes."

"Aye, aye, sir. Beginning battle revolutions smartly but slowly."

The *Retribution* began to spin around Vicky; she leaned back in her high-gee station.

"Helm, prepare to initiate evasive action."

"Evasive action standing by."

"Sensors, jack up the visuals. I want the *Reprisal*'s image to fill that screen."

The sleek, ice-covered hull of the lead battleship leapt at Vicky as the screen zoomed in. Vicky saw deep gouges the *Retribution*'s lasers had made during the last fight as well as the crevasses where its armor had calved and spun off into space as its skipper attempted battle revolutions.

Suddenly, the *Reprisal* began to spin at an appallingly high number of revolutions per minute. Then it vanished from the screen.

"Sorry, sir," Lieutenant Blue said. "She went from one gee to three gees deceleration, and we couldn't keep up with her."

"Are the other ships doing the same?" the skipper asked.

"Right on the same time tick," the lieutenant answered.

A grin spread across Captain Bolesław's face. "Engle, you are as much of a smart aleck as you think you are. And after this, I may just believe you."

"What just happened?" Vicky asked.

"I think I should wait and let Engle explain. He so loves to brag about his practical jokes. I've played the straight man for him way too many times. I think I just did again."

The screen came alive. "Ališ, you there?"

"Yes, Engle. Are you finally free to talk?"

"Free and then some. Those landlubbers have no idea how

to survive aboard ship. The Count of Me thought we were sissies with our high-gee stations since we weren't doing more than one gee. He and his henchmen have been prancing around our ships like they owned them. Now most of them are up against a bulkhead with a broken back, broken neck, or busted head. Amazing, they actually had brains in those skulls. I wonder what they've been using them for."

He paused to glance off screen and grinned. "That wiped the smirk off their faces. What a time I will have telling this story! Oh, and you will get credit, Ališ. You made it quite clear that you could hit my ship where you wanted to and burn right through me on your second salvo. Thanks for not doing it."

"You're welcome. Thanks for not playing the lamb dragged to the slaughter."

"Yeah, it was pretty clear to me and *Revenge* that we'd be toast as soon as you started hitting us with full broadsides. It was pretty clear what side we wanted to be on. Is that the Grand Duchess at your elbow?"

"The full and gracious Grand Duchess herself," Captain Bolesław said, nodding to Vicky.

"Your Grace, I surrender my command to you, having earned the full honors of war. I will lay my sword at your feet, and, if you will allow me, pick it up in your service."

"You always were good at slinging the bull," Captain Bolesław muttered.

"I accept your surrender," Vicky said, formally. She expected that she'd better get very good at this. "I will also accept you in my service. The 16th Marines just surrendered to me but laid down their arms for fear that harm might come to their families."

"I don't think we have that problem. Most of my officers moved their families to Navy colonies when we saw the way the wind was blowing. Strange they still ordered us into the Empress's service, but I think the clowns they've got working for them are not all that up to snuff."

"Let us hope so," Captain Bolesław said. "Captain Rachinsky, please bring your squadron in line behind my squadron. If any of your ships are retaken by Security Contractors, my squadron will be in a position to shoot out its engines."

"If any of those security goons retake one of our ships, we

will shoot it out of space, never fear. We've had enough of being their lapdogs."

They fell in line behind the St. Petersburg squadron, decelerating at one gee. Their vulnerable engines and reactors were submissively pointed at the *Retribution*'s lasers.

Vicky breathed a sigh of relief; Admiral Krätz would be proud of his student. With a little help from Captain Bolesław, she had persuaded the right people in a Marine battalion to surrender, then did the same for a battle squadron. Two sets of commanders had looked at the likely price of victory and found it not worth the blood price of a fight.

You got lucky, girl. Every day ain't gonna be like this.

Vicky suppressed a snort at her cynical self. No doubt worse was coming, but for now, she, and those both with her and against her, had proven more rational than bloodthirsty. Or maybe the bloodthirsty had proven incompetent.

This would not last. There must be some experienced Navy and Marine officers willing to throw in with the Empress for gold or glory.

Make that gold *and* glory.

CHAPTER 23

═══════

THE landings at High Brunswick were carefully done. *Koln* went in first, followed closely by Vicky's *Wittenberg*. Then *Emden* and *Augsburg* berthed at piers across from each other. The *Revenge* and *Slinger* were the next pair. Finally, the *Reprisal* went in, followed immediately by *Retribution*.

Only when all pier tie-downs were locked tight and air locks open did Captain Bolesław breathe a sigh of relief. "I thought we could pull that off. I can hardly believe we did."

"The way you damaged the *Reprisal* and *Revenge*," Vicky said, "you were showing them what you could do while pulling your punches."

"Yes. Engle could have gotten mad and gone all macho on me, or he could see what he faced—and that I wasn't going for his jugular—and do what he did. He's grown up a lot since he was a plebe at the academy."

"Should I formally take his surrender?"

"Why don't we invite him to dinner tonight? I think he'd much rather share a good glass of wine with you than swap his cake cutter. Oh, and if I might suggest, wear one of your Grand Duchess dresses. It will be harder for a captain to admit he surrendered to you if you're showing lieutenant commander's stripes."

"Thank you, Captain, I will follow your advice."

What she wanted to do was invite him to her quarters, strip him bare in a flash, and have her and the two assassins show him what heaven could be like.

Unfortunately, she'd had her computer check his file. He was very married to a lovely woman, doted on his four boys, and worshipped his daughter. She might find him irresistible for a postbattle romp, but he'd likely find the offer far from the Navy Way.

Besides, her computer was becoming most insistent that she was wanted below on Brunswick.

Like a good Grand Duchess, she collected her critical entourage, Commander Boch, Lieutenant Blue, Mr. Smith, and her two bantam assassins for security before heading for the space elevator.

En route, they were held at a police line while a couple of Marines smoked one of the security thugs out of his hiding place. Since those Marines were young and likely had no family at risk, they had happily joined with the locals in flushing out the hated redcoats.

At the elevator station, she was held up further, waiting for a platoon of Marines and another of Rangers to arrive. When finally ready, they were sandwiched between crates of trading goods while boarding, but the VIP lounge was pretty much devoted to them as they began the fast drop to the capital of Brunswick, Laatzen.

Someone was arranging meetings for her, even more bloody meetings as she dropped. Unfortunately, with the battles over, she couldn't kill him.

She was greeted at the beanstalk station by the Governor General, a white-haired gentleman who offered her the key to the planet before a crowd of fawning newsies. Governor General Wilhelm Welf had held his position for nearly twenty years. Father would no doubt include him among his appointments who had gone native and gone to seed. Still, Welf had managed to dodge all the deadly tides of the last few years and hadn't lost his head either to State Security or the Empress's Security Consultants.

That might have changed, had Vicky and her squadron not arrived in the nick of time. Welf knew it, and was rather profuse with his thanks as they waited for transportation to be rounded up for all of Vicky's security escort.

The destination of their quick drive was one of the towering skyscrapers that dotted the center of Laatzen. Again, Vicky was driven down to the secure bottom basement before being whisked up to the penthouse, where she could see all the powers of this world though she was offered little of it.

A Commander Strauss of the Supply Corps was waiting for her at the doorway to the penthouse conference room. He was rather proud of all the meetings he had arranged for Vicky and had no idea how close he came to having Vicky order one of her diminutive killers to take his head off at the navel.

Vicky took in all the burly men with tight haircuts and bulging shoulders lounging about the foyer, and recognized this meeting as not one for her entire team. Captain Inez Torrago, commander of 1st Ranger's Company C, had drawn the job of riding with the freighters. She'd also chosen to lead the platoon of Rangers escorting Vicky today. The Marines had sent a lieutenant.

"Inez, have your Rangers and the Marines secure a perimeter around this room as best you can. Mr. Smith, you, Kit, and Kat see that there are no holes in that perimeter that something slimy can slip through. Commander Boch, you and Lieutenant Blue will secure this door from the inside. Any questions?"

There were none. Vicky allowed Commander Strauss to lead them into a room filled with one huge table with twenty cool men and two women seated around it.

Commander Boch and the lieutenant took station at parade rest beside the door. When the other commander made to follow Vicky, she dismissed him with "Thank you. Please wait outside."

The man looked none too eager to go, but Vicky showed him the door with her eyes, and he left. Turning to face the table, she once again found one chair waiting for her at the foot of the table. She went to it and settled herself comfortably, then eyed those watching her silently.

A full minute went by before the middle-aged man at the head of the table cleared his throat, and said, "That was some interesting fighting you did up there this morning."

Vicky dismissed his concern casually. "We are fortunate that the blackhearted Empress still sees no need to reach outside the ranks of her father's financial empire to hire men competent in commanding other men when battle beckons. No doubt, that will not continue forever."

"No doubt," the man agreed. "Your ships have brought the trade goods we ordered, I see. Is the price going to be more than we can pay, I wonder?"

"The ships with me are not mine. The freighters belong to their owners, who are only too happy to get back in the business of carry and trade. The products are provided by partners on St. Petersburg who hope to open a long and mutually profitable relationship with you."

"And the warships?"

"Some of those docked at your station came with me. Others have just surrendered to me. They took some hard knocks and learned some hard lessons before matters might have become fatal. Now those ships require repairs and a base of operations that will meet their ongoing logistic needs. In return, they will see to your defense."

"We didn't need any defense before you came here," was spat from midtable.

Vicky waited to see if someone else would parry that jab. She didn't have to wait long.

"If she hadn't gotten here when she did, we'd have been bowing and scraping before those damn redcoats next week, and they'd be offering you a few pfennig on the mark for your business, your home, and maybe even your wife and daughter. Come on, Horst, get your head out of the shitter."

"I've got my head on straight, unlike some of you. What happens after she leaves? The Empress will be back, and with more redcoats. It will only get worse."

The man at the end of the table tapped his water glass with a stylus for silence. He got it quickly. "We've been over and over this and gotten nowhere. Your Grace, have you anything to add to our stew?"

Vicky took a deep breath. "You are right. The blackhearted Empress does not give up easily. She's tried twice to take St. Petersburg and twice to take the crystal mines on Presov. My stepmother is a heartless bitch who wants everything and will stop at nothing until she has it all, and the few survivors of her bloody machinations are kowtowing at her feet. So, do you want to offer her your neck or are you ready to stop her?"

"How *do* we stop her?"

"There are a pair of battleships and cruisers parked at your station. That's a start. You have young people. Metzburg is putting them to work at both terraforming and defense. I imagine now that shots have been fired, there will be less tree planting and more battle training. They're creating a Navy from out-of-work merchant ships. If you don't want your battleships, I'm sure they'd be glad to feed the crews and maintain the ships."

"They're ours. Nobody gets them." That came from the middle of the table. The side across from the one who wanted to surrender. Two men glared at each other.

"I think we have first option on those ships," the man at the head of the table said dryly. "Your Grace, we have unused merchant ships as well. Though, if we get trade going again, we may find gainful employment for them."

"You might want to be careful how you balance what you load up with product and what gets 6-inch and 8-inch lasers," Vicky said.

"Yes, we might," he said, making a notation on the computer embedded in the table. "Now, the merchant fleet and the four ships you are willing to give to us are a start on a Navy. What about an Army? Where do we get people to teach our young men to study war?"

"I can't offer you the Marine battalion on the station that surrendered to me this morning. The families of their officers and NCOs are being held hostage on Garnet for their good behavior. Some of the younger other ranks have joined the police force on the station hunting down redcoats, but I don't see the average private training an Army."

"No, I don't either."

"With your permission," Vicky said.

"Please."

"Computer, have Captain Torrago of St. Petersburg's 1st Rangers report."

"She is ordered."

Commander Boch opened the door, and Inez marched in smartly. She presented herself beside Vicky's chair with a stomp that killed any cockroaches within a ten-mile radius and saluted. "Your Grace."

"Captain, these people need an Army. Would you tell them how St. Petersburg found one so quickly?"

"Ma'am. You start with people with a will to be free and who know how to shoot and like long, hard days in the sun: farmers, cowboys, surveyors. You bring them together under the command of people who know the gentle art of killing their fellow man. You start with a few and feed in more who like a challenge, getting up at sunrise and working past sunset. You give them challenges, then get out of their way, letting them have the fun of solving them how they damn well please, ma'am. When you've got a good bunch, you cream off some of the best and dump the next best people you got in their lap and you go from having a battalion to having a regiment. If you're lucky, you have a division before too long. Since I doubt Brunswick has much time, I suspect they'll need to do this fast."

"Ladies and gentlemen," Vicky said, "I offer you Captain Inez Torrago as the lieutenant colonel of your first battalion, Brunswick Rangers. Maybe colonel of your first Ranger regiment depending on how many Marine privates you can hire to join her."

"Ma'am," almost was a squeak.

"Captain, these people need help. Your company is the only help they've got. If they want you, I will order you seconded to their service. Do you have a problem with that?"

"No, ma'am," came out only a bit wilted.

"I'll also see if I can find you a horse."

"It's not a horse I need, but good people at my back, Your Grace."

"It will be up to you to see that they are good."

"Understood, ma'am," had full backbone in it.

Vicky stood. "Ladies and gentlemen, I've offered you the seeds of a Navy and an Army. I've offered you a chance to dig your economy out of the ditch the Empress has driven you into by both giving your young people jobs, getting your factories producing again, and forming up the defensive shield you need from the blackhearted Empress's grasping claws. I wish I could offer you more, but if things were better off, we wouldn't be in the mess we're in. It's up to us to claim our future with our own two hands. The future the Empress offers is bleak and ugly. The future you can see for yourselves is one you'll be glad to hand down to your grandchildren.

"Which one will you choose?"

Vicky kind of hoped there would be a shout or round of applause. Instead, her rousing words were greeted with silence. The man at the head of the table eyed his computer as those around it reached for theirs and did something with a stylus.

You're not voting, are you? Vicky wanted to shout, but it was pretty clear they were.

She waited.

The man stood. "By prior consensus vote, it was agreed that this vote had to be unanimous." He paused to glance around the room. No one disagreed.

"By my tally, the vote is unanimous. Your Grace, I am authorized to offer you our allegiance."

Vicky nodded. "I accept your allegiance to me as allegiance offered to my father, the Emperor, and in opposition to the illegal actions of the Empress against the Imperial Charter. Are these terms acceptable to you?"

"I'm glad to hear you talking in those terms," the man at the head of the table said.

"Then let our people of business continue to complete the trades already commissioned and add any more that now become possible. You will excuse me, but I wish to return to my quarters on the battleship *Retribution*. There have been too many attempts on my life for me to risk much exposure. If you will negotiate with my commander and advance man outside, I will be glad to make a select number of additional meetings if my security can be vouched for."

"I think that can be accomplished."

And on that, Vicky retired gracefully.

CHAPTER 24

THE ride up the space elevator was without surprises. Inez had stayed behind with her platoon to begin the formation of Brunswick's Basic Training Command. Vicky also left Mr. Smith behind to coordinate with the local police and establish a suitable security team for the next time Vicky came to town. The lack of even a police escort from and to the elevator station had shown that the locals needed an education on what happened around this Grand Duchess.

Fortunately, the Empress's claws hadn't been ready this time or had been knocked for a loop when the battle was lost in space and at the station.

Vicky had time for a bath with Kit and Kat and a brief rest before it was time to dress for dinner. Her first choice was the formal dinner dress uniform, but that would show her rank. Captain Bolesław had made it clear it was better for her not to rub a captain's nose in the fact he'd surrendered to someone two ranks his junior. She had several formal gowns. Unfortunately, they showed enough décolletage to distract *two* rooms full of males from any serious discussions.

She had business suits, but they'd work for the next day's meetings. That left one royal blue gown in the back of her closet.

It still flashed her soft and willing breasts, but it came with a cloth-of-gold shawl that could be put to good use. No doubt the men would be removing it with their eyes, but the more mature of them would be able to meet her eye to eye and maintain enough of an IQ to discuss the needs of the future.

She chose that one, much to her assassins' dismay.

"You will not be bringing anyone home to bed tonight with that one," Kit said.

"She can always lose ze wrap or, better yet, wrap it around a nice man and tow him to our boudoir."

"Right by the Marines on guard outside our door," Vicky pointed out.

"Give us a call. We can have the Marines distracted thoroughly before you get here," Kit said.

With a sigh for old times, Vicky wrapped the cloth of gold around her shoulders, covered herself to Navy standards, and let herself out.

Dinner was a delight: a roomful of men playing court to her was something Vicky enjoyed. Captain Bolesław invited the skippers from his own squadron and Rachinsky's as well as Major Burke, whose POW status went unremarked upon.

Vicky listened as old stories and old jokes were trotted out and presented for her entertainment. How these men had survived the Academy and their time as junior officers to arrive at a captaincy and command had to be proof that miracles still occurred.

Major Burke had just finished a story of a training march that went horribly wrong when the digital compass led them deep into a swamp and they had to be helicoptered out one by one when Captain Rachinsky raised a glass in toast to Vicky.

"And how, Your Grace, will we get out of this swamp we are marching into, eyes front?"

The room quickly became very silent.

"Admiral Krätz taught me that any leader taking his country to war should have an end strategy," Vicky answered.

"Admiral Krätz was a very wise man," Captain Bolesław said, raising a glass in memory. "Many of us still have his boot mark on our rear ends."

"Hear, hear," brought several raised glasses.

Vicky raised her glass. "No doubt it will never wear off my rear end, either."

That drew several raised eyebrows but chuckles all around.

"So, *your* end strategy," Captain Rachinsky said, not letting Vicky evade.

The Grand Duchess took a deep breath and let it out. "There is no doubt in my mind that the civil war, just begun today, will end with either me or the Empress dead. Bloody purges will begin immediately thereafter as the winning side assures that there will be no further misbehavior from the losing one."

The room was back to silence. Dead silence.

"At least she's honest, Ališ," Rachinsky said.

"That's why I'm with her, Engle," Bolesław said. "She's honest. She's got guts, and she'll listen to you. She let me fight our battle today without once joggling my elbow. Can you say the same for your Count of Clown?"

"He had his hand jammed up my ass, playing me for a puppet the whole show. You saw how he didn't let me get in a word edgewise before he ordered a cavalry charge. A horse charge, for God's sake! After you showed us just how outgunned we were, he had to order us to wheel around and come right back. Damn!"

"Engle, why didn't you go to battle revolutions before that first shoot? I thought you were better than that. You forget Tactics 101?"

"What could I do, Ališ. He and his guys were prancing around the bridge looking over everyone's shoulders, laughing up their sleeves at us in our high-gee stations as sissies. If I went to battle revolutions, it would be a mess. And yes, my friend, I was kind of counting on you to go easy on us. I figured to go easy on you, but my God, man, you went balls to the wall, if you'll excuse me, ma'am."

"I'm Navy, too," Vicky said.

"Yes, so I hear. Anyway, you were all over the place, and my Guns was having the devil's own time laying a laser on you."

"I had the Grand Duchess on board. You, old buddy, had that political commissar at your elbow, or, as you so gently put it, up your ass. I couldn't count on you going as easy on me as I went on you."

"You call that easy? I've got holes two and a half meters thick in the armor on my bow. Four of them."

"I only gave you an eight-gun salvo to punch those holes.

If it had come to a fight for the station, you'd have gotten a full sixteen-gun broadside."

"You'd have punched through, and I'd be tasting cold space instead of this fine wine," the opposing captain said, and took a sip.

"But how does this end? Do we want the Empress dead? That sounds more like a goal than a plan," the captain defeated this day bore in.

Vicky nodded. "Most civil wars have a pause once the first shot is fired as the two sides shake down and lines are drawn. I figure it will be a month or so before we know exactly where the lines are. Then we'll know how we get to Greenfeld and they how they'll get to St. Petersburg."

"Hmm," Captain Rachinsky said, staring deep into his glass. "Any chance we could help a few of those planets make up their mind?"

"You have any ground forces?"

The *Reprisal*'s skipper eyed Major Burke. The Marine just shook his head.

"Well," went on the twice-turned officer, "you could put a few battleships in a planet's sky and threaten to slag them from orbit. That ought to get a quick surrender."

The whole room held its breath. Vicky might be new at this business, but she remembered that planets had suffered such destruction until a treaty had decreed that any planet that lost the high ground above it had the right and obligation to surrender. Would the Empress's bullyboys follow that ancient treaty?

"I have no stomach for fulfilling the challenge if the Empress's henchmen refuse the locals an opportunity to surrender," Vicky said bluntly. "Worse, I fear that if we once use that option, it will put thoughts in the blackhearted Empress's mind. Knowing her attitude toward me, I suspect that she'll think it good policy to slag a few planets just to encourage the others to come running to her."

"I fear you're right," Captain Bolesław said. Murmurs around the table supported him.

"This is going to be an ugly war," Captain Rachinsky said, draining his glass and reaching to refill it from the decanter.

"Civil wars often are," Vicky said. "You want to crawl under a rock?"

"I chose this profession," Captain Rachinsky said, "though even I'll admit that the long peace made it easy for me to ignore the bloody side of it. But what about our Sailors below-decks? Most of them signed on for a couple of years to get money to buy a farm on an outlying planet or earn an apprenticeship in a good craft. How are they going to take to the sudden discovery that they could be up to their ears in blood?"

Now it was Captain Bolesław who put down his wineglass. "That, gentlemen, will be up to us. Are we fighting just because we chose the profession of the sword and our number came up, or are we fighting to end this bloody tyranny that's blighting our beloved Greenfeld? We can't lead good men into battle if we don't believe it's worth fighting and dying for."

Captain Bolesław raised his glass. "Gentlemen, I give you one hell of a leadership challenge. Here's to leading our fine Sailors and Marines from the front into one damn complex fight."

"Hear, hear!" came as eight captains and one Grand Duchess drained their glasses.

CHAPTER 25

O**N** the station, work proceeded in haste, with unloading and reloading the freighters. The *Revenge*, now back under its name of *Ferocity*, was gently tugged into a repair dock and its armor patched. It was found to be the least damaged battleship. The *Koln* also got first call at the body and fender shop.

It was nice to have a station that had full-service docks for heavy warships. It made Vicky look forward to the day when St. Petersburg would have the same.

Meanwhile, the *Retribution* licked its minor wounds and made itself fit for duty while all six ships not in dock hands stood watch for any incoming hostiles. None came.

Vicky spent much of her time dirtside, waving at people who wanted to see the person in whose name the Security Consultants had been defeated. There had been incidents of rape and robbery on the station while the redcoats controlled it. Word had flown quickly through Brunswick's grapevine of what they could expect when the Security hoodlums landed.

That Vicky had stopped it was cause for celebration.

Vicky did her best to have Inez at her elbow as often as possible. The Ranger captain had done more than Vicky to end it, and Inez would be the one left here to get defenses in place on Brunswick. The people should see her.

But by the same fact of her getting a defense up, she was busy. Inez made a few appearances when Vicky really twisted her arm, but mostly, it was Vicky who waved the flag and took the adulation and allegiance of the people.

The powers that be were another matter entirely.

Those Vicky had met with the first day were there to wine and dine her most evenings, opening their circle wider, bringing in second-tier industrial, financial, and political officials. As Vicky had concluded, Wilhelm Welf was just a figurehead. Her concern was that most of the appointed politicals were little more than straw men as well. That was what her father liked. "The business of this Empire is business," he'd proudly say.

However, Mannie had given Vicky a much wider education on what the political brought to the table. She had learned from her readings in the *Fury*'s library that absolute power corrupted absolutely. Now she was watching as the Empress and her family used the absolute power the Empire afforded business to reach out and gather all to themselves.

Kris Longknife had persuaded Vicky to give Sevastopol an Imperial City Charter. Mannie had used it to blend the people, the money, and industry, along with the elected officials, into something that Vicky was finding worth having. Metzburg and Brunswick appeared to have had no such need to balance anything. Admittedly, its people of wealth were scared that the Empress intended to gut and roast them for dinner. Still, Vicky had no idea how these new planets would fare once she helped them get on their feet.

Vicky weighed what she had seen on the new planets and what she knew of on St. Petersburg. Would fear be enough to motivate everyone to balance their interests with everyone else they shared this planet with? Would the hope of their future hold them together once stepmama was no longer out to rip them to shreds?

If they couldn't, this rebellion might just be the first of many to come.

I need some quiet time to think. This rebellion thing is nowhere as easy as some people thought when they offered me an old flag to wave.

However, Vicky's contemplation came to a roaring halt as her limo did the same. Vicky couldn't remember ever having been stuck in traffic before, at least not in Greenfeld space. Traffic jams were something for Longknife folk to get stuck in.

Vicky glanced around. Traffic was stopped on her side of the street, and almost none was coming down the other side.

"Driver," Vicky said with an annoyed half wave, "pull over and let's jump to the head of this line."

The agent riding shotgun next to the driver spoke on his commlink, then shook his head. "The traffic supervisors don't recommend that, Your Grace. Some gathering of old ladies has gotten out of hand, and the biddies are blocking the road. He suggests you go around."

Vicky scowled. "Old ladies are blocking the road?"

"Something like that," the security agent agreed.

"How often does that happen around here?" the commander asked.

The agent looked pained. "I don't think it ever has."

"Let's get out of here, or we will be late," Vicky said. Several long-term trade agreements had been settled and they wanted her there to sign them, along with the locals and the trade delegates from St. Petersburg. It would not do to keep important people waiting.

The cars ahead and behind Vicky's limo completed a simultaneous U-turn and gunned down the opposite side of the street just as several others drivers got the same idea. They flinched out of the way of Vicky's cavalcade.

Despite the delay, Vicky was right on time.

However, the meeting had taken a decided turn from its agenda.

Captain Torrago was beside the man at the head of the table, and there were major thunderclouds hanging over them.

CHAPTER 26

"**Y**OUR Grace, I'm so glad you are here. Maybe you can make this young woman understand that when her betters give her an order, it is to be obeyed."

"Yes, Your Grace," Inez bit out. "Would you please tell this . . . man . . ." seemed to replace some other preferred word, "that Rangers do not shoot down unarmed women and children in the street."

"They are troublemakers. Rabble-rousers," the man corrected.

"They never would have done this if we still had State Security," one older man at midtable grumbled. "People knew their place."

"And what might that place be?" Vicky asked breezily as she made her way as unthreateningly as possible to the head of the table.

I wondered what this rebellion was all about. I suspect I'm about to discover that rebellion is many things to many people. No need to spook these folks any sooner than I have to. No doubt they're sure they have all the answers.

If I've learned anything, it's that no one does, not even little old me.

Once Vicky was at the head of the table, she stepped between the Ranger captain and the spokesman for the powers that be on Brunswick.

"What seems to be happening that's got you all upset?" she asked, keeping it as open-ended as possible.

"We have a rebellion," the chief citizen of Brunswick said evenly, all unction and oil to *his* Grand Duchess.

"I know," Vicky said, offhandedly. "I seem to have been on the receiving end of its first shots." She smiled her most encouraging Grand Duchess smile.

"Not *our* rebellion, *their* rebellion," the grump at midtable growled.

"Ah," Vicky said, making to appear enlightened. "So it all centers on the pronoun, does it."

"Don't be silly, girl," snapped the grouch. "Jansik, set her straight."

"I will, Wallace, if you give me a chance." The man at the head of the table turned his bright and winning smile on Vicky. "We have a problem with hooligans and troublemakers blocking traffic, destroying private property, and causing mischief. I asked the young woman you suggested be the chief of our defense forces to deploy her troops to support our small force of traffic supervisors. She refused. Would you please tell her to comply with my order?"

Vicky turned to Inez and raised a questioning eyebrow. *No doubt there was more to this story than one side.*

"He ordered me to machine-gun the protestors," the Ranger snapped.

"That's what State Security would have done," Wallace said, getting his oar in the troubled waters.

"Please, Wallace, let the Grand Duchess handle this," said Jansik.

"Okay, okay, I'm just saying," said Wallace as he waved away the head of the table.

"Your Grace," Jansik said.

"Captain?" Vicky said.

"Ma'am, I've recruited some of my best trainees from those projects. I've had two weeks to train them. Many of them have just begun the weapons phase of their training, and this man wants me to order them to shoot down their mothers and grandmothers, their kid brothers and girlfriends!"

That got Vicky's attention. "Who are these people in the street?"

"No one," Jansik assured her back.

Vicky ignored him and kept her attention on Inez. Here was a woman she'd trusted with her life.

"Your Grace, the protestors are the women from the projects. That's where the workers live. The folks that still have jobs. The place is a mess. No running water. Little heat, and these guys raised the rent last month while cutting their husbands' pay for the third time this year. Vicky, the women are protesting because they can't take it anymore."

Vicky listened to Inez with two sets of ears.

One, her father the Emperor's ear, heard what Jansik expected her to hear. Hooligans were making trouble and needed to be taught a lesson. State Security should machine-gun them down. That would teach the likes of such people to accept what they got from their betters.

But Vicky had another set of ears now. Those listened as Mannie would. Here were real human beings, who built with their own two hands everything the people in this room needed. They were the people, like Inez, who would protect them from the likes of stepmommy dearest.

People who had just defended them from stepmom's invasion fleet.

Vicky closed her eyes. *How could they miss the Ranger's warning? If she issued those kids guns to shoot their mothers down, they'd be just as likely to turn those weapons on the officers ordering the murder of their family. On the likes of the people in this room.*

Fools!

Vicky turned to Jansik. "I don't think you've thought this through."

"Thought what through?"

Vicky let her eyes rove the room. The grouch was scowling at her, as were many of those around the table. There looked to be a few who might have put two and two together, but they were few and far between.

Vicky was tempted to just turn on her heels, grab Inez and her company of Rangers, and knock the dust of this place from her shoes.

It was tempting.

Then again, St. Petersburg needed Brunswick as a trading partner. Besides, if Vicky withdrew the fleet, the blackhearted Empress would be down on this bunch with her redcoats in two shakes. They'd be dead, and the lot of the workers would be no better.

"Not long ago, I led a Fleet Marine Force and a task force out to bring food to a planet," Vicky said, slowly. "We had to fight our way through a self-proclaimed duke and his gun-toting henchmen to get starvation rations to people dying of hunger. Inez here fought to make that happen. She's a good warrior," Vicky said, nodding at the captain.

Inez met the praise with a hint of a smile.

"Who has the guns on Brunswick?" Vicky asked. "Who got their hands on the guns left behind by the slaughter of State Security?"

Vicky eyed grumpy, then Jansik.

"I thought the guns were removed by the Navy when they took those thugs away," Jansik said.

"Who checked the inventory?" Vicky asked. "We've found a lot of them still locked up in that planet's armory. That duke fellow blew open the gun vault, and, before long, he had his hands on everything."

"Aren't the traffic safety officers using State Security Headquarters now?" someone around the table asked.

That drew shrugs.

"If they're there," Vicky said, "and you start shooting, whose hands will the guns end up in?"

Several frantic people around the table started talking to their commlinks. Vicky waited patiently for them to find out what cow was eating their cabbage, as some of the ex-farmers in the fleet were often wont to say.

"The gun vault opened at a touch, but it's empty," a woman near the foot of the table announced. "It looks like it was unlocked a while ago and just closed back up."

"So, my fine people, who has the monopoly on violence in your city and planet?" Vicky asked. "There is a thing I read about in one of the books I found on a Navy battleship. Not in the library at the palace, but something the Navy reads. It's called a social contract. Have any of you heard of such a thing?"

Heads shook around the table.

"You come to a green light," Vicky said slow, as if talking to particularly difficult preschoolers. "You drive through it, knowing that anyone coming from the other directions will see the red light and not smash into you. It's the same way with other things. I work for you. I assume that you'll treat me decently. That part of the contract can be a bit harder if you've got the likes of State Security to lean on the worker. The Emperor provided the duress, and you got to stint on the decent-treatment side. Now the machine guns are gone, and you're caught between a rock and a hard place. My stepmother is providing the rock. She's only too willing to smash you down and take what she wants from your dead body. The workers can't help but notice that the guns are gone. They could sure use some decent treatment. Who do you want to bargain with, my mom or those women blocking traffic?"

Vicky settled into Jansik's chair, leaving the fellow standing at her elbow.

The room's silence grew long, but that was too much for grumpy. "A Peterwald is telling us to bargain with our workers. I never thought I'd hear that."

"I bet you never thought a Peterwald would save your sorry ass from another Peterwald, but it happened," Vicky pointed out. "Face it, folks, you live in very strange times."

That drew a lot of surprised glances from around the table.

"Any chance we could bargain with the Empress?" grumpy asked no one.

"Have you talked to any of your family who are stuck in her 'security sphere'?" a young fellow across the table from him said. "The last I heard from my sister, her husband had an offer he couldn't refuse. That was a year ago, and there hasn't been a peep out of them since. Not so much as a small text message. Anyone else hearing nothing, too?"

He eyed the room. Suddenly, everyone was busy looking at the table.

"Yeah, like I thought. Folks, we have one and only one choice. We can pull together, all of us, or we can all get pulled apart. Wallace, I know you won't like it. You were chummy with General Zin before he got tossed out the window of State Security Headquarters."

"He jumped," Wallace insisted.

"Jumped, pushed? He was just a splat on the cobblestones when it was all over. I like this thing the Grand Duchess mentioned. We made our social contract with the Peterwalds and their State Security. They made it easy for us to do pretty much what we wanted to."

The young man looked around the table. "Now we have no guns to back us up, and the Empress is canceling all previous contracts and offering us stuff we can't swallow but can't refuse. So, unless someone has a third option I haven't heard about, we either make our peace with the folks we share this planet with and give them guns to defend themselves and us with, or we kowtow to the Empress and let her do what she wants to us."

Now there was discussion around the table. Vicky figured she'd be there for a long time. She looked up at Inez and drew her close with a quick waggle of a finger.

"Ma'am."

"You want to get back to work?" Vicky whispered.

"Yes, Your Grace."

"And look into those missing State Security machine pistols. You might also want to put some guards around the protestors to see that no one decides to use those machine guns in crowd control. I think I've got this bunch stampeded into a circle, but who knows who is out there and willing to do their unspoken bidding."

At "stampeded," the former rancher smiled, but at the thought of stray weapons wrecking what she and her Grand Duchess had worked so hard for this afternoon, Inez nodded and quick-walked from the room, her commlink already to her lips.

CHAPTER 27

To Vicky's disappointment, she did not find herself standing at several guys' elbows, smiling prettily to banks of newsies, as contracts were quickly signed. Instead, she sat through another long meeting.

It was clear to her what they had to do. Still, no one at the table could find their way clear to get off their rear ends and start making things happen. Thus, Vicky did her best to sit placidly as her tush began to ache and her patience grew shorter while all those around her yapped their way through more long-winded dithering.

She was thinking of leaving. It was good she stayed.

Half a dozen commlinks started flashing at the same time.

"There have been shots fired at Greenfeld Plaza," shouted the young woman who seemed to know more about what was going on than anyone else in the room, or knew it faster. She jumped to her feet.

"Calm down," Vicky ordered in the command voice Admiral Krätz had taught her.

As the admiral had promised his budding JO, people did calm down . . . or at least grow silent. She could almost hear the admiral's words. "People who know nothing are easily dominated by anyone who acts like they know what they are doing."

Vicky's own computer was passing along Inez's report directly.

MY SNIPER HAS TAKEN DOWN ONE PERSON WITH A MACHINE PISTOL. THERE IS NO EVIDENCE OF ANY OTHER SHOOTER. SEVERAL OF MY RECRUITS ARE RACING TO RECOVER THE WEAPON AND RENDER ANY AID NEEDED TO THE GUNMAN.

"Captain, could you please repeat your report to those still in this meeting with me," Vicky ordered.

The Ranger did.

"But, I am told there were several shots fired," Jansik snapped.

"Sir, I am at the scene of the shooting, and my Ranger sniper needed just one shot to put an end to this noise. You are misinformed," was Inez's reply.

That drew quizzical looks Vicky's way. "One Ranger, one target, one round," she said with finality.

That seemed to settle the matter.

"My response team has arrived where the shooter is down," Inez said, updating her report. "We have the weapon in custody. It is a State Security special. We are identifying the gunman. He is Ivan Hollerman, a shop foreman with Galactic Assemblers Limited. He's still breathing."

A siren could be heard in the background.

"Do you locals have anyone you want to take custody of him?" Inez asked.

Vicky just raised an eyebrow.

Instead of an answer, Jansik growled, "You sent your woman to provide guns at the protest?"

"Yes, I did," Vicky snapped back. "And if I hadn't, you'd have blood in the streets and trouble beyond your worst nightmares. Who owns GAL?"

Eyes around the table turned to grumpy.

"Don't look at me. I didn't order that guy to do anything. I've been here all the time." Which said nothing. Vicky had no problems communicating on net while her behind grew more and more pained in meetings. Still, Wallace *might* be that old-fashioned.

"I think we ought to be grateful to that Ranger for saving

us from riots aimed at us for something we had nothing to do with," the young man said.

Slowly, heads nodded.

"Well, maybe you're right, Steve," Jansik finally mumbled. "Still, we should know what's happening here."

"Clearly, you did not," Vicky pointed out.

Jansik forbore any further response.

"May I repeat, is there any sort of police I can turn this fellow over to for questioning, assuming he lives?" Inez snapped on net.

"Our traffic supervisors have been stepping up their game," the young Steve answered.

"You've been waltzing around with no one to handle domestic disputes, bank robberies, anything outside the law?" Vicky found herself saying.

Grumpy scowled. Jansik shrugged. Steve provided the answer. "You didn't want State Security involved in such matters," he pointed out. "There were local ways of handling things in the projects, or so I'm told. As for major crimes, we don't seem to have any."

"People, on St. Petersburg they have their crime families that handle the usual vices. They paid off State Security and ended up allied with the mayors when Security went away. Who's running your black market, prostitution, what have you?"

Those around the table just looked at each other.

Vicky shook her head. "You've been skating on thin ice, sure that you're running things, and you don't know half of what's going on five floors below your penthouses."

Nobody said anything.

"Well, folks, I'll tell you what I'm going to do. Kris Longknife, that Wardhaven princess, once talked me into giving the cities of St. Petersburg their own Imperial City Charters. They empowered them to elect mayors and establish city governance that held up during the hard times we've been having. Computer, shoot these fine folks the contents of one of those charters and the regulations Sevastopol is operating under. The coordination between cities is still kind of loosey-goosey. I suggest you look into something like that."

Vicky let that sink in. "Now, about your protestors. Captain, how's it going?"

"They all ducked when my sniper took out the gunner. Now they're milling about. I think the rumor mill is going crazy, what with a shot fired and an ambulance making its way through the crowded streets. It's not for me to tell anyone in your pay grade what to do, but I'd get someone out here to talk to these folks real quick if I were in your boots," the Ranger said.

"The gal has a point," Steve said.

"Who owns the projects these people are so upset about, and who employs their husbands and has been cutting their pay?" Vicky asked.

No surprise, grumpy slowly raised his hand, but then so did Jansik, and Steve as well.

"Boys," Vicky said, "have I got a deal for you. Trade is open. You're back in business. What do you say that you rescind those pay cuts and housing increases? People don't fight for the people that do them dirty. From the looks of matters here, you're just one blowup from everything coming down around your heads."

"We've liked to think of ourselves as the ones in charge, making things happen our way," Steve said, his eyes roving around the room. Many met him. Others still scowled at where this was leading.

"I'm willing to cut the rent back to what it was and restore pay to where it was last year. The rest of you will have to decide for yourselves."

"If you do that, kid, how can we not follow?" Grumpy growled.

"Yeah, I see your problem, Wallace, but I see my problem as more pressing. The Grand Duchess here is right. We've managed to slide by on a pretty slick deal. Slick for us; not so slick for everyone else. If we don't change the tune, I see us having to pay a pretty angry piper. Just how did your foreman get his hands on that machine pistol?"

"I have no idea," Wallace insisted, almost believably.

"That may be true, but if there's a black market in slightly used State Security machine pistols, I think we need to have ourselves some real soldiers with real weapons and training able to take down a problem in a crowd with one shot."

Finally, the people around the table were working their way toward an agreement.

The Ranger hurried them on. "Well, if you folks can find

your way clear to some agreement, I suggest you get some folks out here to talk to this bunch. My reading of them is these cows are getting real antsy. One hint of another lightning strike, and there's gonna be a stampede."

Vicky stood and headed for the door. It was a short moment before Jansik, Wallace, and Steve joined her. On their heels followed the rest of the room.

CHAPTER 28

DECISIONS were finalized in Vicky's limo on the drive over to Greenfeld Plaza. No surprise; Steve did most of the talking. The two older men usually were content to grunt unhappy agreement. The one time they got vocal was when Steve suggested that the crowd be invited to nominate a committee to present their grievances.

"We're raising their pay and lowering their rent. What more do they need?" grumbled the grouch.

"Do you remember when you were invited to first sit in on the business round table?" Steve said. "I do. I can't tell you how it made me feel. You must have felt it back when."

"I remember," grouch admitted. "I'm not that old."

"Well, we need to know more about what's happening. Happening for real. I agree with the Grand Duchess. Someone is running our black market. Someone opened that gun locker. Unless we want that someone to be heading up our round table, we need to play catch-up, and we need more eyes and ears to do it with. Am I not right, Your Grace?"

Vicky thought back on all she'd learned from Mannie in the last months. All she'd experienced as both the gracious Grand Duchess on St. Petersburg and driving efforts to feed

Poznan and get trade going with Metzburg. "Managing a planet is not something one man can do," she said slowly. "I think the mess my father, the Emperor, is making of the Empire is very telling. I'm not suggesting that we want to go all Longknife with elections every day or such, but we do need to let the people who know how to run things do their jobs."

"And how do we do that?" Jansik asked, not quite in full snide.

"When I figure it out, you'll be the first I tell," Vicky said.

They were at the plaza. Several Rangers and traffic supervisors helped walk the limo through the crowd. It wasn't a problem. At seeing Vicky, her name swept through the crowd. People fell back while others hurried closer. It made for a jam, but a bubble formed around the car, and they were halfway to the inevitable statue of one of Vicky's grand- or great-grandfathers when the car could go no farther.

So Vicky got out and walked. She shook offered hands, and the jam of people seemed to open before her. Or maybe it was the Marines in their green-and-black uniforms. Where they came from, Vicky had no idea but, she was pretty sure she owed their skipper a thank-you.

Steve fell in beside Vicky, shaking hands as well. Jansik and Grumpy were more reticent, but one way or another, they all found themselves on the marble platform before the statue.

Kat produced a bullhorn from somewhere, and Vicky shouted, "Hello."

A long, shouted "Hello" rolled back at her.

"Thank you for letting me visit," Vicky said next.

From a knot of mothers and grandmothers who seemed to have a secure place right in front of her came a "Thank you for coming," that turned into a ragged but powerful response from the crowd.

"It was my honor, and that of the Navy," Vicky continued, "to secure the space above your head. You are now safe from without."

The crowd quieted as Vicky talked.

"The question before you is what to do now."

"Yes," came right back from the group of women at her feet.

"I have someone who wants to talk to you. Will you listen to him?"

The rumble from the women was none too sure, but Vicky

handed over the bullhorn, and Steve began to speak. He played his cards right; he started by praising Vicky and the Navy that came with her. A quick nod to the reopening of trade and more jobs led quickly to announcing the cancellation of the pay cuts. That drew cheers, especially from the back of the crowd. There were more men there. No doubt, absenteeism was high today.

The return to lower rents and a promise to improve the quality of the apartments sent the women into cheers. More of them cheered when Steve handed the bullhorn to Jansik and Wallace, who announced, if less enthusiastically, that they would be doing the same.

The crowd was in a happy mood when Steve got the bullhorn back and played his final card. "I and my friends need to know more about what is happening here, in Laatzen and all the cities of Brunswick. You know a lot about what I don't. Could you nominate a committee to work with us to see that things go better?"

"Why not elect them," came from a gray-haired granny at their feet. That was promptly seconded by several other old gray heads.

"Maybe we will," Steve allowed. "But we need to start with something, and we need to start right now. I'll be back at my office in an hour. If you can get someone to speak for you, I'll meet with them then."

"How will you know that someone who shows up is someone this bunch of yahoos wants?" Grumpy put in as soon as the bullhorn was off.

"I won't, unless they toss that someone out of my office," Steve said.

"Better you start this than me," Jansik muttered.

One or the other of them had summoned a car to get them out of there. They went.

Vicky and Steve hung around, shaking hands and exchanging a few good words with those who wanted to get something off their chest immediately. When one old fellow began a long-winded harangue, two of the grandmothers edged him off until he was talking to two strapping boys who nodded agreement but kept him moving away from Vicky.

That Kat was helping might have added to their speed of departure.

It was a long hour before Vicky and Steve were back in her borrowed limo and driving slowly through a thinning crowd.

"That went better than I'd expected," Steve allowed.

"I'm always surprised when it does. So far it always has. Sooner or later, my luck's going to run out."

"That gas attack at Kiev didn't go all that well," the commander allowed.

"Huh?" Steve asked.

"A long story. Let's save it for another time," Vicky said.

"Hmm. Interesting, I offer them a committee, and someone wants an election right off the cuff. I wonder where that came from?"

"You say the projects handle their own problems."

"So I've been told," Steve admitted.

"And how do those who handle those problems get their authority?" Vicky asked.

"I don't know."

"You might want to find out," Vicky suggested. "I suspect you'll be dealing with them when you get back to your office. And if this really does go into an election for a committee or more, you may find that getting up there and being the face of the round table puts you in places you never thought of."

"Those old farts would never let someone as young as me lead them," Steve said.

"They may have fewer choices in the months to come than they thought they had last month."

"Hmm," was Steve's thoughtful response. "You know, this rebellion idea. It doesn't quit, does it? I figured your saving our rear ends from the Empress's henchmen was great, but I see each step leads to another step. Do you ever know where you're going?"

"Not even a guess," Vicky agreed. "But I know where I'd be going if I went where the Empress wanted. Given a choice between her way and this crazy, unknown way, I'll take the crazy."

"Yeah," Steve muttered. "Yeah."

CHAPTER 29

TWO days later, with nineteen freighters loaded with trade for St. Petersburg, four more than they'd arrived with, Brunswick was disappearing as quickly in the fleet's rearview mirror as Vicky could make it. She left with very mixed feelings about Brunswick that left her wondering how matters were really going at Presov, Posnan, and Metzburg.

Who are you kidding? Do you really think you can make a difference against all the bad karma you Peterwalds have piled up against yourselves and the lackeys that kissed up to you?

Vicky had no answers to her growing doubts. She did know that there were good people working with her. Captain Rachinsky, for example. He'd seen to it that the two cruisers in his squadron had been whipped through the yard quickly and were now ready to answer all bells. The *Savage* and *Ferocity* were another matter.

The *Retribution* had hammered the two opposing battleships pretty hard. The yard had peeled their ice armor off down to bare metal. They'd patched the refrigeration ducts and were slowly spraying layer after layer of new ice on. When they were done, the ships would be as well protected as the day they were commissioned.

The reactors and engines, lasers and electronics were another matter. The fabs on the planet below were putting together a full set of machinery where they could or patching what they couldn't. All that was nice, but it left Vicky with questions she didn't like.

"Is the Navy as rotten as these ships seem to show?"

"I'm not surprised," Captain Bolesław admitted. "Appropriations have been pretty thin, what with your father, our Emperor, building that palace of his. Worse, the ships have spent a lot of time tied up at the pier with the Sailors ordered out to shore parties for knocking heads. That doesn't make for a well-ordered ship or ship's company."

Vicky mulled that thought. "So if we can get our house in order, it just might save our necks when it comes to a fight?"

"Then again, there are those two battleships building. Assuming the yards get them right, they might be a real tough nut to crack."

"You think the yards will get them right?" Vicky asked.

The captain just shrugged. "No doubt, the Empress will see that they get everything they need. Will she be listening to the right people? Your guess is as good as mine."

Messages came in, and Vicky found that she had some very good people working for her.

The Navy had run a team down onto Garnet and spirited away the wives and children of the 16th Marine Battalion before the local security honcho was any the wiser. It seemed a pretty slick operation until word got back that the command top shirt's wife was off-planet visiting her daughter, who was about to give birth to their first grandchild.

A video of the bloody murder of mother, daughter, and a newborn grandson, along with the son-in-law was not slow to arrive in Vicky's in-basket. The warning to Major Burke arrived too late. His command sergeant major had already exacted deadly revenge on the redcoat who had commanded the station as well as his subordinate officers.

"The Gunnys have him out getting drunk," Burke reported. "I've got two in the group who will stay sober and ride herd on the rest. Damn, this is gonna get ugly."

Vicky killed the commlink. There was little she could add.

Over the next weeks, as the convoy made its way back to

St. Petersburg, more reports came in. Metzburg had sent several of its cruisers out with half-trained troops aboard them. They had been enough to garner the surrender of several planets in their trading zone that had recently been invaded by redcoats. Things seemed to be going well until two of the armed liners got into a fight with three *Golden Empress*es. The fight went long. The Empress's ships finally broke and ran for it, but the Metzburg ships had to limp home for repairs, and there were no more planets cut out of the Empress's so-called security sphere in that sector.

There were sketchy reports of planets that rose up and tried to throw off their Security Consultants. A few managed to get word out. The Navy helped wherever it could. Too many, however, suffered bloody repression, no less savage than that meted out to the Gunny's family.

The Empress would either cow everyone to her side or reap a bloody revenge for what she had done.

Only time would tell which would be meted out to her.

CHAPTER 30

WHILE Vicky marked her stepmother's fate as pending, she herself had a rebellion to plan and execute. Kris Longknife might be able to keep vast star maps in her head, but Vicky could hardly keep track of the ever-changing map of the palace.

"Computer, show me a star map of Greenfeld space."

The largest wall in her borrowed admiral day cabin changed from flat crimson wallpaper with golden *fleurs-de-lis* to a 3D volume speckled with lightly tinted dots. There were a lot of dots.

"Ah, computer, take away the uninhabited star systems," Vicky said, and most of the space went blank. The ninety-four planets of the Imperium looked awfully lonely.

There was a polite knock at her door. "Enter," she said.

Commander Boch and Mr. Smith did; they both eyed the map.

"You planning a campaign?" Mr. Smith asked.

"More like I'm just trying to figure out what the Empire looks like from a campaign perspective," Vicky admitted. "Admiral Krätz taught me a lot, but grand strategy wasn't in the curriculum."

"He would have saved that for your fourth year senior project," the commander said offhandedly. "Do you want some input on your map?"

"Please," Vicky said, not keeping the pleading out of her voice.

"Are you using your computer for this?" the spy asked.

"Yes. I didn't want this in the ship's computer."

"Smart," he said.

"Computer," the commander said, "show all jump points that connect the Imperium's planets. Show unpopulated systems in that network with small white blinkers."

Quickly, there were a lot more stars, with thin golden lines connecting them.

Vicky eyed the larger volume. The Empire was a gossamer web in the shape of a rather lumpy dumpling. "That might have sufficed a year ago, but I think we need to look at things a bit differently now. Computer, show the systems trading with St. Petersburg in green."

The map changed. One end of the dumpling now looked covered in green mold.

"How many planets do we have?" Vicky asked the computer.

"Twenty-four at last report," it replied.

"So the Empress has seventy on her side," Vicky concluded.

"That may not be quite true," the spy said.

"How so?" Vicky asked.

"You have rallied the planets around St. Petersburg, Metzburg, and Brunswick," Mr. Smith said. "Planets like Poznan and Presov you picked up because the Empress was content to let them fall into wreck and starvation. Others like Good Luck, Ormuzd, and Kazan, you picked up because you offered them trade before they, too, were in deep distress. Something like this is happening along the entire perimeter of your Empire. Bliven, for example, still had the vestigial institutions of a democracy that they had before voting to enter the Empire. I now have word that they voted to withdraw and associate themselves with the United Society."

"They switched to the Longknifes!" the commander said, incredulous.

"My sources say they have," the spy said. "And they took Fourier and New Kraków with them. In these hard times, those planets had become dependent on Bliven rather than the center of the Empire."

"So the mess we have here is repeated all around the Empire's periphery," Vicky concluded.

"Very much so. Lublin and Kottubus have even realigned themselves with Hispania and the Esperanto League respectively. Sylt is reported to have feelers out to the Scanda Confederacy."

Vicky shook her head. "And if those developed planets go, they'll take their dependencies with them."

"Exactly," the spy said. "The Empress has the center of the Empire around Greenfeld in her tight grasp, but she's letting most of the more distant planets slide away."

"How many does she have solidly in her control?" Commander Boch asked.

"No more than fifty. Possibly as few as forty-two."

"But those forty-two are the heart of the Empire," Vicky said, and had her computer turn the center of the Empire bright red. "The industry and populations of Minsk, Cologne, Dresden, and the space docks of Bremerhaven and Gdańsk. If she turns those to war on the breakaway planets, she could scorch a path through the stars."

"If we give her time to consolidate her holdings," Commander Boch said.

"But we also need time to consolidate," Vicky pointed out.

"This war of yours," the spy said slowly, "may be decided by whoever can get her act together first and strike while the other is still organizing her shit." He was kind enough to smile as he gave Vicky his conclusion.

"No shit," said the commander.

Vicky sighed. "Sadly, you are both right."

She studied the map that now covered her wall. "You know what is missing from this?"

"No," came from both the men.

"The fleet. Where are the battleships and battlecruisers? The cruiser and destroyer squadrons? I know what we need to defend from the Empress and take away from her, but I don't know what tools we have to do the job. We need to think about more than ships this war. We'll need soldiers to dig the redcoats out of their holes and keep them from massacring civilians if I know the predilections of my darling stepmama."

The spy nodded agreement.

"We can't send that kind of hot data round the net for the Empress to intercept, Your Grace. Not with our communications so compromised."

"It would be nice if we had some idea of how many ships had come over to your side, though," the spy pointed out.

"And where the ships loyal to the Empress are," Vicky added.

She held that thought, and she was still holding it when a big chunk of the Empress's ships sailed right into her face.

CHAPTER 31

━━━━

RETRIBUTION cruised slowly up to the last jump before the one into the St. Petersburg system and came to rest only a few hundred klicks from it. Throughout the battleship for the last few days, all the talk had been of home.

Vicky was no exception. She wondered if Mannie might be persuaded to suspend his rule about not getting into bed with a Peterwald for just one night. Or maybe forget the bed and use the sofa. Vicky's daydreams had gotten quite lurid.

She'd suspended her wicked thoughts for a bit and took herself off to the bridge. She had real dreams of commanding a warship in space and wanted to study just how a captain handled the transition from one fraction of space to another a dozen or more light-years away.

Seated in her Grand Duchess chair on the *Retribution*'s bridge, Vicky watched as Captain Bolesław went about his duties with quiet confidence; Vicky had her computer recording. Everything went smoothly. *Sovereign of the Stars* slipped through the jump. There was a brief pause for her to report any problems, then Captain Bolesław took *Retribution* through.

"The jump was nominal," Lieutenant Blue reported from sensors. "Hold it, what's this?"

"What's what?" Bolesław demanded.

"We aren't the only fleet in this system."

"What the hell? Report, damn it."

"I need a moment, sir," the lieutenant replied. "There are a lot of ships, and they aren't squawking. No, they are, just not on the usual frequency. I'm taking them down now, sir. I'll have to match reactors to see what name goes with which ship. Oh, that's a big one."

"How big?" the skipper growled.

"I'm being jammed, but the reactors are making a lot of noise. They have to be as big as ours. Right, there's another big mother. The lead ship is squawking as the *Empress's Revenge.* Following it is the *Empress's Vengeance* and the *Empress's Terror.*"

"Not at all subtle," Vicky noted.

"I can't match these ships with anything in my database because of the jamming. Captain, I'd say we're facing three big battleships, six cruisers, and a dozen destroyers in one formation and a pair of cruisers and another six destroyers escorting what look like five large liners and a dozen freighters."

"That would be the invasion fleet," Captain Bolesław noted.

"No half measures this time," Vicky added.

"What's their course and speed?" the captain asked Lieutenant Blue.

"One-gee acceleration, course set for Jump Point Barbie into St. Petersburg."

"Navigator, plot me a course that gets us to Jump Point Barbie before they do at their present acceleration."

"We'll need to go to at least one-point-two-five gees, sir, to get there well ahead of them. I'll need a minute to give you something more precise."

"Send to fleet," the captain snapped. "The Empress has challenged us to a race. Up acceleration to one-point-two-five gees. Course is for Jump Point Barbie."

The fleet took off at the highest acceleration it could maintain. Vicky had her computer check the incoming data from the rest of her tiny fleet. The battleships and cruisers seemed to handle the extra acceleration. Not so much the freighters. The fifteen Vicky had brought to Brunswick had been chosen for their ability to manage at least 1.25 gees. However, the four freighters added by

Brunswick quickly showed their reactors moving into the yellow. Two ships from St. Petersburg weren't much better.

Captain Bolesław noted that Vicky had activated her board at her command chair and glanced at what she was tracking. "Good, Your Grace. You keep an eye on the civilians, and I'll worry about the Navy."

Vicky waved a hand at her board and it changed to show the warships' condition. "I'm keeping an eye on all of them. I assume we're running because you don't want to fight the Empress's fleet in this system."

"Outnumbered as we are, no," he agreed.

"Hopefully, there will be reinforcements waiting for us around St. Petersburg," Vicky half said to herself.

"Assuming your St. Petersburg Division of the Greenfield Imperial Navy Reserve Fleet has someone home, yes."

"Then by all means, let's run."

"The Empress's task force has upped its acceleration to one-point-two-five gees," Lieutenant Blue reported.

"No surprise," Vicky said.

"The surprise will be who can maintain that acceleration," Captain Bolesław said.

"Mmm," Vicky agreed.

Within the hour, the engineering condition of the other side began to show. First a liner and two cargo ships slowly fell back to one-gee acceleration. One of them even slipped below that. Two destroyers slowed down as well.

"Are they escorting the sick, lame, and lazy?" Captain Bolesław asked Lieutenant Blue.

"I don't think so, sir," the sensor chief answered. He'd been joined by his chief, and the two of them had been poring over their boards like a pair of witches with a strangely boiling cauldron. "Understand, sir, we've never actually done this for real. We've run proof-of-concept tests . . . when no one was looking, but not actually done this in real time. Still, we are showing a lot of distressed reactors over there."

"How can you see that?" Vicky asked.

"It's different frequencies from where the jamming is. Those reactors haven't gotten needed yard time and even less tender loving care from their engineers."

"I wonder what he'd show if he ran his gear on our own reactors," Captain Bolesław muttered to Vicky.

"I have been, sir. I'd say the yard on High St. Petersburg did a bang-up job on your ships before they sailed."

"And we left behind those that were in worst shape," Vicky added. "I wonder if anyone had the guts to tell the Empress's that their ship couldn't answer bells?"

"We're about to find out."

Over the next couple of hours, more of the Empress's ships fell out of formation, including the *Empress's Terror*. The opposing fleet, Vicky couldn't take it into her heart to call them the enemy, and she never heard that word used around her on the bridge, began to look like a poorly strung strand of pearls.

Halfway to their flip-over point, the other commander gave up the chase and slowed the ships still with him to .85 gccs.

"I'm glad he flinched first," Captain Bolesław said, and ordered his fleet acceleration reduced to one gee.

"The *Pride of Darby* will be glad you did that," Vicky said. The *Pride of Darby*, out of Kiel before it was laid up above Brunswick, had been struggling to keep up even as its reactor rose higher into the yellow zone. It was almost to the red when the order came. Over the next few hours, it worked its way back toward green.

"I didn't think any minion of the Empress would give up that easily," Vicky whispered to Captain Bolesław.

"I wouldn't bet that they have. Lieutenant Blue, how many good ships do they have? Ones that might maintain a hard deceleration?"

Blue studied his boards for a good while before answering. "The *Empress's Revenge* is in better shape. Maybe the *Vengeance* could stick with her, as well as a pair of cruisers and four destroyers, sir."

"And we have one 18-inch battleship, a 15-inch battlecruiser, a pair of heavy cruisers, and a merchant cruiser," Bolesław said, tallying up his own force. "If his big guns tie up our big guns, that would give his little boys a free hand to slaughter our freighters."

Vicky could see the ugly picture in her mind's eye. Maybe the cargo ships with desperately needed fabs for St. Petersburg would surrender before the destroyers ripped into them. Even if they did, would the Empress's henchmen settle for that? Was "no surrender" Count Korbinian the only man in that camp proud of the slaughter he'd done?

The two fleets ran down their separate sides of this triangle that ended in the Barbie Jump into St. Petersburg. They were like trains on a track, headed for the same destination and sped on by the physics that would bring them all to a dead stop just before the jump.

"Do we have to hit the jump at dead slow?" Vicky asked Captain Bolesław.

He gave her a look of dismay. "That's standard fleet practice."

"Kris Longknife has been known to take them faster."

"Kris Longknife has Wardhaven-built ships that I suspect have a bigger maintenance budget than our ships have had. Hell, Your Grace, those merchant tubs have been laid up, trailing this or that station, for months. Do you want to trust them to something crazy?"

Vicky felt cowed by his words. Almost, she gave in to silence.

Are you a Grand Duchess or a mouse?

Unlike my dad, I'm someone who listens to those who know better than I do.

And if you listen to the captain, you lose. This rebellion needs a win, and St. Petersburg needs that cargo. Let's show some backbone, Ensign.

Unlike the rest of Vicky's argument with herself, that last was spat at her in Admiral Krätz's voice.

"Captain, if we do what the captain of the *Empress's Revenge* expects, we lose. We lose not only this fleet but maybe the entire rebellion. We can do that, today. He can win it all for the Empress."

"When you put it that way," Captain Bolesław said through a scowl.

"Lieutenant Blue, what kind of risk will the *Empress's Revenge* be taking if it goes to 1.25 gees deceleration toward the jump?"

The lieutenant on sensors worried his lower lip for a long moment, then spoke. "I wouldn't want to be on his ship, Your Grace. From the looks of what I'm taking off his reactors, I'd say there's a real chance he's going to end up with a major engineering casualty."

Vicky arched an eyebrow at Captain Boleslaw.

His scowl didn't waver, but he said, "What do you have in mind, Your Grace?"

Vicky took a deep breath, let it out, and took command of her fleet. "Let's add some uncertainty to this battle."

═══

CHAPTER 32

T HE opposing commander kept up his .85-gee acceleration past the point where his entire fleet should have flipped and begun decelerating. Vicky and Captain Bolesław watched their opponent, allowing for the delay in speed of light.

"I hate not knowing what he did twenty minutes ago," the skipper said.

"Our ships are better than his," Vicky said. "We can make up the difference." She hoped she was right on that.

Finally, most of the opposing fleet flipped and began a one-gee deceleration burn for the jump. Most, but not all. As Lieutenant Blue had foretold, the *Empress's Revenge*, *Empress's Vengeance*, two heavy cruisers, and three destroyers actually upped their acceleration to 1.25 gees.

"Fleet, go to one-point-two-five gees acceleration," Captain Bolesław ordered, and all the Grand Duchess's ships, warship and merchant alike, jacked up their reactors.

"Now we see how this game of chicken will go," the skipper muttered to himself.

An hour later, the *Empress's Revenge* and her reduced task force flipped ship and began a 1.25-gee deceleration burn toward the jump. As soon as Lieutenant Blue reported the change, Captain Bolesław ordered his fleet to do the same.

"Navigator, which of us arrives at the jump first?" the skipper asked.

The man worked his board. Vicky watched as he wiped it twice and ran the calculations three times, then had the chief bosun of the watch double-check his work. Beside her, Vicky watched Captain Bolesław surreptitiously do his own course check. Vicky would have done the same, but she didn't trust her skills. Math was not her strong suit.

The navigator finally spoke. "Sir, it's too close to call. Our two task forces will get there within seconds of each other."

"Assuming we don't blow each other to bits beforehand," Lieutenant Blue said softly, but the silence on the bridge allowed for everyone to hear his observation.

"Yeah," Captain Bolesław said. "We blow bits of them through the jump."

That brought soft "Yeahs" from half the bridge crews.

Captain Bolesław gave Vicky a wink. Once they were on close approach to the jump, they could fight, or they could jump through it and run. They'd know in a few more hours.

The two groups raced down their separate tracks toward that one point in space they both needed to pass through. One of the Empress's three destroyers faltered and went to .89 gees deceleration. It edged ahead of the rest of the ships. The *Pride of Darby* also began to lose deceleration. Its burn fell off slowly until it stabilized at 1.04 gees. It, too, would arrive at the jump well ahead of the rest.

"We'll get to see what the Empress's man intends when the *Darby* gets in range of that tin can," Captain Bolesław muttered to Vicky.

Time dragged. On the *Retribution*, it was filled with drills that kept Sailors busy but left Vicky with time to count the monstrous butterflies circling in her stomach like buzzards. Admiral Krätz had told Vicky a junior officer's job was to look confident and self-assured when everything around the Sailors told them confident was the last thing they should be feeling.

It seemed that a Grand Duchess had pretty much the same job. She smiled confidently when a seaman brought her hot tea. She smiled confidently when a petty officer checked her board to make sure it was in perfect working order. She smiled confidently when a chief petty officer checked her survival pod—and did her very best to hide the choke in her voice when she thanked him graciously.

If Kris Longknife was to be believed, and Admiral Krätz had believed her, it was a defective survival pod that killed Vicky's brother, Hank, and not the laser fire from that Wardhaven princess's cruisers.

Did my new stepmother and her family have their fingers in that bit of sabotage?

There was no way to answer that question now, not after the ship bringing Hank's body home disappeared into a sour jump.

Come to think about it, something as twisted as that almost had to have Bowlingame-family fingerprints on it.

Maybe I finally believe you, Kris Longknife.

Hours and many drills and cups of tea later, the *Darby* was inexorably coming in range of the destroyer's 5-inch lasers. Vicky waited, hardly breathing, to see what would happen next.

"I've intercepted a massage from the *Empress's Revenge*. It's likely orders for the destroyer."

"What's it say?" Captain Bolesław asked.

"I don't know, sir. It's a series of three-digit numbers that don't mean a thing unless you have the codebook."

The captain and Vicky exchanged frowns.

"The destroyer has replied. Again, I can't make much of it, but the sequence nine-seven-three is in both messages."

"Somebody's been told to do nine-seven-three and doesn't want to," Captain Bolesław observed cautiously.

"So what does nine-seven-three mean?" Vicky asked. The captain only shrugged.

"The flag's reply is nine-seven-three repeated three times."

"How do you put numbers in capital letters?" Vicky said.

"No doubt the commander of that task force told his comm boss to do exactly that," said Captain Bolesław.

"They've added four extra numbers," Lieutenant Blue said.

Vicky and the captain exchanged raised eyebrows but ventured no opinion.

Mr. Smith had been quietly observing matters from Lieutenant Blue's elbow. Now he drawled softly, "An interesting codebook that includes phrases for 'I'll hang you up by your balls if you don't execute my orders immediately.'"

"If my stepmother published the codebook, it wouldn't surprise me," Vicky said.

"How could anyone serve that woman?" Captain Bolesław muttered softly, but it echoed around the bridge. Officers and petty officers nodded and returned to their work with a firm set to their lips.

The exact meaning of nine-seven-three was soon revealed. The destroyer fired a broadside of four 5-inch lasers at the *Pride of Darby*. She scored a single hit.

"The fleet's gunnery scores have been lousy of late," Captain Bolesław said, "but that's just flat bad shooting."

It was enough for the *Pride of Darby*. "We surrender. We surrender!" came through on open net from the freighter.

The destroyer sent off a message to the flag with nine-seven-three once again holding pride of place. The Empress's man on the scene shot back the same message as before.

Captain Bolesław whispered a word not fit for a Grand Duchess's ears. Vicky, as a lieutenant commander, echoed it.

The destroyer fired another broadside. The *Pride of Darby* took two hits this time. One to the reactor. The ship began to bloom with survival pods.

The next volley also scored two hits, one aft.

"The reactor containment is failing," Lieutenant Blue said, his voice high and breaking.

A moment later, the *Pride of Darby* began to explode, starting aft and moving quickly forward. Hot gases and fragments of ship or cargo blew out, collided with survival pods, and finished what the Empress had begun.

"Are any survival pods squawking?" Captain Bolesław asked.

"A dozen, sir. I'm getting that same order to the destroyer from the flag, sir. What could they mean by it?"

A moment later, the destroyer fired again. They watched in horror as it took four more broadsides, but they wiped out every last one of the survival pods.

"The bastard," Captain Bolesław growled.

"Message coming in from the *Empress's Revenge*," Lieutenant Blue said, looking rather green.

"Put it on screen," the skipper ordered.

Again they looked at a red-coated Security Consultant in a uniform dripping in gold and silver. This one was taller, thinner, and not at all the type who'd be in line for a coronary.

"I am the Duke of Radebuel, Butcher of Dresden," the redcoat growled. "You have been warned. Surrender now, and you might receive the Empress's mercy. Fail to surrender in the next five minutes, and I will see you slaughtered to the last man, woman, and child."

The screen went blank.

"A man of few words," Vicky observed.

"But those words are bloody," Captain Bolesław said.

"Computer, tell me about this man who styles himself a duke," Vicky said.

"There was no such dukedom when I was last interfaced with the Greenfeld database, but he was mentioned in the data dump we took off the *Golden Empress No. 34*. Giorgio Topalski is another one of the bank managers who came to notice during the suppression of State Security. Among other planets he 'cleaned out,' his own words, was Dresden. He was particularly bloody in the way he killed the State Security types. He also included their wives and children in the brutal slaughter. He sent videos of his depredations back to the Empress and her father and was praised by them. When riots broke out on Dresden over soaring unemployment, he was chosen to go back there with three brigades of Security Consultants and pacify the planet. An unknown number of demonstrators died when his consultants opened fire. A suppressed report from the Radebuel city coroner determined that most of the dead were shot in the back."

"That would get you the nickname Butcher," Captain Bolesław growled.

"That is not why he is called the Butcher of Dresden," the computer corrected the captain. "If the information contained in several letters and two news records from the *Golden Empress No. 34* are correct, once the capital, Radebuel of Dresden, was pacified, some of his guards took over a pub one night to celebrate. They got drunk, then raped several of the barmaids. Three were found dead the next morning, brutally tortured and murdered."

"Now is he the Butcher?" Vicky asked her computer.

"That only starts the story. Seven of his guards, likely not the ones who killed the young women, were found dead two nights later. Topalski pulled seven hundred people off the street, lined them up against the nearest walls, and machine-gunned them. Since he sent his death squads through the financial district during lunch hour, included among the dead were quite a few leaders of Dresden's business community."

"How'd that go over?" Captain Bolesław asked.

"Very well for him. He bought up a major part of the holdings from families that lost their loved ones in that slaughter, but that came later. Three days later, a bomb went off at a club frequented by redcoat noncommissioned officers. Twenty-two died."

"Did he kill one hundred for every one of them?" Vicky asked.

"One thousand for each. Included was a football stadium where a national championship was being played. He sent helicopters over to drop explosives and gasoline on the bleachers. When survivors tried to flee, he had machine gunners waiting for them at the exits. Those that survived by hiding among the dead were then gunned down by his guards. The tally from the stadium did not come to twenty-two thousand, so they pulled people off random buses to fill out the quota."

"Good God," Captain Bolesław muttered. Vicky glanced around the bridge: Jaws had gone slack and lips pale. The stern, battle-ready faces were slipping away.

"So his reign of terror cowed Dresden, made him a wealthy man off the plunder of those he slaughtered, and got him a dukedom," Vicky said, then added, "and now he's the one the Empress picks to soak St. Petersburg in blood."

"It looks that way," Captain Bolesław said.

Vicky knew the Empire would rise or fall on her next words. How she wished she had Kris Longknife at her elbow to give her a hint of what to say.

"He doesn't get his hands on St. Petersburg," Vicky said, biting her words off sharply. "Not on my watch. His bloody trail ends here. We *end* him here."

She looked around the bridge. The future hung by a thin thread as those around her struggled between their fear of what they faced and their duty to those that they defended.

"He may be pretty proud of his record, murdering unarmed

civilians, but now he's up against the Navy. Now he's got a fight on his hands."

"Yes," hissed back at Vicky, and the bridge crew turned back to their work with a determined will.

"I thought we'd lost them," Captain Bolesław whispered from behind his hand.

"They just needed a reminder of who they are. Can we beat that bastard?"

"That all depends on who he's got behind him on that bridge and what he's got on that poor benighted soul."

"We'll find out soon enough."

CHAPTER 33

———

EXACTLY five minutes from when he cut the commlink, Giorgio's sneering face was back on the screen.

"I will take your surrender now."

Vicky stood to face him. "We will blow you to hell."

"Be careful what you say, little girl. This is your last chance to surrender. If you don't, we will take no prisoners when we blow your little toy out of space. St. Petersburg will be next. I do not intend to occupy it. Too many troublemakers there. We'll blast its cities from orbit, and when they are begging for us to land, maybe we will. Maybe we'll give them a chance to see that we enjoy our visit with no complaining from the survivors."

He seemed to be really enjoying his fantasy.

"You get to them through us," Vicky said, heat tempering each of her words. "Know this: Your threats can come back at you. We will give no quarter, either. The crew of your ships can rise up and toss you out the air locks now, or they can die with you. The choice is theirs."

In the background, Vicky could make out a few bridge personnel in Navy ship suits. Several of them faltered in their work as her words struck home.

"You know you're going to lose this fight," she added.

"This idiot had us outnumbered three to one in battleships and cruisers, but he had to come charging down at us alone. He gave us a fair fight. How stupid can you get?"

Now the officers on that bridge were glancing around at each other. A short, thin man wearing captain's stripes stepped into view. "She may be a 'little girl,' but she spotted the mistake I told you you were making."

Giorgio waved his hand dismissively. From off screen came two shots; the captain's head exploded, and he dropped. Giorgio wiped blood and gray matter from the sleeve of his red coat. "That's what happens to those who cross me. Who's next?"

No one on the bridge said a word.

"I mean who's next to run this shit hole of a boat?"

A tall commander stepped forward. His face was unreadable.

"Blow those rebels out of my space," the redcoat snapped.

"Yes, sir," the commander said, dispassionately, and the commlink was cut.

Vicky found she'd forgotten to breathe. Now she took a deep breath and let it out slowly before sitting down and turning to Captain Bolesław. "Do you know those two Navy officers?"

"The captain was a friend of mine, only a class behind me. The commander, I know of. Both are good ship drivers. Likely, they know something about fighting a ship."

"And even more likely, their wives and families are under lockdown by redcoat thugs."

"We couldn't all get our families out of the Empress's grasp," the captain said.

"Captain," came from Lieutenant Blue, "the *Empress's Revenge* is putting on battle revolutions. She's shimmying. No, they've gone back to a steady boat. One of the cruisers had to steady back down as well, but the others are working their way up to twenty RPMs."

"Thank you, Lieutenant. Comm, send to fleet, begin battle RPMs smartly on my mark."

A moment later communications reported, "All ships have reported ready for battle RPMs, sir."

"Helm?"

"Ready upon your mark."

"Comm, send my mark."

"Mark sent."

Around Vicky, *Retribution* began to spin, slowly at first, then faster, until the bridge was spinning at twenty revolutions per minute. Vicky cinched herself tight into her high-gee station. Beneath her, the battleship spun but stayed steady as a rock.

"Good girl," Captain Bolesław was heard to mutter as he patted the side of his battle board.

"The fleet has come up to battle RPMs smartly," Lieutenant Blue reported. "Not a burble," he added.

Captain Bolesław grinned. "Let those redcoats see how the real Navy handles itself."

Vicky grinned, too. "It's always impressive when professionals do it the right way. It's intimidating to amateurs who don't have a clue."

"So quoteth we Admiral Krätz," Captain Bolesław agreed.

"I may have spoken too soon," Lieutenant Blue said, painfully. "The *Slinger* just sloughed off a chunk of her ice armor and is killing her RPMs as fast as she can. She lost more chunks of ice while she was steadying up."

"Tell Captain Mason to get his damage control out there and patch that armor. No, Comm, belay last message. He knows what he needs to do as well as I do. Damn. I thought we could trust the repairs High Brunswick made better than that."

"They may just be out of practice," Vicky said.

"Yeah, aren't we all. Comm, send to *Slinger*. 'Conform your course to the merchants' line.'"

"Will do, *Retribution*. Sorry about this. I thought the yard assured us of its high quality a bit too much. We've got every hand I can spare out filling in the holes in our armor. I'll be back in the battle line as soon as I can manage."

"I'd expect no less from *Slinger*," Captain Bolesław said.

"Did I speak too soon about our bloody-handed duke getting himself in over his head?" Vicky asked.

"It is starting to look more like two-to-one odds than it did before," the skipper admitted.

One of the cruisers remaining with *Retribution* pulled ahead. Now they mirrored the hostiles approaching them. A destroyer led a cruiser followed by the *Empress's Revenge* and *Empress's Vengeance*. The other cruiser and destroyer trailed the battleships.

"He is concentrating his heavies on *Retribution*," Captain Bolesław said softly.

"Is that the duke or your commander or some other Navy officer?" Vicky asked.

"I don't know, but it's going to cause me pain. If I concentrate *Retribution* on *Revenge*, I can hurt her, but that will leave *Vengeance* unmolested. If I concentrate the cruisers on their opposite number, they can get in some licks, but if our fight ends with those two battleships still punching, my cruisers are dead."

"Are their cruisers carrying 8-inch or 9.2-inch lasers?" Vicky asked.

"Lieutenant Blue, you have not been earning your pay. What sort of guns are those ships carrying?"

"I was afraid you would ask," the lieutenant on sensors answered.

"And why might you have that fear?"

"I'm getting more jamming than I've ever had from Navy ships, sir. I've said their reactors seem to be about the same power as ours, but I can't make out the make or model. Same for the lasers and capacitors. Either they've been built with systems that aren't in our book, or something is making hash out of the signals I'm taking off them."

"Have you heard anything about the Empress building an entirely new fleet of ships?" Captain Bolesław asked Vicky.

"There are supposed to be a pair of new huge battleships building, but only two, not three," Vicky said. "Everything else I've heard involves them snatching active ships from the fleet. Also, the new ships were supposed to get captains from outside the Greenfeld fleet. You knew the *Empress's Revenge*'s skipper and XO. I don't think those are the Empress's new toys. So, what is our bloody duck trying to hide?"

"They could be hiding things just for the sake of hiding?" Lieutenant Blue said, eyeing his boards dubiously, much like Vicky was eyed when she claimed innocence.

"Is there any chance that the duke was not talking to us from the lead battleship?" Captain Bolesław asked.

"I thought for sure he was," the lieutenant said, looking up.

"If I concentrate *Retribution* on *Revenge*, and he's on *Vengeance*, I may blow up the one ship I can get for sure but not get the one man I have to kill."

Lieutenant Blue worried his lower lip and started rerunning the communications they had tracked so far, both those to the destroyer that blew up the *Pride of Darby* and the two threats they'd gotten from the duke.

Five minutes later, he shook his head. "You're right, it looks like it's all coming from the lead battleship, but there's something strange about the signal. Something like I've never seen."

Captain Bolesław eyed Vicky.

"We've been playing catch-up in the electronic and computer area with someone in Greenfeld," she said. "Not just us, but Kris Longknife, too. Even her magnificent computer, Nelly, has been jammed during some incidents involving my stepmother's assassins. I don't much care for this."

"I don't care for this at all. I know I can take out one of those ships, but I'm going to be hurting when I switch fire to the next one. If I kill the bastard, the rest may break off the fight. If I don't kill him, it's going to be a coin toss whether or not I can get the second one."

"Lieutenant Blue, put what you've got on our communications with the duke," Captain Bolesław said.

A quarter of the main screen was taken up by six blips. The communications seemed to originate from the lead battleship. "Concentrate on that lead battleship," the skipper said, "and show us the point of origin of those communication signals."

"They sure look like they're coming from that ship," Lieutenant Blue said after they'd watched the communication cycle three times.

"Computer," Vicky said, "measure the location of that battleship and the loci of the communication signal."

"They are not congruent," the computer said.

"By how much?" Captain Bolesław demanded.

"Twelve meters, sixty-two centimeters ahead of the *Empress's Revenge*," the computer said.

"Remind me to ask that computer to do the measurement thing and spare my eyes," the sensor lieutenant said.

"When you're dealing with a corkscrew brain, it helps to have someone with a corkscrew brain," Vicky said. "Is the locus of the comm signal exactly midway between the communication antennae of the trailing battleship and the lead heavy cruiser?"

"Yes," said the computer.

"They're heterodyning the signal," Captain Bolesław growled.

"The cruiser isn't showing anything like a battleship's communications gear."

"They've either suppressed it or modified it to look like cruiser comm gear," Vicky said.

Lieutenant Blue studied his instruments for a long minute. "I sure don't see it."

"Mr. Smith?" Vicky asked.

"I am with the lieutenant. I don't see it either, but I tend to support your conclusion even if I can't find a valid basis for it."

"When we get in range, we target the second battleship in line, the *Empress's Vengeance*," Captain Bolesław said.

"It looks that way," Vicky said.

"God help us all if we guess wrong," the skipper added under his breath.

CHAPTER 34

T HE gunnery officer on *Retribution* updated them as the two task forces decelerated toward the jump, and the range between them closed inexorably.

"Ten thousand klicks until maximum range," he said evenly.

"Bring the task force up to battle revolutions," Captain Bolesław ordered. This time the evolution went smoothly.

Vicky eyed the two lines of dots on the screen. Both were backing toward the single point in space they needed to pass through to get into the St. Petersburg system. Unlike the earlier fights she'd been in with Captain Bolesław, there would be no maneuvering around to get a good shot at the enemy's vulnerable engines and reactors. This fight would be a stand-up slugfest, with the battleships exchanging broadsides first, then the cruisers joining in as the range continued to close. The last man standing would be the winner.

"Five thousand klicks," came from Guns.

"Fleet, prepare to go to Evasion Plan 1," Captain Bolesław said, softly.

"Aye, aye, sir. Evasion Plan 1 standing by," answered the *Retribution*'s Helm. The two cruisers reported ready.

Captain Bolesław pursed his lips. "We'll hold off on the

dancing for a bit. No need to show them what we got," he told Vicky.

She nodded. The fleet they'd fought off Brunswick hadn't shown they knew to use evasive techniques like Kris Longknife did. No need to teach this butcher any tricks before they had to.

"One thousand klicks to maximum range," Guns informed them.

"Give them a two-gun ranging shot when they come in range. Shoot for the lead battleship for that salvo, Guns. We'll switch to the second battleship as soon as we know we have them in focus."

"Aye, aye, Skipper."

Vicky took a long, slow breath.

"We are in range."

"Begin evasion. Guns, ranging fire," Captain Bolesław snapped.

"We have been fired upon," Lieutenant Blue said. "Two broadsides, wide dispersion."

"Put it on screen."

Half the main screen showed *Retribution* and her two cruisers as green dots. Around them, red rays cut the space. It was a wild pair of volleys that didn't manage to focus on anything.

"We scored one hit on the lead battleship," Guns reported. The other half of the screen showed the six hostiles as six red dots of various sizes: small, medium, and large. The third dot, a large one, showed a green ray cutting close to it and another hitting it.

"Guns, use your forward battery to burn one place on the second battleship, your aft battery to give it another deep burn."

"Fire," Guns said.

The three bow turrets that bore on the enemy shot six laser beams from *Retribution* at the target. Aft, three more turrets spat their fire. As *Retribution* rotated, one turret fore and aft was spun out of the line of fire. Others were brought to bear. Bow turret A was spent from the ranging shot, but turret D added its destruction to the mix.

For two seconds, the lights dimmed as *Retribution* poured everything it had at its foe, then, capacitors empty, the turrets fell silent and began to reload.

"One glancing hit forward," Damage Control reported. "No damage. Bots are spraying in water to repair the armor."

"Very good," Captain Bolesław said. "Guns?"

"Got 'em with two salvos as tight as we could get them. At least six of them hit her, three and three. That bastard is spewing steam."

"Aim for the same spots, if you will. Let's get this over with quick," he told his gunnery officer. To Vicky he added quietly, "Before that bastard learns to dance."

Across from them, the hostiles stayed rigidly in line. Vicky eyed their own ships. The cruisers were still out of range of the other cruisers. They had opened the interval between them and *Retribution* to better avoid being hit by a miss.

Still, her two cruisers maneuvered erratically per the evasion plan her computer had put together after watching the one Kris Longknife's computer had her ships doing. As minimal as it was, it could be mistaken for skittish ship drivers having a tough time staying in formation.

With any luck, the Butcher will be too proud to draw the right conclusion before we blow him to bits.

Around Vicky, the bridge team went about their duties in dim battle lighting. Orders were softly given and received. It ran smooth as a drill. That was why a good captain drilled his crew unceasingly; so the real thing would go down just like a drill.

Vicky looked around, as did Captain Bolesław, but both kept one eye on the countdown clock to when their capacitors would be reloaded. *Would the other two battleships reload just as fast?*

"Do you have your target?" the skipper asked Guns softly.

"Dialed in tight, sir."

The timer reached zero.

"Fire," Guns said, and again the lights dimmed.

The screens showed rays reaching out from *Retribution* to spear the second battleship even as Sensors reported they were being straddled by lasers from the opposing force.

This time, *Retribution* took hits. The ship's rotation distributed the lasers' destruction. They burned ice and more ice as the boiling armor was spun away from the laser hits. Still, *Retribution*'s spin went out of true as holes in her armor unbalanced the ship.

Pumps throbbed as they moved reaction mass and reserve water from one side of the ship to the other, struggling to rebalance the hull before its own protection ripped the ship apart as it shimmied and shook.

Vicky found herself holding on tight to her battle board whether to save it . . . or herself . . . she was not at all sure. It seemed like forever, but in a few seconds, Damage Control did what it had been trained to do, and the *Retribution* steadied out.

."The *Empress's Vengeance* isn't doing so well," Lieutenant Blue reported on sensors. "She's bouncing so much, she's tossing off sheets of damaged ice armor."

"Good," Captain Bolesław said. "Guns, how fast can you reload?"

"No faster than the laws of physics allow, sir," came back at him.

Bolesław gritted his teeth and glanced at Vicky. "If I didn't want the Butcher dead, I'd switch my fire to *Revenge*," he muttered.

"But we *need* him dead," Vicky pointed out in gentle Grand Duchess mode.

"Yeah," the skipper grumbled, and turned back to his board.

Again, the timer counted down the minutes until the huge 18-inch main batteries of *Retribution* were ready to speak again. Another part of Vicky's board showed the effort by Damage Control to patch her battleship's armor.

The Empress's lasers had cut deep into *Retribution*'s six-meter-thick armor. This time they'd done more than slice ice; they'd also cut refrigeration coils that kept the ice rock solid. Bots picked their way deep into the crevasse sliced by the lasers to crimp off tubing bleeding coolant into space. They then withdrew while other bots sprayed water into the jagged rents.

In theory, the ice around the hole would cool the water and freeze it in place. In fact, new ice was never as solid as old ice, especially not without coolant coils to encourage freezing.

The gashes in *Retribution*'s protection got better. Would it be good enough?

"Skipper," said Guns, "we're about reloaded. Do you want me to switch targets?" Apparently Fire Control could see the damage to the *Empress's Vengeance* as well as sensors.

"No, Guns. We want that bastard dead. She's still in formation. Someone's holding a gun at her skipper's head."

"Understood, sir," was even. Guns had offered to save

thousands of men's lives. Now their deaths would be on Captain Bolesław's head.

His and mine, Vicky thought, grinding her teeth.

The lights dimmed. Again, the 18-inch lasers reached out for the second battleship in the opposing line. "Hits," Guns reported.

But were they the right hits? Was *Retribution* spending its fire burning off more armor or was it spearing through gaping holes in the ice to pierce deep into the ship's hull? Had they burned through to gut equipment, capacitors, and lasers?

Vicky leaned forward in her survival station to peer at the dots on the screen as if she might see more than the small circles could show.

"She's breaking up," Sensors reported.

"On screen," the captain snapped.

The main screen converted to a picture of one ship. Long and thin, part of its ice reflected back the distant stars. Other parts showed dark as ice spun off it into deep space.

Sections of hull showed gouts of fire exploding out to vanish in the black of space. Well aft, one of the great engines hung at a crazy angle. The battleship began to flip in space as that engine unbalanced the rest and drove the ship where it would.

Even as Vicky watched, mouth falling open, several of the other engines coughed and went dead. Vicky had done a tour in Engineering. The plasma in the reactors had to go somewhere. Aiming the plasma out through the engines was what the huge superconductors that controlled the demon plasma were supposed to do.

The plasma wasn't going out the engines. It had to go somewhere.

Small jets of superheated plasma spouted around the aft end of the battleship. Jets that grew bigger as they opened holes in the ship's ice armor from the *inside*!

The ship began to spew life pods as crew members saw their danger and took to the cold of space to escape heat like the sun now consuming their ship. Vicky gritted her teeth. She'd said she'd offer no quarter. She hadn't really meant it. Her eyes measured the growing number and size of the plasma jets. Even at the limited magnification of the picture before her, she could see pods rocketing into plasma and burning like moths in a flame.

The *Empress's Vengeance* ate itself, starting aft but moving forward with blinding speed. Had Vicky blinked, she'd have missed the mighty battleship's death throes.

It was there, in agony. Then it was gone. Just an expanding ball of superheated gas that vanished away, leaving only small, gleaming bits of hull girders and junk.

Vicky tried to stumble to her feet. Her legs would not support her. "Comm, send to *Empress's Revenge*, 'Will you surrender, now?'"

In answer, the lone surviving battleship fired a full broadside.

CHAPTER 35

"We're hit," Damage Control reported. "Three strikes, fore to aft. Working on them."

Captain Bolesław checked the countdown clock as it approached zero, then snapped, "Fire."

"Five hits," Sensors reported. "The *Revenge* is executing an evasion plan of its own."

"Helm, go to Evasion Plan 3," the captain ordered, and *Retribution* fell out from under Vicky as it did a hard, downward zig.

Captain Bolesław turned to her with a scowl. "That redcoat bastard was on the lead battleship after all," he growled.

For the next half minute, Damage Control did what it could to mend the three hits. Meanwhile, the reactors reloaded the capacitors to the four twin 18-inch turrets forward and the same number aft. A glance at the screen showed the two task forces still backing toward the jump, decelerating all the way. The cruisers were still out of range of each other, and both those escorting the *Empress's Revenge* and *Retribution* had opened up even wider intervals between themselves and the battle being fought by the big battlewagons.

As the seconds counted down to the capacitors' being

reloaded, Captain Bolesław spoke. "Helm, prepare to go to Evasion Plan 4 on my mark. Guns, check out what the evasion plan will do to your firing solution. Use a wider dispersion for your salvos if you must."

"We'll keep it tight," came back a moment later, then "Ready."

As the clock passed two seconds to reload, the skipper said, "Execute Evasion Plan 4."

Retribution leapt up, even as its deceleration dropped off.

"Only one hit this time," Damage Control reported.

"Three hits on the *Revenge*," Sensors reported.

"Good," Vicky growled.

"Still, we've taken more hits than they have," Captain Bolesław growled, "and now our hits are scattered. It will take us forever to peel that ship's ice."

During the next minute, they exchanged two broadsides. They took out two of the *Empress's Revenge*'s forward turrets with a trio of hits, but the *Revenge* got in a good one.

Vicky felt the air pressure drop, and the taste of ozone filled the bridge even before Damage Control reported. "We've got burnthrough aft. Power cables to turrets W and X are cut."

"What shit-for-brains designer put two sets of power cables where one hit could take them out?" Captain Bolesław snapped. "Get a work-around to those turrets and get it now!"

"We're on it."

The captain glanced Vicky's way and shook his head.

"We're just swapping damage. This could go on forever," growled Captain Bolesław.

"We can't afford forever," Vicky said. "Right now, we're one to one, but when the cruisers get in range . . . and the destroyers."

"Tell me something I don't know," the skipper snapped.

Vicky accepted the reprimand. She was wasting Bolesław's time, telling him what he already knew. His time and his temper.

COMPUTER, ANALYZE THE *EMPRESS'S REVENGE*'S EVASION PLAN. DO YOU SEE A PATTERN?

The computer took longer than Vicky expected before answering. IT ONLY SLOWS ITS ACCELERATION. IT NEVER GOES ABOVE 1.25 GEES. ALSO, IN DODGING, IT TENDS TO GO HIGH MORE OFTEN THAN LOW.

"Captain, I have had my computer analyze the jinking

pattern of the *Revenge*. She reduces her deceleration but never goes above 1.25 gees. She tends to sidestep higher more often than lower."

"Pass that along to Guns. We've got seven seconds before the next broadside. Maybe that will help him."

Vicky had her computer talking to Guns's fire control computers before the skipper finished his orders.

"We can use that," Guns said moments before he announced. "Fire."

A moment later, Damage Control announced, "Two hits. No burnthrough."

Sensors reported, "Six hits, none close together. Likely no burnthrough."

For the next long minute, they traded salvos. Captain Bolesław ordered his Helm to switch to Evasion Plans 1 or 2 between broadsides, then ratchet the jinking up to Evasion Plan 4 or 5 just before the clock ticked down to full capacitors. They tried Plan 6 for all of two seconds only to discover that the control jets could not handle it.

Revenge didn't twig to the change. Both ships fired as soon as they reloaded, and the redcoats never seemed to spot any pattern to *Retribution*'s wild jig.

As *Retribution* landed two or three hits for every one *Revenge* scored, the *Empress's Revenge* began to burn. The process was slow but brutally steady. *Revenge* shed ice, first as *Retribution*'s lasers slashed and hacked at the armor, then as the damaged ice gave in to the rotational force of the ship, to spin off huge chunks into space.

Stripped of its defensive armor, *Revenge* began to burn as laser hit after laser hit slashed deep into its hull. *Revenge* was a lucky ship. No reactors gave up their plasma to shoot destruction through the ship at solar temperatures.

Still, *Revenge* burned. Lasers slashed through girders, turning steel to flaming slag, firing electronics and anything willing to burn. Capacitors spent their charges burning around the ship rather than reaching out in laser beams.

Survival pods began to shoot from the ship and jet away, desperately seeking to reach a range safe from the ship's catastrophic end or incoming lasers.

In the end, Engineering must have doused the reactors,

getting rid of the plasma in a controlled dump but leaving the ship powerless, burning in space until vacuum was let in to rob the fire of oxygen, quenching it.

No longer decelerating, the hulk of the *Empress's Revenge* shot ahead of its escorts.

"Grand Duchess?" Captain Bolesław said.

Vicky stood. "I once more offer you a chance to surrender. We have destroyed both of your battleships and killed the Butcher of Dresden. Surrender and live."

The redcoat's face appeared on the screen, none the worse for the fight. "It will take more than you've got to kill me, you little bitch."

On the portion of the screen always dedicated to the tactical situation, the two cruisers veered sixty degrees from their course and went to 1.78 gees, opening the range from *Retribution*. The two destroyers followed suit, trailing them.

"Damn it," Lieutenant Blue snapped. "The Butcher was always on the lead cruiser."

"Get me a target," Captain Bolesław ordered.

"Both cruisers evading madly," the lieutenant answered. "They are also swapping out the lead. The destroyers are now trailing chaff. I can't track which ship is which."

"Guns."

"The way they're dancing around, I'm not sure either. Targeting is a crapshoot."

"Shoot," Captain Bolesław ordered.

"Ranging with our forward battery. It's only five strong."

The lasers reached out, but the four ships were dancing wildly.

"No hits, Skipper," Guns reported. "Reloading forward. I'm holding aft to see if they settle down."

Vicky joined Captain Bolesław watching the jinking dots on the screen. They'd been opening the distance by steering a good thirty degrees off *Retribution*'s course. That had protected their engines and reactors from a straight-up-the-kilt shot. Now they came around full perpendicular to Captain Bolesław's course, opening the range as fast as they could.

"Fire the aft battery," Captain Bolesław ordered. "Aim for the closest heavy cruiser."

"Closest cruiser targeted. Fire."

The aft battery was reduced from eight to four lasers.

Retribution reached out with what she had. Three were clean misses. The cruiser might be presenting its bare tail, but it was still doing a jig. The one hit was only a graze.

"Guns, follow that one and target it for the forward battery when you can."

"Will do."

The reload clock for the forward battery reached zero. Again, five lasers blasted away at the trailing heavy cruiser.

A split second before they fired, the cruiser jigged up and veered back to the sixty-degree course that made it a bigger target but gave more protection to the critical reactors and engines.

It also slowed to one-gee deceleration.

"We overshot," Guns reported. "Damn."

"The destroyers are popping chaff all over the place. The two cruisers are swapping the lead back and forth behind all that gunk. Skipper, I'm not sure which is which."

"They're getting out of range," Guns added. "I've got a shot from our aft battery, then maybe the forward guns."

"Do it," Captain Bolesław snapped. "Pick the one you think it is and nail it."

Vicky shook her head. The cruiser was a smaller target. It was bouncing madly around and again going hell for leather at close to 1.75 gees deceleration, opening the distance not only by course but also speed.

Twice *Retribution* fired half a broadside. Twice it missed hitting any of the Butcher's ships.

The pair of cruisers and destroyers pulled out of maximum range. Vicky knew they could continue shooting at them, but the lasers at that range could hardly do any damage.

They were also approaching the jump. They'd be going through it at close to fifty thousand klicks an hour as made no difference.

"*Slinger*," Captain Bolesław ordered, "lead the convoy through the jump."

"Aye, aye, sir."

In single line ahead, *Slinger*, *Sovereign of the Stars*, and eighteen freighters shot through the jump, each ship holding steady as a rock to avoid turning this into a horribly wrong jump from which they might never return. The jumps orbited more than one sun, some as many as five or six. Treat the jump with disrespect, and you might end up at any of them.

Taking a jump fast was disrespectful. The skippers compensated by being very steady.

Retribution was about to rocket through the jump, backward as it continued decelerating, when Mr. Smith, seated next to Lieutenant Blue, let out a low whistle.

"The Butcher of Dresden has reinforcements," the spy said.

"Reinforcements?" Vicky whispered softly.

"Battleships are jumping into the system," the lieutenant said, "and they're squawking. The *Empress's Fury, Empress's Rage, Empress's Wrath, Empress's Reprisal, Empress's Avenger, Empress's Punisher, Empress's Vindication.*"

Lieutenant Blue quit reporting as *Retribution* ducked through the jump into the St. Petersburg system.

CHAPTER 36

No sooner had they shot through the jump than the *Augsburg* appeared behind them.

"One more battleship showed up after you left," its skipper reported. The *Empress's Chastiser*, if you will."

"Any more after that?" Captain Bolesław asked.

"Hey, we were the only friendly in that system with a whole lot of overeager, unfriendly types. We jumped."

Vicky gnawed her lower lip as Captain Bolesław seemed to meditate on that answer. "For a St. Petersburg paper mark, I've half a mind to reverse course, jump back in, and keep an eye on that bunch," he finally said. "As soon as I can work the energy off the ship."

They had jumped at forty-five thousand klicks an hour. That return might take a bit. What might happen in that system while they were doing that?

"Are we in any shape to fight if they want to?" Vicky asked.

He shook his head. "No. Comm, send to convoy, set course for St. Petersburg. One-gee acceleration if you can make it."

The convoy took off for St. Petersburg.

"Your Grace, you should tell them we're coming and what's following us home," Captain Bolesław said.

Vicky winced but stood, composed herself, and spoke, "St. Petersburg, we are safely returned from Brunswick with a load of requested cargo and more, as you can no doubt see. Unfortunately, we were intercepted by a battle squadron from the Empress and had to fight our way through the last jump. Some of our ships will require repair. At last count, there were nine battleships in the next system and enough attack transports for a division-sized invasion force," she said, carefully vague about her own ships' battle damage on an open net. No need to be vague about the size of the Empress's fleet.

With a sigh, she sat down, message sent. Around her, the crew set about repairing what damage they could while under way. While she waited for any response, she and Captain Bolesław caught a quick bite to eat in his wardroom. They returned just in time for an incoming message from Admiral von Mittleburg.

"Glad to see you back. We will have space docks waiting for you as soon as you arrive. Can you tell us more about the Empress's forces in the next system? Better yet, can you maintain any observation presence on that side of the jump?"

Vicky's brows formed a questioning V. Captain Bolesław shook his head firmly.

Vicky stood and faced the screen where the final frame of Admiral von Mittleburg's message still held primacy of place.

"Thank you for holding the docks for us. The Empress's forces are jamming any assessment of their ships, so we can't tell what size they are until we get within visual range, unless, of course, she wants to intimidate us with the number of battleships she has. Even that must be viewed with some doubt. We had to fight them to discover they had 18-inch lasers as large as *Retribution*'s. There are at least one battleship and several heavy cruisers picketing their side of the jump. Captain Bolesław strongly, repeat, strongly suggests that we not go back there with anything less than a battle fleet."

Vicky surreptitiously ticked off on her fingers the three main issues the admiral had raised. She'd answered all of them. She nodded, and the message was sent.

The time for a reply came and went that evening. Apparently, Admiral von Mittleburg had no more interest in gabbing with his Grand Duchess. Since she had nothing to say, she was just as happy to let matters rest.

Better yet, behind them, the jump stayed quiet, coughing up no *Empress's Nasty This* or *Mean That*.

The end of the journey was blessedly uneventful. The freighters were directed immediately to unloading piers. They were not the only ships unloading at the station. Apparently, the Grand Duchess had indeed inspired trade to begin again.

Retribution and *Slinger* were pointed directly to vacant space docks that hadn't been there when they left. St. Petersburg was doing well by its Navy.

What was more important for Vicky and her revolution now aborning were the number of battleships and cruisers occupying the Navy piers.

The Empress would not get this station without a fight.

CHAPTER 37

VICKY returned to her quarters to check on her two assassins. They'd done a perfect job of packing. Mr. Smith was also waiting patiently to be her shadow as she left *Retribution*.

Commander Boch appeared before Vicky could leave to pay her respects to Admiral von Mittleburg. "The admiral is headed over here to meet with you. He asks that you wait for him."

Lieutenant Commander, Her Grace Victoria, once again found herself wondering at the admiral's honoring her with a visit rather than waiting for hers, but settled into her armchair to await him. Captain Bolesław joined her as soon as he had his ship firmly settled into the space dock.

"I've got my XO going over our needs with the yard bosses. It's quite amazing what they seem prepared to handle." He paused, then added, "I'll believe it when I've finished a post-yard shakedown with no write-ups."

They had not long to wait. There was a rap on Vicky's door. "Enter," she said, and a JG with a JOOD's armband led a vice admiral and Rear Admiral von Mittleburg into a room that was busy snapping to attention.

"As you were," the vice admiral said.

Vicky relaxed but did not sit down.

"Your Grace," Admiral von Mittleburg said, "may I present Vice Admiral Albert Lüth, Commander, Battle Squadron 22. He led his four battleships into the system a week ago, and we were most glad to see him."

"How did you happen to find your way here, Admiral?" Vicky asked, shaking an offered hand.

"I was about to be asked to surrender my command to the scrappers or maybe the pirates. I got wind of it and polled my skippers. We are honored to present to Your Grace the Greenfeld Imperial starships *Implacable*, *Adamant*, *Merciless*, and *Hunter* of my own squadron. Along the way I picked up a few more. *Vigilant* and *Unrelenting* were both headed for the breakers, and they kind of tagged along."

"Tagged along," Captain Bolesław said before Vicky could. "A captain doesn't just decide to get up plasma and sail off into the sunset."

"No, you have to push the button," the new admiral said, and had the good sense to cough at that oversimplification. "Your Grace, you have friends at Bayern who not only let us know what was headed our way like a runaway sun but arranged for certain 'off-the-book' options to open up for us. We ran for your territory, picking up a half dozen cruisers and a score of destroyers on the way. The nice folks at Metzburg were kind enough to give us food, fuel, and reaction mass and send us on to you."

"They didn't want you to stay?" Vicky asked.

"No, it seems they had just survived a small invasion of their own. The Empress sent two battleships to intimidate them. Metzburg already had acquired four by fair means or foul. Now they have six. Strange how that happens."

That drew a chuckle all around.

Vicky took in a deep breath and let it out slowly. "So the opposition to the Empress grows."

"And not just with the ships that have managed to slip across into your territory. Ships that have been boarded by the Empress's redcoats and ordered to sail against you suddenly develop the worst case of broke and can't be fixed that you've ever seen. Not that the fleet hasn't been run roughshod and given little enough maintenance support. Interesting how the shoddy workmanship done on new Navy construction is coming back to bite the Empress on her tiny little butt. The word has gotten out. Skippers and crews do not want to go up against you, Your Grace. Not after what you've been doing to the Empress's sallies.

"Our crews are motivated to not cross swords with you, and the redcoats don't know the first thing about a warship. It's amazing how a good chief can screw up the works. I mean, they're the ones I count on to keep the ships in space. Now they're pissed off, and what they can do to turn a ship into sick, lame, or lazy is totally beyond the ken of a bank clerk."

"What goes around, comes around," Admiral von Mittleburg said with an enthusiastic grin.

"Yes," Vicky said, "but there's still a lot coming at us that we need to do something about."

"Can I ask how bad things are with the two battleships you just brought in?" von Mittleburg asked.

Vicky tossed that ball off to Captain Bolesław.

He shook his head. "*Slinger* took some solid hits before we could win the fight around Brunswick."

"You had to fight your way into the Brunswick system?" Admiral Lüth was more than surprised.

"The redcoats were already there and in control of the station," Vicky said. "Captain Bolesław and his tiny squadron fought a brilliant battle that let the opposition know they faced destruction if they didn't come up with some way to surrender. The jumped-up bank clerk was so busy prancing around the bridge that he didn't bother to sit down and fasten a seat harness. When the flag captain put pedal to the metal on his flagship, along with the rest of the fleet following, he kind of broke his neck against the bridge's aft bulkhead. Hard to keep a gun to a skipper's head when gravity is slamming you around."

"He didn't?" Admiral von Mittleburg said.

"You know old Engle Rachinsky," Captain Bolesław said. Von Mittleburg nodded. "You still can't trust him when there's a good practical joke in the wind."

"I don't see him with you," Von Mittleburg said.

"I left him at Brunswick," Vicky said. "He's the seed of their Division of the Greenfeld Imperial Navy Reserve Fleet."

"Good, good, good," Admiral Lüth said.

"His ships did get a couple of good hits on the *Slinger*. We thought the yard at High Laatzen had repaired her, but as soon as we put on high acceleration, she started sloughing off ice. *Retribution* had to fight two 18-inch battleships to clear the way to the jump into this system."

"You hurt bad?" Von Mittleburg asked before the senior admiral could.

"I got at least one turret badly damaged. Two more are down with sliced cables. Who came up with the design that runs two turrets' power cables side by side, I ask you?"

"No doubt it saved money," Vice Admiral Lüth growled.

"No doubt," Vicky agreed dryly. "How fast can these new space docks make things right on these battleships? There's trouble on the other side of the jump and no telling when it will drop into our lap."

That turned the conversation around to Admiral von Mittleburg.

"The yard has been doing some pretty good work on our ships," he said. "Redoing the armor on the *Slinger* is something they should be quick about. The question is what major parts will we need to set the damage on the *Retribution* right? I asked the mayor of Sevastopol to be up here, both to welcome you back, say thank you for all the goodies you brought, and see if there was anything he could do to speed up fabrication downside on any parts your battle yacht needs."

"Good," Vicky said. She would very much like to see Mannie.

"His shuttle should be coming alongside the station any minute now," Admiral von Mittleburg said.

"One more thing before we bring civilians in," Vice Admiral Lüth said, eyeing the spy.

"He is with me. What I know, he knows, especially if it keeps me alive," Vicky said.

The admiral made a face at that but took a breath and went on. "Certain friends of yours agree with your decision to wave the flag of rebellion. They don't all agree with your timing, but since they couldn't agree on the best time to do it, your choice is as good as any of theirs. However, now that you've done it, they would appreciate it if you would kindly keep your head down. Every time they hear a report of a battle, you are in the center of it. Now that you've done what you've done, they can't afford to lose you."

Vicky eyed the man, wondering how much battle experience

he had. Around Vicky, fights just happened. Vicky had heard Kris Longknife comment on that dryly. "It's not like I go looking for fights, they just break out wherever I am," she remembered the Wardhaven princess saying.

Vicky fixed the vice admiral with a flinty eye and quoted Kris Longknife, without attribution.

"Ah, yes, Your Grace." The vice admiral gently coughed.

"I told you," Admiral von Mittleburg said, not quite under his breath. "She's a fighter. You do not want to pick a fight with her."

"So it seems. Still, Your Grace, the powers that be wish you to be more cautious with yourself," Admiral Lüth said evenly.

There was another knock at the door, and Mannie came in with his infectious smile. "I'm so glad to see you back, Your Grace. I hear that you brought us all sorts of goodies."

"And a battle fleet from my loving stepmama," Vicky added.

"Yes, I heard about that, too. Is your yacht in space dock for maintenance, or did you bang it up again?"

"I'm afraid I once more got it bent and dented. You know how traffic is." Vicky found herself smiling at Mannie and loving the fellow's way with words. Now, if he'd only lean over and give her a nice peck on the cheek.

She waited, but it didn't come.

So she went on. "I was just having a little talk here with Vice Admiral Lüth. Have you met him?"

"Your good Admiral von Mittleburg suggested he drop down to St. Petersburg for dinner with several of the nice people paying to keep his ships supplied with food, spare parts, and walking-around change for his crew," Mannie said with a not-at-all-sly smile.

The admiral rolled his eyes. No doubt it was an informative evening for a Greenfeld Navy officer.

"Well," Vicky went on, "he thinks I should keep my head down and try not to be around when my loving stepmommy's thugs start fights, battles; you know, those things with loud noises and blowing-up starships."

Mannie made a face. "Don't you just hate it when that happens?"

Vice Admiral Lüth made a different face. "It's rather hard to maintain a rebellion if the center of it gets herself blown to pieces."

"Yes, and I would dearly hate for that to happen to our Vicky," Mannie said so quickly and with such sad eyes that Vicky actually found herself believing him. "However, Admiral, people can't follow someone into battle who is hiding in some bunker way behind them.

"Take for example, the first time her loving stepmom tried to blow up our Vicky. She'd just walked out of a meeting with quite a few important people from around Sevastopol, and we were quite upset when she walked back into our meeting, mad as a wet hen. She got exactly what she wanted after that.

"Then there was the time her stepmommy dearest sent thugs to kidnap our Vicky and leave her tied up to die of thirst. Vicky, of course, got out on her own before any Prince Charming wandered by, and the whole attitude on our planet changed after that. Our people will not so much as let someone look cross-eyed at our Vicky without going to her defense.

"And then there was the invasion fleet that Vicky single-handedly stopped."

"Stopped," Lüth yelped.

"Gave the redcoat in charge such a runaround that he died of a heart seizure," Mannie pointed out, innocently.

"I can see that possibility," the new admiral said dryly.

"Happens all the time around the girl," von Mittleburg said. "I take my meds religiously."

"Tell me who your doctor is. I may need a referral."

"As you can see," Mannie went on, ignoring the table chatter, "our gracious Grand Duchess is quite a handful, and she is most capable of taking care of herself."

"With a whole lot of help from my friends," Vicky said. "I include most everyone in this room among those who have helped me stay alive and, no doubt, will soon be adding Vice Admiral Lüth to my list of saviors. By the way, Admiral, how do you propose to keep the blackhearted Empress's latest move against St. Petersburg from burning its nice people to cinders?"

"Cinders?" Manny asked with a bit of a gulp.

"She's sent us the Butcher of Dresden this week. He's bragging that he'll laser you from orbit right down to bedrock."

"Not a nice man," Mannie said, then turned to the newly arrived vice admiral. "You do have a plan, don't you?"

"Not one I will be sharing with civilians," he snapped.

"So you don't have a plan, huh?" Mannie said.

"Not one that he's shared with me," Rear Admiral von Mittleburg said.

"Admiral!" Lüth huffed.

Vicky turned to the newest Navy officer she would have to bear. "Admiral, I've followed Princess Kristine Longknife. She never went into a fight without everyone with her knowing just how she intended to fight her battle. Not that any of them went the way she planned, but she seemed to think that the more her folks knew about her intent, the more likely they would be to improvise something new when the wheels came off. Now, Mannie here is very likely to be dirtside looking up at some very nasty lasers. I think we can count on him to be just as concerned about our operational security as you and I will be. Admiral, how do you intend to see that the Empress's nine battleships don't get into orbit around St. Petersburg, where they can lase the planet to fire and dust?"

The admiral was most disappointingly quiet.

"What are the chances we could hold the jump point?" Vicky asked.

"During the Unity War and the following Iteeche War, no one ever tried to defend a jump point," Admiral von Mittleburg said, no doubt saving his superior from having to cross swords with Vicky.

"Yes," Vicky said. "Admiral Krätz explained to me that no one wanted to float around the jump point with no gravity."

Both admirals nodded at her most sagaciously.

"Of course, when he was gallivanting around in the train of Kris Longknife, it involved a lot of waiting for her in orbit with no station and no gravity. Admiral Krätz came up with an idea for hitching two of his battleships together with a long beam and letting them swing themselves around each other. The feeling of down wasn't perfect, but it beat all to hell no down at all."

The two admirals exchanged glances. Neither of them was willing to say the obvious. *Why didn't I think of that?*

Then von Mittleburg shook his head. "That might be a good idea once things settle down, but for now, with those battleships liable to come through the jump at any time, it would not be a good idea for us to go charging off. There's a reason why most battles in space take place around or near a planet."

"We could find ourselves just getting to the flip point on our way to the jump, and they'd come through," Captain Bolesław said. "It would be a mess, what with us breaking for the jump as they started accelerating toward St. Petersburg."

"We'd be in worse shape than that idiot polo player I teased into charging us," Vicky agreed. "Okay, we don't go chasing off to the jump. But we don't want to end up waiting here in orbit for them. Nine battleships have to be stopped well away from Mannie's farmhands and fab workers."

"Yes, definitely, as well as my dear *grandmadre*. She wants to go shopping with you."

"Then we definitely make sure those wonderful dress shops are not burned to dust by any nasty lasers."

"Nasty, nasty lasers," Mannie agreed.

"So, Captain Bolesław, is there any planet between here and the jump we could swing around and use to put us on a parallel course so we could slug it out with the Empress's battleships?"

Her skipper was shaking his head before Vicky finished. "None close by," he said.

Vicky frowned in thought. "I know you used a high elliptical orbit both times you had to fight an incoming force," she said slowly to Captain Bolesław. "Didn't Kris Longknife once use a swing around a moon to get her more fighting time?"

"I haven't read too much about her fighting tactics," *Retribution*'s skipper said.

"I've spent a lot of time studying her file, both on my own and with Admiral Krätz's assistance," Vicky admitted.

"You didn't seem to think much of her after she got back from losing Admiral Krätz's battle squadron," Admiral Lüth said. "Not that I saw your interview. I just heard about it."

For someone who claimed to have only heard about Vicky's time on the news, his eyes quickly slid from her face to her chest and what she'd showed off to get her extra time on the air.

Vicky chose not to contradict the admiral, though now, every man in the meeting seemed to have developed an intense interest in the overhead.

"I learned a lot from Kris Longknife," Vicky said. "I wonder where she is now."

Mr. Smith cleared his throat. "She was not at Wardhaven when I was last there with your shopping list. I understand she ended up at Musashi for some reason. They put her on trial for starting the war with the alien space raiders without getting proper permission or something."

Vicky snorted. "As if she had anyone around who might have given her 'proper' permission."

"That seemed to be the sticking point," Mr. Smith agreed. "They could neither find her guilty nor innocent."

"Who could ever find that woman innocent?" Admiral Lüth agreed. "She killed your brother."

"I'm finding that harder and harder to believe," Vicky said. That got her both admirals' attention. "Admiral Krätz was in that battle and agreed with Kris Longknife that whoever sabotaged Hank's survival pod was who killed him. Now I find myself wondering if the Empress and her family's grab for power can be traced back to my brother's death."

"You think so?" Admiral von Mittleburg asked.

"No way to prove it, but the coincidences are piling up, aren't they?"

That left the two admirals deep in thought.

"Again speaking of Kris Longknife," Vicky went on, "where is she now?"

Mr. Smith seemed to wait for the admirals to say something before going on. "There were rumors of her getting a ship from Musashi, one of the new, Smart Metal frigates. After that, she seems to have disappeared. No." The spy snapped his fingers. "King Raymond later took off for the other side of the galaxy. You know that planet you were fighting to save?"

"Yes." Vicky nodded. "I always wondered what happened to it."

"It seems that King Raymond's long-lost wife was out there. He went off to bring her back home and came back rather empty-handed."

"It would take a Longknife to tell a Longknife no," Admiral Lüth muttered.

"Did Kris come back with him?" Vicky asked.

"Not that I heard," Mr. Smith said.

"There are reports of a lot of new Navy construction," Admiral von Mittleburg said. "Not just in the US but also in clusters associated with them. Why are you asking, Your Grace?"

"I'm not sure," Vicky said slowly. "It seems that if we are ever to find a way to end this civil war short of mutual annihilation, we may need the good offices of some middle person. I'd trust Kris Longknife. She saved my dad's life once. I doubt he'd trust anyone with his fate, but if he would, it could be Kris Longknife."

"And your stepmother?" the spy asked.

"Not a chance," she said.

The looks the men gave her pretty much confirmed that.

"Okay, so we shelve that idea. Now, we've got a planet of our own to save."

The admirals looked at Vicky. Vicky looked at them.

When no one opened his mouth, Vicky opened hers. "I agree we can't send a battle fleet out to guard the jump, what with the Butcher of Dresden likely to come through at any moment. However, if we sent two destroyers out there with a long beam and orders to zap anything that came through the jump to take a peek at our side, it might equalize the challenges of our situation. We don't dare stick our necks through the jump to get a look at their forces. If they send anything through smaller than a destroyer, it won't live long enough to report back. Any problems with that?"

The admirals eyed Vicky like she had grown a second head. Then Admiral von Mittleburg spent a long moment gnawing his lower lip. "That might just work," he finally said.

"A pair of cruisers might be better," Vice Admiral Lüth said.

Five minutes later, they had agreed on a pair of old light cruisers.

"Now, what else can we come up with?" Vicky asked.

CHAPTER 38

════

A N hour later, they were no further along than when they had started. They hadn't been able to think of anything better for when the Empress's forces came than to have Vice Admiral Lüth lead the battle fleet in a loop out and around St. Petersburg's one moon. Even that assumed the Butcher didn't wait too long, and the moon moved out of place. A high loop around the moon would give them a longer running gunfight than they'd get from just a loop out from St. Petersburg. The problem remained that it would be a *long*, running gunfight with a lot of blood and guts all over the place.

"Kris Longknife says the only fair fight is the one you lose," Vicky said. "What can we do to make this an unfair fight for them?"

That drew her blank stares from the Navy officers.

"What can we do to get ourselves an advantage?" she clarified.

Still no response.

Vicky ran a worried hand through her hair. "I seem to recall both Admiral Krätz and Kris Longknife saying something about water making a better reaction mass than just free hydrogen."

"Yes," Captain Bolesław said. "The weight of a water molecule is nine times heavier than a pair of hydrogen atoms. If you heat both of them to the same temperature, you'll get nine times the specific impulse, but it likely won't get you any real value."

"It won't?" Vicky said. "They seemed to think it was worth the effort."

"It might be," Admiral von Mittleburg said, "if you could make use of the extra reaction mass, but our ships can't take much more than two, maybe two-point-five gees without breaking something." Admiral Lüth nodded, but seemed distinctly uninterested in crossing his Grand Duchess again.

Vicky knew where she wanted to take this, but she kept it slow for the seniors present.

"Agreed," she said, "assuming we don't want to bend or break anything, but what if we were moving greater weight around? Might we benefit from heavier reaction mass if it was moving a heavier ship, just at the same acceleration?"

"Why would we want heavier ships?" Admiral Lüth couldn't avoid jumping at that one.

"What if we added a half meter or more of ice armor to our battleships?" Vicky said, as offhandedly as she could manage.

The admirals did not jump down her junior officer's throat, so she continued.

"We've got a shipyard here, and the planet below gives us access to water to thicken our ice armor and stoke our tanks with heavier reaction mass. They're likely refueling on the other side of that jump from a gas giant. An ice giant if we aren't lucky. Either way, they've got the armor they came with and we just peeled that armor off two 18-inch battleships and blew them into gas clouds."

"We do have the LCAs from the Marine transports," Admiral von Mittleburg said slowly.

"We're holding on to them to move cargo down from the station," Mannie filled in. "Other than bringing up some of the spare parts you need, Your Grace, we could have them lugging water up on the return trip."

"And there are four slips that could be used to thicken the ice coatings on the eight battleships we have," von Mittleburg agreed.

"We have eight battleships?" Vicky asked.

"Ten, if we include the two dinged-up ones you brought back," the station commander corrected. "I was down to just the *Stalker* and the *Scourge* before Albert here showed up with his six homeless waifs."

"And glad you were to see me," Admiral Lüth said, not quite elbowing von Mittleburg in the ribs. "Still, Your Grace, battleships are designed to support their armor under acceleration. You add too much weight to a hull, and you could collapse a strength member. Hell, you increase the weight of a turret, and the machinery for rotating the lasers and ice could cave in on you."

"Yes," Vicky said, "so we look carefully at how much we add, and maybe go a bit easy on how much we honk these ships around. Captain Bolesław, did you notice that the Empress's ships attacking us seemed to have a harder time maintaining their acceleration than we did?"

"They most definitely were being delicate with their acceleration and deceleration, and at least one destroyer and one battleship couldn't hold to the fleet acceleration we had our freighters doing."

Admiral Lüth shook his head. "The Navy has spent too much time tied up at the pier. But what else could we do, what with the stingy maintenance budgets we got."

"And the need to use Sailors to bash civilians' heads," Admiral von Mittleburg added.

"That, too," Vicky said. "So, do we have anyone to do the calculations as to how much armor we can pile onto our battleships and how quickly we can get it done?"

Mannie coughed softly. "We sent out feelers for anyone who might be interested in coming to St. Petersburg to work in our shipyards."

"You mean everyone wasn't just totally scared to do anything that might displease my darling stepmommy?" Vicky said, batting her eyelashes at Mannie.

"Sad to say, we found quite a few," Mannie said. "That, and a couple of retired officers from the Navy colonies who were only too willing to get back in harness. Admiral?"

Von Mittleburg nodded. "I was wondering how it happened that so many yard types were dropping by and offering me a hand. So it wasn't just my sparkling personality?"

"No doubt it was," Admiral Lüth said dryly.

"I'll have my flag secretary call a meeting in my office in half an hour," von Mittleburg said, talking into his commlink. "That should give us a better idea of how much extra armor we can pile onto our war wagons."

"There's another matter," Captain Bolesław said. "My Gunnery Officer thinks he can tighten up our gun cradles so that we can fire more focused salvos. Hitting the Empress's battleships nearly in the same place destroyed the *Empress's Vengeance*. It would have been nicer if we could have gotten the *Revenge* just as quickly."

"I see the agenda for my meeting growing," said Admiral von Mittleburg.

"And if you don't mind, while you're doing that, Admiral," Mannie said, "I would like to squire our Grand Duchess downside to receive the thanks of a happy and bustling economy. Oh, and she might want to visit some of the fabrication plants that will be putting together what you need to fix up her ride."

"Already?" Vicky asked.

Mannie eyed his wrist unit. "I understand they have already made scans of the turrets that are still working and have transmitted them down to the fabs at Sevastopol and St. Pete. They'll be laying down the base parts tomorrow and printing the fine points as quickly as they can make it all happen. You did say there were some very bad people on the other side of the jump into our fair system, didn't you?"

"I said it, and I saw them," Vicky said.

"Then I know some people who very much want to wine and dine you tonight, maybe even fill up your dance card."

Vicky nodded to her two admirals. "Then I will leave the heavy lifting to you gentlemen, where our warships are concerned, and do all I can to keep the worker bees happy making us the honey we need."

"Isn't that sweet of you," Admiral von Mittleburg said, and, hand on Admiral Lüth's elbow, led him from her quarters.

Which left Vicky and Mannie staring at each other. She wanted to fold herself into his arms for a long hug and delightful kiss. Did he look just as longingly at her? But they were not alone. A moment later, the two of them left, with her spy and two assassins leading the way. Commander Boch provided a rear guard with a chief and several seamen strikers lugging what they would need dirtside for a few days of public adulation.

The walk through the yard was educational. Last time Vicky had passed this way, it had been a sleepy place, with only a handful of civilians and Navy types going about their business with purpose, but not a lot on their hands. Now, the place was bustling with yard hands towing flatbed trucks with huge chunks of ship and machinery, none of which looked like anything Vicky had yet seen aboard a ship. No doubt because she, as an officer, was not supposed to get her hands dirty.

Now there were supervisors and officers hurrying in every direction and deep in conversations that Vicky only caught a snatch of, but "repair," "fix," and "damn mess they made of a fine ship" were prominent.

"Quite a growing economy," Mannie said with pride.

"Quite a growing base force," Commander Boch put in.

"Quite a target the Empress will no doubt want to destroy," Mr. Smith said darkly.

Vicky found she had no trouble agreeing with all three of them.

The shuttle ride deposited Vicky not at St. Petersburg or Sevastopol as she expected, but in the bay surrounded by Kiev.

"Why here?" she asked.

"You kept your promise to them," Mannie said. "You remember you said Kiev would get the next load of imported heavy machinery and fabs to make up for what went to St. Pete after the delivery from Metzburg proved hard for Kiev to get up and working."

"Yes. St. Pete had the space and the workers to get them working immediately," Vicky said.

"And they did. Some of the assemblies needed to repair *Retribution* will be coming from those Metzburg-provided fabs now up and running in St. Pete," Mannie told her.

"I kept my word. I always knew I would. Didn't they trust me to?"

"They did. Other people, maybe not so much. Now that you have, they want to make sure everyone knows that you did. There will be quite a show tonight."

Vicky frowned at the Sevastopol mayor.

Mr. Smith cleared his throat. "While you, Your Grace, had

every intention of keeping your word, there are plenty of people who find the very concept of a Peterwald whose word can be trusted as something strange. It is also equally strange, that you, Your Grace, a mere slip of a girl, can make a pledge and see that it is kept."

Now Vicky was the one making a face. "I think I must thank you, Mr. Smith, for your unique take on matters. I doubt if there are many who would risk telling me such truth."

"I tried," Mannie said.

"You did try. I just found it more understandable coming from someone who is superb at telling lies."

The mayor of Sevastopol just shook his head.

Before Vicky could devote any more time to mulling the strange ways of representative government, the shuttle's hatch popped open, and a roaring cheer invaded their space.

"You have an adoring crowd waiting for you," Mannie said, and, offering Vicky an elbow, led her out to a lineup that started with the mayor of Kiev and included most of the city council, all of the business owners, and finished with the two kids Vicky had helped beat a carnival game. Again, the young girl had flowers.

Vicky had heard of parades. She'd even seen a few of them from the palace windows. She'd never been the center of one before. The cheering throng at the shuttleport gave way to sidewalks full of more cheering people. Vicky waved. They waved back as she passed.

Police and boys and girls from the Guide Escadrilles marked off the sidewalks and kept the crowds from pushing forward. And up on the rooftops, Kiev militia soldiers could be seen with rifles at the ready.

While Vicky waved, Mr. Smith, Kit, and Kat eyed everyone.

There was no incident. Kiev was celebrating. People here still remembered who had used them to try to kill Vicky. They were taking good care of her.

At the fabrication plants, Vicky saw shiny new equipment being lowered into place or plumbed in. Happy faces were everywhere.

How long will this last if the Butcher gets his way?

At times, it took effort to keep her smile in place.

Much later that night, installed once again in the Imperial Suite, after an evening of dining, dancing, and meeting half of

Kiev, or so it seemed to Vicky's sore right hand, she poured Mannie a glass of wine and joined him on the couch. He at one end, she at the other.

They finally had the suite to themselves.

"Did you miss me?" she asked Mannie, taking a sip of a surprisingly good local Riesling.

Mannie took a sip before he essayed a response. "Yes. I'm surprised at just how much I did miss you. Did you really have to fight your way onto the station at Brunswick?" he asked.

Why are you changing the topic? Still, Vicky followed where he led.

"All I did was talk this jumped-up bank clerk who claimed to be a Count into getting his whole fleet out of orbit and charging right at us. Captain Bolesław did most of the work after that."

"That's not what I heard. While you were busy shaking hands and smiling, I checked back with your captain. He said you did all the talking and made it easy for him to dot a few i's, cross a few t's, and finish what you started."

Vicky watched the swirls of liquid in her glass. "I've always been good at driving people crazy."

"You don't drive me crazy," Mannie said, then hid himself behind his glass as he took a deep swallow. "Except when you're off and maybe getting yourself killed. *That* drives me crazy."

Now it was Vicky's turn to take a long sip. "We could all get ourselves killed if we can't hold off that invasion fleet."

"Are you afraid you can't?"

Vicky focused on her drink. "If I told you I was, does that mean we could eat, drink, and be merry tonight because tomorrow we won't have anything left to worry about?"

Mannie didn't take his focus from his drink as he replied. "It is very tempting."

"But not a smart move," both said, together, then shared a laugh.

"Maybe I should go," Mannie said, not putting down his glass. "You've got a pretty good record on staying alive. It would be a shame to mess everything up tonight and live to regret it all tomorrow."

"Hmm, let's see if I can talk you into staying," Vicky said.

Mannie's eyes got wide with alarm, but he still didn't bolt for the door.

So Vicky told him about the people who thought they owned Brunswick and their attempt to hire Inez and her Rangers to "keep the workers in their place."

"Those are our allies?" Mannie yelped.

"Seems like it. How have you folks on St. Petersburg managed to keep things balanced between all your players?"

Once again, Mannie swirled his wine. "'Balanced' is the key word. Workers, capital, farmers, politicians like myself, General White, and our new Army. Also, the Navy we're trying to build. All have to be kept in a delicate balance. So far, all of us know we need each other if we're going to survive this."

"Hmm, kind of like I've learned. I need all of you if I'm to stay alive," Vicky said, taking a small sip.

"Exactly. An old rebel from back on Earth, I forget his name, said we must all hang together or we will end up hanging separately."

"That was what I tried to explain to the wealth of Brunswick," Vicky said.

"Your dad had them in his pocket. They did what he wanted, and he did what they wanted. Of course, for the rest of us, it was a lousy deal."

Vicky chose her next words carefully, not at all sure where she was going or would like where she ended up when she arrived. "Are you thinking of turning our Greenfeld Empire into some kind of Longknife democracy?"

There, I said it. Now she needed a big gulp of wine.

She almost emptied her glass as she watched Mannie swirl the liquid in his own. She began to wonder if he'd actually heard her. She was about to repeat the question when Mannie whispered an almost inaudible "No."

"No?" she echoed, but hardly louder than him.

"No," he said, shaking his head. "Longknife space, Wardhaven, the US, whatever you call it. They've been doing their thing for some two hundred years. Lots more if you consider where most of them came from on Earth. They do it because they've been doing it that way, just like we've been doing whatever it is that we do, for a long time."

"Or thought we knew what we were doing," Vicky pointed out. "At least, what I've been seeing out here in the real world is nothing like what my father bragged he was in control of when I was an impressionable little girl batting my eyelashes at him."

"Yes," Mannie agreed. "I don't know how the Longknifes run their end of space. When I get media reports through smugglers bringing trade in from their distant colonies, it appalls me what they do there, but somehow, they keep on managing to do things that we can't." The mayor shook his head.

"Their Smart Metal ships," Vicky noted.

"Yes, but it's not just their scientific advancements. It's also the way they grow their economy and give everyone a share in it. How do they do it? How do they keep everyone from eating each other alive?"

"Like my stepmother is doing?"

Mannie nodded. "Yes. How can we get something like that but not that?"

"If you don't know, I don't have any hope that I'll ever know," Vicky said.

Mannie snorted at that. For a long minute, he stared into his glass. "When you were a kid, did you ever ride a bike?" he finally asked.

Vicky's brows came down in question, but she just shook her head.

Mannie scratched the back of his neck. "I did. The thing about a two-wheel bike is that you can't stop. You stop, you fall down. You have to keep going. Keep moving. Keep heading wherever it is that you're going. So long as you're pedaling your little legs, the bike is balanced. You stay up, and you go someplace."

"We can't stop," Vicky said slowly. "We've got to just keep going."

"And you don't always go where you want to go," Mannie said, smiling at some memory. "A little kid just learning to ride a bike has to go where the bike wants to take him. You have to turn into a fall, catch yourself, get your balance back, maybe some more speed, then turn it the way you want to go."

"You make it sound like a good way to break your neck," Vicky said. "No wonder I wasn't allowed near the killing things."

Mannie's smile got even wider. "When you are a kid, it's not that great a fall. I swear, kids have rubber for necks. Anyway, I learned how to ride and got a lesson I have now passed along to you. We are riding a bike, and we can't stop; nor can we go exactly where we want to go. We've got to go where it takes us."

"Gee," Vicky said, sharing his grin, "and I thought we were riding a tiger."

"A lady may ride a tiger. We guys must settle for bicycles," Mannie said, then sighed. "So, how do we arrange for everyone to learn to ride a bicycle?"

"I was about to ask you that," Vicky said. She suddenly noticed that both her and Mannie's glasses were empty. She stood and turned to the wet bar only to hear the click of a glass firmly being deposited on the coffee table.

She turned back to Mannie.

"If I allow you to refill my glass, I fear that I will fall off of more than a bicycle," he said, and turned, empty-handed, for the door. Vicky set down her own glass and followed him. He paused, his hand on the doorknob.

"We sent trade delegations to both Brunswick and Metzburg," Mannie said slowly. "I'm thinking now that we ought to have sent more people. Politically astute representatives from General White's staff. Folks who are coordination with the Navy, people from both business and labor who don't have axes to grind . . . on each other's skulls. We're kind of thin on the ground where political types are concerned. Your old man was hard on us."

"Will you need to send similar teams to the smaller planets in this sector?" Vicky asked. "Finster, Ormuzd, Good Luck, and the like?"

"I don't think so. They've been trading as much with US colonies like Pandemonium as with us. The Longknife way of doing things can be contagious if you get it when you're small."

"Those rubber necks that you say kids have that don't break?"

"It looks like it. No, we'll have enough trouble finding people for Metzburg and Brunswick. Hopefully, that will be enough. For now."

They were standing so close. Maybe Vicky leaned in closer. Maybe it was Mannie. It could have been both of them. One moment, Vicky was holding her breath, and the next moment Mannie's lips were on hers, and she wondered if she'd ever need to breathe again.

They stood there, just lips touching for the longest time.

"That was wonderful," Vicky said as she did discover that she needed to breathe.

"Yes," Mannie breathed softly on her, and she found her whole face tingling with the touch of it.

Vicky gulped hard. "If you don't go out that door this minute, I don't know that I'll be able to let you out it in the next."

"I don't want to go."

For long seconds, they looked at each other, leaning closer, leaning into the next kiss that would not end with his leaving.

Vicky gritted her teeth, and found Mannie's jaw tightening even as hers did. She turned away.

"Until tomorrow," Mannie said to her back, and the door closed between them.

Vicky listened for his footsteps as he left, but the door or the carpet silenced them. She threw herself down on the sofa.

"Stepmother, this has got to end. You are ruining my life!" she screamed into the cushions. "We have got to get this over with so I can get a life."

CHAPTER 39

═══

THE next morning started with a quick, suborbital hop from Kiev to St. Petersburg. On the flight, Vicky was briefed that today she'd be smiling and waving at many of the people who were working around the clock to turn out the subassemblies *Retribution* needed to be restored to battle readiness. There were also several steel-fabrication plants extruding special beams to strengthen the hulls of all the battleships that would be getting extra armor.

"I definitely want to smile at these folks," Vicky said.

No sooner had the lander rolled out of the water and onto the port than she found herself meeting a lot of serious faces. The local mayor greeted her with a delegation of business and financial leaders with one and only one question on their mind.

"What's this we hear about an invasion fleet?"

Vicky chose honesty for her answer.

"The Empress has one in the next system out. Our convoy escorts fought with its lead elements to get the freighters through from Brunswick. Your fabs are putting together things that will give us a leg up when we next fight them. Do you have a problem?"

"Yes," one large banker said, shouldering his way to the

front. "The commander of this force, the guy we hear is called the Butcher of Dresden, why didn't you kill him the first time you fought him? Can you kill him?"

"When we fought his forces the first time, we blew away two battleships. He got none of ours," Vicky said succinctly.

"I heard they got a freighter?" came from the back of the crowd of worried civilians.

"One of our merchant ships suffered an engineering casualty and couldn't decelerate with the rest. It was picked off by one of their destroyers," Vicky said curtly. "Apparently you've been talking to someone who got scared the first time they saw a battle. I've seen a few, and it wasn't all that scary. We'll be ready for them just like we were the other two times the Empress tried to take your system."

"It didn't seem like we were all that ready," again came from the back.

"We fought. We won. They lost. That's why you have a fleet, to see that they are the ones who die and we are the ones who live. I'm scheduled to say a few words to the folks making our ships better than their ships. What do you say that we stay on schedule?"

There was plenty of grumbling, but none of it rose to a level that Vicky had to pay attention to. A limo was waiting for her, and a small motorcade got under way.

"I'm glad we lost that bunch of little old ladies in long skirts," Commander Boch noted as the fleet of large black limos took off in their own direction, leaving Vicky's the only one with an escort of police and military SUVs headed for the industrial side of town.

"Who's been talking to them?" Vicky asked no one in particular.

"It's kind of hard to keep merchant Sailors from talking," Mannie answered. "It's not like we have state security to lock people up."

"How *do* the Longknifes keep people from blabbing?" Vicky said, suspecting she and Mannie were continuing their talk from last night.

"Perhaps they trust them to keep their own mouths shut and maybe they do. Sailors have been talking in bars for several thousand years," Mannie pointed out.

"Merchant captains have been telling their owners what they saw for just as long," Commander Boch added.

"Well, at least we still have people waving at us," Mr. Smith noted with a wave of his hand, and Vicky took the reminder that she should be waving and smiling at those people. The crowd here wasn't as enthusiastic as the folks lining the streets in Kiev. There also weren't as many of them. Vicky took that as a sign that their itinerary might not have been blasted all over the media.

She was about to mention that to Mr. Smith when all hell broke loose.

CHAPTER 40

━━━━

VICKY caught the flash out of the corner of her eye. A car parked on the side of the street had been there a moment ago. Now pieces of it were flying at her.

And pieces of the people she'd been waving at.

Time seemed to stand still.

The limo flew up into the air like a cat toy. Vicky reached out to grab hold of the door and found it coming her way in a hurry. When it hit her arm, it was pure agony.

Someone was screaming. Likely her.

The limo had been steady as she entered it back at the spaceport. Then, she'd taken it for heavily armored and been glad of it. Now it rolled over twice as if it were paper blown by the wind and came to a halt on the other side of the street against another parked car.

The door she'd been reaching for was now leaning hard against her shoulder. Pain lanced into her. Mr. Smith and Commander Boch were calling to her, reaching for her.

She couldn't hear a word they said.

Kit and Kat were squeezing themselves out the far door, even as blood flowed from their eyes and ears. Kat had a jagged piece of metal sticking out of her butt that she ignored.

A moment later, both of her assassins were standing in the gaping hole that had been the limo door, Kat faced out with a gun leveled. Kit strained for a moment as she struggled to haul the door off Vicky.

The shattered armored-glass cut into Kit's hands, but she didn't so much as flinch as she pulled the heavy door off Vicky. It might have helped that Commander Boch was pushing from the inside as well.

Vicky gritted her teeth and did her level best not to scream as the door came away but the pain didn't.

Mr. Smith touched her shoulder. From the look on his face, he was doing his best to be careful.

The pain was still excruciating. Vicky wished she could pass out, but though the world got hazy, it would not go away.

She blinked blood out of her eyes and found herself focusing on Mannie. The mayor of Sevastopol had been tossed against the opposite door. Kit and Kat had walked right over him to get out that side. He seemed to be recovering, shaking his head as the dazed look in his eyes was slowly replaced by his focusing on her.

He said something. She couldn't make it out, but at least she heard something.

Movement caused her to turn her head. Big mistake. A wave of nausea swept over her, but she swallowed down what came up.

Reinforcements were now arriving. A pair of Rangers, rifles at the ready beat three cops to the door that Kat guarded. She kept her pistol aimed at them. They kept their weapons aimed high and turned around to face out with Kat. Only then did the diminutive assassin relax—a smidge.

Two medics arrived. At least the bags they carried showed Red Crosses and Red Crescents prominently. At the collection of firepower aimed at them, they opened their bags enthusiastically and were allowed to pass through the cordon only when the contents matched the advertising.

Both headed for Vicky, but she pointed at the bloody hunk of metal sticking out of Kat's rear end. The two assassins took in the wound, apparently for the first time. In Kat's case, it took some twisting around before she could spot what Vicky was pointing at.

Kat shook her head. Vicky could still not make out the words, but it was clear Kat had no intention of leaving her post while Vicky's condition was still unknown and an assault might well be in the offering.

Kit nodded and turned her back on her friend, motioning Vicky to see if she could stand up.

Vicky tried to pop the five-point harness holding her to her seat. It wouldn't budge. Since she and the harness had gotten quite personal during the two flips the limo went through . . . and it would be a while before Vicky let anyone else touch her lady parts . . . Vicky could only shrug to those around her.

Mr. Smith produced a wicked-looking knife and began to carefully cut Vicky free. The commander left Mr. Smith and the medics to work with Vicky and joined the growing layer of guards around the banged-up limo.

Vicky found herself free. She reached for Mr. Smith and failed to swallow a yelp. Her right arm would not move. One medic gently touched the shoulder and shook her head.

"You've got a dislocated shoulder," she shouted with careful enough enunciation that Vicky could understand. "We've got to get you to a hospital."

The other medic was checking Vicky's scalp. "You're cut. Maybe concussed. They'll want to keep you tonight for observation."

Mr. Smith scowled at the medical advice. "Do you want them to set policy for a Grand Duchess, or do you decide what needs doing?"

It took Vicky three tries, but she finally got out a hoarse, "What do you have in mind?"

"You came here to tell some workers that what they were doing was crucial. Clearly, the Empress doesn't want you talking to anyone. What do you intend to do?"

What Vicky wanted to do was crawl in bed and have Doc Maggie make all the hurts go away. Vicky squeezed her eyes shut.

Where is Maggie? When did I let her go one way and me go another?

After two slow breaths, Vicky opened her eyes. Everyone was here. Mannie and the commander, Mr. Smith and Kit and Kat. They were who she counted on now. All of them looked to her, waiting for her to give the order. *What does a Grand Duchess do?*

What would Kris Longknife do?

Not crawl back in bed, Vicky answered herself.

Vicky squared her shoulders . . . or at least started to before the pain made her gulp down a yelp.

"Let's go talk to some production workers." She intended the words to be hard. And they might have been, if her voice hadn't cracked so badly.

"Let's see what I can do about that shoulder," Mr. Smith said, and gently led Vicky to a nearby light post. "Hug that thing like it was Mannie here," the spy said.

That got a giggle from Kat. Mannie turned quite red in the face.

"What are you going to do?" one of the medics asked before Vicky could get her tongue around the question.

"Fix that shoulder so she can do a day's work."

"Let me at least give her a shot," the other medic said.

"You want to be stoned, or stone-cold sober when you talk to those workers?" Mr. Smith asked Vicky.

"I hate this macho shit," Vicky said, and hugged the lamppost with her good arm, offering her spy the bad one gingerly.

He took off his leather belt, folded it twice, and put it in her mouth. "Bite down hard." Then he took the arm gently, and carefully felt up around the shoulder as he moved it ever so gently.

Maybe this won't be so bad, Vicky was just starting to think.

And screamed as she nearly bit through the belt. The two-faced secret agent man had yanked on her arm with all his might, almost walking away with it. Once more, the world was turning black. Vicky did, indeed, hold on to the post for dear life.

"If you told me you were going to do that," the senior medic said, "I'd have gotten one of these Rangers to shoot you. We don't do that kind of crap anymore."

"We do what we have to do to finish the job," Mr. Smith said curtly.

"Don't worry," Vicky mumbled, "I'll shoot him later."

"You are so gracious, Your Grace," Mr. Smith said through a grim smile.

"Well, at least take these painkillers," the medic said,

offering Vicky two familiar pills that she was not averse to using when her monthly went long.

"Will these do any good?" Vicky asked, but only as she was swallowing them down with the offered water.

"You'd be surprised, deary," the woman medic said. "Hold this ice pack on your shoulder. It's going to swell like the blazes in a few minutes."

"It already is," the other medic said, and wrapped Vicky's arm in a restraint that also managed to keep the ice pack in place. That done, one turned to work on Vicky's bleeding forehead while the other began to examine Kat's butt.

Only now did Kit allow her focus to waver toward her comrade. Her worried gaze flipped back and forth between Vicky and her sister assassin. Vicky waved Kit away.

Several ambulances arrived, lights flashing. Only after Vicky saw them did she hear the sirens. And only then did she take in the slaughter that surrounded her.

The stench hit her, forcing her to struggle to keep her stomach down.

The police SUV ahead of her limo had been even with the car bomb. The explosion had flipped it over. It hadn't been as heavily armored as Vicky's ride. It was stove in and had caught fire. It didn't look like any of the five people in it had gotten out alive.

So that was the horrible stench.

Or maybe just part of it.

Around the car bomb were people and parts of people. Vicky had thought the crowd was starting to thin out. Maybe it had. Maybe it could have been worse.

Just now, she couldn't see any way it could have been better.

More ambulances arrived, more medics. The two who had first helped Vicky were ready to move Kat. Kit gave her hand a final squeeze, then returned to Vicky's side.

"That bitch is so dead," she whispered, more to herself than to Vicky.

A Ranger captain appeared at Vicky's elbow. "I need to get you out of here."

"You need to get me to where I was going?"

"Ma'am?" had "you crazy?" all over it, but she didn't blink, and he led her and her team to a SUV that was three back from her limo's wreckage. He shouted orders while Vicky gingerly got herself seated and secured in the back. Her team surrounded her and held on tight when the rig got under way, with tires squealing.

They backed up, found a left turn, and took it, drove two blocks, and took a hard right. Somewhere along the line, they picked up a squad of motorcycle cops who raced ahead and halted traffic just long enough for them to zoom through intersections without slowing.

Up front, it looked like the Ranger captain was flipping a coin every time they came to an intersection. Sometimes they raced through it. Other times, they took a hard right or left. Vicky doubted anyone knew their route, not even their driver.

CHAPTER 41

THEY charged through a gate at an industrial plant just as it was opening. Apparently, even the guards weren't informed ahead of time about the arrival of their honored guest. The rig came to a stop at the large doors in the front of the fab building.

Vicky tried to get out but found the world going gray again. Mannie came around, and between him, Kit, and Mr. Smith, she managed to get on her own two feet. A glance down told her that she had been through a bombing. Her undress whites were speckled and streaked with blood. Most of it was someone else's. Some was hers.

Leaning heavily on Mannie, she stumbled up the two steps to the fab's many double doors. Several managers in suits were there to meet her but seemed suddenly turned to stone.

Mr. Smith took the lead. "The Grand Duchess is here to talk to your workers. I doubt she can do much walking. Do you have a place where she can talk to a bunch of them?"

Several of the managers recovered enough to form a sort of huddle that ended quickly with, "Follow me," and they did.

Two others joined them, each with an armful of white, clean-room bunny suits.

"Forget that," the lead suit snapped. "We'll use the Atrium."

"I thought we kept that clean," came from one of those buried under the bunny suits.

"We like to, we don't have to. We'll let Rabati show us just how good her air scrubbers are. She's always saying they could clean up after a herd of water buffalo."

The young woman with the other pile of bunny suits took in the Grand Duchess and her entourage, and her eyes grew wide.

The Atrium turned out to be a large room with a raised stage on one side. It was slowly filling with people, most in white clean-room suits. Many only glanced up from screens they were keeping an alert eye on when Vicky entered the room.

One look at her and those with her caused a low murmur to sweep the room. As Vicky was helped up the three steps to the stage and the few paces to a small podium and microphone, the room took on a deathly hush. Many of those holding screens held them up to record Vicky. Off to her left, what looked like a pair of newsies used top-of-the-line gear to do the same.

Make this good, Vicky breathed to herself.

"Go ahead," Vicky said. "Take a good look. It's real blood. My blood, and that of my friends. It could be blood from your friends, too. A car parked along the side of the road with a bomb in the trunk doesn't give a damn whose blood it splatters all over the place. Just like my stepmother, the blackhearted Empress, doesn't give a damn how many she blasts to bits, so long as what she's clutching at the end is all hers."

Vicky paused for a breath. In front of her, people were reaching in their clean suits for their phones. She waited as the room filled with a babble as calls were made, answered. Most sighed in relief.

There were two shrieks of grief.

Beside Vicky, the senior manager nodded at two of those around him, and they quickly left the stage to go to the side of those who had received bad news.

One woman was led out of the room.

"Get a car ready for a fast run to the hospital," the boss manager whispered into his commlink.

The situation around the other, a man, was different. He tossed off the consoling hands that reached for him. "No, damn it. I want to hear what she has to say. What my daughter's blood paid for her to say. It better be good."

Through all the pain of cuts and bone that Vicky had felt, a new agony flushed through her. Here she was, face-to-face with someone who would be paying for her visit here every day of his life with an aching void in his world.

What do I say? What can I say, as a survivor to the bereaved?

Vicky took a deep breath . . . and plunged in. "Sir, there is nothing I can say to you that will make this day anything but horrible for you and your family."

He nodded angry agreement.

"Neither you, nor I, nor anyone in this room, had anything to do with what happened. The Empress ordered it done and, despite the best effort of the police and military, someone got the bomb where the Empress wanted it."

There were soft murmurs of agreement around the room, but none from the man who stood, arms folded on his chest, glaring at Vicky.

"All of you here are doing your best to stop the Empress from doing to every one of you and your families what she managed to do to two of your coworkers. You are fabricating the weapons and gear needed to repair the ships that fought through the Empress's invasion fleet and brought through the industrial equipment this planet needs to defend itself and put an end to her murderous greed."

Vicky paused again to catch her breath and to let her eyes rove the room. As much as that one man's grief dominated her, there were others here. Others who were making the contributions to the coming victory that they all desperately needed.

"We can cower before the blackhearted Empress, or we can stand up to her. We can let the evil that is her wrap its cold tendrils around our hearts until we are frozen in place, good for nothing except trembling obedience to her every whim. We can do that, or we can fight.

"Waiting at the station above you are Sailors. You are extruding the steel to strengthen their ships and give them an edge fighting the ships the Empress has sent here to destroy us. They will fight, with or without what you can add to their strength. It will cost them in blood and sacrifice, but those Sailors stand ready to make it.

"You can give them an edge. You can give them protection that will let them keep on hitting the Empress's battleships long after they might have fallen silent. The Navy stands ready to defend you. Do you stand with the Navy?"

"Yes," came at Vicky like a wave.

"Are you with me?"

"Yes," was even louder.

"Thank you," Vicky said. "Thank you from all the Sailors and Marines who will be following me into battle to beat the Empress again and again until we have beaten her for good."

The room disintegrated into wave after wave of cheering, but it slowly fell silent as first one person's eyes, then another's were drawn to the grieving man, still standing like a rock, arms held tightly across his chest.

Vicky could hardly stand; she'd given it all she had, but she held on to Mannie with her good arm and watched the man watch her.

When the room was again silent, he said, "I heard tell this morning, at least, someone said, the Empress had sent the Butcher of some-place-or-another to blow us all away from orbit."

"The Butcher of Dresden made such a brag to me," Vicky admitted.

"Can you take him?"

"We blew away two of his battleships, but he slipped away from us," Vicky admitted. "We're counting on what you're making here to give us a better chance of nailing his hide the next time we see him."

The man nodded.

"Okay, Your Grace, I'll make what you and your Sailors need," he said.

"You want us to take you to the hospital now?" the manager asked.

"Don't you need me? Don't the gracious Grand Duchess here need me to make my machine dance? That's what my daughter called you, this morning when she told me she was going to slip away with some of her best friends to see you. See the gracious Grand Duchess."

He was crying now. Vicky wondered if he could even work his fabricator.

"I'll take your fab if I have to," the boss said. People on the floor made a show of cringing at the idea of the manager doing real work. Maybe they were joking. Maybe they weren't.

"Oh hell," the manager said, "I'll haul the union rep's ass out of his office and see what he can do to handle a dance or three with your jig."

"Haul me out, hell," a big fellow in a plaid shirt and jeans said as he headed for the man. "I'll cover your jig, Fryderyk. You go look after your daughter."

One of the guys with the bunny suits joined them, then hollered for the other one. They needed a bigger suit to cover the union rep.

Vicky prayed that Fryderyk would find his daughter among the living. There had been an awful lot of bodies down and not moving when they left.

"Now, if you'll excuse me," Mannie said, "I need to get our gracious Grand Duchess to the hospital herself before she keels over on me."

Vicky found she could not argue with Mannie. If she didn't walk out now, she might have to be carried out. Slowly, she turned and let the mayor and the spy help her from the stage.

At the bottom of the steps, the two newsies were waiting for her. A middle-aged reporter with a huge paunch and a young woman.

"You did very well, Your Grace," the guy said.

"Every market on this planet was carrying you live," the woman added.

"You're really much more newsworthy when you don't shrug out of your dress," the guy added, and got a swift jab in his big gut from his female associate.

"I told you not to say that to anyone but me," she growled at him.

"I live and learn," Vicky said. "Thank you for being here and getting the word out."

"Just part of our job," the woman answered, and they fell behind as Mannie and Mr. Smith moved Vicky along as quickly as she could pick her feet up and put them down.

"I deserved that," Vicky whispered to Mannie.

"As you said, you have lived and you have learned. Learned a lot, I might point out."

Vicky ignored the praise as she concentrated on not falling

on her face. She went from leaning on Mannie's arm to leaning her head on his shoulder. Somewhere in her stumbling walk to the rig, Mannie reached down, picked her up, and carried her.

Do I have to just about get myself killed to have this man hold me, Vicky thought, but she enjoyed just lying in his strong arms and resting her head on his shoulder.

Tenderly, he set her down in the rig, and buckled her in almost lovingly. Sadly, she felt so bad she couldn't enjoy the feel of his hands as he pulled the straps around her.

Halfway through the drive to the hospital, she passed out.

CHAPTER 42

MANNIE'S "You going to rejoin the living?" were the first words Vicky heard as she regained consciousness.

She opened her eyes to see a very worried mayor beside her bed. A cautious look around, careful not to move her head, told her the rest. "I'm in the hospital, right?"

"Got it in one," Mannie agreed as he leaned over and kissed her cheek.

Only after he sat back did Vicky's gaze take in the window behind him. There was blue sky out there. Daylight. "How long was I out?"

"Only a couple of hours. They managed to get a scan of your shoulder with you only moaning a bit. There's no permanent damage though they have started a lottery to see who gets to hang Mr. Smith from whatever delicate part of his anatomy is available for what he did to you."

"He got me in good enough shape to do what I had to do," Vicky managed to get out through parched lips. "Is there water anywhere around here?"

Mannie retrieved a small cup and straw from a table beside her bed and held it to her lips as he said, "That's what he said, and I couldn't disagree with him, or you."

Vicky allowed herself three sips before she tackled her next question. "About that guy, Fryderyk. Is his daughter here?"

Mannie shook his head, his eyes sad. "She was not one of the lucky ones who survived the bomb."

"Damn," was all Vicky could think to say.

"Twenty-two people died on that street. Eight of them were cops or Rangers. "

Vicky closed her eyes. "They got too close to me. What is it Kris Longknife says? 'Don't get too close to one of those damn Longknifes.' They got too close to a damn Peterwald."

"No one blames you, Vicky. Now there are a whole lot of people who want a piece of your stepmom's ass. While you were sleeping so peacefully . . ." Mannie smiled and seemed to lose his train of thought. "Do you know you look angelic when you're asleep?"

"I never had anyone who slept with me tell me that," Vicky admitted.

No reason not to let this delusional fool in on the evils of my past.

"Later we'll discuss this more. Anyway, while you were out cold, my deputy mayor called from home. We've passed a resolution to fund four Navy ships from Sevastopol's city budget. We'll support one of the battleships and heavy cruisers in orbit. We'll also foot the bill for converting two hulls into merchant cruisers. We'll make the lasers and gear at our own fabs."

"Keep the money close to home," Vicky noted.

"Why not? Charity—or defense—is always easier when it stays in your own backyard."

Vicky closed her eyes again and tried to think. Between the pounding in her head and the throbbing in her shoulder, it was kind of hard to keep any train of thought from going off the rails and taking a roll through the woods. "Any chance you could get some of the other cities to adopt part of the fleet?"

Mannie's grin got wide and so like a little boy's. "Kicv has already bought into another four." He glanced at his wrist unit. "Moskva should be voting on the same proposal anytime now. St. Pete is the only council dragging its feet. We may have to prop you up and run you by their talkfest on the way to the spaceport."

"What's their complaint?" Vicky asked, trying to get comfortable. That only ended up making her hurt worse. A nurse rushed in, gave the two of them a dirty look, then helped Vicky get pretty much back to the way she'd been lying before.

"Don't wreck all our good work," she scolded Vicky as she left.

"But my ass hurts," Vicky whispered, but only after the door swung shut.

"I would dearly love to make your ass feel better," Mannie said.

"You had your chance, lover boy, and you walked away from my ass," Vicky growled at him. "Did they give me pain meds?" she added, wondering how her tongue had gotten so loose around Mannie.

"Yes, they gave you a shot for the pain," Mannie said, "so today you can blame your loose ways on the drugs. And yes, I did blow a great chance to show you how nice I could make your ass feel, but those two midgets of yours scared the bejesus out of me. I was half-afraid they intended to jump in bed with us."

"No doubt they would have if you gave them half a wink."

"Oh."

"Scandalized?"

Mannie made a face, more terror than leer. Vicky had never seen quite that look on a man before. "You hear stories about the wicked ways of the capital. I know you're no reluctant virgin, but . . ." seemed to be the end of Mannie's thoughts.

"Dear mayor, I was never reluctant, even when I was a virgin, and yes, things can get very, *very* wicked around the palace though I hear that most people on Greenfeld lead very staid, normal lives."

"So, will I have to live your way," Mannie said, "or are you interested in living my way?"

"That is something we will have to talk about at length, once this rebellion is over and we have a chance to do something with the rest of our lives," Vicky said, then frowned.

"What were we talking about before I got confused?"

"Supporting the fleet?" Mannie said.

"Right. Now why is it taking St. Pete so long to decide to do what you nice people of Sevastopol are doing? What's the holdup?"

"Words," Mannie said. "Words, words, words, signifying something."

Vicky closed one eye and looked at Mannie hard. "I don't think my ears are working. You want to say that again."

"You heard me right. St. Pete doesn't mind adopting a battleship, they just don't want to pay for a battleship with a name like *Retribution*, *Merciless*, *Hunter*, or *Relentless*. They want to spend their money on something nice."

"Nice!" Vicky squeaked, and was immediately rewarded with a shooting pain behind her eyes.

"Yes, something like *Success*, *Prosperity*, *Defender*, or maybe *Enterprise*."

Vicky closed her eyes and did her best to slow her breathing. Maybe even the pounding of her heart. "Let me see if I get you. You want us to rename Imperial ships. You want to give the Empress all the opportunity she could want to go before my dad and tell him we're in full rebellion out here and renaming *his* warships."

"The Empress is renaming ships. Do you think renaming the *Merciless* to *Defender* is going to bend your dad all out of shape?"

Vicky took three seconds to show that she was seriously considering his question, then answered. "Why, ah, yes!" she could have said without thought. "And don't tell me that the Empress's renaming her ships is a precedent. I'll put my whole fortune up against a single pfennig that Dad knows nothing about his wife's renaming his ships."

"You're probably right," Mannie said. "Your dad doesn't just live in a bubble. She's got him in a concrete dungeon where he never sees the light of day."

Again Vicky found herself closing her eyes and thinking. Maybe thinking more about Dad than she ever had. "He was always in a bubble," she said slowly. "Nothing I've seen since I left the palace, first with the Navy, and now, running for my life, has been anything like what he bragged about to me of his world of business and power. The Empress and her family have only turned his bubble into a marble-and-gold prison that shows him exactly what he wants to hear. My dad is a blind fool," she said finally.

Mannie sat silently, listening as she spoke more to herself than to him. She took a deep breath and let the moment of introspection vanish away as she exhaled. "I think Kris Longknife would be . . . intrigued . . . that this fish has discovered water."

They would have a lot to talk about, her and that Ward-haven princess, if they lived long enough to cross paths again.

"However, Mannie," she said, coming back to the problem that might eat them alive just now, "we're walking on eggshells here. Anything we can avoid doing is something we shouldn't do."

"Even if we did something as innocent as rename the *Retribution* something like *Victory*?"

Vicky might have laughed if the very thought of it didn't bring pain to her skull. Instead, she took three deep breaths before going on. "I'll make you a deal. The minute our little rebellion is over and victorious, I'll rename that tub *Victory*, but not a minute before."

"Same for the others?"

"You tell them to pick the ship names they find offensive and make up a list of what they'd like to have them changed to. You run them by me, and I'll see what I can do. No Sailor worth his salt will want to serve on the *Posey*, but I'm willing to look at them. And the merchant cruiser conversions, they get to name them. They may have to crew them as well if they get too over the top on the names, but the conversions are theirs."

"I'll tell them they have to run those by you to get the Navy's approval," Mannie said. "Do you mind if I talk to St. Pete's mayor for a moment? This might save you a trip."

"Anything that keeps me out of the shooting gallery," Vicky said, and closed her eyes.

Her rear end really was tired of lying the way they had her. It seemed that all they were doing to keep weight off her shoulder was putting weight on her butt. She tried fidgeting a bit, then switching her weight from one side to the other. Her temper was rising with her pain. She was thinking of ordering up her guards and storming out of the place when a young doctor ducked into her room.

"How are we doing?" was the wrong opening.

She answered his question with a full broadside.

He didn't even flinch. "I could increase your pain meds," he offered.

"Mannie thinks I may have to arm wrestle your city government for a quartet of warships."

"Then I would suggest using your left arm," the doctor said with a disarmingly boyish grin.

"And the pain in my butt?"

The doctor strode up to the bed, and began his examination, checking her vitals with a glance at the readouts, then lifting an eyelid and staring deep into her eyes. Vicky returned the advance only to discover that the doctor had the most amazing blue eyes.

"It may be," he said distractedly as he continued his check of her head and shoulder, "that the pain in your rear is a distraction for the pain in your shoulder."

Vicky flinched as his gentle probing of her shoulder brought agony. "I'd say it's more competing with all the other pain for first place."

"I've been told that before," the doctor agreed, stepping back. He glanced at Mannie, who had just finished his phone call, then turned back to Vicky. "I'd like to keep you at least one night for observation, so I can medicate you enough to stop all those pains from getting together and singing a delightful four-part harmony. We really do need to stop the cycle of pain causing muscle spasms causing more pain. You can get well quickly and be done with the pain, or you can draw this out. Do you like pain?"

Vicky said a most unnoble word.

"I thought so. Well, you talk to the mayor here and see if I can have all the dances on your card tonight," the doctor said. Stepping back from the bed, he cast Mannie a dirty look.

"Don't scowl at me, Doc. I come bearing good news."

"I could use some," said Vicky.

"St. Pete has just voted to support two Navy ships and convert four merchant hulls to cruisers, assuming we can find four appropriate hulls. They also upped the ante and said they'd pay for one-quarter of *Retribution*'s upkeep, assuming you promise to rename it *Victory* as soon as you think it is politically doable."

"Tell them they have a deal if it lets the good doctor fill me full of joy juice for the night."

"I hope you won't mind, but I accepted their proposal on your part."

Vicky studied Mannie through narrowing eyes. "You starting to think you can speak for me?" came out sounding dangerous. Vicky liked the sound of it.

"This one time, with you flirting with the good doctor here,

I thought I might overstep my boundaries and do what I thought you'd do yourself."

Vicky took a deep breath and let it out with a sigh. "I guess I can give you a pass this one time, but don't make a habit of it. I make a habit of never ever being predicable. Now, Doc, give me one more call to clear my dance card, and I'll take those shots. Computer, get me Admiral von Mittleburg."

"Von Mittleburg," came in a second.

"Have you heard about my latest misadventure?"

"From your arrival to the boom to your giving quite a speech, you all bandaged up and covered with blood. How much of that was yours?"

"More than usual," Vicky said sourly, "but still way too much from other people."

"It always is."

"So, I've got a doctor down here who wants to keep me for observation tonight and float me with joy juice to stop the pain. I'm not averse to either. Do you need me topside?"

Vicky was surprised by the long pause that followed.

"Are you safe?" the admiral finally said.

"The hospital hasn't blown up while I've been here."

"We've made this place secure," Mannie put in.

"Would you mind if I added a company of Marines?" the admiral countered.

Mannie sighed. "The last time I went out of Her Grace's room, I was tripping over police and Rangers every step I took."

"I'd prefer you were walking on cops, Rangers, and Marines for every step you took."

"Send down the Marines," Vicky said, putting an end to this testosterone-driven "mine's bigger than yours" contest.

"They're already on their way," the admiral said. "I'm also fielding a lot of requests for merchant hulls to convert to cruisers from folks dirtside. You know anything about this?"

Vicky quickly filled him in on what Mannie seemed to have pulled off.

"So, the more blood you show on camera, the more fleet I get."

"It seems that way."

"Don't get me wrong, I like the ships, but we need you. Be careful about that blood thing."

"You say the nicest things, Admiral. I will do my best to keep my blood off my clothes and inside me, where it belongs."

"You do that, Your Grace. Now let that doctor give you a shot and call me when you wake up, assuming you're in a better mood."

"Will do."

The doc already had a syringe waiting. He glanced at her, Vicky nodded, and he added it to her drip with a "Sweet dreams." He stood there for a long moment.

"Don't you have someplace to be? Some things to do?" she asked Mannie.

"Nope. I'm going to be right here by you."

"There's a couch over there," the doctor said, pointing, "that's good to sleep on."

"You get some rest," Vicky said through a yawn. "It sure looks like I will."

"I'll be right here with you."

"And here I figured the first night we spent together would be so much more fun than this."

"I'll make up for it next time."

"Promises, promises," Vicky said, but her eyelids were drooping. Mannie took her left hand and began making nice circles with his thumb on it. "Nice," she said, but that was all she got out.

CHAPTER 43

VICKY came awake feeling almost decent. She wondered how long that would last and did her best not to move anything.

She opened her eyes to daylight and Mannie. He was asleep in the chair beside her bed, his hand still on hers. For a moment, Vicky allowed herself to consider what it would be like to wake up next to this fellow every day for the rest of her life.

It would be a change.

A change like the Empire needs?

Maybe one of many, she concluded.

A nurse came in silently. Vicky risked cracking a smile.

"We thought you were awake," he whispered. "The breakfast cart just arrived. You hungry?"

"Starving. You got steak and eggs on that cart?"

"Scrambled eggs and some nice Jell-O."

"Torture," Vicky spat through a grin.

"So I've been told. Are you up for company?"

"It depends on who."

"Cute gal. Pint size but, ah . . ."

"Deadly," Vicky provided.

"Might be."

"She is, trust me. Kit, you out there?" Vicky called, raising the volume of her whisper but hopefully not enough to wake Mannie.

Kit appeared at the door. "Are you okay, Your Grace?"

"Thanks to a lot of you, my stepmother has once again failed to remove me from the line of succession."

"Someone should remove her," the assassin growled.

"She's not in the line of succession. Only her newborn son."

"Him, too," Kit growled.

"Now, now," Vicky said, "we've got to be better than her."

"I assure you, I am better at killing than her hired flunkies."

"Are we discussing strategy, policy, or just gossiping?" Mannie asked.

"So, you are going to join the living," Vicky said, echoing Mannie's own words.

"It seems like I must."

"Good nurse, do you have two of those abominable breakfasts?" Vicky asked.

"I think it can be arranged," the nurse said, and disappeared.

"How is Kat?" Vicky asked.

"Good," Kit answered. "Well, more like embarrassed. We want our scars in the front. She'll have a hard time explaining that one to any good guard type she lets pet her rear."

"Maybe we can find a good plastic surgeon," Vicky suggested.

"And hide that nice scar? How can she brag about taking a hit for you, Your Grace, if you make it disappear? Now she'll be dropping her pants every chance she gets."

"No doubt," Vicky admitted.

"You want to see my scars?" Kit said, leering at Mannie.

"Maybe when we're at the beach, and you gals are in skimpy bikinis," the mayor allowed.

Kit shook her head. "Where did you find this man?" she asked Vicky.

"He found me," Vicky allowed.

"Toss him back. He's no fun."

Vicky looked at Mannie and found herself smiling fondly. "No way. It took me forever to find a man like him."

Mannie actually looked surprised by her answer. He settled back in his chair and proceeded to mull her words for a bit. She got a squeeze to her hand a moment later.

Vicky squeezed back.

"Admiral von Mittleburg asks if you are awake," her computer said.

"Admiral, I am among the living," Vicky allowed. The nurse entered with two breakfast plates. Vicky made a face. Her plate had a lot less food on it than Mannie's. "Though I may starve to death on the chow they're giving me."

"Doctor's orders," the nurse said cheerfully, and bustled about, setting the tray on a table and rolling it over in front of Vicky. Mannie winked at Vicky, seeming to promise her some of the steak, eggs, and potatoes on his plate.

"Your, or Admiral Krätz's idea, of swing ships along a beam works. We hardly had the old light cruisers *Halum* and *Ferwert* anchored fifty thousand klicks back from the jump when some longboat poked its nose through. They blew it away. Only a few moments ago, I learned that a destroyer had tried the same and been hit so hard it's now rolling dead in space."

"So the Butcher is getting no reports on what we're doing?" Vicky asked.

"None."

Vicky thought about that for a long moment, then asked her own question. "What's taking him so long? Why hasn't he come charging through the jump? I know I would have."

"You would not have lost two battleships, then run away from the fight on the cruiser you were hiding your, ah, excuse me. Hiding in."

"No, I would not have run away from a fight," Vicky said with determination.

"But he did, and that's no way to impress Navy officers, even those with machine guns at their heads. I imagine there's a lot of talk going around that fleet about how and when to fight the next battle, and your poor Butcher is finding it hard to persuade everyone to do his bidding."

Mannie looked perplexed. "He's got machine guns aimed at their heads?"

"Yes. That worked for him the first time," the admiral answered. "Now, imagine you're holding that machine gun at some admiral's head. Also imagine you lost a lot of friends who held machine guns at the heads of the officers Vicky and company blew away. Are you sure you want to do no different than they did? Even thugs with machine guns want to live long enough to spend their paychecks."

"Right," Mannie said.

"I listen to my Navy officers," Vicky said. "He shouted at his, then ran away when he got them in a mess. That doesn't encourage anyone to follow him the next time."

"Yes, Your Grace," the admiral said. "Now, how are you coming along? I admit that I'm torn. If you're down there when the Butcher sticks his nose through the jump, I get to fight my battle with you safe on the ground. No doubt, Admiral Lütz would like that."

"No doubt," Vicky said sourly.

"Yes," the admiral said quite firmly.

"Any idea when our frightened bunny rabbit will bring his twitching nose through our jump?" Mannie asked.

"None whatsoever. You want to have Our Grace wave her bloody shirt some more?"

Mannie made a face, half worry, half regret, all pain. "I think I can persuade our mayors to skip parading Her Grace around the planet. This last hit was a bitter surprise to us."

"I wanted to open trade," Vicky said. "But now you never can tell what my stepmom will have hidden among the next cargo."

"Sadly, true," Mannie agreed.

"Are you suggesting that I take her up here and get her out of your hair?" Admiral von Mittleburg asked.

"As much as I love her smiling company, I'm afraid I am," Mannie said.

Vicky allowed herself a plaintive sigh. "Visit me often?"

"You know I will, but you know it won't be as often as either of us want."

Vicky's sigh this time was resigned.

"Get me some clothes," she said. "I can recuperate on the station as well as I can here, and maybe on the station, I can use my pull to get some decent food."

"No doubt our doctors will consider your rank when they fill out your meal card," the admiral said.

"In a pig's eye," Vicky allowed, to much laughter. None of it was hers.

CHAPTER 44

───

VICKY found her mind wandering as the shuttle took her up to the station. She had a problem. *How do I stop a whole lot of warships, way more than I have in my fleet?*

Was the Butcher really prepared to slag a planet as well developed as St. Petersburg? Especially with all the empty planets out farther in the sector that could use its production?

The Empress's family was crazy, but where money was concerned, they weren't stupid. Or wasteful.

Vicky continued thinking and was ready to stand as an equal with her admirals by the time she landed on High St. Petersburg. Bandages and all, she marched into Admiral von Mittleburg's day quarters.

No surprise, both admirals were there.

After a few moments spent inquiring on how she was feeling, the admirals seemed to expect her to sit in a corner and tend to her knitting.

"You mentioned yesterday that you were getting a whole lot of merchant ships being offered for arming as merchant cruisers."

Von Mittleburg seemed surprised she remembered. Vice Admiral Lüth certainly was.

"Yes, we're up to twenty-three ships, Your Grace. I don't know where we'll get enough lasers to arm them. Not in the time the Empress will grant us."

"No doubt," Lüth agreed.

"So we don't put lasers on them," Vicky said.

"What do we arm them with?" both admirals asked in two-part harmony.

"Rockets," Vicky said. "I remember reading something about rockets in Kris Longknife's file. Have either of you looked at her file?"

Von Mittleburg shook his head. Admiral Lüth looked like he'd swallowed something poisonous. "I know nothing about that Wardhaven princess except what I occasionally hear in the media. None of it is good."

"Well, I did pay good money to get a copy of her file. It seems she managed to blow away six of our largest battleships," Vicky pointed out, "with only twelve mosquito boats, a pair of destroyers, and whatever armed civilian ships she could lay her hands on or load up with what weapons she could beg, steal, or borrow. It was quite an accomplishment."

"It was never proven that those were our battleships," Admiral Lüth said sternly.

"Kris Longknife knows, and I know, who those ships came from, and you likely know in your heart of hearts why there are so many empty seats at Academy reunions the last few years."

Vicky waved off any further discussion. "What is important to our situation is what Kris Longknife managed to lay her hands on. She loaded several freighters full of obsolete Army rockets and used them to, ah, what is the word?"

"Swarm," her computer supplied.

"Right, swarm those battleships' defenses. Admirals, do your battleships, cruisers, and destroyers have antimatter torpedoes?"

"Yes, but you can't use them for much of anything," Admiral Lüth pointed out. "Any warship worth its salt has secondary batteries to swat such torpedoes before they can do any damage. However, if a ship is seriously damaged, you can use them to finish it off if its captain won't surrender."

"That's not going to be our problem. We need to slam those

ships and slam them good. We need our torpedoes to do serious damage."

"That's impossible," Vice Admiral Lüth growled.

"What do you have in mind?" Rear Admiral von Mittleburg asked. And drew a dirty look from the senior admiral. If this kept up, Vicky might end up using her Grand Duchess card to have them swap jobs.

"First, computer, can you come up with some evasion plans that push our antimatter torpedoes to the maximum of their capabilities?"

"Yes, Your Grace."

"Please begin calculating at least six of them immediately."

"Processing."

"Now, Admiral von Mittleburg, how many of those merchant ships can you arm?"

"Maybe half of them, Your Grace. We were already working on arming several liners. They make much more capable warships than the freighters. Not quite as good as a light cruiser, but not all that much below them."

"And the rest?" Vicky asked.

The admiral shrugged. "We might turn some into raiders. The Empress's pirates have been raising Cain with our trade. Why shouldn't we issue a few letters of marque and see how they like it when the shoe's on the other foot?"

"A good idea," Vicky said, "but not this week. On the way up here, I had my computer search through some easy-to-build rockets with guidance systems that could be made from phones or game units. It found a few good ones. Computer, retrieve the rockets."

Several rocket designs appeared on the nearest wall screen. "They're fairly easy to build. The solid rocket motors can be poured to form and will allow for some hard acceleration. They can't maneuver quite as hard as a standard Navy torpedo, but the aluminum powder in the fuel leaves an interesting smoke screen, making it easier for your smart rockets to home on the last known location of a target and only become a target when it breaks out of the smoke."

"You can't be serious?" Lüth demanded.

"I think she is," von Mittleburg said, rubbing his chin thoughtfully. "I think she very definitely is."

"We've got eight battleships. At last count, they had nine. Likely more by now. They outnumber us in cruisers and destroyers. We need something to give us an edge. Why not?"

"Because that plan is crazy," Vice Admiral Lüth snapped.

"I do see some weakness," Rear Admiral von Mittleburg said. "A merchant ship is no speedster, Your Grace. How will these swarm ships keep up with the fleet?"

"Here is where I hope to get help," Vicky said.

"And your head examined," Lüth suggested. "Both of you."

Vicky and von Mittleburg exchanged glances that went right by Lüth.

"Merchant ships are usually heavily loaded," Vicky said. "No owner wants to carry a lot of unused space around."

"Right," von Mittleburg said.

"So we don't load the ship up anywhere close to its full load. Better yet, we whack off the bow, forward of the bridge, and only load rockets in the aft holds."

"Cut them almost in half?" Admiral von Mittleburg sounded incredulous.

"We park the bows trailing the station and the owners can weld them back together once things are back to normal. For now, we save hull weight we don't need and only load the top half of the aft holds, not the bottom."

"One-quarter of what they normally carry, huh?"

"Something like that. We can do the hull separation in a slip and load as many rockets as St. Petersburg can ship up. We push through as many ships as we possibly can as fast as we can."

Vice Admiral Lüth put his foot down, firmly. "I will not risk my battle squadron around anything so crazy as this idea."

"Then I won't ask you to," Vicky said, bringing herself up to full Grand Duchess. "Admiral von Mittleburg, you may assume command of the St. Petersburg Reserve Battle Fleet. Admiral Lüth, you may assume command of the High St. Petersburg Station."

"You can't do that," was Admiral Lüth's sharp reply.

"Admiral Lüth, the Navy has charged me with raising this rebellion. They trusted me to decide what is and is not a manageable risk. I find your attitude toward the risks involved here way out of line. I'm offering you a place in our movement more in keeping with your tastes."

"You can't do this," he repeated, only this time he was shouting. "I command Battle Squadron 22. Those are *my* ships."

"No, sir, they are not. You received them from the hand of my father, the Emperor. Rather than surrender them when the Empress demanded it of you, you brought them to me, Grand Duchess Victoria of Greenfeld. Now I find that the rebellion is better served by their being led by Admiral von Mittleburg."

"We'll see about that."

"Commander Boch," Vicky said almost softly. All deadly.

"Yes, Your Grace."

"You will call the Marine guards from outside, and you will escort Admiral Lüth to the brig. There you will see that he is comfortably detained while he awaits my pleasure. He will have no visitors. Understood?"

It finally dawned on Vice Admiral Lüth that Vicky meant exactly what she was saying and was about to do exactly what she said she would.

"Heinrich," he said, pleading with Admiral von Mittleburg.

"Albert, it is not a bad plan she has come up with even if it is likely borrowed from that whore Kris Longknife."

"But she's just a girl," Lüth half shouted, scowling at Vicky.

"That is wrong in so many ways," von Mittleburg said, shaking his head. "Albert, it is better that you quit while you are behind. Commander, see to it that he is made comfortable."

"Yes, sir," Commander Boch said. "This way, sir."

The vice admiral was still muttering under his breath as the commander led him out.

Vicky waited until the door was closed, then turned to Heinrich. "Did I do wrong there?"

Admiral von Mittleburg worried his lower lip. "You did what you had to do. Albert is a good man under normal conditions. What we have here is nothing like normal. You have imagination. Likely more than any of us old men who have come up doing what was done by those who came before us. I like your idea. We will have to work on it a bit."

"No doubt. I'm looking forward to your suggestions."

"For now, we will have to delay refining your idea. It seems that I must go advise a chief of staff that he is now working for me and not Albert."

"Will that be a problem?"

"I do not know. Once you choose to join a rebellion, all the normal things that hold military discipline in place are strained. No doubt, your relieving their commanding admiral will add to that strain. However, you have shown yourself to be a competent leader and that you can learn from others. Captain Bolesław has seen to it that that word got around the station. I think this will work. We will see. You might consider an all hands address to the battleships' crews tomorrow morning."

"I'll give serious consideration to that."

"Now, Your Grace, if you will retire to your own quarters, I will see to what needs to be done here."

Vicky had only Kit and Mr. Smith to get her back to her quarters aboard *Retribution*. She noticed that Captain Bolesław had already doubled the guard at the gangway and in the passageway outside both their quarters.

Vicky stepped inside, intent on spending the rest of the day looking into how to improve her swarm boats and what she might say to the battleship Sailors the next day.

CHAPTER 45

I T wasn't long before Vicky began getting a steady stream of visitors intent on helping her improve on her crazy idea. It seemed that Admiral von Mittleburg kept it about as secret as an erupting volcano.

Captain Bolesław was the first to drop by and begin talking about the idea as if it were his to begin with.

"Where'd you hear about this?" Vicky got out, as much surprised as startled.

"It's not often one hears of a vice admiral being hauled off to the brig. I dropped by to see if he needed anything, and he wouldn't stop shooting off his mouth about your "insane, stupid ideas" long enough to let me know if I could get him something. I don't think the man noticed when I left, he was so intent on yelling at the bulkheads and overhead of your many deficiencies as an officer and a Peterwald."

"So my relieving him is no secret," Vicky said with a sigh.

"Not by an old-fashioned mile. But I have to tell you, you couldn't have picked a better flag officer to test your newfound powers on."

"Huh?"

"Albert is known around the fleet as the showcase of the

brown-nosing, narrow-minded types that have been promoted to flag rank of late."

"Like captain what's-his-name that had the *Retribution* before you?"

"He would have finished his career with four stars whereas yours truly would have retired after the joy of commanding a heavy cruiser."

"You enjoying a battleship command?"

"Greatest fun I've had with my clothes on if you'll excuse the phrase, Your Grace."

"Excused," Vicky said with a smile.

"Only thing that could make it better is to be shut of some of the crazy passengers I have to chauffeur around the Empire."

"Sorry, you're not getting out of that job. When we sortie to take down the Butcher of Dresden, I'm going right along with you."

"No doubt. Now, about this crazy, insane idea of yours."

Vicky filled him in on the details. He called in a pair of his officers and a chief.

The senior, a commander, listened, then seemed to knock the whole idea down better than Admiral Lüth had. "Do we really want to be sharing space with a bunch of whacked-off merchies who can't steer straight? Why not hang those rocket launchers off our cruisers and battleships? That way, we'd for sure have them right where we want them when we launched our good torpedoes."

Vicky turned to Captain Bolesław, none too sure she hadn't been bested.

He considered the idea for a long moment, then shook his head—and Vicky started breathing again.

"No, Hyman, not a good idea. Do we really want all that propellant and those explosives dangling off our ice armor when the Butcher's battlewagons start popping off? I don't see lasers and rockets mixing at all well. If we got one huge explosion just outside our armor, it might dish in our hull all the way to the central ladder."

"Right," the commander said, rather sheepish.

"But keep thinking, folks," Vicky said. "I much prefer solving our problems before they start eating us alive."

That got her a "Yes, Your Grace," all around, and the designers Captain Bolesław had provided quickly knocked out a set of preliminary sketches.

The officers might have gold-plated the design, but the chief would politely get an elbow in their face with a, "Begging the officer's pardon, but I think the Grand Duchess here wants us to Sailor proof it as much as we can, sir, and that's going to just clog up the works."

"And slow down production and jack up the costs," Vicky would add every time.

It got to where one officer would finish the chief's sentence for him before he'd gotten much more than, "Begging the officer's pardon." Then the other would finish with Vicky's line.

They got quite good at mimicking the two of them before they had something like a final design.

Then Vicky got Mannie on the line, who extended the call to include some engineers and production people. Before she went to bed, a small fab had already turned out the first rocket and test-fired it. More followed the test article as production ramped up at several different fabs on St. Petersburg.

Admiral von Mittleburg himself dropped in late in the afternoon, saw what was going on, and gave it his blessing. "If only Albert could see this."

"You want to invite him over?" Vicky asked.

He was shaking his head before she finished. "I dropped in to see the vice admiral. They have a Gunny on watch to see that things don't go sideways. I was told he hadn't stopped shouting, except to demand a glass of water, since he arrived in the brig. He didn't stop shouting the whole five minutes I tried to visit him. If the fellow doesn't calm down, he's going to give himself an aneurism."

Vicky winced. "I'd hate to have that on my conscience."

"You needn't worry too much about him. I couldn't find a single man on his staff or flagship who wasn't glad to see him crash and burn. He's a stickler for details and cuts no one an inch of slack . . . except himself. What I did find out was that neither the Navy nor the Empress had any room for him. The Navy told him it was the beach for him once his ships were gone, and the Empress's folks wanted nothing to do with him. They just wanted his battleships. Hard to believe that bunch would pass up an experienced ship commander."

"So his only future involved bringing his ships to me," Vicky said.

"Something like that. The skipper of his flag, the *Implacable*, said he was really hot to trot for them all to come over to your side. There are a lot of officers over there who still aren't sure they chose the right side."

"Oh," Vicky said. "So the thought that was growing in my mind that you had done a great job of solving one of my problems has a whole new problem following on its heels."

"Yep, Your Grace, you need to sell this rebellion to a whole lot of Sailors and officers who are none too interested in buying in."

Vicky sighed through tight lips. "If you sailormen have this insanely crazy idea of mine well in hand, I think I will start thinking about just the right words to bring some more hands on board."

"And I need to start hacking the bows off freighters and turning them into boats that can carry your rockets right alongside the battle line," Admiral von Mittleburg said.

"Tomorrow will be another busy day," Vicky said.

CHAPTER 46

N EXT morning, the chief bosun's mate of *Retribution* piped his ancient tune, then added, "Now hear this, now hear this, all hands, this is the Grand Duchess speaking."

Ensign Vicky Peterwald had heard other people piped: captains, admirals. She'd never expected her own words to be piped to all hands. Never had she felt so much the rebel.

She stood before the microphone. Her words would be transmitted not just to the four battleships of BatRon 22 but also to the other two battleships that had come out with them. At the last minute, Admiral von Mittleburg extended the hookup to include all the cruisers and destroyers that had just joined them on St. Petersburg.

Then he shrugged. "We might as well pipe your message to all ships in the system. If we don't, scuttlebutt will, and get it all wrong in the process."

"I agree," Vicky said. Having relieved a vice admiral, she was not about to disagree with the only admiral she had left.

She suppressed a smile. *Take that, Kris Longknife. You relieved your skipper in your first battle, a mere commander. I've relieved a vice admiral.*

Vicky trembled inside at what she'd done.

Vicky did not dare tremble on the outside just now. She did not clear her throat, or tap the mic, things she had heard captains do that did not impress the listeners.

"Sailors, Marines, and officers of the St. Petersburg Division of the Greenfeld Imperial Navy Reserve, our time has come to stand with my father, the Emperor." There, she'd gotten it all out in the open in her first breath.

"We stand together, against the usurper, committed to defending every man, woman, and child on the planet below. The blackhearted Empress has sent the self-proclaimed Butcher of Dresden. He bragged to me personally that he and his battleships will slag St. Petersburg down to bare bedrock.

"We. Must. Not. Let. Him. Do. That," Vicky said, forging her words with deadly calm.

"You may have heard that we are outnumbered. But remember, Captain Bolesław of *Retribution* fought two of the Butcher's battleships. They are now atoms in the cold of space. The *Retribution* will be joining us in a few days after the High St. Petersburg docks finish patching her up and making her even more deadly.

"The Butcher of Dresden knows how to slaughter unarmed civilians. He doesn't do so well when he goes up against experienced Sailors who know how to use the lasers they've trained with."

Vicky paused for a moment, then added, "Besides your own ships, we are forging some surprises for the Butcher. Even as I speak to you, fabs on the planet below are turning out weapons that the Butcher knows nothing about—weapons that will give us the edge he only imagines that he has. He sits in a cold, lonely system, one jump out from St. Petersburg. He sits, burning reaction mass, adding wear and tear on equipment, growing weaker.

"We orbit a planet that is making us stronger every minute he delays. He is in for a very deadly surprise."

Now Vicky took a deep breath. "I want to finish on the same note I started. We are the loyal servants of my father, the Emperor. We serve Greenfeld, not the grasping, greedy blackhearted Empress and her family, who have bled our Empire, sucked its lifeblood, and stolen everything that they haven't destroyed. The Empress has tried to assassinate me so many times I've lost count. I'm still here.

"She tried to take down St. Petersburg twice, and she missed both times. Now she's trying for the planet below us one more time. I say three strikes, and she's out. Stand with me as she swings and misses one more time. Then we'll all send her packing with the pack of dogs that passes for her relatives. There is no room for them in our Greenfeld."

Around Vicky, on the bridge of *Retribution*, there was applause, cheers, and even a few loud whistles. She noticed that the mic was still live, carrying that encouragement out to her fleet.

Captain Bolesław was standing next to the comm officer. Likely it was his job to see that this unusual behavior on his bridge got transmitted. Then the chief of the comm watch lit up in a wide smile, and, making a fist, raised his right hand in the air.

Captain Bolesław pointed at the chief, and he twisted some dials. Suddenly, the bridge was filled with more clapping and shouting.

Vicky's eyebrows raised with a question.

"Ours isn't the only live mic. That's coming from the bridges and mess decks of all the ships in your fleet. I definitely think you have them."

Vicky blew out a breath she didn't know she was holding. She just managed to stumble her way to her station chair next to the captain's.

She'd talked several ships into coming over to her side. With any luck, the Butcher of Dresden would not surprise her in the worst moment of the coming battle by talking any of her own ships over to his side.

Vicky crossed her fingers and sent up a silent prayer to whoever it was that granted people like her luck. She was going to need a whole lot more than her misspent youth had earned. But from the sound of things just now, she might be getting it anyway.

CHAPTER 47

═══

B Y that afternoon, Vicky was invited to rechristen the *Silver Flyer* and the *Diamond Flyer*, freighters of the High Flyer Lines. When they sailed next, they would be the Imperial rocket boats *Gnat* and *Spider*. There was no busting of a bottle of champagne on the now-missing nose of the former cargo hauler though Vicky did spill a half glass of the liquid on the deck plates of what now passed for a quarterdeck.

She got a tour of the *Gnat*.

"Our fire control system is pretty basic," the skipper of the *Gnat* told her as he guided her through his truncated ship. He had been the skipper of the *Silver Flyer*. "We plan to get a firing solution tight beamed over from the nearest battleship and slave our rockets to their attack. We have jacked up the minimal optical and radar sensing gear we had as a freighter with some stuff we knocked together from ships on the Middle Sea. We're binding it all together with computers pulled out of gaming consoles if you can believe that. However, if worse comes to worst, and we lose our link with the battleship we're working with, we can still launch some sort of attack on our own."

Commander Boch shook his head in dismay, but he said nothing against it until he and Vicky were alone. "These guys have a whole new brand of courage, to go into battle on something as clapped together as those things."

"It may save the Navy's bacon," Vicky said.

"Yeah," he agreed. "We've come to the point where the Navy has cobbled together rockets and patched them into a weapons system with fishing gear and kids' gaming stuff. My dad was an admiral, like his dad before him, and they'd both be laughing their fool heads off if they knew their kid was going into battle holding his breath for support like this."

"A win is a win, no matter how you get it," Vicky pointed out.

The commander just shook his head.

A tour of the engine room got her a briefing on how they expected to get extra speed out of the old cargo hauler. "We're taking on the best reaction mass the station can give us. They're hauling up water from St. Petersburg to give us as much oxygen in our reaction mass as possible. There's even some nitrogen in the mix. I figure we can boost the old girl with a bit of the heavy stuff if we got to punch it to keep up with those battlewagons. They're also out there welding an extra half meter to lengthen our six rocket engines. With any luck, keeping the plasma in the bell for a few extra nanoseconds will give us that extra push."

The chief engineer seemed happy with his prospects.

The commander turned to the captain who'd let the plasma jockey handle this show. "Can your *Gnat* take three gees?"

Vicky found herself holding her breath, something she seemed to be doing a lot of lately. The answer to this question might make or break her "crazy, insane" idea.

"Don't you worry, sonny, you don't need to teach this old granny how to suck eggs," said the former merchant skipper, now wearing an Imperial Greenfeld Navy green shipsuit. "The first thing I asked for was some testing equipment to go over my hull strength members. We'll make sure we don't have any bum welds and see exactly how thick they are, what they can bear. I got engineers going over the results of those tests even as we speak. They'll have all the bad welding spots fixed before we move over to the fitting out pier in a couple of hours.

"If that ain't enough to keep you and me happy, they're bringing in reinforcing strakes to buck up the old girl. She'll be pulling gees like her old owner never intended me to, and she'll be dancing just fine with your big war wagons. Don't you worry none."

To Vicky's surprise, the commander did look much less worried.

"No worry, Navy, we've thought of the stuff you have and a couple more besides. We'll do our job. We won't let the Grand Duchess down. You just make sure the Navy gets its shit together."

The commander allowed himself a chuckle at that. The skipper and the chief engineer of this bucket of kludged-together bolts joined in.

The rest of the tour went quite well.

Vicky was invited to Admiral von Mittleburg's wardroom for lunch. She found him surrounded by a dozen captains, Captain Bolesław among them. He was in the middle of how they had talked Engle Rachinsky into switching sides by a combination of good shooting and Vicky's words.

At Vicky's entrance, the conversation died as all eyes turned to her. The old her would have licked up the attention. Now, she would have preferred to find her seat quietly and listen to Alîs tell the tale and observe the captains' reaction to it.

"I assure you," she said, as she took her seat next to the admiral's vacant chair at the head of the table, "Engle's changing sides had a lot more to do with Captain Bolesław's cagey shooting than anything I said."

"A Peterwald giving credit where it's due," one captain said. "Now I can die. I've seen everything."

"Be nice to our gracious Grand Duchess," Captain Bolesław said. "I've sailed with her, and you can bet your last gold mark that we'd all be in a pickle if we didn't have her. She's one unique woman."

Vicky found herself blushing at the look he gave her.

She never would have believed it was possible for anything to make her blush.

Before she could stammer anything in reply, someone shouted "Atten hut," and chairs scraped as the officers got to their feet.

"As you were," from Admiral von Mittleburg stopped the movement before anyone could rise. The admiral quickly strode to his chair, spread a linen napkin in his lap, and told the chief steward's mate at the door to begin serving.

"Unfortunately, it's goulash again, but there is plenty of it."

"Can't we get anything better out of that planet?" one

captain said. "God knows, we're all that stands between it and their being lased to dust."

"That planet is all that stands between starvation and cannibalism for several planets in this neighborhood," Admiral von Mittleburg said. "That includes the one that is shipping us crystal. Have you all read my report on how this economic crash was created?"

The officers nodded.

"Then you know that we're all riding a thin margin. I'll settle for goulash if that planet below us also ships me up the weapons and gear we need to patch up our fleet. Captain"— now he studied with hawk eyes the officer who wanted better fare—"how long has it been since your *Relentless* had a serious yard period?"

"Not counting the one we just had here, four years, sir."

"Right. Every one of our ships has gotten some serious yard time, thanks to the equipment that planet turned out, using the fabs that the Navy helped them ship in from places like Metzburg and Brunswick. We wash their hands, they wash ours."

Steward's mates began placing bowls of goulash before the officers. "Enjoy it, gentlemen, there are a whole lot of people only a few jumps away that would gladly have a few spoonfuls of what we have today."

There were no more remarks on the table the admiral set as the officers turned to and made the food disappear. Only when the last of the goulash had been chased by the last of the delicious brown bread did the admiral pat his lips with his napkin and lay it on the table.

"Grand Duchess, gentlemen, I didn't call you here to discuss my table. We have a problem. No doubt, any of you could list me a dozen problems we have, but I am concerned now with only one of them."

The captains listened silently.

"The Grand Duchess here has come up with an idea that may give us an edge in the coming battle. Your Grace, I am told you were given a tour of the newly commissioned *Gnat*."

"Yes, I was. The captain demonstrated several ways they had improved upon my simple idea, far beyond the basics I thought of. Commander, your thoughts?"

The commander quickly briefed them on the backup fire

control, the tweaks being made to the engines to get them extra acceleration, and the reinforcement of the hull. "I think the former merchant captain has a good team of engineers and technicians doing everything possible to make that ship a decent war fighter."

"Good," the admiral said. "Now, how do we fight such a sawed-off runt of a ship? It brings rockets to the battle that may serve as a distraction. They may even make a few hits. Who can guess how the ships of the Empress will do against a swarm attack? But, having a ship is not the same as fighting a ship. What doctrine do we use? What fleet evolutions will allow those ships to support the battle line? Gentlemen, the Grand Duchess needs ideas. I expect us to give her those ideas before suppertime. You will earn your goulash tonight."

The last was delivered with a smile and met with groans from the captains, but, as one, they turned to with a will, forming themselves into four groups.

Vicky watched as the severe, white bulkheads of the wardroom turned into screens. Each group gathered around one of the screens and began to operate it as if it were a battle board. Ships formed into lines and swept across virtual space, doing battle with each other.

First they tried one way, then another. Admiral von Mittleburg offered Vicky his arm and guided her from one group to the next. They said nothing, only observed. The officers said nothing to them but went about their business.

Vicky watched silently as some of the more oddball ideas were tried and found wanting. Gradually, as the battles repeated themselves, the formations the four different groups used became more and more alike.

Admiral von Mittleburg nodded. Soft, "good, good," became his comment to all four groups.

An hour before the supper goulash was due, the four groups had three different formations. Now two took the role of the Butcher and formed the ships they knew he had into a standard attack formation as taught at the Imperial War College outside Anholt in the shadow of the palace.

The other two formed up the ships they had in orbit above St. Petersburg and swept them out to swing around the moon and take the Butcher under attack as quickly as they could.

They did well—sometimes.

Other times, things went sideways in a hurry.

"We need to do better," Admiral von Mittleburg said firmly. "What was it that made things go so well?"

"Luck?" a doubting Thomas suggested.

"The way we held the rocket boats in close to the battleships," Captain Bolesław offered tentatively.

"I think so," the admiral said.

"But what if they break down, or suffer a casualty and ram my battleship?" one captain said.

"They are doing all they can to become a reliable part of our battle array," Vicky said. "It seems untrusting of us to assume they will not hold up their part of the battle plan."

"No battle plan survives contact with the enemy," one captain offered Vicky.

"No doubt this one won't survive any better than the rest," Admiral von Mittleburg said, then turned his agreement around. "Still, there is no reason not to make the battle plan as good as we can make it. Let's assume our truncated little boys can bear up under the burden of what we need if we are to win."

Vicky watched as the whole collection of captains took a deep breath.

"We are betting the entire effort to save the Empire on this battle," she said, careful to avoid the word "rebellion." "Let us assume that every ship and every man will strive to do his utmost for his future and that of the Empire."

On that, they returned to their chairs at the table and partook of yet another bowl of goulash. This one, at least, had lamb for its base. Vicky was not the only one getting tired of beef.

CHAPTER 48

═══════

FOR the next week, the High St. Petersburg shipyard maintained a frantic pace. *Retribution* and *Slinger* were no sooner clear of space docks than the newly arrived *Ravager* and *Trouncer* slipped into their vacated spots. Both were new 18-inch battleships and should have been in good shape. Remarkably, both had had no yardwork done in the last four years.

"I still have a page's worth of discrepancies I made up on builders trials that no one's looked at," one skipper told Admiral von Mittleburg. The fabs down on St. Petersburg had gotten a long list of gear that needed repair or replacement. They'd been working on it for a week. Much of what was needed was already waiting at the space docks.

But time was what they needed most.

How much time would the Butcher of Dresden give them?

Vicky wasn't the only one who wanted to know.

"I've had the artificers knock this together," Lieutenant Blue told Vicky and Captain Bolesław. In the palm of his hand was something the size of a grasshopper—but no grasshopper ever looked like this. It was black as space, such a deep blue-black that Vicky could almost see rainbows in its multifaceted sides. There were no ninety-degree corners—every one of them was angled in or out at odd degrees. Vicky bent down to look at the end that faced away from the lieutenant.

"Are those rocket engines inside it?" she asked, seriously puzzled by the what's-it.

"Yes, the shrouding around the engines should give it a very small radar cross section even from aft on," the lieutenant said. "The bulges along its sides are antennas. If everything goes according to plan, they'll take a snapshot of all electro-magnetic activity in the system beyond the jump."

"We've shot up everything they've sent through the jump," Vicky pointed out.

"The Butcher seems to have given up on scouting our defenses," Captain Bolesław added.

"Yes, I know," Lieutenant Blue said. "That's why we designed this little bug. We send it through the jump back-ward, let it coast for two seconds, then the rockets cut in, and we're back through the jump in a second, no more. We're back with three seconds of data on their radio traffic and reactors. Three seconds is all they get to spot this little bit of nothing. It gives almost no radar reflection. It's passive, so it has the tiniest possible electronic signature. There's nothing iron in it, so it has nothing for a magnetic anomaly detector to latch onto. The best part is that it only weighs fifteen grams. No gravity detectors will spot it."

"Will it get enough data?" Vicky asked.

"We'll definitely get readouts on the ships around the jumps. The data about the more distant ships, like the Empress's battleships, will be attenuated, what with only three seconds to gather it. Still, we should get something."

"And if they don't shoot it up, we can always send it back for a longer visit," Captain Bolesław said.

"Precisely."

"Can one of the cruisers on duty at the jump point print one of these out?"

"Yes. We only built this one as a proof of concept," the lieutenant said.

"Then let's go see the admiral," Vicky decided.

Thirty minutes later, with the admiral's chop on the order, a message went out to the cruisers on guard station with a file attached.

Six hours later, the *Mischievous Pixie* accelerated itself slowly toward the jump, flipped, and coasted through it. Three seconds later, it was back. It downloaded its data to the *Halum*. Four hours later, Vicky was rousted out of bed to see what there was to see.

"They've got no guard ships at the jump?" Vicky demanded, out of breath from an 0200 hour trot from *Retribution* to admiral's country on the station.

"Not so much as a merchant ship with a peashooter," Lieutenant Blue assured Vicky, Admiral von Mittleburg, and Captain Bolesław.

"What can you tell me about the Butcher's fleet?" the admiral demanded.

"Not a lot from this three-second scan. If the first peek was a success, the *Halum* had orders to send the *Pixie* back for a ten-minute look, then, after reporting back, it will stay an hour."

"They have *nothing* at the jump that can burn our tiny spy down to atoms?" the captain asked again as he turned and paced a few steps away, then back.

"There is no question from this scan that there are no ships within a million klicks of the jump," the lieutenant assured them.

"There were few who came back from Kris Longknife's Voyage of Discovery who would know about Admiral Krätz's idea of mooring ships together," Vicky pointed out.

"We haven't used it until now," Captain Bolesław said, nodding.

The admiral briskly rubbed his chin. Vicky had never before seen him in need of a shave. Some of the bristles were gray. "So another report with better information is likely already on its way here."

"Very likely," Lieutenant Blue assured him.

"Then I suggest we order up some tea," Admiral von Mittleburg said, settling into a comfortable armchair in his day quarters. Vicky took the chair across from the admiral. Captain Bolesław and Lieutenant Blue took the other two. The coffee table between them went from a dark teak to an even darker representation of the system on the other side of the jump.

A chief steward's mate brought in water for the admiral's samovar. When he was satisfied that the temperature was just right, he filled four small, individual teapots. Before he could finish his "tea ceremony," Lieutenant Blue muttered something that might have been "Hot damn!"

The admiral allowed the young officer's overenthusiastic remark to pass unremarked upon. His eyes were fixed on the table's screen. A moment before, it had only shown an empty system: a few rocky planets in the middle distance from an unremarkable red dwarf. Close in was one large gas giant. Well out, there were more gas giants and one ice giant surrounded by a sparkling white ring of ice crystals.

Now, beside the gas giant closest to the jump, a window opened, and a long list of names cascaded down. The first twelve were the battleships Vicky expected, then the list went longer. *Empress's Retribution*, *Terrorizer*, *Pounder*, *Hammer*, *Slammer*, *Trouncer*.

"Now she's stealing names from us, her *Empress's Retribution* and *Trouncer* just like we have," Vicky said.

"Get used to it," the admiral said. "I doubt she's expecting our ships to be around long."

Empress's Smiter, *Anger*, and *Ravager* had been added while Vicky talked. The list now switched to heavy cruisers.

"These seem to still have the names of the cities they carried in the Greenfeld Navy," Lieutenant Blue said. "Their reactors are a match for the ones installed when their class was built." He paused to eye his readout carefully. "Though they do not appear to be operating nearly as efficiently as they should."

"You can tell that?" the admiral snapped.

"I can get just enough of a rough readout to make that call. Remember, this is only what we were able to capture during a ten-minute survey. I can tell you more, and it will be more reliable, when the one-hour report comes back."

"Excuse me, Lieutenant," Captain Bolesław said, "but when we were fighting that bastard, we couldn't make heads nor tails of his fleet. How can you read them now?"

"Before, sir, they were jamming my sensors. I could read nothing. Now, they seem to have their jammers off. Maybe they're broke. Maybe they're saving them."

"You're sure?" the captain said, the clear skeptic at the moment.

"Sir, they can jam me. They cannot deceive me."

The captain pursed his lips, eyeing the junior officer, then nodded, and said, "Okay."

Admiral von Mittleburg cleared his throat. "When you get to the end of the quick search, tell me just what is the present size of the Butcher's force."

"Yes, sir."

They all watched intently as the list grew longer and longer. Heavy cruisers gave way to light cruisers, then to armed merchant cruisers followed by destroyers. Finally, they were into the attack transports."

"God, if they have all those troopies locked down in zero gee, the barracks bays on those ships must be unmitigated hell from the stink alone," Captain Bolesław said, then added, "Begging Your Grace's pardon."

"I'm Navy, too, Captain, and the observation seems to fit the situation. Do they have any Marines?"

The admiral shook his head. "They haven't had much luck where they are concerned. Here and there, she manages to snap up a battalion by duress or holding families hostage, but the Navy managed to pull a lot of them back from the center of the Empire. 'What need have you of these ruffians?' Several of the battalions where she managed to suborn the officers emptied out the first time the men were given liberty. They're young and creative, most had no stomach for breaking heads on riot duty. Some went sour and are taking her silver marks, but they are few. They're Marines, not murderers. Few had attachments that the Empress could hold over their heads to keep them in line."

"We saw that on Brunswick," Vicky said. "The officers and senior NCOs had wives and families the Empress held hostage to their good behavior. They surrendered and asked to be locked up. But a few days later, when Brunswick decided they needed an Army, the lower ranks of the battalion stood up to provide the skeleton of the training command. Then the Navy managed to break out the wives and kids, and the battalion was active again."

"Be that as it may be," the admiral went on, now steeping his tea under the watchful eyes of the chief steward's mate, "anyone holding on to their bunks to keep from floating away aboard those hell ships is likely some recent civilian who joined up for a paycheck and a chance to terrify unarmed subjects. They are little more than civilians themselves."

They passed a few quiet minutes steeping tea to their own

preference and smelling the delightful result. After taking his first sip and nodding his satisfaction to the chief, the admiral looked around the table.

"So far, what does this tell us?"

"They have powered down their jammers to save wear and tear on them, or they have no fear of us," Captain Bolesław said. "They showed that when they did not keep so much as an armed merchant cruiser at the jump. They expect that they will be the ones to invade the St. Petersburg system, not the other way around."

The admiral nodded his agreement.

Lieutenant Blue went next. "By my count, and it is one I have a high confidence in, we now face nineteen battleships, most of them with 16-inch or 18-inch batteries, although there are a few old 14-inchers in there. The butcher has twenty heavy cruisers, eighteen light cruisers, and a dozen merchant cruisers armed with a mix of 4-, 5-, and 6-inch lasers. He has about forty destroyers, and they are accompanied by some twenty-five transports of various sizes. I'd estimate a ground force of at least two divisions, possibly three or more if they made no accounting for their comfort."

"I doubt they would," Captain Bolesław said through a scowl.

"I do not doubt at all," the admiral said, then turned his eyes to Vicky.

"I do not wish to claim too central a place of importance," Vicky said, waving a casual hand at herself, "but it appears that my darling stepmom is throwing everything she can lay her hands on at St. Petersburg. Could her interest in the place be because poor little *moi* is here?"

Neither the admiral nor captain moved to gainsay her. "Kill the spider at the center of the web, and you have put an end to everything," Captain Bolesław said.

"To kill a rebellion, you take off the head of the largest rebel," the admiral added.

Vicky gulped noticeably.

"As much as I hate to agree with Admiral Lüth," the admiral said, "he did have a point. The smart thing to do would be to put you on a fast ship to Metzburg."

Vicky shook her head. "Are you sure the good citizens of Metzburg don't have a few among them who would be only too happy to deliver me gift-wrapped to my loving stepmother?"

The two senior officers exchanged a droll glance.

Vicky went on. "Besides, I would be depriving you of your flagship. Unless, of course, you put me on a destroyer or merchant cruiser and kept the *Retribution* for yourselves."

"That might very well deliver her gift-wrapped to that bitch if a pirate cruiser chanced upon her," Lieutenant Blue dared to essay.

"Too true," Captain Bolesław agreed.

"Any chance we could talk you into staying dirtside with that nice fellow, the mayor of Sevastopol?" the admiral asked.

"Not only would I not want to go, but Mannie has already made it clear that the Empire has been ill served by one Peterwald falling into bed; no need for another to repeat the folly."

"I wasn't suggesting that," the admiral sputtered, then ground to a halt as Vicky eyed him.

"Okay, that option is out for now," Captain Bolesław said, "though I have to question the man's logic."

"I question the man's self-control," Vicky said dryly.

"Moving right along," the admiral said. "Do we attack them, or do we continue to wait for them to come to us?"

"They outnumber us five to three," Captain Bolesław pointed out. "We can barely hope to fight them to a draw if we defend, maybe a bit more if Her Grace's missile boats pan out. We've got to hold here."

Vicky leaned back in her chair and gazed at the overhead. "Where is the Empress getting all these ships?"

"She seems to be scraping up everything she's got to send here," Captain Bolesław agreed.

"What are you thinking, Your Grace?" the admiral asked.

"It's just that there haven't been a lot of planets coming over to either of our sides. The original frantic switching back and forth is done, what with both of us garrisoning the planets and picketing them in orbit. But now she's pulling ships from here and there, concentrating them on the other side of our jump and not getting a lot to show for her effort. If she's all that strong here, could she be a lot weaker other places?"

"While we maintain a refused center here . . ." the admiral said slowly.

"Do you think the staff on Bayern would be interested in that kind of idea?" Captain Bolesław asked the admiral.

"I think it's enough to order a destroyer away from the pier this instant and get it headed there with all that we know of our situation."

"Tell them not to reinforce here though I wouldn't mind some help," Vicky said, "but we'll achieve more eating away at the Empress's flanks than going head-to-head with her here."

"Are you teaching your grandma to suck eggs?" the admiral said.

Vicky must have turned a pale shade of white because the admiral went on, "Your thoughts of late show you paid attention to Admiral Krätz's lessons. Good."

Vicky relaxed. It was so hard to find the middle ground the Navy expected of her. She could usually manage to be the proper field-grade officer, but when they brought her into strategic planning like tonight, it was impossible not to jump in and run with an idea.

Then Vicky paused. *They are pushing my idea up to the Navy staff. If they approve, the entire rebellion will be following my strategy.*

Not a bad thought.

Vicky leaned back, kept her mouth shut, and watched as the admiral and captain taught her crazy idea how to run.

CHAPTER 49

FOR the next several weeks, Vicky watched as the rebellion unfolded on two tracks: what was happening here in front of St. Petersburg and what developed along the edges of the battle line between Empress-controlled space and her own.

The destroyer *Cobra* was away from High St. Petersburg Station within an hour of Admiral von Mittleburg's decision. It quickly accelerated to four gees and didn't flip ship to decelerate until it could coast through the jump at the maximum 50,000 kph.

It would refuel at Metzburg. Vicky and the admiral hoped the folks there would use their own fleet to start the pressure on the Empress. They had eight refugee battleships at last count and an Army of several divisions, only half-trained, but they'd likely be more effective than the "Security Specialists" the Empress was defending with.

The first Vicky learned that her plan was accepted was when a pair of battleships showed up. The *Sachsen* and the *Baden* were old 16-inch battleships from when her grandfather was still naming battleships after planets. They'd been shot up pretty badly attacking Arkhangelsk.

The Empress had left four old battleships there. Metzburg

had risked sending an invasion fleet built around six battle-ships, two of them fairly new. The battle had been hard fought until the *Bavaria* blew up, taking the fight out of the Empress's other three. Still, the *Sachsen* and *Baden* were hard hit.

So they were sent to St. Petersburg as reinforcements, thank you so very much.

When Vicky remarked upon that, Admiral von Mittleburg just laughed.

"You should see the three battleships that surrendered. They'll be joining the Metzburg Reserve Fleet as soon as they can patch them back together. I made sure the fleet at Metzburg learned of Captain Bolesław's little trick of targeting the same place on their opponent's hide. I'm not sure they did as well as the *Retribution* did around Brunswick, but it was good enough. By the way, the *Cobra* just jumped back into the system, right after our new battleships."

"Wrecks of battleships," Vicky insisted.

"Well, I think the *Cobra*'s dispatches will cheer you up. I am to be a vice admiral, and your Captain Bolesław will raise a rear admiral's flag on *Retribution*."

"Good for him," Vicky said. "Will I be rousted out of the admiral's quarters to make way for him?" From her time in the Navy, Vicky had learned that few fair winds didn't blow somebody ill.

"He can't. You outrank him, Your Grace. Admiral Waller has promoted you to vice admiral, a fraction of a second ahead of me."

For one of the rare times in her life, Vicky found herself speechless.

"Lieutenant commander to vice admiral in one long jump," she finally stuttered.

"I've heard that historically, revolutions tend to leave sudden promotion openings for those who don't lose their heads."

"Yeah," Vicky said, still trying to take the measure of this sudden gift.

"Face it, young lady, you have been amazingly successful in your direction and timing of this bit of political theater. You haven't done at all bad using what few ships you had."

"It was Captain, I mean Admiral Bolesław's idea that won us the battle at Brunswick."

"Yes, and you didn't joggle his elbow but used his tactics

and victory to allow you to bring another important planet onto our side."

"Keeping my mitts off the control stick has been my main job," Vicky pointed out.

"Keeping your mitts off the machinery is something you have learned to do, as well as knowing just the right moment to put your nose into our business. You have done well. Admiral Waller has chosen to promote you. Enjoy it while you can."

Vicky chose to change the subject. "Admiral Waller managed to make it out of Anholt ahead of my stepmother's Imperial Guards?"

"Barely." Admiral von Mittleburg got suddenly serious. "His wife was caught during her escape. The Marines escorting her out died to a man defending her. The Empress slit her throat personally and sent the video to Bayern."

"The bitch," hardly seemed strong enough.

"The Navy is now fully in the rebellion," Admiral von Mittleburg said softly.

"All of the Navy?" Vicky asked.

"Sadly, no. There are those who have chosen her side. No doubt they are confident she will prevail. We have heard that she is paying very high bounties to any captain who brings his ship over to her side."

"We must see that they do not live long enough to spend her largesse," Vicky said, and only as she heard the words realized just how evil she could be.

"We may need a general amnesty when these troubles are over," Admiral von Mittleburg said softly.

Vicky eyed the admiral and realized that she had likely just received the best advice she would ever hear. It made her stomach rebel, but she said. "Yes, we will. If we don't, this war will drag us all down, and the aliens, if, no when they show up in our sky, will find that we have already made of it a wasteland."

"The aliens had slipped my mind," the admiral said, "but yes, they, too, argue for clemency."

"Once you've seen a planet wrecked by the alien raiders, they can never be far from your waking mind because they haunt your every night."

The admiral paused to let the station's ventilators clear that black miasma from the air. Then he continued.

"Lieutenant Blue just reported that the Butcher is changing his habits."

"I hadn't heard anything for a while."

"There was nothing to hear. However, now there is. Six attack transports under heavy guard of four battleships as well as cruisers and destroyers have withdrawn from his system."

"Where will they go?" Vicky asked.

"I'd very much like to know, but I've got nothing I can risk to feed my curiosity. We'll just have to wait and see."

"Strange. He's keeping most of his force there but sending a major part of it out."

"If I were a betting man," the admiral said, "I'd bet that he has been persuaded to give some of those poor damned souls shore leave."

"God help the planet he picks," Vicky said.

"And may the gals there have fast running shoes," the admiral said, extending her prayer to something more practical.

"How long before we know what he's up to?"

"Your guess is as good as mine," the admiral said.

"Well, I better call Mannie and see what he can do to get these busted-up battleships patched up quickly."

"He's coming up to see for himself. Why don't you show him around?"

"Are you trying your hand at matchmaking?" Vicky asked.

"I think what I'm suggesting is high and aboveboard, but if you think the shoe fits, I would suggest you try it on."

Vicky did meet Mannie as his shuttle came in. She stayed at his elbow as the skippers of the two pranged-up battleships and their dock bosses showed him the worst of it. Mannie had several fab managers following him around. They got specs for the damaged equipment and measurements for the bent bulkheads, strength members, and hull plates. The fab managers left immediately after their tour, but Mannie stayed for a nice dinner in Vicky's own quarters. It was quiet and candlelit even if it was just goulash. Vicky could never chase from her mind the closeness of her bed in her night quarters next door.

Is Mannie thinking what I'm thinking?

But the table talk was of the coming battle and what might follow.

"I hope we can avoid fighting over every planet in the

Empire," Mannie said, as Vicky served dessert from a tray that offered way too many choices. Goulash for the main course, yet this fancy dessert tray. How strange.

"I hope we don't have to dig the security thugs out of every planet, too," Vicky said, then told Mannie of her plan to nibble around the edges of the Empress's holdings. "Those two dinged-up battleships were from a fight at Arkhangelsk. We captured three old battleships and blew up one. I'm told that the next system in had not one ship picketing the main planet. They took it without a fight. Bayern is launching a similar thrust."

Mannie gave his skull a fast and hard rub with both hands. "Yes, I'd heard something, nothing as precise as what you just told me. Still, the older planets near Greenfeld have their mothballed battleships from the Iteeche War. They may only have 14- and 15-inch lasers, but there are a lot of them. If the Empress puts a crew aboard them, there will be hell to pay."

"I know. Dad always said those old ships couldn't get under way to sail to the breakers, but I guess if the Empress really put her mind to it . . ."

"Yeah. I've been losing sleep over those ships for a while," Mannie said, forking a nice bit of cherry pie *à la mode* into his worried mouth. Vicky settled for a lemon tart and barely nibbled at it.

"Have you given any thought to how we might end this?" Vicky asked Mannie.

"One idea might be mediation."

"My father let someone *else* decide his fate? You must be joking. Besides, I can't think of anyone my dad would agree to for a mediator that I'd like. Come up with a better idea."

"I think there might be one person you'd both accept," Mannie said, and filled his mouth with pie so he could munch while Vicky mulled the unlikely. No. Impossible.

"I give up. Who?" she finally said, as Mannie's fork reached for another piece of pie.

Mannie stopped, fork halfway to his mouth, then said, "Kris Longknife. She saved his life, and she's your friend."

The words said, he stuffed his mouth with pie and left Vicky to carry on the conversation. Or say nothing.

She chose nothing for a long minute.

Kris Longknife. Might it work?

Dad would never allow it. Annah would have a stroke.
Though that might not be a downside.

Would I trust that Wardhaven princess as an honest broker?

Better yet, would I be willing to bet everything that Kris could come up with something that my dad and the people who are backing me would be willing to accept?

The longer this war goes on, the higher the price in blood and treasure and the less people will want to settle for anything less than total victory.

Isn't that an argument to get this war over quickly?

"Any idea how Kris might end this war in a way acceptable to both me and my dad, not to mention his wife and her family?" Vicky asked.

Mannie had another fork of pie almost in his mouth. He held it there as he thought for a bit. "I haven't the foggiest. It's a lot easier to start a war than end one, or so history seems to demonstrate."

"Yeah," Vicky said, and nibbled her tart.

Mannie still held the fork short of his mouth. "But I've known it to happen that if you put enough people in a room, and don't let them out for dinner, they can solve impossible puzzles."

"You would, no doubt, hate to miss dinner."

"You bet," Mannie said, and finally took his bite.

"So, how would this work? Should I send a flag of truce across the lines between us and suggest we get Kris Longknife here from wherever she has wandered off to?"

"Oh, God no," Mannie said, speaking for the first time with his mouth half-full. He swallowed the rest of his bite. Something went down the wrong way, and he started choking. He reached for a glass of water, took a long swallow, then caught his breath.

"For God's sake, Mannie, don't die on me. At least not before you finish your last thought."

"I thought you were going to say 'before you got me in your bed,'" he said with a mischievous gleam in his eyes

"Well, that, too, but you've got my curiosity up. I know I've been more concerned with winning this next battle than ending this war."

"I hear it got you an admiral's flag. Why aren't you wearing all the extra gold braid?"

"I could say I've been too busy to have my blues sent out to the tailor."

"You're wearing whites. All you have to do is change the shoulder boards."

"Suddenly you're all Navy."

"Maybe I want to know more about the world you live in."

"Really?"

"Really." Mannie paused. "Watching you bloody, but not bowed. Delivering that fighting speech, then consoling that poor man. You were wonderful. You were courageous. I wanted to take you in my arms and tell you I loved you, and I will to the end of my days."

Vicky gulped. This was what she wanted to hear, but hearing it was terrifying.

Mannie went on. "Then, when you were stumbling out of there, leaning on my arm, then my shoulder, I did pick you up and hug you to myself."

"That was wonderful," Vicky managed to get out. "I mean, I was hurting and at the end of my rope, but your picking me up and carrying me. That was so special."

"I know," Mannie said.

They paused at that, staring into each other's eyes. Vicky found herself thinking lustful thoughts of that oh-so-very-near bed.

Maybe Mannie was, too, because he changed the topic. "Now about this crazy idea of getting Kris Longknife as a mediator."

"Yes, about it," Vicky said, following where Mannie led even if it wasn't to her bed.

"I do still have some contacts in the capital. Maybe still in the palace. People who might help your dad think the idea of getting Kris Longknife out here was his idea."

"I don't much care for your plan," Vicky said curtly

"What problem do you see?"

"I've about had enough of this advisor or that good lay getting the Emperor's ear or other body part and twisting him around their little finger."

"How would you do it?" Mannie asked, cautiously.

"The way it should be done in an Empire. Up front. My dad and I making the call. None of this greasy, under-the-table stuff. And none of this almost democracy stuff. We will not turn Greenfeld into some sort of Longknife votearama. It's bad enough that we're talking about hauling in Kris Longknife from wherever she's hiding. We've got to do this our way."

"Ah, when would you try to do it your way?"

"After this next battle. If we win it, that would give us the right to say 'you've got to listen to us' to the Emperor."

"We could lose the next battle," Mannie pointed out.

"Yeah, I know. If that battle is here in the St. Petersburg system, we could likely lose the war as well."

"I'd hate to lose you," Mannie said.

"I'd hate to lose you, and me," Vicky added, with a gulp.

"There are some times when you really scare me, Your Grace," Mannie said.

Vicky nodded. "There are some times when I scare myself. Do we have time for after-dinner drinks?" Vicky asked, changing the subject.

Dolefully, Mannie shook his head. "If I stay for one drink, I'll stay for a second, and maybe a third for the road. Then I'm likely to just stay, and we both know we can't do that. At least not yet."

"Not yet?" Vicky said, arching her eyebrows.

"What I'm doing may be the most stupid thing of my entire life, and I may live to regret it, but I will not risk our future for a few moments today. And if I lose out because I do this right thing," he said, ruefully shaking his head, "it will just prove to my *grandmadre* that the rest of her grandchildren got all the smarts there were to be had in this generation."

Vicky took a deep breath and let it out. "I'm willing to wait if you are. You be careful."

"*Me* be careful?" Mannie said. "*You're* the gal that needs to ride around in a great big battleship. A battleship headed for a great big battle. What have I got to worry about?"

Vicky covered the few steps that separated them and wrapped him in her arms so fast that he seemed taken by surprise. "Don't you know, you've gotten too close to me? My stepmother hates me. If she can't get to me, who do you think she'll kill?"

"Oh," escaped as if by surprise. "I never thought of that."

"Well, think about it, you lovable lunkhead." Vicky squeezed him tight. Now his arms were around her, gently rubbing her back.

"I'll make you a deal," he finally said.

"Yes?"

"I'll increase my security team and be as careful as I know how to be, and you be as careful as you can be in the coming fight."

Vicky found his words absurd. Not that he'd increase his security. She was glad of that. No. How was she to keep herself any safer when battleships started blowing up? She opened her mouth anyway. "Yes. You take better care of yourself, and I'll eat my vegetables and do everything I can to make myself safer when the lasers start buzzing." Despite herself, a soft chuckle escaped her.

"Good," Mannie said, and, reaching down, raised her chin up to face him. With one hand so deliciously firm on the back of her neck, and the other caressing her chin, he kissed her. Vicky had locked lips with guys before. Lots of times. This wasn't like one of those.

This kiss started softly, gently, just a brush of his lips on hers. She opened for him, and his kiss became more demanding, more urgent. She met him demand for demand, urge for urge. Vicky's knees began to go weak, and the thought of falling back on the couch and wrapping her legs around Mannie was galloping to the forefront of her mind when Mannie broke away from her lips, breathing hard.

"Thank you," he said, breathlessly.

"For what?" Vicky said, and found she was just as breathless.

"For letting me give you a warrior's send-off. For giving me a warrior's send-off. For letting me know what I want to come back to. I don't know what all, but I liked it."

"I loved it." Vicky paused, gathered up her courage and went on. "I love you, Mannie. You take care to be here when I get back."

"Oh, I will, trust me. And you take care of yourself, love."

"Love?"

"Yes, love of my life. I can't see living my life without you," Mannie said as he opened the door.

Together, not arm in arm, Vicky walked with Mannie to catch his shuttle down.

CHAPTER 50

━━

NEXT morning, after breakfast, Vicky joined Admiral von Mittleburg, make that Vice Admiral von Mittleburg, for a review of threats and progress. These meetings had become a standard part of their morning.

As Vicky arrived, the admiral was receiving congratulations all around, which he was happily sharing with Rear Admiral Bolesław, who sported new shoulder boards.

"Atten hut," was announced as Vicky entered. She looked around, puzzled by the action.

"Are you going to stand us down, Vice Admiral, Your Grace?" Vice Admiral von Mittleburg said, a tight but huge smile on his face. "And, Your Grace, you are out of uniform."

"As you were," Vicky said, trying not to sound too timid. "I haven't received any *written* orders to change my uniform."

"Rear Admiral Bolesław, if you will bring me the orders from my desk," von Mittleburg said, and a message flimsy, along with a pair of shoulder boards appropriate for a vice admiral, were soon in his hands.

"Your Grace, if you will step forward."

Vicky found herself battling an attack of vertigo, but she did manage to step forward.

"Report yourself, Commander," Vice Admiral von Mittleburg had to remind her.

Saluting, she snappily announced, "Victoria Peterwald, reporting, sir."

"This is the last time I will return your salute," the admiral said, returning that honor.

He looked at her, almost like Vicky thought a proud father might look at his daughter. There was much more pride in his eyes than Vicky had ever seen in her own father's. "When you arrived here, Your Grace, I didn't know what to do with you. I foresaw all kinds of trouble. I never would have thought that you would pull off the things that you have. Save planets. Maybe save our beloved Greenfeld. You have earned this promotion differently from any officer I know of, but you have earned it as well, if not better than most. With your permission, Your Grace."

"Permission granted," Vicky said, voice steady. Somewhere during the admiral's words, Vicky had found something deep inside herself. Call it her center. Gone was the scared, insecure little girl who was overjoyed just to receive a new dress. She'd survived kidnapping, attempted murder, and rape. She'd somehow managed to talk bankers and businessmen and politicians into her own wild scheme that had saved the lives of hundreds of thousands, if not millions. She was preparing to fight a battle, and her victory just might turn on a crazy idea that she had come up with herself.

Kris Longknife, thank you for all the help, but next time we meet, we meet as equals.

The room broke into applause as Admiral von Mittleburg finished removing her second lieutenant commander's shoulder board and affixed the one with the broad stripe of a flag officer and the two narrower ones of a vice admiral. She saluted him again, or maybe he saluted her. It was hard to tell.

"For what it is worth, gentlemen," Vice Admiral von Mittleburg said, "her promotion was cut a few seconds ahead of mine, so if there is any question as to who is senior officer present, it is Her Grace. Let there be no doubt about that."

The "Yes, sir," from all present was solid though there might have been some puzzlement around the edges. Exactly how this would all play out, no doubt, would be a matter of some concern among the captains. Vicky had no doubt. When it was time to say ship right, ship left, it would be Vice Admiral von Mittleburg giving the orders.

"Now, Your Grace, gentlemen, if you will all take your seats, I think there are a few things of interest this morning. Commander Blue."

Commander? There must be a lot of promotions going around.

Sure enough, the lead of the sensor team was now a division head sporting the two stripes and one half stripe of a lieutenant commander.

I'll have to give him a set of my old shoulder boards. He and his crew did a lot to earn me my new ones.

"The good news is that two battleships and four destroyers jumped into the system about fifteen minutes ago. They are old tubs, the *Krasnoyarsk* and the *Karelia*, but they were of the first class to sport 16-inch lasers, so they will, no doubt, be a grateful addition to the Grand Duchess's fleet here. That is, after they get some yard time."

The yard superintendent glanced at his commlink. "We're receiving a long list of equipment that needs replacing. No doubt, the mayor of Sevastopol will be making a trip up to look it over."

Vicky neither blushed nor ducked her head. She glanced around the room; heads nodded with concern, but none wagged in her direction.

They better not. I'm being a good girl, and I hate it!

Admiral von Mittleburg nodded. "It would appear that our Empress is losing the race to get reinforcements here."

The nods now were accompanied by happy smiles. Nobody likes being outnumbered. With fourteen battleships to the Butcher's nineteen, the odds were a whole lot better. Even assuming the square root of each force, it was less than two to one, well below the critical three to one that a good commander might hope for to assure victory.

"In the other direction," Commander Blue continued, "the Butcher continues to send his ships out for a bit of shore leave. It hardly takes a genius to figure out that he won't be attacking while a quarter of his forces and invasion fleet are off somewhere spending time learning to walk again."

Again, heads nodded.

Vicky was not so sure. Sooner or later, the Empress was

going to hear that her personally chosen Butcher was fiddling while Vicky and her rebellious friends were burning them all along their flanks.

But matters held together as one week stretched into two. Work on the final refitting of the *Trouncer* and the *Ravager* continued, with the yard workers sure they'd have them ready tomorrow. And then tomorrow. And then tomorrow again.

Vicky kept her mouth shut and let Admiral von Mittleburg take the yard superintendent for a walk. A long walk.

The refitting of the *Sachsen* and *Baden* started out fine, then got worse. Every time a new piece of equipment was installed, something beside it broke, or spinning up the new gear blew out something further down the line. Dirtside, the fabs worked around the clock trying to fabricate on their night shift what had shattered into a dozen pieces on the yard's morning shift. Tension rose as frustration added to fear of what was going on somewhere else in the Empire.

Good news came back from Bayern and Metzburg. They had broken through the Empress's crust defense into "the chewy middle," as some wag put it. Every week, two or three more planets were coming over to Vicky's flag. That assumed their change of allegiance was sincere and not because rebel battleships were in their sky and rebel troopers walked their streets.

Vicky did not like what she was hearing through back channels. Some of the families she'd met with on Metzburg were seeing that their corporate holdings were returned to their uncles and brothers, sisters and aunts. If there was truth to some of the dark rumors Vicky heard, not all of the holders of those properties were the thugs who had stolen them. Properties had often changed hands; sometimes several times. Were the holders of the deeds who got rousted out of them just as undeserving as those who stole it in the first place?

This rebellion needed to get over, and soon, so that some semblance of normal and proper comity before law could be returned to Greenfeld.

Assuming it ever had such a foundation, Vicky thought bitterly.

The four battleships that had been so long in the yard began to cast off their moorings and make slow cruises around the moon and back, even as the *Krasnoyarsk* and *Karelia* slipped into their places. Unfortunately, the four returned with long lists of things that hadn't survived even that gentle voyage.

Once again, Mannie was called up to get the fabs working faster than any sane man had a right to expect. Still, the workers on the planet below did what they had to do.

Then everything changed. The Empress threw them a curveball.

CHAPTER 51

T HE day started so nicely. At the morning staff meeting, Commander Blue advised them that the Butcher of Dresden's latest liberty party should be coming back that evening. The next batch of warships, the last to finally get time dirtside, had eagerly boosted out of orbit and were already making a good gee and a half toward the jump.

"When do you expect the swap out to take place?" Admiral von Mittleburg asked.

"Of late, the returning party has only gotten through the jump an hour or so before the next ships jump out. This time, the next leave party looks like a bunch of eager beavers that can't wait. I would be surprised if they didn't jump out before the next batch get here."

"Too bad we can't do a bit of damage to them while they're at half strength," Admiral Bolesław suggested through a wolf-ish grin. "It would be nice to see how many of them we could cut out while they were missing half their fleet."

"It would be nice, but I see no way for us to do that before they could concentrate again. Too bad you didn't think about that idea a week ago."

"We didn't have fourteen battleships a week ago," Admiral Bolesław pointed out.

"True," seemed to finish it.

It had to, the room had taken on a deathly pall.

Commander Blue had his right hand to his earbud and was slowly raising his left. "We're getting a message from the *Halum*. Those ships we expected back from liberty later today are jumping into the Butcher's system *now*. They've got a good thirty thousand klicks on them coming through the jump."

"Somebody is in an all-fired hurry to get to their own funeral," Bolesław said.

"There are more ships coming back than went out," Blue said.

To Vicky's surprise, Vice Admiral von Mittleburg muttered a word she would not have expected to hear above the mess deck. Every eye was on Commander Blue.

"Trailing the returning liberty party through the jumps are the *Empress's Attacker*, *Empress's Striker*, *Pursuer*, *Beater*, *Ferocity*, *Shooter*, *Scourge*, *Annihilator*, *Conquest*, *Wolf*, *Lion*, *Sword*, *Mace*, *Lance*, *Javelin*, *Battleaxe*, *Dirk*, *Spear*. Now we're into cruisers. In the middle of them there's a huge space liner, the *Golden Empress*. No number to that one."

"Could the bitch have come here herself?" Vicky asked, expecting no answer.

"Maybe so," Admiral Bolesław said. "How better to get the lead out of the Butcher's britches?"

"You might have a point," Admiral von Mittleburg said. "Commander Blue, can you tell us the origin of the *Golden Empress*? She's stolen most of her ships. Who'd she steal this one from?"

"Excuse me, sir, do you want me to interrupt this report to get that?"

"Hang the cruisers," Admiral Bolesław said, "Let's see what she's gallivanting around the spaceways in."

"Yes, sir. Break, break. Chief, can you make out the origin of the *Golden Empress*?"

"Got it, now get back to the hull count. Are there any more transports?" Blue asked, then turned to Admiral von Mittleburg. "Sir, it is difficult to determine what the *Golden Empress* began life as. We have the *Spaceway's Spirit* in our database.

She's supposed to be the largest passenger liner at one hundred fifty thousand tons, half again as big as a battleship. The problem is, the *Golden Empress* is at least half again as big as the *Spirit* and has more reactors and rocket motors."

"Computer, are you aware of any larger ship being built by the Spaceway passenger line?" Vicky asked.

"There are no reports of the Spaceway line's building a larger ship. However, the Green Flag line laid down a ship to take away the pennant for the largest, most luxurious liner from Spaceway. When last any press release or media report was made on the ship, all work had stopped on it due to the economic downturn. Still, the size and number of reactors Commander Blue described would fit the potential Green Flag *Majestic*."

"So the Empress snapped it up for a song and made it her yacht," Vicky concluded.

"A bit different from yours," Admiral Bolesław said.

Vicky grinned through a lot of teeth. "I like my ride a whole lot more than hers."

"No doubt your ride will more likely be in the thick of a battle," Vice Admiral von Mittleburg observed dryly. "What is she doing here?"

"I have no doubt that she's come here to see that everything is done to her expectations," Vicky said. "The Butcher hasn't been moving fast enough to please her. Worse, too many ship captains have been figuring out a way to surrender to me and mine. She intends to make sure she has them under her eyes when they fight next."

"But her eyes will be well to the rear," Admiral Bolesław pointed out.

"No doubt, she's sure she can throw crockery from there to wherever they are standing."

"So she stomps her foot, and men risk their lives beyond all reason," Admiral von Mittleburg observed.

"My dad does," Vicky pointed out.

"One must not extrapolate extraneous conclusions beyond the limits of their application," Admiral Bolesław said.

"No doubt."

"Well, Your Grace, gentlemen, no doubt we have a battle to prepare for."

"No doubt," Vicky agreed.

The men in the room grew stern and firm as, one by one, they laid out just what they would do to assure that Vicky didn't throw any crockery at them.

"My stepmother does that. I don't," Vicky said. But after the third denial she gave up and, with a grin, started keeping a teacup close at hand.

The men around her were tense, but they never failed to enjoy the joke when she threatened them with a teacup.

CHAPTER 52

I F Vicky had considered the pace at the shipyard and the fabs frenzied before, she was amazed at the level of effort they set themselves to now.

Ships that had any discrepancies were pulled into one of the repair slips and given a quick going-over. And it was quick. No ship went into a slip before its list of discrepancies had been shipped down to St. Petersburg and the fabs had generated exactly what it needed, then shipped them back up to the station. The yard hands, now aided by any rigger with some sort of experience in space, would have the ship in and out within two shifts, three at the most. Another battleship, cruiser, or destroyer would be drifting in space just short of the slip, waiting for the buffed-up ship to slide away so that it could slip in and start its own high-speed refit.

The record between one ship's undocking and another ship's taking its place was six minutes.

Vicky was glad they'd managed to hold on to the *Anaconda* and the *Crocodile*. Their LCTs hardly took a break. If they weren't dropping down to the planet, they were climbing up to the station. Some of the heavy equipment for the ships in dock maxed out the landing craft. Other boats were topped off with missiles for the rocket boats. If there was any spare weight left over, they pumped in water to heavy up the reaction mass. No matter the load, all were lifting back up to orbit within the hour. Some less.

Everyone, Sailor, Marine, civilian, did whatever they could to prepare the fleet for battle.

Unfortunately for Vicky, the need to ship critically needed gear up to the station meant that there was no weight left over for other essentials, like Mannie, to make a visit in person.

He spent a lot of time on the commlink, though. Problem was, Vicky could find no excuse to be added to his calls when he talked to the yard superintendent or Vice Admiral von Mittleburg. She had to satisfy herself with a few stolen minutes late in the evening when both of them were exhausted from the day.

"This being a good girl is the pits," she muttered to herself after one all-too-short and very frustrating call.

"Can I help you?" Kit asked.

"Sorry, Kit, you're not the man I'm looking for," Vicky said, and settled for a cold shower.

Next morning, Commander Blue reported that all the Empress's ships were in orbit around the gas giant, and destroyers were dropping down to skim the huge planet's atmosphere for more reaction mass.

"No doubt they'll top off their tanks before they head for us," Admiral Bolesław said.

Once again, Commander Blue found himself interrupting his briefing to listen to a hot report.

"Two merchant cruisers have just detached themselves from the rest of the fleet and are headed for the jump."

"How big are they?" Admiral von Mittleburg asked.

"They've got 6-inch and 4-inch lasers with 18-inch pulse lasers," came back quickly.

"The *Halum* and the *Ferwert* ought to be able to take them," Admiral Bolesław said. "Their 24-inch pulse lasers should pick them off as they come through the jump."

"Tell me again why our fleet isn't out there ready to pick them off as they come through?" Vicky asked.

"There is no yard out there, Your Grace. Our ships have benefited mightily from the time we've been here."

Vicky nodded, now remembering why they had made the

choice to fight it out close to St. Petersburg rather than attempt the first-ever meeting engagement at a jump. *Oh, and there is always the chance that the jump will do a jump itself and her fleet could be left guarding an empty bit of space while the Empress's fleet charged into the system somewhere else.*

She wished she'd kept her mouth shut.

Vice Admiral von Mittleburg laid in a fleet exercise for the next day, just a quick duck around the moon and back, but it would get the fleet some practice operating in his proposed battle formation. There would also be a practice shoot. Hopefully, it would show how well the changes made to tighten up the gun cradles had tightened up the salvos. Vice Admiral von Mittleburg would command the first task force. Rear Admiral Bolesław would lead the second. Bolesław would have *Retribution*, with its 18-inch guns. In addition, he'd have the *Ravager*'s and the *Trouncer*'s 18-inch guns, *Scourge*, *Sachsen*, and *Baden* with 16-inchers, and the 15-inch battlecruiser *Stalker*. Von Mittleburg's Task Force 1 would have the 18-inch guns of BatRon 22's *Implacable*, *Adamant*, *Merciless*, and *Hunter* as well as the *Vigilant*'s and *Relentless*'s 16-inchers. He would also have the other battlecruiser, the *Slinger*. If the *Krasnoyarsk* and *Karelia* got out of the yard in time, they would join Bolesław's battle line, adding more to Vicky's protection.

The twelve heavy cruisers and eight lights, along with twenty merchant cruisers, thirty-one destroyers, and twenty-eight rocket boats would also be divided evenly between the two squadrons.

"My intention is to have the battleships form a line with the cruisers and destroyers above and below them, closer to the enemy, so that the cruisers can defend us against their destroyer attacks. Our destroyers will be in position to take advantage of an opening to charge in and hit them with their pulse lasers and missiles. The rocket boats will form up in two columns, one high and one low on the unengaged side of each battle line. We'll order them forward when we intend to salvo torpedoes at the Empress's battle line. Any questions?"

There were none. With the exception of the deployment of the rocket boats, this was the standard battle formation for a fleet of this size, one that the Greenfeld Navy had used for a hundred years or more.

The sortie notice was dispatched to the fleet, and the officers left to prepare for what, no doubt, would be a fun and challenging day. Vicky waited until only Admirals von Mittleburg and Bolesław were still in the room.

"Do I need to move off *Retribution*?"

"Are you willing to raise your flag on the station?" Admiral von Mittleburg shot back.

"No," Vicky said flatly.

"No surprise," Admiral Bolesław said.

"Then I assume you will stay safely on *Retribution*," von Mittleburg said. "It is our largest warship."

"Admiral Bolesław?" Vicky asked.

"I will be staying on it as well," he answered.

"I have the admiral's quarters. You have the captain's quarters, still."

"And I will still have them," Admiral Bolesław said. "Willi Neumann can stay in the quarters he had as XO. They are more palatial than most captains have on a battleship. *Retribution* was intended for both a flag and something political when it was designed."

Vicky nodded. "Then it is settled."

"Yes," Admiral von Mittleburg said.

Vicky was likely the only tourist as every man jack on the station turned to, intent on their ship showing its best colors in the morning.

CHAPTER 53

T HE sortie could be called a success. All the ships got away from their piers on time. Mostly. No ship bumped another. Barely. There were no explosions aboard any ship, and all of them made it back to their assigned piers. Fortunately, the number of ships that had to be directed straight to space dock did not exceed the two available.

The number of ships wanting one of the repair slips was another question. Admiral von Mittleburg called a meeting to discuss the general status of the fleet. The skippers of all the battleships, cruisers, and destroyers were invited, along with the division commanders of the merchant cruisers and rocket boats.

It could have been a zoo.

Vicky might have been the only one who was keeping her eyes on the clock. She was not surprised when Commander Blue walked up and interrupted Admiral von Mittleburg by whispering something into his ear.

"Well, damn it, son. Put what you have on the screens."

Clearly, Admiral von Mittleburg was feeling the stress of his situation.

A picture of the jump appeared from a camera mounted on the *Halum*, according to the date stamp.

"The *Halum* kept a probe on the far side of the jump until the Empress's merchant cruisers came within 6-inch range, then it withdrew."

"Don't we have more than one probe?" Admiral Bolesław interrupted.

"Yes, Admiral, we have four. Two that are on station on either side of the jump and two that are rotating with them after a refueling and maintenance period on the *Halum*."

"Logical," Admiral von Mittleburg observed. "Continue, Commander."

"The *Halum* pulled the probe back because we don't know that they've spotted the pixies, and we didn't want them to. Anyway, as you can see here, two hours later, a longboat came through the jump. It was annihilated."

On screen, something that looked like a liberty launch that had sprouted a small grove of antennas appeared and just as quickly disappeared, with little wreckage to show it had ever existed.

"Jumping ahead fifteen minutes," the commander said, and a second longboat appeared to vanish quite quickly.

"And five minutes later," a third appeared and disappeared.

"Not having learned anything," the commander quipped, and the screen showed three launches appear ten seconds apart and just as quickly be blown apart.

"But they learn."

Not ten seconds after the last launch, an armed merchant cruiser appeared at the jump. It needed time to acquire a target, get a firing solution, train its lasers out, and take the target under fire.

Both of Vicky's cruisers knew exactly where the jump was and where any ship that came through it would be. While the Empress's cruiser paused to acquire the situation, 24-inch pulse lasers slammed into it, tore its guts out, and left the hull rolling drunkenly in space.

The next cruiser came through five seconds later.

It rammed right into the wreckage of its leader.

Then it got lucky.

The wreckage of the first cruiser masked the second one. The helmsman of the second also did a bit of a dance, yawing first right, then left, wrecking the light cruisers' firing solutions by dodging into, but then away from, a clear line of sight and field of fire.

Then the Empress's ship fired its own pulse lasers.

The *Ferwert* took three direct hits; more hits than a light cruiser's thin armor could handle. The *Ferwert* came apart at the exact same moment the *Halum* got a good firing solution on the enemy merchant cruiser and took it apart with four pulse-laser hits as well as a broadside of 6- and 5-inch lasers.

The Empress's ship got off a few more shots from its 6-inch guns, but the next salvo from the *Halum* put an end to that noise.

Where once four proud warships had sailed, now stood only one slowly moving amid the wreckage, retrieving survival pods.

"So, they came, they didn't see anything, and they won't be making any claims to be conquerors," Admiral Bolesław said dryly.

"It seems that way," Admiral von Mittleburg said. "Commander, has the *Halum* reported anything from the far side of the jump?"

"My chief reports that they will deploy a pixie through the jump as soon as they have collected as many survivors from the *Ferwert* as possible."

Vicky was ready to jump down the skipper's throat, but she kept her mouth shut long enough to think the situation through. She remembered that the Empress's merchant cruisers had been forty thousand klicks away from her light cruisers. *Halum* would need to pick up all the survivors it could find there before closing on the jump, where they might retrieve the Empress's survivors as well as send a pixie through the jump.

Both of the other admirals seemed to know intuitively what took a long minute for her to figure out, but the pall of death hanging over the room for that minute delayed them from going on and Vicky from going off.

I've got a lot to learn.

"The *Halum* did not report that the rest of the Empress's forces were moving out, did she?" Admiral Bolesław asked.

"Her destroyers were still sucking up reaction mass, sir, when we got our last look. I think it's safe to say that the *Halum* will have a pixie on the other side well before they can distribute their reaction mass, re-form their destroyer squadrons, and break orbit."

"Good. Walter, do you still think your division is the best in the fleet?"

He commanded the newest destroyer division.

"Yes sir," the captain said, jumping to his feet.

"Order two of them, not your flag though, out to relieve *Halum*. She'll need to come back. With all the survivors, they're likely to be taking turns breathing in and out."

"Sir," Captain Walter Oseau said, and departed the room, already speaking into his commlink.

Now the room got down to the ancient military art of making do with way too little. There were skippers pleading for space on a slip for their ship. The yard superintendent already had their list of failed equipment that needed replacing. He also had the list from dirtside of what gear could be produced by the fabs quickest and which would need more time.

To no one's surprise, the two did not fit together. It wasn't even close. Over the next hour, compromises were struck, and those facing a long wait for spare parts began to haggle among themselves to see how they might rob from Peter to get Paul away from the dock.

Vicky saw two skippers actually playing rock, paper, scissors. The loser took it like a man. He was quickly set upon by others who were sure that now that he was missing a major component of his power plant, there wasn't any reason that he shouldn't give up more gear.

The *Vanity* ended up stripped down nearly to its hull plates.

Next, skippers began bidding for his crew like some ancient slave auction. Every ship in the fleet was undercrewed. The skipper was a good sport, especially after Admiral von Mittleburg took him and another captain aside who had just been diagnosed with a rare, untreatable cancer.

That ailing skipper was in tears, but he surrendered his command. "You take good care of *Caprice*. She's a damn good ship with a good fighting crew."

"Trust me, Konrad, I will."

"You do, or I'll hunt you down in hell and make it worse for you."

Vicky stepped outside to put a call through to Mannie. "Have you gotten the word?" was all she said.

"That your fleet did one of those day-trips to the moon and a lot of stuff broke?"

"So you got that word."

"There's another word?"

"The Empress had two of her merchant cruisers try to force the jump, first with a few longboats loaded with sensors, then with the two cruisers."

"How'd that go?" Mannie asked.

"She lost two cruisers, we lost one."

"I guess that's a good trade."

"Maybe it was," Vicky said, remembering the black pall of the officers. How many of them had seen men die in their rise to command ships? It had been a long peace.

Do these men really have the stomach for war?

Then Vicky remembered the skipper reduced to tears when ordered to turn his command over so that another man might sail it into the teeth of death.

Her ships had fought battles. How many had the Empress's fought?

Vicky shook herself and focused on what she had to. "The Empress is coming for us. Maybe not today or tomorrow, but she's coming soon. Whatever St. Petersburg can manage to give us, we need it. We need it badly, and we need it fast."

"I hear you. I'll get on it immediately. I may not get back to you today, but I will when I can come up for air."

"You have time to breathe. You must be slacking off," she said, but softened it with a bit of a chuckle.

"Anyone ever tell you about that Peterwald sense of humor you have?"

"Most people tell me that we Peterwalds don't have a sense of humor."

"Yeah, that's what I said," and now he chuckled.

"Maybe you can help me find one when all this is over."

"I'd love to try to find a lot of things you have hidden away."

Now he was talking like a lover. Had anyone ever talked to her like that?

"I'd love to let you find a whole lot of things I keep hidden, but for now, we both know what we have to do."

"I'll get right on it," Mannie said.

Was there a hint of a soft kiss as the line went dead?

Vicky decided there was.

Then she returned to Admiral von Mittleburg's meeting.

CHAPTER 54

———

FOR the next two days, Vicky found herself with nothing to do while everyone around her was frantic. Growing up in the palace, there had been a lot of times when she had nothing to do. But then, those around her also seemed to have little to do.

Maybe her smaller self hadn't understood what her dad really did with his hands on the wheels of power. Then again, maybe Dad had only thought he was making things happen. Vicky remembered the time when she'd been allowed to sit on Dad's lap and put her hands on the steering wheel of the small electric get-about that he used to drive around the gardens. She'd been so excited to actually "drive" the cart.

She was left brokenhearted and screaming when Hank pointed out that Dad had had his hands on the top of the wheel the entire time she had her hands on the bottom.

Was she just sitting on someone's lap as they really controlled where they were going?

She thought about that and came to the conclusion that if her dad were here, he'd be throwing his weight around everywhere—and likely making a mess of everything.

Vicky remembered a book she downloaded from the

library of Kris Longknife's ship. It had introduced Vicky to the idea of a "constitutional monarchy."

Was she becoming some sort of castrated constitutional monarch? "Castrated" was the word Father used when he talked about Ray Longknife. "He's not a king. He can do nothing. He was a great man, once. Now he's let them cut his balls off."

Vicky gave that a long thought.

I'm the one who chose to come to St. Petersburg. I'm the one who raised the flag of rebellion. I'm the one sitting here like a stalking goat for the Empress while our ships cut her flanks to ribbons. I chose my course.

However, she'd chosen it carefully—with advice and input from some very smart men.

Am I smarter than my dad?

That was a hard thought to tackle, but it did bring up something worse.

Dad! Where are you?

Could the Emperor have come out with the Empress?

Heaven knows that luxurious tub is big enough to hold the entire palace.

What if the fleet came through the jump waving the Imperial flag and announcing the presence of His Imperial Majesty—lay down your arms or face his full displeasure?

Could Vicky order her fleet to fire on her father, the Emperor?

That was a question that required parsing. Could she give such an order? How would her captains and crews react to it?

Vicky was none too sure about the first half of the question. About the second half, she was even less sure.

Fire on the Empress. No problem. Vicky could give the order, and every gunner in her fleet would gladly jump to it.

Fire on her father, the Emperor? Fire lasers with the intent of killing Dad or at least killing men fighting for him?

Vicky found the question distasteful. No doubt she'd find the actual situation even more revolting.

Vicky smiled. She'd started a revolution and now found that if she faced the question at the heart of the matter, it was revolting to her.

"The Empress was the one trying to kill me. Dad, you've become little more than a middle-aged buffoon in my mind's eye. But what will I do if I'm faced with you in all your buffoonery?"

Am I already facing it?

Vicky went looking for Commander Blue. She found him in his witch's cave off the main corridor, the one with the unmarked door. She knocked. A second-class petty officer answered, then immediately let her in. Commander Blue was at a workstation.

As Vicky came in, the commander, a chief, and two first-class petty officers blanked their screens and stood to attention.

Vicky ignored the lack of trust, or the need to look at the raw data before letting their betters know how consulting the entrails had enlightened them.

"As you were," she said, then added, "Commander, is there anyplace where we may talk in private?"

"This is a totally secure room, Your Grace."

"I need to talk to you *alone*."

Commander Blue nodded. "Chief, I need this room. Take the crew out for coffee."

"Aye, aye, sir," the chief said, and followed the junior petty officers out of the room. He personally pulled the door shut, got a solid click, then tested it before leaving.

"What do you want, Your Grace?"

Vicky took a seat next to the commander. "I want to hear the message traffic that was exchanged between our light cruisers and the Empress's merchant cruisers."

"I don't think there was any," he said.

"That's what I need to know. Was there any traffic, and if there was, what did the Empress's cruisers have to say for themselves before they died?"

"Give me a moment, Your Grace," the commander said, and turned to his station. He called up the visual he'd shown the assembled captains and admirals. It had no sound. He called up a second file that was rather more sketchy, but still had no attached audio file. A third file, even more visually degraded, came with audio.

"When do you think the bastards will quit yanking us around and do something for real?"

"Who's that?" Vicky demanded.

"That's the comm watch on the *Halum* and *Ferwert*. This recording covers all guard channels."

"Keep your cool, Hermann. They will come when they come."

"Do you think there were any people in those launches? For Christ's sake. Would you volunteer to man something like that? Do you think that doll of a Grand Duchess would make us? Would you volunteer to do it if she offered you a night . . ."

"Shut up, Hermann. We're supposed to guard these channels, not fill them up with your fantasies. Beside, we're recording all traffic."

"You're recording all this?" ended with Hermann's voice breaking with a high-pitched squeak.

"Yep."

There was a long pause. "Could you maybe edit me out, at least that last bit?"

"No, and are you sure that your leading chief isn't recording your traffic?"

There was quiet for a very long time.

"Here they come," broke the silence. It was said simultaneously on several channels.

Then there were several kinds of statics, crackles, and pops.

"We got the bastards," came only a few seconds later.

There was a long pause, and you could almost hear the panting of men trying to catch their breath. Realize they were still breathing.

"Here comes another one," was again shouted by several voices.

"Damn!" "That wreck's in the way!" "I can't get a firing solution! Between its moving and the hulk's rolling, the fire control computer can't get a fix on the bandit."

It went like that for a matter of seconds, then there were screams on several nets, cut off abruptly.

On other channels, there was a curt, "I got a solution."

"Fire."

"Thank God we got it," came a few seconds later.

Vicky listened as the last few shots were fired, as some hits slashed into the *Halum*, but from the Empress's ship on net she heard absolutely nothing.

"Can you isolate just the outside channels that we're supposed to guard at all times? Rescue, contact, and the like?" Vicky asked.

The commander adjusted his board. Only four lines ran

across the screen. They never wiggled for so much as a tiny spike, much less an entire message.

"They transmitted no message," Vicky said finally.

"That is where we would have copied it, and there is nothing there, Your Grace."

"Thank you, Commander."

"You're welcome, Admiral."

Without saying another word, Vicky stood and headed for the door. He asked her no questions and she told him nothing, neither lie nor truth. He had no interest in what she needed to know. He would follow her orders because she gave them.

And she would give the orders she had to give.

So the Empress is being just as silent as those bug-eyed monsters that chased me and Kris Longknife across the galaxy.

But would that change?

Worse, would the Empress meet them with some computer-generated demand from Dad, the Emperor, for them to lay down their weapons and submit?

At the door, Vicky turned back to the commander.

"If we received an audio message, how long would it take you to examine it and find out whether it was a real message or had been patched together from a whole lot of speeches?"

"That would depend. If I had the data on the person already organized, I could do it in less than a minute. If I had to search the video file, it could take longer."

"Call up all your files on my father, your Emperor."

"Oh," was all he said.

"Yes," was Vicky's response.

As she left, Commander Blue was on his commlink. "Chief, I need you to do a little search for me. I need you to do it yourself and keep it under your hat."

Vicky was none too sure of what the future held, but she was preparing for it.

I am no castrated constitutional Grand Duchess. I'm in the decisions for this rebellion right up to where they will put the noose around my pretty neck.

CHAPTER 55

═══════════

VICKY wasn't sure where she was headed after her talk with the commander. Maybe she would just walk a bit. Think things over.

Several Sailors ran by her. One of them knocked her elbow. "Sorry, ma'am. Admiral. Sir," he stammered, but ran on.

An officer dashed by her at full speed. He had his act together enough to say formally, "By your leave, Admiral." He even kind of saluted as he passed her at full gallop.

"What's the all-fire hurry?" Vicky asked, but softly, half to herself. There had been no all hands announcement over the 1MC.

Her computer provided the start of an answer. "Admiral von Mittleburg requests your presence in his day quarters immediately, Your Grace."

"You know why?" Vicky said as she turned and headed for *Retribution*'s quarterdeck.

"The destroyers *Wolverine* and *Wombat* have taken up station as jump-guard ships. The *Halum* was coming in at one gee. She's now upped that to 1.5 gees. A priority one message just came in from the *Wolverine*."

"And it said?" Vicky asked, not caring for how long this conversation was taking.

"I do not know, but the landline usage on the station and ships is about to overload the system."

Another officer dashed past Vicky, leaving her fast-walking in his wake. He didn't even remember to exchange courtesies.

Vicky reflected on how overloaded with survivors the *Halum* must be. The max she could push herself couldn't be more than 1.5 gees.

Vicky took off at a full gallop. If anyone noticed a hard-charging Grand Duchess, they better just get out of her way.

On the quarterdeck, those coming aboard were being rushed in with little formality. Honors rendered to the OOD and the flag were hardly more than perfunctory. Vicky exited just as informally. The gangway going ashore was being used for more crew to come aboard.

Someone shouted "Make a hole for the admiral!" and a lot of Sailors and officers ducked to the left-hand side of the brow and came to attention.

"As you were," Vicky said, and jogged quickly past them. She'd heard of fish that struggled to swim upstream. None had it as easy as her.

Aboard the station, there were a lot of people: Sailors, Marines, officers, and civilians racing from where they were to where they needed to be. Vicky joined the mob but soon found her way cleared by shouts of "Admiral coming through." "Make a hole for the Grand Duchess," and similar variations on those themes.

She got to Admiral von Mittleburg's day quarters out of breath but fast.

He was alone with the yard superintendent, but he had Mannie's face on a screen.

"What's happening?" Vicky got out through gasps for breath. She hadn't been working out nearly enough. She really needed to find a way of exercising with her security team that didn't end up in bed.

"The Empress's forces are breaking orbit and heading for the jump," the admiral said.

"So that's what all the hubbub out there is about. People are running all about."

"I haven't given any orders," the admiral said through a frown.

"Well, trust me," Vicky said, "out there, it's all hands forward lay aft. All hands aft lay forward. All hands amidships, stand by to direct traffic."

The admiral blew out a breath. "I wonder who leaked it."

"Does it matter?" Vicky said. "We've got a lot of eager sailormen who can't wait for a fight. That sounds good to me."

"Yes, yes. It is good. Now, Mr. Mayor, how much can you jack up production of rockets? Do you think you can get antimatter missiles into production?"

Vicky raised an eyebrow at Mannie. *So you found out before me?*

He was focused on the admiral, and something off screen and didn't even look her way. *I guess that's good.*

"The rockets are no problem," Mannie answered. "We've got a new chemical plant coming online and two fabs to load both the rocket bodies and the warheads. We've even got that new proximity fuse. Antimatter missiles is where the rub comes in."

"We got you the specs and plans for them."

"Yes, but you only got them to us last week. We've been modifying every reactor on this planet to catch more of the occasional bit of antimatter, but catchment is just starting to pick up. Other than that, we've got the rocket motors ready to go into production and the warhead-containment vessels and ignition gear ready as well. But you have to understand: You'll be trading antimatter missiles for conventional rockets. If we don't have the antimatter, your missiles will be stuffed with high explosives, and that's inefficient. The rockets carry a five-hundred-kilo warhead. The antimatter warhead, even with the weight of the superconducting containment vessel removed, can barely handle a hundred and fifty kilos of regular explosives."

"I know, I know," the admiral said. He looked tired and frustrated . . . and maybe a bit scared. "Build your antimatter missiles to meet your highest assumption for antimatter production. If we get them, it might just let us fight outnumbered two to one and win. If the reactors don't come through, we're hardly worse off than when we started."

"We will do that, Admiral. Vicky, how's it going?"

"I'm running as fast as I can, and I'm just barely keeping pace."

"Yes. I hope to see you when this is over."

"Me too," Vicky just managed to get in before Mannie

disappeared from the screen. Then she turned to Admiral von Mittleburg. "How much time do we have?"

"It's hard to tell," he said. "It depends on how much weight the Empress is willing to put on. One gee might give us as much as a week. The more gees, the less time we have to get those rockets we need and our ships cycled through the yard."

He briskly rubbed the tension in his scalp. "Do we polish our ships in the yard? Dial them in as best we can? Or do we take another spin around the moon, polish our ship handling—and risk breaking a few more? Damn, but this war shit is a bitch."

"You want to retire to that vineyard?" Vicky asked.

"No. This is what I've lived for my entire life. I know a lot of my classmates who would part with their right arm to be in my seat."

He glanced at Vicky, eyes gleaming. "This is what I was born for."

"Then what's it going to be, a quick trip around the moon to drill your captains, or sitting here, polishing our lasers?"

"Put that way, there's no real question, is there?"

"Then if we're going to do it, shouldn't we get it over with before the Empress is looking over our shoulder?" Vicky said

The fleet sortied at 0900 the next morning. A few of the casualties from the last exercise were left behind in the yard, but they were the only ones to miss the last chance they'd have to practice what they would be doing for real before the week was out.

CHAPTER 56

THE Empress held her fleet to a comfortable one gee. Why was anyone's guess. That left Admiral von Mittleburg's ships plenty of time to fix and mend what broke during the second practice run.

Wolverine and *Wombat* fell back well before the Empress's fleet came through.

It was tempting to leave them there at the jump. They could have easily picked off the first destroyers to come through: two, four, maybe even six. If they were light cruisers, however, its 6-inch lasers would quickly range in on the destroyers and shoot them to pieces.

Vicky knew that in the next couple of days, she might be asking destroyers to make suicidal charges, but to ask two to stand in place, just forty thousand klicks from the jump, was a death sentence she wasn't willing to sign.

Apparently, neither was Admiral von Mittleburg.

The destroyers fell back to well out of 18-inch range and stayed there.

No sooner had they reached a safe position than the Empress's fleet began jumping through and forming in full battle formation. Four battle lines of nine or ten battleships held pride of place, surrounded by cruisers and destroyers. The assault transports held at the rear of the fleet, guarded by merchant cruisers and destroyers.

Only after all this was arrayed in perfect order did the Empress's barge stick its nose cautiously through the jump.

Immediately, it blared out an order from the Emperor to lay down their arms and submit to their proper liege lord.

Vicky was prepared for that. As Commander Blue and his leading chief ran the message through their voice recognition analysis, Vicky stood, in full vice admiral and Grand Duchess mode, and demanded, "Can you authenticate that order?"

It took quite a while for her question and the Empress's answer to bounce out and back.

"What do you mean, authenticate it? You heard the order. Obey," the Empress demanded right back several hours later.

"Verbal orders have been known to be faked," Vicky said. "Words can be patched together like a quilt. I say again, can you authenticate this so-called order?"

A conversation this elongated could not raise blood pressure half as high as Vicky wanted, but it served its purpose and bought time. She already had Commander Blue's answer.

"You little bitch. You know the Emperor's voice. You claim to be his obedient daughter though I've seen none of that. Submit."

"Commander," Vicky said, handing off her center place to an expert.

"Every one of the words in the Emperor's order has been taken from one of nine speeches the Emperor made recently. One speech had a lot of applause behind it. It was his birthday speech. The applause has been wiped, but if you check the audio very carefully, you can spot those words for the lack of background noise. This is no order. This is a collage."

"Thank you, Commander Blue. Now I have a word for the Navy units that just covered the Empress's ass as she tiptoed through that jump. Lay down your arms, and you will be received readily into our fleet or allowed to go home unharmed. Fight for that blackhearted bitch against me and my father, your Emperor, and a lot of you will die. Pull out while you can."

"You can quit talking, Your Grace," Commander Blue said. "The Empress has closed down this frequency and is jamming it."

"How much got out?"

"Not much after that blackhearted-bitch remark. She can dish it out, but I don't think she likes to have it thrown back in her face."

"No surprise there," Vicky said. "Commander, can you get me a secure landline to Admiral von Mittleburg?"

A screen blinked. The admiral was already looking at Vicky.

"Did that go as well as you hoped?" he asked her.

"About as well as I could expect. We countered her claim to have an order from the Emperor. I got an offer out to all her ships, assuming everyone was monitoring that channel."

"I think you can count on that. From my check of our own ships, just about every comm unit was turned to you two's slow tête-à-tête."

"So. What do we do now?"

"What we've been doing," Admiral von Mittleburg said. "Load every weapon your friend down on St. Petersburg can squeeze out of his fabs or reactors. Have the yard dial in every ship so that we can get every ounce of effort out of them when the battle comes. For you and me, that means waiting patiently and killing any snake that can't be handled below our pay grade."

Vicky allowed herself to worry her lower lip. "Can I say that I hate this?"

"You can, but I can't help you."

"You've done more than anyone could have expected of an admiral in these trying times," Vicky told him.

"And you, Your Grace, have surprised me more than I ever thought a Peterwald could."

"Now you're just being nasty," Vicky said through a grin.

"Right back at you. Now, let's get to work."

CHAPTER 57

THREE days later, the Empress's fleet was braking at a comfortable one gee toward orbit around St. Petersburg. The moon was a bit out of the way to provide the perfect pivot for Vicky's fleet, but they'd used it to swing out and around, blast themselves high above the moon and toward the incoming fleet. They turned on a course that would take them back to St. Petersburg a bit ahead of the Empress's ships. They'd have a clear shot up their vulnerable aft end with its engines.

The Empress had her jammer back on, so it was impossible to determine exactly how her force was organized, but before it went up, the pixies had gotten a good read on her battle line. More than half of her battleships, twenty-three in all, were ancient hulks from the reserve fleet. They carried twelve 14-inch or 15-inch lasers, much less powerful and shorter-ranged than the 16- and 18-inch guns on the sixteen newer ships.

Proof of the poor maintenance aboard the Empress's ships was clear for all to see. Three of the old battleships and several of the cruisers and other ships had suffered engineering casualties on the acceleration and deceleration toward St. Petersburg. A couple of them trailed the fleet. Those that had failed while decelerating had veered well away and would have to make another try at getting into orbit around St. Petersburg.

What the Empress still had outnumbered Vicky's two to one.

None of her ships had broken down and fallen out. The next few hours would tell if the extra maintenance and rocket ships would make enough of a difference.

During the long approach, the Empress and the Butcher of Dresden had treated the people of St. Petersburg to a series of bloodcurdling threats. They talked, screamed, or shrieked in livid details about what they would do when they got there. It did them no good.

The fantastic production levels from the fabs below did Vicky's fleet quite a bit of good.

It also got her six more ships volunteered to her service.

There was no time to run those hulls through any kind of conversion. Also, there were some strings attached to the offer. So the merchant ships were loaded with containers full of coarse gravel, large river stones, granite boulders, and other things you did not want to meet in space. These ships, and their owners, would sail from the station and head for the jump to Metzburg. Along the way, they would dump their load, spraying it along the path the Empress's fleet would sail.

Buried in with all the rocks were contact explosives, no bigger than stones, as well as some rockets with homing devices that would only activate if their passive sensors picked up a nearby signal. St. Petersburg's outer orbits would be a mess; they'd have to be swept clear of all this. It was unanimously agreed that was a bridge they'd blow up when they came to it.

For now, anything that promised the Empress a bad day was good.

The Empress's battleships, cruisers, and other ships that could not decelerate went zipping by Vicky's fleet, desperately trying to vector themselves out of range. The Empress was heard to scream on her command net that the ships should take the chance to charge the rebel fleet, but the ships that were already down with engineering casualties seemed uninterested in seeing if the rest of their systems worked any better.

Vicky put them in the "they'll surrender later," column and ignored them.

For this battle, she was sharing Admiral Bolesław's flag

bridge on *Retribution* one level up from the captain's bridge. She sat in her station chair, her high-gee station parked at her elbow. Admiral Bolesław had the place fully manned and equipped to let him track half of Admiral von Mittleburg's fleet as well as the goings-on among the Empress's ships.

He agreed with Vicky that Commander Blue and his magic boxes were something he wanted. The new skipper of the *Retribution* would have to make do with the division's leading chief covering the station on his bridge until Commander Blue trained up an officer replacement.

Strange how something no one used to think about was now essential. *Thank you, Kris Longknife, for showing me that one.*

The Empress's remaining thirty-six battleships had reorganized themselves into four balanced battle lines, well apart. The middle two were a bit more distant than the upper and lower ones.

"I think she's going to try to envelop us," Admiral Bolesław muttered, half to himself.

"Why not. We've been doing it to her strategically for the last month," Vicky said.

"You may have taught her something."

"Who commands over there?" Vicky asked Admiral Bolesław.

"I don't know. What I do know is that over half her ships are antiques left over from the Iteeche War."

"She's already breaking the reserve battleships out of mothballs and sending them out to fight?"

"It would appear so," the admiral said, rubbing his chin. "It doesn't seem to have helped her all that much. The ships that broke down are all reserve wrecks."

"She's got a lot of destroyers and cruisers stretching out her line toward St. Petersburg. Fewer in the rear," Vicky observed.

"Somebody over there knows something about how you fight a battle in space."

"Huh?"

"We want to get some good shots at the aft end of her battleships, where the vulnerable rockets and reactors are. That's why we're braking toward St. Petersburg a bit ahead of her. Obviously, she doesn't want us to do that."

"Understandably. Kris Longknife was always trying to get a shot at the alien's reactors."

"Smart girl," Admiral Bolesław said, clearly not happy praising the Wardhaven princess. "Anyway, the Empress's fleet is deployed heavy aft. Lots of her cruisers and most of her destroyers are back there, between us and her battleships' aft ends. This way, if we try to cross her T, cut across her vulnerable rear, she can order the destroyers to launch a high-speed run in, get close enough to fire their pulse lasers, and do us a lot of damage."

"Won't we just pick them off?" Vicky asked. She'd learned a lot from Admiral Krätz. This hadn't been covered.

"A few. Maybe a lot. And we'll order our destroyers to make a fast run in themselves, to get a pulse-laser hit on those aft engines and shoot up the attacking destroyers. The Empress's cruisers will take a stab at our destroyers and cruisers while our cruisers are rendering honors to theirs. It will be a wild melee battle with no one quite sure how it will turn out."

"When will our destroyers and cruisers go in?"

"When Admiral von Mittleburg gives the order. The Empress has the wind gauge, so to speak. She's braking; all she has to do is order her ships to reduce their deceleration, and they'll overtake us. There's a disadvantage to ordering the first attack. Your ship might build up more energy on the boat, but the battle will take place closer to your enemy's battle line. Our battleships will be better able to support our destroyers with our secondaries."

"But won't that tend to let them get in range of our battleships?"

"Maybe, but remember, it's their vulnerable sterns that are hanging out. Their destroyers are attacking our bows with thick meteorite catchers as well as armor."

Vicky frowned at the screens showing the two fleets closing. "As you say, a melee battle."

"Yep."

===

CHAPTER 58

"THE Empress has issued a signal," Commander Blue said, almost in a whisper. "All ships acknowledged what I take was an order. The Empress just issued an execute." There was a pause. "All destroyers and cruisers have changed their vector from deceleration to closing with us."

"Any orders from Admiral von Mittleburg?" Admiral Bolesław asked.

"None, sir."

"Comm, send to squadron. Prepare to execute orders."

"Acknowledged, sir," said the young lieutenant serving as the flag comm officer.

Vicky glanced at his board. Each ship in Task Force 2 had sent a digital reply just as the lieutenant finished the order.

Talk about eager beavers.

"Signal from Admiral von Mittleburg. All Cru, and Des-Rons, prepare to close with the enemy cruisers and destroyers when I issue execute."

"Comm, pass along to the squadrons. Execute on *my* order."

Vicky tried very hard not to smile. Rear Admiral Bolesław was not about to allow Vice Admiral von Mittleburg to usurp his prerogative.

On the screen, Vicky could see destroyers and cruisers from all four of the Empress's squadrons closing on her two lonely ones. She held her breath while Vice Admiral von Mittleburg sweated out the hardest decision of his life.

"Don't wait too long, Heinrich," Admiral Bolesław whispered through clenched teeth.

Then all the Empress's cruisers and destroyers began to skew their courses, aiming for the *Retribution*.

"That gold-plated bitch," Admiral Bolesław said. "Now don't you wish you'd stayed at home by the fire?"

"No." Vicky had nothing to add to that.

"Yeah, I know. Life's a bitch, then you get bitches like her. Come on, Heinrich. She's showed her hand."

"All Cru and DesRons engage the ships closing on *Retribution*. Execute now."

"Pass that order to all ships," Admiral Bolesław said. "Give my execute."

In the blink of an eye, the comm board turned green as all Task Force 2's ships acknowledged the order. In hardly more time, destroyers changed their deceleration and vector, shooting out to engage their own kind. The cruisers were a bit slower, but they were not far behind.

Vicky eyed the board. The two battle fleets were a good two hundred thousand klicks apart. At the rate they were closing, they'd likely be within range of her 18-inch guns in less than a half hour. The 16- and 15-inch lasers in both fleets would likely take a few extra minutes. The old 14-inch guns in the Empress's fleet would take even more time.

The *Retribution* was at the head of the column of battleships backing down toward St. Petersburg. That put it closest to the Empress's fleet. Its secondary battery included twelve 6-inchers and another twelve 4-inchers. That was the biggest secondary armament Vicky knew on any battleship.

It was about to get a workout.

Vicky tried to keep her eyes on the Empress's battleships as they closed the range, and watch the battle of the destroyers and cruisers between them. She found herself in danger of going cross-eyed.

"Can we ignore the battleships and just shoot at the cruisers and little boys?" she asked Admiral Bolesław.

"Not if you want to come out of this with your hide relatively intact. You got to watch them both."

"I was afraid you'd say that."

"Maybe I can save you some trouble. Computer, warn me if the Empress's battleships change direction or acceleration. Warn me when they come within one hundred twenty thousand klicks of any friendly battleships."

"Orders logged. I will follow your instructions."

"See, that takes a bit of the work out of your day and mine."

They both turned back to concentrate on the developing battle.

"Uh-oh," the admiral said.

"Do we have a problem?" Vicky asked.

"The Empress tried a sneak," Admiral Bolesław said. "We sent every cruiser and destroyer we had into the fight. She was holding back sixteen destroyers to escort her transports. She just had them cut all deceleration and use maximum acceleration to close the distance with us."

Vicky did the numbers in her head. She had thirty-one destroyers closing on the Empress's battle line. The Empress had thirty, allowing for the two that had broken down. Things were about even. These extra sixteen destroyers raised the Empress's odds to three to two.

Vicky checked the cruiser count. The Empress had most of her light cruisers, sixteen of them, backing up the destroyers. She was holding most of her heavy cruisers with the battle line, only releasing four to this wild charge. "Admiral von Mittleburg has committed all his cruisers. The odds are even," Vicky muttered.

"Or maybe better," Admiral Bolesław said, with a bit of a smile.

"Better?"

"The Empress is coming at us balls, er, pedal to the metal, Your Grace. Three gees."

"You mean balls to the wall, Admiral."

"That, too. Anyway, Heinrich has our destroyers holding to just one and a half gees."

"He's letting them get closer to us for the meeting clash."

"Exactly. We'll have our main battery at least in range. Maybe our 6-inchers as well."

Vicky let her stomach taste the idea that she was being used as bait. She was not surprised. *Why not?*

"When they get in close," the admiral said, "I intend to drop *Retribution* back to the end of the line. They will have to come through every battleship I've got to get at you."

"I'm the carrot dangling in front of the donkey," Vicky said.

"And we must keep the carrot out of the donkey's reach as long as possible, right?"

"What does the carrot say?" Vicky asked.

"It says nothing. It just allows us to make the best use of her that we can."

"So that's what a Grand Duchess is worth today?"

"We asked you to stay dirtside. I think there may have even been an order to that effect. You refused. Now you're used."

"Foolish me."

"Enough of this prattle. The battle is about to begin. Do you want to order in some popcorn? You are just going to watch, Your Grace. Right?"

"Right. But I'll pass on the popcorn. Is there any tea to be had?"

"Chief steward's mate?"

"Here sir," and a cup of the requested beverage appeared.

Admiral Bolesław sipped his tea so calmly, eyes flashing as he took in every movement on the screens.

Vicky took a deep breath, a sip of tea, and did her best to stay calm.

Like a good carrot should.

CHAPTER 59

⸻

THE Empress's heavy cruisers opened fire first. They hit nothing, but their fire did make the belt of crud sparkle.

"I bet that's a surprise," Admiral Bolesław said.

"But it was one we wanted to save for her battle line," Vicky said.

"No way to avoid her destroyers finding it."

Vicky nodded. It had been a long time since there had been a serious battleship engagement. No doubt a lot had been forgotten. And she, of course, was trying several new twists.

That's what I get for experimenting.

Vicky went back to the screens. Her destroyers began a gentle jinking pattern as they came in range of the cruisers 8-inch guns. That accounted for the misses. The Empress's were still coming straight in. When Vicky's heavy cruisers opened up, several of the Empress's destroyers took hits. One exploded, but the others seemed none the worse for the wear.

Then the Empress's destroyers began a random pattern, bouncing up or down, right or left. Vicky frowned. That would make the cruiser's firing solutions harder.

Three of the Empress's destroyers came apart or bent in the middle.

Admiral Bolesław barked out a laugh. "Got you now," he snapped.

As Vicky watched, her cruisers made several more hits. The damage gave the destroyers a cruel choice. Reduce their wild maneuvering and risk a second hit, or keep it up and risk bending in half.

Most chose to keep up the jink pattern and abandon ship quickly when the inevitable break came.

"They'd rather break and abandon ship than risk our fire," Admiral Bolesław observed. "What does that say about their eagerness to die for their Empress?"

"Not much," Vicky said.

Now the heavy cruisers were in range of each other. The destroyers were handed over to the light cruisers. Their 6-inch lasers could reach the destroyers, just not each other.

Here, the Empress paid the price for keeping her heavy cruisers back with her battle line. Outnumbered three to one, the four Empress heavies took hit after hit. Vicky's heavy cruisers had begun Evasion Pattern 2 as soon as they came in range. The Empress's cruisers took a few extra seconds to realize their steady course was a death warrant.

By the time the four heavy cruisers threw themselves into a mad evasion effort, it was too late. Two cruisers bent in half. They spewed out survival pods even as they lost way and became rolling hulks in space.

One ship took a series of direct hits, one after the other. It exploded. The last began to shed ice, then lost all control as chunks of the ship followed the ice overboard.

That one, also, abandoned ship. "Check fire. Check fire on the heavy cruisers," Admiral von Mittleburg ordered. "Transfer fire to the light cruisers."

The last heavy cruiser must have had some maniac or one of the Empress's fanatics aboard. Or maybe a firing circuit closed on its own. However it happened, one 8-inch laser fired after the check fire order. It was a lucky shot.

Painfully lucky.

It took the *Augsburg* right on one of its forward turrets. The explosion carried backward up the power lines, and the entire forward battery vanished in one cascading explosion.

"Dear God," Admiral Bolesław muttered.

"Help them," Vicky added to the prayer. She doubted that she could pray. Yet. But she could piggyback a few of her thoughts on someone else's.

"That wasn't supposed to happen," Admiral Bolesław said, half to himself. "I hope whatever that was isn't in all our ships."

Vicky said nothing, but the Empress's cruisers had died so very quickly. Would hers vanish into smoke just as fast?

Vicky's remaining heavy cruisers turned their fire on the Empress's sixteen light cruisers with a vengeance.

Someone, however, was learning quickly. These cruisers had begun to dodge about well before they came under fire. Since they hadn't programmed their jinking into their fire control computers, their fire became wild while Vicky's cruisers were just as deadly as before.

Vicky's ships jinked according to a pattern laid into the ships' nav computers and shared with the fire control system. The computer was able to predict exactly where its own ship would be when it came time to fire. The targeted Empress's ship was the only variable. Vicky's cruisers didn't hit every time, but they hit a lot more than the Empress's ships did.

As the cruisers fought it out in a painfully even fight, the destroyers came in range of each other. It could have been a massacre, with Vicky's ships outnumbered three to two, but her destroyers had one advantage.

They had not yet reached the junk field. Admiral von Mittleburg had timed it perfectly. The Empress's destroyers charged into the minefield Vicky's last bunch of volunteers had strewn just as the Empress's destroyers needed to take their opposite number under fire.

It was a disaster for them.

Initially, they fired at Vicky's destroyers. With both sides jinking, the results were pretty much a wash. One of Vicky's destroyers took a hit but kept on going.

Then one of the Empress's destroyers ran into a rock that exploded. Two others ran into dirt, but the hits were in good places.

"I'm getting talk on a scrambler I can read," Commander Blue announced.

"Put it on," Admiral Bolesław ordered curtly before Vicky could say, "Please put it on."

Oh, well.

"What the hell is this stuff?"

"I don't know, but I've got a small hull breach. Thank God it wasn't five centimeters more forward, or I'd have lost my reactor."

"Use your main battery to sweep the space in front of you," came the voice of someone in authority.

"Doing it," came in several voices.

On the screen, Vicky saw several destroyers begin to fire at the space not ahead of them but where they intended to go next.

"Do you see what I see?" Vicky said.

"More importantly, I think our destroyer skippers have spotted it, too."

Half a dozen of the Empress's destroyers took hits when they zigged into the space they'd cleared.

"Quit that!" came in a shrill female voice. "Don't you see, you're giving yourself away? Charge! Get that willful bitch!"

"I think my loving stepmom is taking tactical command," Vicky said.

"It's not a bad order."

"Not bad?"

"Sometimes the best way past a minefield is through it," Admiral Bolesław said. "Just ask a Marine. If the way around it is swept by fire, you just have to suck it up and go."

"Close up your intervals," came in that authoritative male voice on the Empress's net. "This damn thing can't be too thick. Close up and go through."

"A smart man. Too bad he's not on our side," Admiral Bolesław observed.

Vicky acknowledged him with a scowl.

On screen, the destroyers closed up into divisions of four and bored through, returning Vicky's little boys' fire.

Small explosions flared as bits of crud and small mines did their damage. Bigger explosions showed where Vicky's destroyers hit them. Several of the Empress's destroyers fell out of their tight formation. Some continued to fight their way forward. Three abandoned ship.

With an effort, Vicky tore her eyes away from the battle of the little boys to check in on the cruisers.

Nothing seemed to be happening there.

The twenty cruisers continued to exchange fire. There was the occasional hit, but no sudden, catastrophic end to a ship. No ship going slack and seeding space with survival pods.

Vicky checked the board that reported the status of all ships. The battleships were, of course, solidly in the green. The cruisers were a different matter. All of the ships had one or more systems tending to yellow. A few, like the *Augsburg*, glared red.

The cruisers were taking punishment. Unfortunately, there was no way to tell if the Empress's cruisers were getting as much, or worse, than they gave.

"Am I missing something?" Vicky asked.

"I don't know, Your Grace, but I think I've just spotted something. Comm, get me a secure line to Admiral von Mittleburg."

In a second, he was connected. "Admiral, are you seeing what I'm seeing?"

"If you mean the failure of the Empress's cruiser gun line to fall back on the battle line and concentrate on our incoming destroyers. Yes, I just spotted it."

"The golden bitch really does want to get Our Grace here, doesn't she?" Admiral Bolesław said.

"It looks like it. If her cruisers keep our cruisers tied up, it could go hard on you, Ališ."

"Yes, it could," Admiral Bolesław said. "I'm prepared to pull *Retribution* back to the tail of our line. Make those destroyers come down through every gun I have to get to Her Grace."

"Can you use the battleships' main battery to hit the destroyers?" Vicky asked.

"It would be like swatting flies with a twenty-pound sledgehammer, Your Grace," Admiral von Mittleburg said.

"But if the battlewagons' main batteries took out their cruisers?" Admiral Bolesław said.

"Then our cruisers could concentrate on their destroyers," Vicky said.

"That sounds like a plan," Admiral von Mittleburg said. "Let's keep this line open, shall we, Ališ?"

"Good talking with you, Heinrich," and the two admirals hung up.

In a moment, the orders came down. "Battleships, engage

the hostile cruisers when they come in range of your main batteries. Engage destroyers with your secondaries as soon as they come in range."

Admiral Bolesław passed along the order, adding a "fire at will," to the Admiral von Mittleburg's order.

"Now we see what hell we can give them," Bolesław whispered. "We've sure as hell trained as much as we could."

Vicky checked the board on her battle line. All the ships' main batteries were solid green. It had taken over a month to get the board that way, and a lot of hard work from the fab workers on St. Petersburg.

I wonder what the blackhearted Empress's board looks like?

Hell, I wonder if she even has a board.

Vicky smiled at her private argument with herself, then went back to the destroyer battle.

Five more little boys had fallen out of the fight: four destroyers on the Empress's side, one on hers. Between the engineering casualties, the guns, and the rocky minefield, the Empress was down sixteen ships, one-third of her force.

These were just the ships that had given up the charge. There was no telling how many still coming were limping, lame, or wishing they were somewhere else.

On the cruiser gun line, one of the Empress's cruisers was out of the fight, spewing survival pods as it drifted in space. Unfortunately, the *Augsburg* was pulling out of the line, still under some sort of control but letting its own inertia carry it away from the fight.

Vicky did a check: the *Retribution*'s main battery was sixteen 18-inch lasers. They had a range of one hundred thousand kilometers. The Empress's destroyers were coming in range. The cruisers were twenty thousand klicks behind them. It wouldn't be long before the *Retribution*, *Ravager*, and *Trouncer* could open up.

"You hungry?" Admiral Bolesław asked.

"I'm afraid if I ate anything, it might come back up," Vicky admitted to him in a whisper.

"Good black bread and butter will do you good," he said, smiling jovially. "You have to keep up your energy. It's not like we hack at each other with battle-axes anymore. Still, this can take nearly as much nervous energy out of you as swinging a good sword."

Vicky allowed that might be possible, and the chief steward's mate disappeared, only to return with the black bread, butter, and a squeeze bottle of honey.

"Ah, perfect, Sergei. Once again, you have read my mind."

The chief just smiled and cut the bread for them. The admiral slathered on the butter and honey. Vicky followed suit, going light on the toppings.

The chief offered a slice of bread to Commander Blue. He took one, added nothing to it, and munched it without taking his eyes from his boards.

Together, Vicky and Admiral Bolesław munched their bread and watched as the battle developed. A few more destroyers fell out of the charge: two of the Empress's, one of Vicky's. Two cruisers, one from each gun line, fell out.

Then the destroyers got in range of the approaching cruisers' secondary batteries.

All hell broke loose.

CHAPTER 60

═══

THE cruisers continued to hammer each other with their 6-, 8-, or 9.2-inch lasers. Now they reached out for the little boys with their secondaries of 4- or 5-inch lasers. Six destroyers, evenly divided, were swatted down immediately and left crushed in space. Still, the gunfight continued between the cruisers. Another two, one Vicky's, one the Empress's, fell out.

Then the Empress's cruisers crossed the hundred-thousand-kilometer line. In a blink, Admiral Bolesław's *Retribution*, *Ravager*, and *Trouncer* opened fire, as well as BatRon 22's ships in Admiral von Mittleburg's squadron: the *Implacable*, *Adamant*, *Merciless*, and *Hunter*. Eighty-eight 18-inch lasers spoke almost as one.

The cruisers had just reached the crud field and closed up, dividing their secondaries between shooting at destroyers and doing their best to sweep the space ahead of them.

They were not prepared for 18-inch guns with the best dialed-in fire control systems in the fleet.

Two cruisers vanished as if grabbed by the fist of an angry god of old. Other cruisers were staggered as they took hits not intended for their class. Some wandered into explosives they hadn't noticed or reacted to in their distress. Others settled on a straight course as bridge crews were distracted by more pressing matters.

The second broadside was worse than the first.

Four cruisers vanished in the blink of an eye.

"We're getting surrender offers from two, no three," Commander Blue said. "No, make that all of the cruisers."

"Comm, connect me with Admiral von Mittleburg." The admiral immediately appeared on screen.

"Have your sensors picked up the surrender offers?"

"No."

"I have. Will you hold your fire while I attempt to negotiate a surrender?"

"Make it quick."

"Comm?"

"You're on the guard net."

"Cruisers on net, who is asking to surrender?"

The reply was garbled as they all tried to speak at once. Admiral Bolesław shouted, "Report in alphabetical order of your ship's name. Damn it, we don't have much time."

"*Bielefeld*," came through clear and strong, followed quickly by, "*Dusseldorf*," "*Gdynia*," "*Krotovo*," "*Mlawa*," "*Tychy*." "*Utena*," finished up the list.

"Please don't shoot," *Utena* pleaded. "We know we don't stand a chance."

So, of course, the Empress broke in, screaming invectives and ordering that all traitors be shot. She screamed for the security experts on each ship to shoot the cowardly captains.

No security type appeared on screen to execute the Empress's rant.

The skipper of the *Utena* rolled his eyes at the overhead. "See what we've had to put up with. Who do you think begged me to give up? What do you want us to do?"

"Empty your lasers and do not recharge them," Admiral Bolesław said. "I'd order you to dump your reactors, but that planet ahead of us is coming up fast. Disable your lasers as best you can." Bolesław rubbed his chin. "There are a lot of people in survival pods who aren't going to make it if they aren't collected. Don't make me regret this, but you are ordered to pick up as many survivors as you can."

"Understood. That's a job I'm glad to accept."

"Wait one. Vice Admiral von Mittleburg, have you been following my negotiations?"

"I have and am satisfied with what you offered. Tell them that I have personally reserved some 18-inchers for them if they go back on their word."

"I understand," said the skipper of the *Utena*. "My leading chief has successfully rendered my fire control system unusable. I have ordered all ships to follow our lead. If someone stupid tries to do something, I assure you it will be as ineffective as possible. Oh, someone just smashed the main bus to the lasers. I swear to God, you have nothing to worry about from us."

"Commander Blue, can you confirm any of these actions?" Admiral Bolesław said.

"Unfortunately, no, Admiral. However, I can say that the fire control system is down and the lasers have no charge."

"Let me know if that changes," Admiral Bolesław said, then turned to the screen with Admiral von Mittleburg. "The cruisers are out of the battle."

"Then God help the destroyer men. All ships, put those little boys out of action before they hurt one hair on the head of our Grand Duchess."

Vicky's destroyers, now picking their way carefully through the cloud of crud and past the cruisers that offered them no opposition, were well out of range of the Empress's destroyers. The defense of Vicky's battle line was totally in the lap of the cruiser gun line.

They spoke. The larger 8-inch lasers on the heavy cruisers had a tough time tracking the rapidly jinking destroyers. The light cruisers' 6-inch main batteries were more nimble. The secondary batteries on all the cruisers had an easier time tracking the destroyers and taking them under fire.

The Empress's destroyers burned, bled, and exploded.

"I've cracked a scrambled net channel," Commander Blue said.

"On speaker," Admiral Bolesław ordered.

"We can't take much more of this."

"Could we just blast the cruisers? They're almost in range."

"Don't you dare waste your main punch." The Empress was on this net now, screaming like a banshee. "You told me those ship wreckers of yours could take down battleships! Now you will take down the battleship that little traitor is on! Get that bitch, or I'll have your heads on pikes right next to those cowardly cruiser men!"

One destroyer fired on a heavy cruiser anyway. One 21-inch pulse laser shook the ship hard, but it held its course.

The Empress's scream was soul-shaking.

The Empress's destroyer next to the one that fired took it under fire and blew it to pieces.

Three more destroyers were hit by the gun line and fell off, powerless.

The destroyer that had blown up its mate suddenly came under fire from the two destroyers nearby. It disintegrated in one huge fireball.

"We can't keep this up," came a voice on net. "We've got to surrender, like the cruisers, or we'll all be dead."

Another destroyer turned its fire on the ship beside it.

"Thus to all traitors."

Two of the destroyers—and four of Vicky's cruisers—took that one under fire, leaving another glowing ball of hot gas where it had been.

"We can't keep killing ourselves as fast as they're killing us. I quit," said a disembodied voice on net. On screen, a destroyer cut its acceleration down to almost nothing though it continued to dodge.

No one shot at this one.

"Don't fire at any destroyer that powers down," Admiral von Mittleburg said on net. On his private channel to Admiral Bolesław, he said, "Are you getting a request for surrender?"

"They're a bit leery of going on net asking to surrender since the last two to try got shot up by their mates," Admiral Bolesław said. "Let me see what I can do."

The admiral turned to Vicky. "You want to stand next to me? It might help."

"I thought I was the carrot," Vicky said.

"Maybe I'll use you as carrot cake. You ever have a slice of one? I loved my mother's."

"About that surrender," Vicky said.

He turned back to the screen. "This is Admiral Bolesław. I

have Her Grace, the Grand Duchess Victoria, at my elbow. We are prepared to offer asylum and protection to anyone who chooses to stop shooting at us. Empty your lasers. Disable the power buses to them and join your brothers on the cruisers picking up any survival pods you can find."

"All but one destroyer has powered down."

"Which one is the holdout?"

"The *Following Wind* is still armed and dangerous."

"Pass its position to the gun line."

"Passed."

"There is one of your number who is still loaded for bear. Rest assured, this bear is locked and loaded and aimed at you. Either disarm, *Following Wind*, or you will die on a count of three."

"One."

After only a medium pause. "Two."

Admiral Bolesław shook his head.

"He's powering down. The *Following Wind* has emptied its pulse lasers and 4-inch guns."

"Very smart of you, *Following Wind*," the admiral said.

"We had to persuade our 'political officer' that it's better to surrender to the Grand Duchess than to get blown to bits in the service of that bitch of an Empress we have."

Said Empress, no matter what her genetic makeup, was now screaming on the net. Commander Blue suggested switching to another channel, and the destroyer men did. There, uninterrupted, they settled the conditions of their temporary parole.

Vicky, however, went back to the channel with her darling stepmommy. "Hello, bitch," she said when the woman finally had to stop for air.

She waited while Annah screamed to her heart's content. When she finally had to gasp for another breath, Vicky got some words in edgewise. "You sent your cruisers and destroyers at me. We blew them away, and those that were smart surrendered."

She had to pause again while her loving stepmum exhausted that breath. "Now we'll handle your battleships, bring the smart ones over to our side, hunt you down, and put you out of your misery," Vicky finished.

The Empress went back to her raving. Vicky found herself thinking about what she'd just said.

I meant to say I'd hunt her down and kill you. Instead, I

flinched away and settled for putting her out of her misery. Am I going to do the same when Retribution *has her pleasure barge in its sights?*

I'll need to have a black heart in my chest when that time comes.

CHAPTER 61

━━━

"**R**ECALL the destroyers," Vicky ordered.

"What?" Rear Admiral Bolesław said.

"Is that line to Vice Admiral von Mittleburg still open?" Vicky asked comm.

"Yes, Your Grace."

"Vice Admiral von Mittleburg, will you be so kind as to recall the destroyers?"

"Your Grace, ah, Vice Admiral Peterwald, may I ask what you have in mind?"

"Yes, you may, Vice Admiral. We have just seen how an unsupported attack, cruisers and destroyers against a force of destroyers, cruisers, and battleships came to grief. Just now, our destroyers have no support. Please recall them. Next time we unleash the ship wreckers, I suggest we do it when everything we have is at hand keeping all that the Empress has left very, very busy."

"Understood, Your Grace, the Grand Duchess Vice Admiral Victoria. Comm, recall the destroyers. Your Grace, they had gotten quite close."

"So had the Empress's destroyers, all brave Sailors, Admiral. There is no question I could be making a mistake, but after what we've just seen, the first destroyer attack in some eighty years, I think we need to rethink their use."

"You could be right, Your Grace. I certainly cannot say that you are wrong. The little boys have turned about and are returning to our fleet."

"Very good," Vicky said. "Now, let's think a bit about what happens next, shall we? I think we have some time."

Fifteen minutes later, the Empress's battle line was closing into 18-inch laser range. Vicky and her admirals had gone through several options for handling the coming slugging match. Vicky had discovered how useful her computer could be when it came to quickly running alternative battle plans. They'd watched a good many times as their battle fleet was destroyed.

The plan they were about to execute had been passed down to the smallest ship through coded tight beam. Now they'd see how it worked.

For the moment, Vicky stood before the main screen on *Retribution*'s flag bridge and ordered Comm to hail her opposite number.

A wiry, white-haired man wearing the stripes of a grand admiral took her call.

"I am Her Grace, the Grand Duchess Vice Admiral Victoria, and I command here."

"I am Grand Admiral Kuznetsov, and I have orders to take your surrender or destroy you. Which will it be, young lady?"

"Uncle Vitaly," came from a second screen, where Admiral von Mittleburg was observing Vicky's sally. "Did they drag you out of retirement?"

"Is that you, Heinrich? What are you doing mixed up in a thing like this?"

Admiral von Mittleburg shrugged stoically. "These are difficult times, Uncle. We find ourselves making choices that, on another hand, we would never think of making. Are you really with the Empress?"

"Of course he is," the Empress said, joining the conversation. "All right-thinking men obey the oaths they have taken. Unlike some brats."

"Have they got a gun at your back, Uncle Vitaly?"

"I would not quite say that," the old grand admiral said.

"But he's got me with him." The Butcher of Dresden smirked as he stepped up beside the grand admiral.

"How sad to see you again, Butcher," Vicky said with as much cheer in her voice as she could fake. "How did your officers take to you getting two battleships blown away? Is that why it took you so long to finally come visit us?"

"I'll finish now what I came here to do," the Butcher said darkly.

"Enough of this," the Empress snapped. "Admiral, get on with this."

Vicky shook her head. She appreciated being called admiral because it jumped her up another rank to full admiral. But to address a grand admiral that way was to demote him. Her stepmother knew nothing of the Navy officers she was bossing around.

"May I have your surrender?" the old grand admiral asked.

"I'm sorry, Grand Admiral Kuznetsov, but no," Vicky answered, then added, "No doubt you have noticed that my forces are not easily defeated. You have lost all your destroyers and light cruisers and several of your heavies. Many have chosen to surrender rather than fight to their own destruction. Would you be interested in considering the terms I might offer you to surrender?"

"You little shit!" the Empress screamed, but did not become visible on net.

You really do need an anger management intervention, Vicky thought but did not say.

The Butcher was on the flagship and looked ready to vent his own spleen, but the grand admiral raised a restraining hand.

"You face two-to-one odds, young lady. I have only to cruise along as I am doing, and I will make orbit and capture your station and begin to threaten the people on the planet below. You must come to me. I assure you, I will not make the mistake the destroyer men made of underestimating you."

"I do not expect that you will, Grand Admiral. However, my battle fleet will not surrender. Please remember as the day's events unfold that I have taken two surrenders today. I will not delay in taking a third."

"We'll be taking your surrender if we haven't blown you to bits," the Butcher snapped with all the equanimity of a five-year-old. The screen went dead.

After a pause for everyone to catch their breath, Vicky turned to Admiral Bolesław.

"That didn't go so well," he said.

"I don't know. Every ship that was monitoring that channel now knows I'm willing to accept its surrender, and we now know who is trying to command that screwed-up situation over there. Admiral von Mittleburg, who is your Uncle Vitaly?"

"We are not blood relatives, but my father fought with him during the Iteeche War, and he used to own a vineyard next to my grandfather's. I don't know how they got their hands on him."

"Is he good?"

"One of the best," Admiral von Mittleburg assured Vicky.

"Then we will have to hope that he is good enough to separate his Sailors from the Empress's butchers so that many of them won't have to die today," Vicky said evenly.

The two admirals looked at her and nodded sadly.

CHAPTER 62

_____

THE battle began to develop very much along the line that Admirals von Mittleburg and Bolesław had foreseen. But not entirely.

Vicky's fleet was a good fifty thousand klicks closer to St. Petersburg, braking with their well-armored bows aimed in the general direction of the Empress's forces. Those forces were also braking to make orbit, but the bit of extra distance they had to go meant Vicky had a good shot at their vulnerable rocket motors and reactors.

Vicky had the advantage.

For her part, the Empress had twice as many battleships as Vicky. Formed into four battle lines of nine battleships, they could spread out and engulf Vicky's smaller force, concentrating their fire two to one against her two battle lines of seven and nine.

The Empress began to use that advantage five minutes before the biggest battleships would come in range with their 18-inch guns. Grand Admiral Kuznetsov had his four battle lines stacked an even distance from each other. Now they began to spread out. The lower line dropped lower and edged closer. The upper line went higher and also closer. The middle two squadrons held back.

"It's time we do something about that," Admiral von Mittleburg said. "Ališ, you take the high squadrons, I'll take the low ones."

For a few minutes longer, the grand admiral kept his formation as it was, then the two middle ones began to edge up, following the top squadron, the one that was trying to outmaneuver Admiral Bolesław's lone squadron.

"No surprise there," Admiral von Mittleburg said. "Execute Redistribution Plan 3," he ordered.

The destroyers that had returned to the battle line had been used hard, some more than others. Admiral von Mittleburg had them reorganize themselves into four divisions with the Fourth Division holding all the badly dinged-up destroyers that could still answer bells.

On his orders, Fourth Division took station in front of his battle squadron. The other three divisions moved over to support Admiral Bolesław. The two least damaged divisions formed up on the engaged side of the battleships, one forward, and one aft of them. The Third Division settled in among the rocket boats, ready to support where they were needed.

The twenty-eight rocket boats had been evenly divided between the two battle lines. Now, Admiral von Mittleburg's rocket boats split in half, one group staying with him, the other following the destroyers over to join Admiral Bolesław's battle line.

It was clear that the Empress was aiming everything at Vicky. Now, Admiral Bolesław's line was enlarged to defend her.

The Empress's two middle battle lines were now well on their way to closing on Vicky's battle line as they came in range of the *Retribution*'s 18-inch lasers.

"For what they are about to receive, may we be truly grateful," Admiral Bolesław said softly, then his voice boomed. "Task Force 2 and accompanying ships, begin Evasion Pattern 2."

Around Vicky, the task force began to jink according to one of the moderate dodging patterns.

Now the Grand Admiral did something to reduce the vulnerability of his battleships. One minute from 18-inch range, his remaining twenty heavy cruisers cut their deceleration and shot out, coming in range of the battle line well before they could hope to use their 8- or 9.2-inch main battery.

"Battleships with 18-inch lasers, fire at the heavy cruisers.

Transfer fire to the battleships when they come in range. Cruisers, close on the hostile cruiser line," von Mittleburg ordered.

Fifteen of the heavy cruisers were supporting the three battle lines engaging Vicky. Five were in the smaller force covering Admiral von Mittleburg. *Retribution*, *Ravager*, and *Trouncer* reached out with their first broadside. Fire was widely spaced; Vicky's gunners expected the cruisers to be dodging, and they weren't wrong. But they were prepared. All they needed was one good hit on a heavy cruiser's armor to swat it down.

Two cruisers across from Vicky and another two facing Admiral von Mittleburg were speared through by laser light and left drifting or struggling to keep way on. One exploded.

The seven biggest battleships in Vicky's force reloaded. It took thirty to thirty-five seconds before they got off their second salvo at the remaining sixteen heavy cruisers. The *Trouncer* was the last. This time, von Mittleburg's BatRon 22 aimed for the cruisers across from Vicky. Again, four heavy cruisers died. The hostile cruiser gun line was down to twelve.

Vicky's ten heavy cruisers and six light ones should be able to keep them out of mischief. Better yet, if Vicky ordered a destroyer attack now, the Empress would have few cruisers to protect her battleships.

Again, the battleships reloaded. When next they fired, they'd be exchanging shots with the Empress's 18-inch battleships.

"Commander Blue, how is the Empress's jamming going?" Vicky asked.

"Not so good, Your Grace. I think some of the cruisers we blew away had jamming gear on them."

"So what can you tell us?" Admiral Bolesław asked.

"I have a good idea which battleships are the 18-inchers."

"Then it's time to hit the big ones," Admiral Bolesław said as he gave *Retribution* and his other two big-gunned battleships orders to fire at the closest 18-inch battleships held in thrall to the Empress's power.

At the end, he added, "Willi, you make sure Guns concentrates his salvos. Go for four hits on the same spot. Two hits almost burned through Engle's ships off Brunswick. Let's see what four can do."

"You bet, Admiral. You can count on the *Retro*."

"I do," Ališ said softly as he rung off.

CHAPTER 63

O F the twenty-seven battleships in the three squadrons closing on Vicky's Task Force 2, seven were 18-inch battleships, none as big as the *Retribution*. The nine facing Admiral von Mittleburg had only two. Not only were the odds, seven to nine, the best Vicky would face today, but the distribution of the two forces was a bad mismatch.

However, Vicky's ships had something the Empress's ships didn't have.

Battle experience.

The gunnery officer on *Retribution* had let his assistant handle the cruiser shoot while he studied the battleships. The *Empress's Rage* had trouble getting up to battle RPMs and its jinking was pretty pathetic. The gunnery officer didn't need a computer to figure what that one would do next.

When the captain asked Guns to pick a target, he chose *Rage* and advised the other battleships to leave her be. *Retribution* had eight guns forward in four turrets and the same battery aft. The aft battery could be swung out just enough to engage *Rage*. As he'd been ordered, Guns targeted two turrets, four 18-inch lasers, at one spot on *Rage*'s aft end. He had a total of eight turrets; he targeted them for tight salvos against four spots where he expected burnthrough on the *Empress's Rage*. He was not disappointed.

On his command, all sixteen lasers fired: twelve immediately, four more as the ship's rotation brought them to bear. It was difficult at one hundred thousand klicks, but optics seemed to show steam boiling off *Rage*'s ice hide in four spots. Then there was a flash aft, a reactor lost containment, and, a blink later, there was nothing more than a ball of gas to look at.

Vicky and Admiral Bolesław stared at the screen as *Empress's Rage* was eaten by her own plasma. "God help those poor beggars," Bolesław prayed.

"Amen," was all Vicky could add.

Ravager and *Trouncer* had fired at the next two larger battleships. BatRon 22's two ships concentrated on the two opposite them. They hit them, but nothing as spectacular as *Retribution*'s blasting *Rage* to gas.

All seven 18-inch battleships across from *Retribution* concentrated on Vicky's flagship. It danced out of the space it had been headed for and suffered only one hit that singed the meteorite catcher.

The remaining eight largest battleships in the Empress's fleet reloaded their lasers, as did Vicky's seven.

"Task Force 2, prepare to go to Evasion Plan 4," Admiral Bolesław ordered. Vicky had known the man long enough to taste the tension behind his words.

"*Ravager* and *Trouncer*, concentrate your fire on three places on your target battleships. That's what your new gun cradles are meant for."

"I thought we were," said the skipper of the *Ravager*. "They may not be jumping around like us, but they're a bitch to predict."

"Check with Guns on *Retribution*. Find out which target he's chosen, then pick ones you think are jumping around the least."

"Understood."

The tracking clock at the top of the screen counted down to when the battleships should be reloaded. It was based on when the *Retribution* last fired and how long it would take to reload. All the other battleships in Vicky's fleet took more time to recharge their lasers. Now they would discover if the Empress's battleships could meet the standard thirty-second reload.

Then Grand Admiral Kuznetsov made a smart move.

CHAPTER 64

━━━━

THE opposing battle lines cut their deceleration and shot down. In one bold move, they came even with Vicky's ships, put their vulnerable sterns out of reach, and cut the range.

"Execute Evasion Plan 4," Admiral Bolesław snapped. "*Scourge, Sachsen, Baden, Krasnoyarsk*, and *Karelia* fire!" The last two of the 16-inch ships that now joined the fight were making their shakedown cruise right into a fight.

Among Admiral von Mittleburg's ships, *Vigilant* and *Relentless* joined in.

Now, only two of Vicky's ships, the battlecruisers *Stalker* and *Slinger*, with their 15-inch lasers, were still out of the fight.

Against Vicky's fourteen engaged ships, the Empress had fifteen: eight surviving 18-inch ships and seven 16-inchers. Her twenty remaining battleships were old boats hauled out of the reserve fleet to pad the Empress's numbers. She would soon find out how worthless they were.

The rolling salvos from both fleets were a bit ragged. There was a good ten-second interval between *Empress's Fury* firing its 18-inchers at *Retribution* and the last of the 18-inch battleships across from Vicky, *Empress's Ravager*, getting off its broadside. Possibly the sudden cut in deceleration tumbled their firing solution.

Maybe they just took too much time to reload.

The next salvo would tell more.

Retribution again jinked out of the space it had been headed to, seeded that direction with chaff, and went somewhere unexpected. The 168 shots filled a lot of space: one nailed a 4-inch turret while five just burned ice.

"Thank God for the extra meter of ice," Admiral Bolesław prayed.

Five seconds after the last of the 18-inch lasers fell silent, *Empress's Punisher* got off the first 16-inch salvo. Six more added their fire but only managed to fill the space where the *Retribution* had been.

"Every battleship is firing at me," Vicky muttered.

"So it would seem. But look on the bright side. We got *Fury*."

Vicky sardonically raised an eyebrow. *Empress's Fury* had been so intent on getting a solid firing solution that it had held its course a few seconds too long. *Retribution*'s guns made it pay the price for its intense focus on killing Vicky.

Now the Empress had only seven 18-inch battleships.

"I wish I could aim something at the Empress," Vicky half muttered to herself.

"We still have twenty-two armed merchant cruisers," Admiral Bolesław pointed out.

Together, the two of them looked at where the merchant cruisers were in line, half behind Vicky's battle squadron, the others behind von Mittleburg. There were a lot of enemy merchant cruisers and attack transports between them and the bloated passenger liner where the Empress was, no doubt, buffing her nails.

"If the Empress turns and runs?" Admiral Bolesław started but did not finish.

"If she's aiming for me, why shouldn't we aim for her?" Vicky said. "Admiral von Mittleburg, I wish to detach the armed merchant cruisers and have them attack the liner with the Empress aboard."

"You do, do you?" came back pensively.

"We've got twenty-two merchant cruisers. They've got sixteen," Admiral Bolesław pointed out.

"How many of those attack transports have some kind of popgun on them?" came back.

"I don't know," Admiral Bolesław admitted.

"Do we want to kill a lot of those troops?" was the next question.

"I would prefer to keep the slaughter to a minimum," Vicky said. "Still, if our merchant cruisers could keep their distance as they go around the invasion fleet . . ." Vicky left unfinished.

"Captain Kyrillos of *Rostock*," Admiral von Mittleburg snapped, "you will detach yourself from the present cruiser gun line. You will take command of all the armed merchant cruisers not yet engaged and do your best to destroy the command ship with the Empress aboard. In doing this, you will attempt to avoid excessive destruction of the attack transports."

"Understood. I have a hunting license for one *Golden Empress*, but don't let myself get up to my neck in the blood of those dumb schmucks trailing after her for a paycheck."

"I would have expected you to put it no other way, Drugi," Admiral von Mittleburg said.

Quickly, one light cruiser put on extra power, boosting its way up and away from the present cruiser battle. Putting Vicky's battleships between it and the Empress's battle lines, it headed for the armed merchant cruisers, which had already gone to two and a quarter gees, aiming for the side of the invasion fleet away from the Empress's battle line. Eight armed merchant cruisers shielded that side of the transport fleet. No doubt, they would soon be hard-pressed all around.

The battle fell silent as the big ships reloaded their lasers. Vicky had time to notice that Admiral von Mittleburg's ships had concentrated their fire against the ships across from her. Both side's cruisers had cut their deceleration a bit more and were having their own little battle farther along toward St. Petersburg, staying clear of the behemoths trailing them.

The Empress's four battle squadrons had stopped trying to swing around Vicky's two. Apparently, someone had noticed that if the Empress's ships got too far out trying to surround Vicky, they risked being defeated in detail.

Grand Admiral Kuznetsov seemed content to fight it out here. The Empress seemed content to let the Grand Admiral call the shots so long as almost all her battleships sent salvo after salvo ranging against Vicky's flagship.

Sooner or later, they would have to get lucky, *Retribution* would run into a few shots, and once damage began to accumulate, things would go downhill in a hurry.

"How do we change this?" Vicky asked no one in particular.

"All ships," Admiral von Mittleburg announced, "prepare to cut deceleration for thirty seconds to point-five gee on my mark."

Admiral Bolesław got a happy grin on his face. "We change things by playing their game better than they do."

As the clock counted down to the next broadside, Vicky found herself holding her breath.

"Announce to Second Battle Squadron that we go to Evasion Plan 5 on Admiral von Mittleburg's mark."

"Order transmitted," Comm reported.

"Will this get messy?" Vicky asked.

"I hope it does," the admiral said through a jolly laugh. "We stay alive if they mess up."

"You think it will joggle Guns's elbow?"

"Not Ulryk's elbow, it won't."

Vicky tightened her five-point harness on her station chair. The high-gee station stayed empty.

"Mark," Admiral von Mittleburg announced.

The bottom fell out of Vicky's stomach as *Retribution* cut power. Still, it kept up its bounce to the right or left, a bit slower in the fall or faster. *Retribution* reached out for the *Empress's Punisher*, a 16-inch battleship. Hammered hard, it fell out of the line and lost all deceleration. It began to spew survival pods. Four turrets did manage to fire, but their shots were ragged and went wild.

Several of the Empress's ships were either showing the effects of hits or poor maintenance. Two big battleships in the low squadron were hammered by four of von Mittleburg's ships. Their course grew erratic and their fire less effective.

Again, the Empress's ships aimed for *Retribution*. They didn't seem prepared for the sudden drop in deceleration. Even those who did failed to allow for the dodging and weaving.

Still, three shots caught Vicky's flag. Two were just glancing blows. One however, got burnthrough forward.

"Hull breach. Hull breach," rang throughout the ship.

"Damage control parties responding," reported the flag comm.

"We surprised them that time," Bolesław still crowed. "They didn't see that one coming."

For their part, they didn't see the trick Grand Admiral Kuznetsov now pulled out of his sleeve. As they reloaded, his entire fleet changed the direction of their deceleration, pointing their nose over forty-five degrees toward Vicky's ships and blasting their way to close the range.

"He wants to get those 14-inch battleships in range before he runs out of bigger ones."

Vicky eyed what the grand admiral had done. She studied what showed on her board and made her decision. "Admiral, it's time to order the destroyers forward."

"I think you're right. You want to pull the rocket boats up?"

"No, not yet. I'm none too sure those truncated merchies can stand in line with the battlewagons. At least not for too long. We aren't ready to launch our antimatter missiles. Hold the boats back, but advise Admiral von Mittleburg that it would be nice if his destroyers could join with mine."

A few quick words were exchanged, and three of the destroyer divisions were aimed nearly bow on to the Empress's battleships, accelerating in their direction as they still decelerated toward St. Petersburg.

"Permission to join the attack," came from the commodore of the Fourth's destroyer division with the hard-hit and crippled little boys.

"You don't belong out there, Cibor," Admiral Bolesław said.

"We sure as hell don't belong back here, Admiral."

"Be it on your head, my old boy. You have my permission to go."

The Fourth Division edged over, aiming itself gingerly at the approaching battle line. As they passed below the battle line, Vicky could hear a cheer rise in *Retribution* and likely in all the battleships.

"It's a death's ride," Bolesław said softly.

Back at the battle lines, another ragged volley rolled up and down the battleships' lines. The salvos from many of the Empress's big-gunned ships were weak. Lasers were out of action or masked as they closed in on Vicky's ships.

The Empress lost two ships: One, a 16-incher across from Vicky's squadron, exploded, *Retribution*'s fourth. One of the 18-inchers engaging Admiral von Mittleburg fell out of line, lost power, and began to drift.

Retribution took two hits: one knocked out a 6-inch secondary turret. The other made a deep gash in her armor, but the extra ice kept it from burning through.

"We may be able to get one more broadside in before the old battlewagons come in range," Admiral Bolesław said.

"Should we wear away from them to keep the range where we want it?" Vicky asked.

"That would be the smart thing to do," Admiral Bolesław said.

"I do hate to run away from a fight. I don't want to be like my stepmom, using everyone else as a shield for my body."

"You do need to be alive to win this little rebellion we're involved in."

Vicky sighed. "Wear away, but make sure we can bring all guns to bear."

In a moment, Admiral Bolesław had given the order, and the entire battle squadron did a smart turn away.

A moment later, Commander Blue said. "I have the Empress on a clear channel, screaming at Grand Admiral Kuznetsov."

"Put it on screen."

The Empress was up, her face livid with rage and large in the camera. "Chase that bitch! Don't let her get away! Tell your Sailors they can have her warm body when I'm done with her. That ought to get them off their duffs."

Grand Admiral Kuznetsov stood ramrod tall and looked pained. Almost disdainful. "As you wish," and right there on an open channel, he ordered all of his battleships to aim themselves for Vicky's battle line and go to two gees.

On Vicky's screen, the Empress's battleships were now chasing her as fast as she was running away. All their aft main batterics were masked—and they were closing on Vicky's destroyers as fast as the destroyers were closing on them.

Worst, half their secondary guns were masked as well.

"Is he doing this intentionally?" Vicky asked Admiral Bolesław.

"He's doing exactly what she demanded, and damning her badly."

"That bitch is attacking me!" the Empress suddenly shouted. She'd paced away from the camera, but she had her nose in it again. "She's trying to kill me! Do something, Admiral."

On the screen, the Imperial barge had gone to two gees deceleration and was pulling away from the braking fleet.

"Yes, Your Imperial Highness," the grand admiral said blandly. "But what?"

"Order some battleships back here to protect me."

"Which would you have me send? Our newer battleships with larger guns have accumulated a lot of battle damage. While we've concentrated on *Retribution*, they've hammered all our firing ships very hard. The old battleships you had hauled out of mothballs are hardly in any condition to attempt more than one gee. One and a half at the most. I see you are now running away at two gees. Can your liner maintain that deceleration?"

As if to answer the grand admiral, the liner's deceleration began to fall off—1.98, 1.95, 1.92.

"Admirals," Commander Blue announced in a loud, clear voice, "I have a message coming in from His Imperial Majesty, Emperor Henry I."

"The Emperor?" Vicky echoed, and managed not to add. *What the hell is he doing here?*

"Put it on screen," Admiral Bolesław ordered.

CHAPTER 65

═══════

THE screen showed the bridge of a light cruiser. The skipper sat in a high-gee station. It looked like he hadn't shaved in a week.

"I am Commander Bonaventura of the cruiser *Smolensk*, and I bear a message to all parties from His Imperial Majesty Henry I." In a moment, the commander disappeared, and the Emperor himself stood before them stiffly, in full regalia.

"You are all hereby ordered to cease immediately this distaff strife," he said, "and stand aside from each other under the pain of my severest displeasure."

"Distaff?" Admiral Bolesław asked.

"Womanly," Commander Blue said.

"Dad's been reading Shakespeare again," Vicky said with a sigh.

"It pleases me to have your discord submitted to mediation, so that I may have harmony in my palace once again."

"Mediation? Who?" Vicky said. And was shocked to hear her stepmother ask the same thing on her net.

"Who could mediate this?" Admiral Bolesław asked. "Really mediate this, I mean."

Vicky shook her head. "I have no idea."

"It pleases me to request from another noble monarch the services of Princess Kristine Longknife of Wardhaven. She saved my life, and I would willingly place my trust in her now. She brought you, Grand Duchess Victoria, home from much risk and travail. This pleases me, and I hope it will satisfy you, Victoria."

"That bitch!" the Empress screamed. Someone cut the feed.

"Doesn't that woman know any woman she doesn't think is a bitch?" Admiral Bolesław asked Vicky.

"Nope. I don't think so," Vicky said, but her mind was on something else. She really thought she had this battle won. Given a few more minutes, they might blow the Empress's barge out of space.

Dare I keep this battle going for a few more rounds?

Vicky shook her head. "Comm, put me through on a channel to Grand Admiral Kuznetsov."

The old man looked flummoxed. "I never heard of a battle ending like this," he was muttering.

"But it behooves us to end this battle or risk His Imperial Majesty, my father's, wrath, don't you think?"

"Yes. Yes I do."

"Admiral von Mittleburg, I am ordering all the ships loyal to me to stand down, cease fire, and set a course for High St. Petersburg Station. Grand Admiral, I hope you will excuse me if I ask that your ships avoid coming close to that station."

The grand admiral pursed his lips and studied something off screen. "It appears that my fleet all have sufficient reaction mass to swing wide of St. Petersburg and return from whence we came."

"Would you mind terribly if I asked you to discharge your capacitors while you make your approach and exit?" Vicky asked.

"Would you be willing to do the same?" the old grand admiral countered.

Now it was Vicky's turn to worry her lower lip. "I really don't want to," she finally said.

"Your Grace," said Admiral von Mittleburg, "I can understand how, in the past, you have benefited from a certain amount of cautious paranoia."

Vicky met that with a rueful rolling of her eyes.

"However," Admiral von Mittleburg said, going on, "Grand

Admiral Kuznetsov still has his ships encumbered by certain Security Specialists who seem most enthusiastic to carry out any little order that comes in from the Empress."

Now it was the grand admiral's turn to roll his eyes.

"It seems to me that it would be better for us all if our lasers had empty capacitors. We should be able to tell the second any capacitor, ours or hers, begin to power up and take actions accordingly."

Vicky glanced at Commander Blue, who stood at his station out of view of the camera. He nodded. Vicky drew in a deep breath and let it out slowly. "We thank you for your thoughts, good admiral, and it pleases us to follow your advice," she said.

"Good God, I'm deleting your copy of Shakespeare," Admiral Bolesław muttered softly.

"Oh no. I don't read that old guy. I like trashy period romances," Vicky said. Feeling like a ton had been lifted from her shoulders, she headed off the flag bridge.

At the hatch, she paused and glanced back. "Oh, Admiral Bolesław, please lay in the fastest course for St. Petersburg. I have a bone to pick with a certain mayor."

The admiral raised a questioning eyebrow, but Vicky was already turning away. She desperately wanted a bath and a bit of sleep.

———

CHAPTER 66

"WHAT the hell did you do?" Vicky demanded, as soon as Mannie walked into her day quarters aboard the *Retribution*. She'd been on a slow burn ever since she got blindsided by this mediation idea. For this meeting, she'd sent everyone away.

"And what might it be that you think I did?" Mannie asked as he approached her, so innocent that platinum might melt in his mouth.

That act didn't work on Vicky. She knew Mannie too well. Hands on hips, she let him have it. "Don't be cute with me. You hornswoggled my dad, your Emperor, into letting Kris Longknife mediate this thing between us," Vicky spat. "He's the Emperor. I'm the Grand Duchess. *We* decide how things are done in this Empire."

"He does now, does he? I hadn't noticed him doing much of anything of late."

He had Vicky there. *But still!*

"I thought we had an understanding between the two of us. We are an Empire. We don't put everything up for a vote like they do in Longknife space. You democrats tricked him."

Mannie paused only a few feet from Vicky and pulled himself

up to his full height. That made him just about eye to eye with her. He paused, took two deep breaths, then said, "I am the duly elected mayor of Sevastopol. *I* have no authority over *your* Empire. No one does, except your father, as you are quick to point out."

"I'm glad you're willing to admit that," Vicky snorted.

"And for the last several years, your father has been sniffing around your stepmother and letting her family wreck everything that your forefathers and a hell of a lot of other good people built. Am I not right?"

Vicky let out the breath she'd been holding, and admitted, "We've agreed on that."

"So, the Empress goes running off to make sure that you are blown into tiny bits by one honking-big battle fleet, and it just so happens that some other people manage to get a word in the Emperor's ear."

"Democrats," Vicky spat, making it sound like a dirty word.

"I suspect that the people who managed to sell your father on this entire mediation idea came with a whole lot of agendas, some of which I would, no doubt, find distasteful. I am told that a functioning democracy is very messy. From what I've seen on St. Petersburg, I think they got that right."

"But we're letting Kris Longknife in!" Vicky almost screamed. "She'll likely try to turn Greenfeld into something . . . something . . . all Longknifish," Vicky said, with a shiver.

"Would you rather your father mediated between you and the Empress?"

"What would *that* do?" Vicky growled.

"Likely keep the war going much, much longer, piling up the bodies," Mannie said.

"Couldn't any of you think of anyone else?"

"Can you?"

Vicky found herself stumbling to a roaring halt. Mannie had her, point, set, and match.

Who could *mediate between me and my stepmother?*

After a long moment for reflection, Vicky found herself deflating like a pin-pricked balloon. A couch wasn't too far away; she stumbled to it and folded herself into it.

In a moment, Mannie joined her on it, seating himself about as far away from her as the overstuffed bit of furniture allowed.

"You know," Vicky said softly, aiming her words at no one,

"we almost won that battle. We had the Empress running for the jump and a whole lot of your merchant cruisers on her tail."

"I'm sure our merchant Sailors would have been only too happy to open the gates of hell for her."

"I was pretty sure I could give the order for them to do it," Vicky said.

"Only pretty sure?" Manny asked with a highly raised eyebrow.

Vicky allowed herself a loud sigh, and, if possible, deflated even more. "I've seen a lot of people die. Ships vanishing in a blink. Thousands of good men dying without even a moment to know it was coming."

Mannie nodded. "It must have been horrible. How do you keep your sanity in such an insane situation?"

"I'm not sure I did," Vicky admitted. "When the cruiser showed up with Dad's message, I was of half a mind to ignore him. To order the merchant cruisers to keep baying after the Empress until they caught her."

"Why didn't you?"

Vicky shrugged. "I'd really be the rebel then, now wouldn't I?"

"The victorious rebel?" Mannie offered.

"Are you sure? Do you think your, ah, unctuous rats at court could have kept Dad from disowning me, from declaring me in rebellion? Where would that have left us?"

"With you leading a rebellion marching on Greenfeld. Likely one of those unctuous rats, as you named them, would slip a knife in your father's back before we got there."

Vicky turned to Mannie. While they'd been talking, somehow the distance between them had grown smaller. "I didn't think all that through, but I think I knew in my bones that that would be the endgame if I didn't take the chance those rats had given me."

"Given us," Mannie added.

He'd leaned back on the couch, one arm resting on its back. It was almost touching Vicky's shoulder. "Given *us*?" she repeated.

"Us," Mannie said. "The people of the Empire. You and me." The smile he gave her warmed her in places she hadn't been warm in a very long time.

With a sigh and a smile, she folded herself into his arms. His lips were waiting, and she took them. The first kiss was tentative, just a brush of hers on his. When he answered that touch with a soft kiss of his own, Vicky pulled his head to her, eager to see where this might lead.

Just before she let the universe disappear, one last thought floated by.

Good luck, Kris Longknife. You're going to need more of that legendary Longknife luck than anyone has a right to expect.

ABOUT THE AUTHOR

MIKE SHEPHERD grew up Navy. It taught him early about change and the chain of command. He's worked as a bartender and cabdriver, personnel advisor and labor negotiator. Now retired from building databases about the endangered critters of the Pacific Northwest, he's enjoying some fun reading and writing.

Mike lives in Vancouver, Washington, with his wife, Ellen, and close to his daughter and grandchildren. He enjoys reading, writing, dreaming, watching grandchildren for story ideas, and upgrading his computer—all are never ending.

Look for *Kris Longknife: Bold*, coming from Ace in October 2016, to see what happens when Vicky and Kris cross paths again. Mike is also hard at work on Kris's next book for October 2017.

You can learn more about Mike and all his books at his website mikeshepherd.org; you can e-mail him at Mike_Shepherd@comcast.net or follow Kris Longknife on Facebook.

From *New York Times* Bestselling Author
MIKE SHEPHERD

. . .

The Kris Longknife Series

MUTINEER
DESERTER
DEFIANT
RESOLUTE
AUDACIOUS
INTREPID
UNDAUNTED
REDOUBTABLE
DARING
FURIOUS
DEFENDER
TENACIOUS
UNRELENTING

. . .

Praise for the Kris Longknife novels

"A whopping good read . . . Fast-paced, exciting, nicely
detailed, with some innovative touches."

—Elizabeth Moon, *New York Times* bestselling author of
Crown of Renewal

mikeshepherd.org
facebook.com/acerocbooks
penguin.com

M905AS0815

FROM *NEW YORK TIMES*
BESTSELLING AUTHOR

MIKE SHEPHERD

VICKY PETERWALD
TARGET

When her brother was killed in battle by Lieutenant Kris
Longknife, Vicky Peterwald, daughter of the Emperor,
had to change her life from one of pampered privilege to
one of military discipline. Though the lessons are hard
learned, Vicky masters them—with help from an unexpected source: Kris Longknife.

PRAISE FOR MIKE SHEPHERD AND
THE KRIS LONGKNIFE NOVELS

"A fantastic storyteller."
—Midwest Book Review

"Fabulously written and frenetically paced,
the Kris Longknife series is one of the
best in science fiction."
—Fresh Fiction

mikeshepherd.org
facebook.com/acerocbooks
penguin.com

M1505T0614